The Spare Who Became the H\

The Head, the Heart, and the Heir

Broken Sons

The Heir Rises

THE HEIR RISES

THE HEIR RISES

ALICE HANOV

Gryphon
Press

Gryphon Press

Published by Gryphon Press
Waterloo, Ontario

Copyright © 2023 by Alice Hanov

First Edition

Paperback: 978-1-998835-02-7
Hardcover: 978-1-998835-03-4
Special Hardcover: 978-1-998835-04-1
Ebook: 978-1-998835-01-0000

Edited by Intrepid Literary and Gryphon Press
Cover design by The Book Designers

Dedicated to Marissa.

Part fairy godmother, part angel, part bookworm.
You are ferflucsing amazing!

Dear Reader,

Please be aware that this book deals with sensitive subject matters including mental health struggles, trauma, abusive relationships, and miscarriage. I handle them in a way that helps the characters learn and grow, but I understand that many of these topics are troubling for readers.

If you'd like a list of what exactly this book will touch on, please see my website, AliceHanov.com or scan the code below with your phone.

Happy reading, and take care of yourself.

Alice

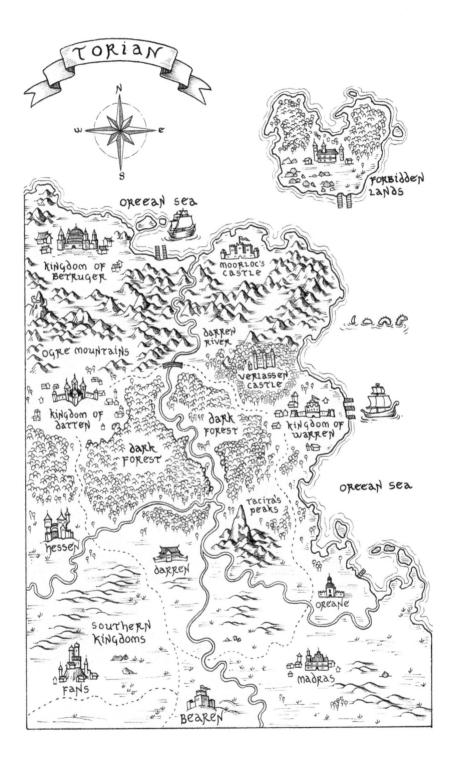

CHAPTER 1
ALEX

Blood, sweat, and death. Alex closed her emerald green eyes and inhaled deeply, hoping to replace the stench that memory always brought. The details of the battle they'd survived—the one that had brought her home—haunted her even now. Moorloc's bloodied face flashed in her mind, and the betrayer's mark on her arm burned even as the cool summer night air kissed her skin.

She smelled earth, pine, and flowers—the comforting smells of summer in Torian's Dark Forest.

Alex opened her magic well and her eyes, ready for her training.

It took her a moment to adjust to the darkness in the clearing where Stefan and Michael had left her. Once she did she realized she was near her castle. *Didn't even bother to go beyond walking distance? Either you aren't expecting me to put up a proper fight, or you don't want to hobble back when I'm through with you.*

She smiled mischievously and tossed her chestnut brown braid over her shoulder. She listened for her attackers, but all she heard was the wind blowing through the trees. As a cloud blocking the moon moved on, the clearing lit up, and for the briefest moment, a glimmer flashed across the grass.

Found you!

Straightening her back and core, Alex twisted her hips and thrust her arms straight out. Soundlessly, vines slithered away from her toward the surrounding trees and returned with a chest plate. A loud bang resounded behind her. She feigned turning toward it, then pivoted in the opposite direction in time to see a blast of fire coming her way.

Flames raced across the ground, encircled her, and erupted upward. As they crackled around her waist-high, Alex turned toward the forest where the attacking sorcerer was grinning at her. "Nice job, Megesti," she shouted. "Our practice is paying off."

Water, wind, or earth? Which will keep you down? Before she could decide, an arrow flew past her hip.

Michael.

Alex dropped her hands and flicked her fingers, drawing water from the air to douse the surrounding flames. A second arrow flew past. Her entire body was illuminated with golden light as she turned toward the archer. "*Ferflucs!*"

Stefan coughed, a trick Alex knew he used to mask his laughter. Since she'd returned home, her temper rarely set things on fire. Instead, it made her glow gold like a torch in the halls. It was dangerous for her to glow every time she got angry, so as her faithful friends and protectors, Stefan and Michael were helping her learn to manage her temper, and Megesti was helping her try various remedies from their family journals to keep her from glowing.

Megesti. Despite his ascension to Titan of Merlin eight months ago when they freed Alex from Moorloc, Megesti hadn't once glowed violet. As much as it annoyed her, Alex understood that at sixty-eight, Megesti had more experience; he controlled his powers. Alex's powers still controlled her.

Around them, the woods came to life as the night animals began their evening routines. A fox cried, sending its prey scattering, while an owl welcomed the night with its questioning *who*. The sounds would serve as a convenient distraction.

Alex was ready for Michael's next arrow. She threw her arms up, and her wind sent his arrow off course. She squatted and brushed the grass with her fingers so the scorched earth became lush and green again. Scanning the tree line, she figured out where Michael and Megesti were, but Stefan was still hidden. He was always good at staying out of her line of sight.

Alex sent a breeze through the trees in different directions until the smell of musk hit her. *Got you.* She lowered herself to the ground, and all at once, the three of them attacked. They'd realized she'd found them and thwarted her attempt to grab them with her vines. Michael shot another arrow, but Alex deflected it with the same wind she used to send Megesti's next blast back at him. She followed the wind with water, dousing the flames that grabbed Megesti's cloak. She spun and found Stefan behind her with his sword out.

Alex knew he'd wait for her to draw hers. Wiggling her fingers over the hilt, she focused on the blade Aaron had picked out for her from Datten's collection. It had belonged to Emmerich before he became King of Datten, a fact he delighted in telling her anytime she wore it around him.

She unsheathed her blade, gripped the hilt with both hands, and stared at Stefan. Her golden glow illuminated his pale face and fiery hair. He stalked toward her with an intense smile, his brows drawn together.

"Brothers," Alex groaned as she stepped back to circle him.

Behind her, Michael laughed, and Stefan's smile grew larger.

He enjoys beating me, but he won't today!

Alex and Stefan circled one another until she was ready. She opened her well again, and her soft glow became a blinding light. Stefan groaned and shielded his eyes, and Alex leaped into action. She charged him and smashed her blade into his. Stefan's grip was stronger than hers, having been built for battle, so even one-handed, he didn't drop the sword. So Alex dealt the low blow Michael had taught her. She kicked him in the knee, and he cried out. His sword landed in the grass with a dull thud.

"I surrender," Stefan said, holding his hand up.

Alex's chest heaved. It was rare she won, so Stefan giving in so easily surprised her, but then a vine grabbed her ankle, and she slammed into the ground, the wind knocked out of her.

"You forgot about us," Michael said, walking over with Megesti.

Her sword lay in the grass, just out of reach. Michael looked down at her, and his messy black hair almost covered his blue eyes. He drew his bow and aimed at her chest. Lowering the flat arrowhead, he gently tapped her forehead.

"We win tonight."

Alex groaned and covered her face with her arms.

"Don't be discouraged, Alex. You did great," Stefan said as he stood. He held out his hand, and when Alex took it, he pulled her off the ground with a single tug.

"That wasn't great. I should be better." *Stronger, faster, more ... me.*

Michael dropped his hand to her shoulder, and Alex felt her golden glow fade as a feeling of safety filled her.

"They starved and tortured you for six months. You've only been home eight." Michael's tone was curt but soft. "Your father's physician made it clear—*at least* two to three months of healing for every month you were there. Stop being so hard on yourself."

"It took you years to learn your fighting skills the first time," Stefan said, slipping his arm around her. "Why do you expect yourself to master these new skills so quickly?"

Alex looked at each of them. "Because I won't be that vulnerable again."

"You won't have to," Megesti said. "Our uncle is dead, and we have the family journals now. We'll keep learning to wield our powers, and you'll get better. Little by little."

Alex sighed. *I know you mean well, Megesti, but it's not the same learning alone. It's harder and takes longer. I wish* Gryphon *were here.*

"All right, I think it's time to head back for bed," Stefan said, ushering her toward home.

Alex crossed her arms as they headed across the clearing.

Verlassen Castle wasn't huge, but it was the perfect place for Alex to hide from everything while sorting out her powers and dealing with the aftermath of her time at Moorloc's castle. Upon her return, she'd tried to stay in Warren, but there were . . . mishaps. Too many people watching her while she struggled to adjust to life outside Moorloc's control. While she'd been gone, her father had the royal builders repair everything and even made a few additions. Now her mother's castle was as beautiful as it had been all those years ago. Her father, King Edward, had suggested she come here, and for the past eight months, this had been her home.

The builders kept the tree that had broken through the hall alive, and it now grew in the small courtyard. The broken ceilings were all fixed, and they'd remade the library shelves. It was everything Alex ever could have dreamed of. However, besides new bedding and cushions in her favorite color, her mother's room was unchanged. The predominant colors of Warren were silver and blue, but there was a lesser-used green, and Edward had proclaimed that since Alex hated blue, everything given to the crown princess must be Warren green.

The large hall was her second favorite room. There was no evidence of the vortex that had almost cost Stefan and Aaron their lives. That history was long ago, and all of that damage was now erased. The walls were covered in paintings, new and old. Those depicting Moorloc had been destroyed. Her favorite painting had been gifted by Aaron's mother, Guinevere; it was Datten's copy of the last painting made of Alex with her parents before her mother died. Seeing it made Alex smile and reminded her how fiercely her mother loved her. Aaron's favorite part of the painting was how regal her parents looked while Alex's expression was the scowl of a furious little girl who hated the blue dress they had forced her into.

They crossed the moat to the castle, and Alex stopped at the main doors. "I'm going to check on Flash. You three head inside."

Stefan said, "I'll have your food sent to your room."

"I'm fine, Stefan."

"I'm still having food sent. You're supposed to eat a little all throughout the day since you can't handle full meals."

Alex stuck her tongue out at him. She'd never admit it, but having Stefan and Michael fuss over her was nice and felt like home.

She walked around the perimeter to the small stable attached to the castle. Edward had extended the moat and kept most of the horses in stables on the other side. Flash, Thunder, Elm, and a handful of other guard horses were kept nearer to the castle. There was a door that connected the castle to the stable, but Alex took the longer outside route and nodded at Julius, who was making rounds. When she arrived, she slipped silently through the small side door used by her stable master.

Aaron was standing between Flash's and Thunder's stalls, holding a carrot out to each of the horses. His golden hair sparkled against his pinkish skin. No matter how much time he spent outside, he never tanned. Alex snuck up behind him, wrapped her arms around his waist, and kissed his back.

"Hello, my love," Aaron said.

"What are you doing hiding in the stables?"

"Waiting for your training to end. I wanted to hear how it went. We've both been so busy this week, the only time we spend together is in our bed sleeping or doing other things."

"You mean *my* bed. Your room is on the second floor."

Aaron chuckled and turned around. He cupped Alex's face and kissed her. The scent of pine, dew, and hay nearly overwhelmed her. Gripping his hips, she pulled him closer to deepen their kiss.

"I may have my own room in your castle, but I haven't spent a single night in it since we moved here, and you know it," he teased.

"Are you finished in here?" Alex asked, reaching out to stroke Flash.

"Almost. How was training?"

She groaned.

"Lost again, I see."

Glaring, she reached out to pinch Aaron.

He laughed and hugged her. "I know you're frustrated with your lack of control, but you'll get it back."

"Some days I have full control, and others it feels as if my powers are a pot boiling over with a clattering lid."

Aaron caressed her arm. "How did the last memory spell go?"

"Other than sneezing blue pebbles out of my nose? Nothing. Have I said anything new in my sleep?"

He huffed and rubbed the back of his neck. "Same as the last eight months. You cry for help and call his name."

Alex wrapped her arms around Aaron. "What if I can't get them back? Will you be able to live with it?"

His blue eyes sparkled like the sea as he looked down at her. "I'd learn to."

That isn't reassuring. "*Ferflucs!*" she grumbled.

"Now who has the temper?"

"Still you. I'm going to go to the lab and try one of those last spells I found."

"Want company?" Aaron winked as she stepped away.

Alex giggled. "You're a distraction, not help."

"It's not my fault I'm so handsome." Aaron kissed her cheek. "Go to the lab. I'll finish here and go to our room. Come up when you're done."

Alex cracked herself out of the stable and into her lab in the bowels of the castle. The fireplace and torches roared to life as soon as she arrived. She removed her sword and tossed it to the side, cracking it at the same time so that it landed on the table in her bedroom. *Why can I only control useless things?* Alex glanced at a decimated chair in the corner, the latest victim of her uncontrolled power. Shaking her fear away, she snatched her notes from the desk and flipped through the last few pages.

"Only one more book to try." *A few more chances to get my memories back.*

She went to the bookshelves, and an icy chill hit her. She looked up and saw Daniel, the ghost of Aaron's brother, staring at her with a frown and crossed arms.

"Don't look at me like that. I know you don't want me to get the memories back, but Aaron and I decided. You don't get a vote."

Daniel stepped aside. She undid her braid, scratched her head, and put her hair back up in a bun her lady's maid Jessica would be ashamed of. Scanning the books, she found the last one she needed to review.

"Then tell him the truth," Daniel said.

"It doesn't matter if I'm scared of what I'll learn. We agreed."

After she'd become a Returned One for a second time, Alex found she could *hear* ghosts in addition to seeing them—but only if she focused. Whenever she did, it quickly drained her, but Daniel was the exception.

She grabbed a book written by Merlin, her great-grandfather and the founder of the Merlin line. All the sorcerer lines had at least seventeen generations of sorcerers, all except the newest line of Merlin. He'd only had one son, Hermes, and that sorcerer only had three children: Moorloc, Merlock, and Victoria. The remaining children of her generation were the last of the line. Megesti and Alex were using these ancestral journals to help them with their powers, but no one knew where Alex's cousin Lygari was. They hadn't heard any news of him since she'd accidentally banished him during the battle at Moorloc's castle.

She plopped the book down and rested her elbows on the table. There had to be another spell she could try. She flipped through the pages, but the closest she could find was a spell that could return lost things. She sighed and collected the needed herbs from the shelf behind her. Once everything was on the table, she filled a cauldron with water and swung it over the fire.

It took her a few hours to grind the herbs, mix the ingredients, and wait for the mixture to heat. Once it started bubbling, the potion turned a swampy green and began smelling of compost.

At this point, the spell required she add an element of what she wanted to bring back. *What do you add to bring back memories?* She watched it bubble while she pondered and then pricked her finger, hoping her blood would help her remember where her scars had come from. The potion swallowed up the drops and turned bloodred. It smelled grotesque.

Alex lowered a jar into the cauldron and lifted it out full of the burning hot concoction. She wrapped her hands around it and used her Poseidon powers to cool the potion.

Icy wind hit her, and she spun around, expecting to see Daniel, but it wasn't him. Startled, Alex dropped the jar, and it shattered, sending glass and thick red potion all over. Her heart pounded.

Her mother pointed at the cauldron and scowled. Then she sighed, and her shoulders dropped. She floated toward Alex and shook her head gently.

Alex swallowed. "*What?* You don't want me to get my memories back?"

Victoria stoically stared at her.

"Why? What happened that you don't want me to remember?"

Victoria frowned but stayed silent.

"I can hear you now, so stop being cryptic."

Alex's cheeks grew cold when her mother reached out and caressed her face. Ice prickled her forehead as Victoria softly kissed it and vanished.

She looked from the empty space where her mother had been to the bubbling potion. "I want the truth. No more forgotten memories."

She grabbed a new jar, scooped the potion into it, and chilled it slightly. When she sniffed the brew, she had to turn her head away to avoid gagging. It smelled worse cold, worse than the dirty stables on a hot summer's day. She shuddered, plugged her nose, and chugged the entire jar of the foul concoction.

It tasted even worse than it smelled. Alex retched. The jar fell from her fingers and smashed on the floor, and she rushed to a bucket in the corner to throw up. Only a little of the potion came up. It was as though it had coated her insides. She rested her back against the wall and was wiping her mouth when she heard the sound of a whip cracking.

She stumbled to her feet and rushed into the hallway. The torches roared to life, but no one was there. She climbed the stairs to the main hall and found that it, too, was deserted. She ran through every part of the main floor, but she found nothing out of the ordinary.

The hairs on her neck stood on end as she returned to the still-empty hall.

Crack. She turned and ran so fast she slipped on the smooth stones outside the library. She rushed to her bedroom's secret door. *What is wrong with me? I must be hearing things.* With her hand on the book that triggered the door's opening, she covered her mouth and struggled to calm herself.

Finally feeling safe, Alex pulled the book, and her door opened. The fireplace was still glowing, providing a bit of light. Aaron was sound asleep, and her sword rested on the table with their matching crowns.

She draped her wet, potion-splattered clothes on the toy chest she'd brought from her suite in Warren and put on her nightdress. She lifted the soft green quilt and slipped into bed. Before she could worry any more, Aaron rolled over and embraced her. Alex snuggled into him, inhaling the relaxing scent of pine and letting his warmth lull her to sleep.

CHAPTER 2
GRYPHON

The ground was damp and freezing. Everything about the dungeon cell was wet.

Ares! I hate being wet.

Gryphon sat up and cracked his neck. His side and ribs throbbed from the beating Phobos had administered. This was a cell designed for Ares and Mystics sorcerers. Clearly, his hexa had planned this and put him in a cell between the Ares and Mystics wing and the Salem wing. Even if he hadn't been restrained, the dampness meant he couldn't use his fire powers to escape.

He'd been locked in the dungeon for a month now with a red steel bracelet on each wrist. It didn't surprise him that they'd gone to these extremes. Usually a punishment from his parents meant not leaving the castle, but this time the Heart was involved. After Lygari arrived and ratted him out, his parents, Garrick and Imelda, had locked him in his bedroom and starved him for a week before they questioned him about how he'd found her. He pretended to give in, but he only confessed to helping her. After that, Garrick ordered his son to stay away from the mortal world and from Alex, and Gryphon agreed. Then, the first chance he had, he'd cracked to her.

She was by that old little castle that had Victoria's magical essence all over it. He'd discovered her and Megesti in the nearby forest. They'd been holding a book and working together to learn a Salem spell. When it got out of control, Alex conjured water to put it out. They clearly weren't discouraged and kept trying over and over.

Alex was still malnourished, but with a book in her hand and Megesti at her side, she seemed happy. He'd watched them for hours until her cheeks grew pink from exertion. Satisfied that she was safe and content, he'd returned home, not wanting to interfere in her life any more than he already had. That was when his father's sycophant Phobos had caught him, resulting in his new accommodations.

After learning his son had helped Alexandria, Garrick had been furious in front of the other sorcerers, but since being locked down here, Gryphon learned he'd played right into their hands. His family had plans for Alexandria. Eris, his mother's mother—his maternal hexa—was a proud Ares sorceress, and she had suspected Gryphon's generation would be the one to bear the sorceress Heart. She was desperate to get Alex bonded to him so they could create the next sorcerer generation while she was still alive. Eris told of an old Ares legend about an Ares and a Cassandra coming together to make the most powerful sorcerer who would ever live. Gryphon had read all the Ares books in their library and never found this legend, but clearly his hexa's premonition had been correct.

It seemed his family had known where the Heart was all along, but they had repeatedly failed to retrieve her, enraging his hexa to no end. Nevertheless, she claimed to have played a successful role in their plot, but wouldn't say more. Garrick had attempted to retrieve Victoria when she was pregnant with Alex, but had failed because Victoria had fallen in love with Edward by then. Imelda had been sent to find Alex as a child, but she'd also failed since Alex was so well hidden because of her magical necklace. Thus, the job fell to an unwitting Gryphon. By answering Alex's call for help, he'd accidentally played right into their hands. Thanks to Lygari's big mouth, they knew about Aaron, how powerful Alex was, and her mother's castle.

Gryphon had tried everything to keep from revealing Alex's weaknesses, but his father was still the most powerful Mystics sorcerer alive, and once the bracelets were on, he could force himself into Gryphon's mind. He fought back—which made the process excruciatingly painful—and managed to keep a few things from his father, namely Alex's beloved brothers and ladies. When he failed to extract the information he wanted, Garrick locked Gryphon in the dungeon, hoping it would get him to talk. But Gryphon would rather die than help them hurt Alex.

Footsteps echoed in the hallway outside of his cell. He knew it was his parents before they even reached the door.

"Have you come to your senses, Gryphon?" Imelda asked. His mother was a voluptuous woman with pink skin, strawberry blonde hair, and blue eyes. Gryphon had towered over her by the time he was thirteen. She wore the Tiere titan cloak even though she'd given up her title to marry his father and become the mother of the next Head. Gryphon found it laughable, considering how little work she'd done raising him. She'd left the hard work to her adopted sister, Birch.

As usual, Imelda had her sleeves rolled up to her elbows, a habit she developed as a young sorceress to keep her cloak clean while working with animals. It also showed off the scar that ran down her left forearm. She'd never told him where it came from.

Glaring, Garrick didn't speak. It only took one glance to see Gryphon was his son, a fact that Gryphon himself loathed. His two-colored black hair came from his father; except Gryphon had a streak of blond through his black hair, an inheritance from his mother, whereas his father's streak was gray. They had the same bronze complexion, and their eyes were the same golden color.

"And just what am I to come to my senses about, Mother?"

Imelda sighed and placed her hands on her hips. "You know why you're down here. We're finished playing games with you. The Heart is dangerously powerful for her age. She needs our help to learn to control her powers before she hurts herself or, worse, someone she loves. We need you to convince her to come to us. It would be better for everyone if she came willingly."

Gryphon scoffed. "Meaning you can't force her to come here, so you need me to manipulate her. Why is that, Mother? Afraid you'll fail again?"

"Catch your tongue, or you'll regret it," Garrick snapped. He was in a foul mood, but Gryphon didn't care. He knew his family too well, and they were up to something. He'd never agree to be part of whatever plan they had to hurt Alex.

"Take off my bracelets, and we'll see if you can make me regret it."

"We're giving you one last chance to come to your senses," said Garrick. "One last opportunity to help us bring *your* Heart home. I lost my Cassandra to a mortal. Are you willing to lose yours too?" His father spoke with the same haughty smugness Gryphon had used when he talked to Aaron and Alex's mortal friends.

"Nature rarely gives sorcerers a bond with the same depth as that which occurs between a Head and Heart," Imelda said. "You can't ignore it, and you can't possibly want to wait for that mortal mutt who has her now to grow old and die. Ares sorcerers *take* what they want."

"I'm well aware of what Ares sorcerers do, Mother."

Someone else answered, saying, "I hardly believe that, youngling."

They all turned to find his hexa standing in the doorway. Eris's once powerful body had withered with age. Her skeletal physique made her appear weak, a dangerous assumption that she would use against anyone foolish enough to underestimate her. Despite being nearly three hundred years old, Eris stepped proudly into the room, never once taking her eyes off Gryphon. One eye was gold, and the other was blue. Most lines loved having their hexa or hexen alive to teach the younger sorcerers —but they didn't have the Ares's violence or craving for power. Eris shuffled toward him and grabbed his face between her bony fingers.

"Remind me again what your dominant power is, Gryphon."

"Ares."

"Do you consider yourself worthy of that title? You let that mortal boy leave with *your sorceress*. You should have killed him the moment you laid eyes on him and taken your Heart. Are you aware of how our bonds work?"

"Of course I am." Gryphon tore himself from her grasp. "We can lock a nature bond several ways, but the fastest is by establishing a connection."

"And how does a sorceress connect?" Eris asked.

Gryphon looked at the dirt floor. He wouldn't give them the satisfaction of answering.

"With intercourse," Garrick answered. "All you had to do was take her once, and she'd be yours. Even if the mortal part of her still wanted that simpleton, the sorceress part would know better."

"That isn't how I'm going to win her. Alex deserves better."

"Alex? You call the Heart by a nickname? Perhaps you didn't fail as much as we thought." His mother smirked at him as she crossed her arms and cocked her head to the side. "Tell us more about *Alex*."

"No." Gryphon slunk back, his throbbing ribs reminding him of Phobos's beating the night before. Phobos wasn't with them, which meant they weren't planning physical abuse this time. His parents wouldn't bother getting their own hands dirty.

"Darling, you thought that was a request?" Imelda grinned at him as his father stepped forward, his hands extended.

Garrick gripped Gryphon's temples, and a sharp pain bored into his head to find the secrets he'd kept from them. Gryphon used all his Mystics powers to fight back against his father, sending dreams, useless information, and outright lies into the mix of memories his father was hunting through.

Gryphon's head was on fire as he fought the red steel on his wrist, but his powers were draining quickly. Just when he felt he couldn't hold out any longer, alarm bells echoed in the hallway.

"What now?" Eris snapped.

Garrick released Gryphon and turned to Imelda. "Your useless sister is in my library. No doubt trying to steal more of her father's books."

"Leave Birch alone." Gryphon lunged for his father, but the red steel had weakened him so much that all his father had to do was grab his shoulder. Garrick's hand seared through his tunic and skin, and the stench of burning flesh wafted in the air before his father slammed him to the ground. Gryphon had to fight back tears.

"Leave him," Eris said. "We'll deal with Birch and come back. It's not as though he can go anywhere."

The three sorcerers cracked away, leaving Gryphon alone in his cell. He closed his eyes and tried to summon his Salem power to extinguish the burning in his shoulder. Soon, he heard a key unlock his door. He looked up and saw two figures in gray cloaks.

"Kharon?" he asked.

The first sorcerous dropped their hood, revealing black hair, blue eyes, ghostly pale skin, and a kind smile. "Who else could sneak by unnoticed? No one ever pays attention to Hades sorcerouses," Kharon said.

"Considering your robes match the stone walls, I'm not surprised," Lynx said, pulling off her own hood. Even in the dull light, her golden hair sparkled against her tan skin, though her brown eyes were full of fear as she looked Gryphon over.

"What are you doing here?" he asked.

"Isn't it obvious? We're breaking you out," Lynx whispered.

"Birch went to the library to distract your parents and hexa," Kharon said.

"Give me your wrists," Lynx said.

Gryphon held up his hands. Lynx took them in hers and yipped and snarled at the bracelets.

"Of course Mother used wolf magic," Gryphon groaned as the bracelets fell off.

"Did you expect her to *not* use her Tiere powers to bind you? Do you know her at all?" Lynx asked, shaking her head as Kharon helped Gryphon to his feet.

"Can you crack?" Kharon asked as they slid their arm around Gryphon's shoulders. Lynx supported him from the other side.

"I don't think so. I used up everything I had left to keep my father from finding out anything more about Alex."

Kharon and Lynx nodded to each other and cracked them

all to the worn stone path that led to Birch's cottage. A moment later, Birch appeared behind them.

"That was an adventure. I got two books this time!"

"You actually stole books?" Lynx asked.

"Naturally. Can't have them thinking I had anything to do with this escape. Now bring him inside so I can look him over. I suspect he's starving."

"And he was roughed up," Lynx added. "Phobos was in too good a mood this week."

They had to turn sideways to navigate the narrow path. A menagerie of plants had taken over the yard around Birch's tiny cottage. Once inside, Kharon brought Gryphon to the couch, and the friendly little birds that lived there chirped and rushed to him, sitting on his head and shoulders. Birch handed Gryphon a large mug of foul-smelling liquid. He groaned.

"Drink it," she said. "Your mother and hexa haven't found my new home in decades. If you want to hide here and be safe, we need you hidden from Mystics and kin." She paused. "I added apple blossoms!"

Gryphon sighed and chugged the entire thing as Lynx hurried back from the kitchen with a mug of water.

"Do you have anything for his wrists?" Kharon asked Birch.

Birch grabbed Gryphon's hand and gasped when she saw that the skin where the bracelet had been was completely raw and blistered. "Your parents put you in a red steel bracelet?"

Gryphon nodded and showed her his other wrist. Birch went ashen as she bit her bottom lip. He knew that look well; she was trying not to cry. She hadn't let go yet, and he gripped her hand as she hiccuped.

"Thank you . . . for getting me out," he said. "All of you. I know you risked everything, and I have no way to repay you."

"Don't mention it," Kharon said. "No one will ever suspect I was involved. Hades sorcerouses are boring."

Lynx sat beside him and gently took his free hand in hers. "You'd have gotten out eventually, and they would have accused Birch and me of helping you escape even if you did it on your own. At least this way I'm actually guilty of it, and I can sleep at night knowing I didn't leave you to rot down there."

Birch tossed Lynx a tin of ointment. When she opened it, both she and Gryphon wrinkled their noses and turned away. The overpowering scent of peppermint stung their eyes.

"Put some on his shoulder too," Birch said. "I can smell the burn from here."

Gryphon removed his shirt, and Lynx sighed as she rubbed the ointment into the blistering red handprint that had been burned into him.

After the ointment soaked in, Birch handed him a drink.

He raised his eyebrows. "Another?"

"For sleeping. I'm no Cassandra, so you're going to have to heal the old-fashioned way—with rest."

Gryphon plugged his nose and chugged the potion. As he handed the mug back to Birch, he could already feel it kicking in.

"Rest up, Gryphon." Lynx's voice became softer and more distant as it vanished into silence. "You're safe now."

CHAPTER 3
ALEX

I ce surrounded her, crushing her so she couldn't move her arms. She struggled to freeze more water even as the flames, now inches from her face, grew into an inferno. Lygari's wicked laugh echoed all around while the ice melted and streamed down her neck. She couldn't keep up, and her tears joined the melting ice. *I'm failing. I can't do it. He's going to kill me. Gryphon!*

Alex shot up in bed soaking wet and gasping for breath. Sobs erupted from her as the nightmare started to fade from her memory even before Aaron could get his arms around her. He held her close, trying to comfort her as she shook uncontrollably. There was a soft knock on the hall door.

"Come in," Aaron said. He climbed out of bed and helped Alex to her feet.

Michael and Jessica quietly entered the room. Michael went straight to the bed and stripped off the wet sheets. Her lady's maid was behind him with clean ones, tucking under the corners with amazing efficiency.

"I'm sorry."

Everyone turned toward Alex when she spoke. Jessica handed Michael the sheets, then pulled Alex away from Aaron and into a big hug. "No, Alex. We're sorry. No one should have to endure what you've been through. As long as you need us, we'll be here. We're honored to be part of your recovery."

Michael opened her wardrobe and tossed Aaron a clean nightdress.

"Good night, you two," Aaron said. "We'll see you at breakfast."

Michael nodded and led Jessica back out the door.

Alex looked down at herself and sighed, dragging off the soaked nightdress. Aaron helped her into the dry one, and they slid back into bed. He put his arms around her and was asleep in no time, but Alex couldn't silence her thoughts. She tried to forget the dream, but it was one she had too often. It terrified her and left her wondering what was in those lost memories. She lay awake, listening to the sounds of the castle, and heard another whip crack.

She bolted up in bed, making Aaron mumble in his sleep. After a second, he rolled over. Alex slipped her feet onto the rug on her side of the bed and tiptoed to their wardrobe. She changed into her sparring clothes and hurried into the hallway to hunt down the mysterious sound.

Despite walking around the castle for an hour, she heard nothing out of the ordinary and didn't find anyone who wasn't supposed to be there. She needed some fresh air to clear her head, so she grabbed her journal from her time at Moorloc's castle and headed to the rooftop garden. Sitting on the edge of one of the large planter boxes, she conjured an orb to help her read the words. Alex read the entire journal, starting with the first day, when she'd arrived and settled in, through to the day that she worked with the armies to free herself.

Every time she came across a torn-out page, she ran her

finger along the ragged remnant and wondered what had made this day so much worse that Gryphon had to take the page. There were fights with Moorloc, sparring bouts with Lygari, and the horrible things the mercenaries said. What could be worse than that endless abuse? *Based on the scars all over my body, someone injured me. But what if I hurt someone?*

Lost in thought, Alex shrieked when someone squeezed her shoulder. She looked back and saw her other lady's maid, Edith.

"What are you doing up here?" Edith asked.

"Thinking. The fresh air helps. What time is it? Did I miss breakfast?"

"No. I come up here sometimes to think too. The flowers make me happy."

"Such a Warren lady," Alex said.

"True. The flowers remind me of my mother's garden."

Alex's smile fell. "Do you miss Warren? If you're unhappy here, I—"

"Stop it." Edith sat beside Alex, giving her the stern look that she inherited from her father, General Randal Nial. "I never said I was unhappy here. You're always trying to take care of everyone, but all we want is for you to let us take care of you. You're the one they took from your home. We missed you."

"I'm scared."

"Of what?" Edith tucked her raven hair behind her ear. Her sandy-colored skin looked pink in the orb light.

Alex grew quiet and played with the hem of her shirt, but Edith didn't pry. She sat in patient silence.

Eventually, Alex asked, "What if I get my memories back and learn something I can't live with?"

"Such as?" Edith asked.

"What if I was the monster?"

"You aren't your grandfather. You're not capable of what he was."

"How do you know?" Alex asked.

"Because we know you," said Aaron.

They turned around to find him standing at the top of the stairs.

"Looks like you have cuter company." Edith winked at Alex and patted her shoulder. "Just let me know if you ever need to talk. We're all here for you."

"Thank you."

"Your Highness." Edith nodded to Aaron as she headed down.

"What was that about?" he asked.

"As if you didn't know," Alex said, glaring at him. "Next time, don't send one of my ladies for information you could ask me for."

Aaron sat beside her, and she playfully pushed him. He ran a hand through his hair and looked pensive. She knew he was trying to decide how to say what he was thinking.

"I've tried, Alex. I've asked repeatedly since you got home to talk to me about what it was like there, but you won't."

"That's not fair. I've answered all the questions I can. You've read my journal." Alex dropped it in his lap. "I told you about every day I can remember. But you're fixated on the handful that I can't."

"Because I believe that sorcerer did something to you, and I'm not talking about Moorloc. He kissed you on the last day. What if that wasn't the first time?"

"You don't get to obsess over this and not explain yourself."

"Alex, I lost you!" Aaron shouted. "And I'm not willing to let that happen again."

"Aaron, you didn't lose me. I left."

"I know ... but that makes it worse for me. I need to know

what you went through so I can help you heal from it and move on. It's been eight months. You don't sleep, you barely eat, and you won't talk to any of us."

"Just because I don't talk to you doesn't mean I don't talk to anyone."

"If not me, then who? I know you aren't talking to your ladies or your adopted brothers, so who, Alex? Who's left?"

Tears shimmered in Alex's eyes as she stood. *I can't fight about this anymore.* "Who I talk to doesn't matter, but know that I am talking to someone who understands that the deaths caused by this choice are on *my* soul, not yours. You came to get me back, and you did. Your conscience is clear, but mine isn't, and I can't risk adding any more deaths to my count. I'm done. No more spells. No more potions. If my memories aren't back yet, I'm done trying."

Aaron went silent for a long time. Alex picked at her shirt until he took her hands. "If that's what you want, I'll support your choice."

"Truly?"

"Yes. I'll learn to live with not knowing, so long as you promise to marry me."

Alex chuckled. "The wedding is in less than a week, and you're still worried? We're leaving soon. Are you packed?"

"No. I was thinking you should go alone with Stefan in the morning. Have a bit of time with your father before the rest of us show up."

"I'd like that."

"WHY ARE we taking the horses? We should just crack," Stefan said as he struggled to saddle his horse.

Alex laughed. "Elm clearly needs the exercise. Besides, I

miss my long rides with Flash. Since I learned to crack, we never ride anymore."

"It takes hours."

"Do I have to order you?" Alex smirked as she mounted Flash.

"No, princess," Stefan said and followed her out of the stables.

As they clopped along, they chatted about plans for the knights at the training school they'd set up in Moorloc's castle, the new book Alex finished, and how her new guards were working out. The sun was well into the sky, but the woods went eerily silent. The air suddenly became heavy, the way it did on a muggy summer night. The hairs on Alex's arms and neck stood up. She slowed Flash to a walk as Stefan sat straighter on Elm and slowed too. They scanned the trees for beasts. Alex heard three cracks of a whip again, and her heart raced.

Stefan noticed her tense. "Alex?"

"Did you hear that? The whip cracking?"

He cocked his head. "What? No."

"Do you feel like we're being watched?"

"I do," he replied.

"Observant little witch, aren't you?" A figure wearing a long maroon cloak that reached the ground walked out of the trees ahead of them. The cloak was similar to the kind worn by Gryphon and Moorloc. The figure pushed down her hood, revealing long, fiery red hair, pale skin, and golden eyes. Alex was drawn to the marks on her neck. Even though she couldn't see them perfectly, somehow she knew that one looked like a stylized flame and the other a small hill.

A man came out of the woods from the other side of the road. "I didn't expect her to be so clever." His cloak was the same hideous burnt orange as Gryphon's, but when he pushed back his hood, Alex saw he had black hair, copper skin, and red eyes. His beard badly needed a trim. Had they met at the pier or any other casual meeting place, Alex would have laughed at his beard and cloak. Instead, she trembled as she stared at the marks on his neck. They depicted a small gravestone and the same ax that Gryphon bore.

Alex sensed the power emanating from both of them the same way she had that first day on the beach, when Gryphon had arrived. But whereas Gryphon's power had excited her and given her control, these two made her feel scared and sent her magic into chaos.

Stefan positioned Elm in front of Alex and Flash and stared down at the two sorcerers.

"Move aside, and no harm will come to you," Alex ordered, forcing herself to sound more confident than she felt.

"It isn't us that the harm will come to," the sorceress said. A wicked smile spread across her bloodred lips, sending a shiver through Alex.

"Who are you?" Alex asked. She spoke in a commanding tone despite the quiver that jittered through her.

The sorcerer said, "How rude of us. I'm Phobos, Titan of the Line of Ares, and this is my bonded partner."

"You would call me a wife. As if I'd ever be subservient to anyone."

"Ember is the Titan of the Line of Salem," said Phobos.

"So where's your little friend?" Ember asked.

"Which friend? I have many," Alex said.

"Gryphon, you witch. They sent us to retrieve the next Head. He's vanished, and his poor mother and hexa are distraught. They figured he'd seek you out."

"Clearly he hasn't," Stefan said.

"Ah! It speaks. How amusing to have a pet that talks,"

Phobos said. "Well, in that case, we're supposed to bring you back to our Head as bait."

"He's simply dying to meet you after hearing about you from Lygari and Gryphon," Ember said.

Alex felt her bravery drain at the mention of her cousin Lygari. The betrayer mark on her forearm burned as the image of Moorloc dying at her hand came unbidden into her mind. *Breathe. It was you or him. Gryphon promised. He won't let Lygari hurt you again.*

"No. He wouldn't betray me," Alex said. She urged Flash back a few steps, her adrenaline spiking and her breathing quickening with fear.

Ember chortled as she took a step toward them. "Enough talk. My patience wears thin."

Phobos snapped his fingers, and a whip appeared in his hand. Before either Alex or Stefan could react, he cracked it, striking Elm. Despite his best efforts, Stefan lost control, and Elm nearly bucked him off. Alex leaped from Flash and rushed for Stefan as Elm bled and stamped all over the place. Phobos struck Elm again. The terrified horse reared, throwing Stefan backward into a tree. Alex tried to calm their horses as Stefan staggered to his feet, groaning in pain and holding his shoulder.

Ember appeared beside Alex and grabbed her arm. Her skin sizzled beneath the sorceress's grasp, and Alex wrenched her arm away. Fueled by extreme terror, her powers took over, and a gale force wind erupted from Alex and threw Ember back. Fury swept over the sorceress's face as she slammed into the ground.

"A child will not beat me." Ember's eyes glowed and became bloodred.

Sweat dripped down Alex's face as a wall of heat flew through her. The tree Stefan was using for support burst into flames. Alex sensed the tree's change an instant before the magic struck, and she grabbed Stefan's arm. They only made it a few steps away before the entire tree exploded.

Pieces of burnt wood struck them. Phobos cracked his whip again, and the horses panicked. As they charged around, Elm collided with Alex, knocking her back. Stefan stumbled, clearly in pain, but he pulled Alex behind him, doing his duty to protect her.

Ember smirked as she raised her hands above her head. She gently clapped, and all the trees around them burst into flame. With a menacing giggle, she flicked her wrists and made them all explode. She hurled the broken limbs like javelins, striking Flash and Elm.

The horses collapsed on the path, blood pouring from their wounds. Alex tried to run to Flash, desperate to save him, but Stefan yanked her back. Ember's hands were flaming again. Phobos's eyes flashed, and he gave a knowing smirk to Ember while his hands glowed orange.

"Get us out of here," Stefan said to Alex through gritted teeth.

Ember and Phobos stalked forward like wolves toward prey. Alex's chest heaved as she pulled her eyes away from the sorcerers and back to Flash. *I'm sorry.* Ember dove for Alex; the heat from her hand sizzled Alex's skin just before she squeezed Stefan's hand and cracked them both away.

CHAPTER 4

ALEX

Fear propelled them forward. Alex didn't have time to concentrate on a location. Only on the need to get as far away as possible, and one thought popped into her head—*Harold.* They slammed into the courtyard as if someone had shoved them through an invisible door. Alex lost her footing and hit the rocky ground. Pain ripped through her back as she landed. *How could we . . . we just left Flash and Elm. I don't think they'll survive that.*

Stefan held his good arm out to her, and Alex took it. They were in a small, unfamiliar courtyard. Before Alex could say anything, guards rushed out of the main building, swords drawn. Stefan stood in front of her, holding out his hand to the men.

"Don't attack! You all know me, Stefan Wafner—General Wafner's son. I fought with King Harold to get back our stolen princess. The princess standing behind me right now."

The guards shifted their eyes from Stefan's red hair to his Warren-crested tunic. Alex watched them quickly assess the scene, and then she realized her pale skin was streaked with blood. She looked up and saw red seeping down the side of Stefan's shirt.

"Stefan?" Alex moved his arm to check his front, realizing what the guards had been staring at. "You're bleeding."

Stefan glanced down at his chest, but his eyes widened when he looked at Alex. "You are too."

Alex examined herself and found nothing until a breeze hit her, and she felt slickness on her back.

"We need to see Harold. I need his help," Alex pleaded to the guards.

The young guards looked at one another nervously. Finally, one ran into the castle. A minute later, Harold, his curly black hair bouncing, came running out as he chastised the guard. "Never keep Warren or Datten nobility waiting!"

"Princess!" He held out his hands to greet her, but his face immediately fell. "Fetch Macht and my physician at once. Bring them to the infirmary."

"No," Alex said. "My father needs to hear from us what happened. No one else."

Harold exhaled but nodded. "Macht, to my room. Can you tell me what happened?"

"It's a long story," Alex said, feeling weak.

"Can you walk, Stefan?" Harold asked, his violet eyes full of concern.

"Yes, if you can help Alex. You'll likely need to carry her."

Alex opened her mouth to argue, but her knees wobbled, and she grabbed Harold's arm. Harold scooped her up as gently as Stefan would have, and he brought them inside to his room.

He placed Alex on the edge of his gigantic bed. Unlike her father's, Harold's chamber had only a single level. The decor was minimal but elegant. A giant table with six chairs stood off to the side, but Alex's gaze lingered on the bookcase. The shelves bowed from the weight of all the books. The fireplace was the only reasonably sized thing, and she could see through it into another room.

"What?" Harold asked, watching her take in his room.

Alex smiled. "Your room's green. I love it."

"The queen's suite next door is yellow. They are the colors of our crest—other than brown, of course."

Alex suddenly felt dizzy. Stefan rushed over and squatted beside her.

"How bad is it?" she whispered.

"Worse than falling from the pine tree but not as bad as the river."

Sir Macht and the physician arrived moments later with supplies in hand.

"Who should I fix up first?" the physician asked as Harold and Macht cleaned Alex's and Stefan's wounds.

"Start with Her Highness," Stefan said.

"Stefan—" Alex started.

Stefan shook his head, his jaw clenched.

She knew better than to argue with that face. "Then at least let me heal you," she said.

"No. You brought us to Harold instead of your father or Emmerich. Something is happening with you, and you're not healing me until you can control your powers."

Alex felt her stomach drop. Stefan had trusted her, even when she was a child. *Does he know? Do they know?*

"You can heal the scar later," Stefan said. He grabbed her hand while pressing the towel Macht had given him to his wounds.

"Do you prefer I stitch you up, princess, or cauterize it?" the physician asked.

"Cauterize it," Alex said.

"Are you sure?" Macht asked. "That leaves a big scar."

Alex sighed. "Look at my back, Macht. The entire thing is

scars thanks to . . . well, I don't know what happened, but one more won't make a difference. I can only heal what I can touch, so I've accepted my back will always be hideous."

"Scarred or not, you'll want to have something to hold, Your Highness," the physician said. "This will be painful."

Alex squeezed Stefan's hand as Harold stepped up and offered his own. Alex accepted. Harold and Stefan locked her arms with theirs.

Harold smiled reassuringly as the physician pressed the fiery blade into Alex's wound. Her screams shook the castle as magic raced through her. Tears streamed down her face. It took an unimaginable amount of energy to keep her Salem powers from escaping. Stefan and Harold didn't even flinch and stayed strong for her the entire time. When it was done, the golden light spreading through Alex illuminated Harold's bronze skin and almost immediately faded, and the pain left her.

Stefan also requested his wounds be cauterized. He took the stick offered by the physician and bit down on it. Harold, Macht, and the physician each took a blade while Alex used magic to hold him down. In one round, they sealed all his wounds. Then Macht held Stefan as the physician popped his dislocated shoulder back into place. Afterward, the physician packed up his things and left the room with only a nod, and servants scurried in to change the bloodied bedding.

Stefan groaned as he got off the bed.

Once they were alone again, Harold asked, "What happened?" Stefan lowered himself into a chair at the table and motioned for Alex to do the same. She ignored him and watched the fire. Although it was lit, she was so cold her teeth chattered.

She said, "We were due in Warren for wedding preparations, but on the way, we were attacked." Alex swallowed hard. "Sorcerers . . . they were sorcerers. They attacked with fire and killed our horses . . . they killed Flash." Her voice faltered as she spoke.

"Why not crack? It would have been faster," Macht asked.

"I missed riding," Alex said, holding back tears.

"Where is His Highness?" Macht asked. "I can't believe he'd let you go anywhere alone after last year."

"*His Highness* hadn't finished with the work he needed to do before leaving," Stefan said, and Alex shot him a warning look.

She said, "Aaron wanted to give me some time alone with my father."

Harold considered her for a moment. "I'm sure our guests are hungry. Macht, bring Stefan to our kitchen to pick some food for them. We'll meet you in our hall shortly."

Stefan hesitated. His rich brown eyes betrayed his distress; he didn't want to leave Alex after what had happened. Macht jerked his head, and finally Stefan nodded to the royals and left. Alex stopped pacing and sat down on the edge of Harold's bed.

He crouched, took her hand, and stared into her eyes. "Talk to me."

Alex exhaled a deep breath and told Harold everything: how frustrated she was that she couldn't get her memories back, how chaotic her powers were being, and how terrified that made her. In her mind, she heard a whip crack, and Alex flinched.

"How often have you heard this whip?" Harold asked.

"At least eight times now."

"The marks on your back—they look like lashes from a whip. Do you know how many there are?"

Alex sighed. "Thirty. I've overheard Aaron count them at night when he thinks I'm asleep."

Harold moved to sit beside Alex, letting her cry on his

shoulder. It took longer for the tears to stop than she'd ever admit. She felt so defeated. All she wanted was to get healthy and strong, be happy with Aaron, and settle back at home. *I am failing him in everything. He risked his life to get me back . . . all I have to do is be happy.*

"I wish I could move on from my time at Moorloc's. I drank all these disgusting potions to bring the memories back, and now I'm hearing things. What if remembering everything breaks us? What if I did something unforgivable?"

Harold turned to Alex. "You were held captive and did what you had to in order to survive. No one should punish you for that, and nothing you did would be unforgivable—not to my people."

"You say that now."

"I say that as your friend and ally."

"Thank you, Harold, but you don't have to." Alex stood to straighten her shirt, then stopped and laughed.

"What?" Harold asked.

She shook her head. "I'm straightening my shirt, and there is a giant rip down the back."

Harold chuckled, walked to his wardrobe, and returned with one of his tunics.

"I can't take that, Harold."

"You'd rather walk around with your back showing? I know you're sensitive about your scars."

"You and Aaron talk too much," Alex said, accepting the shirt.

"I'd like to go to your Verlassen Castle, if you don't mind. I can help Aaron decide what to do about this attack. Your fathers would likely summon me anyway."

"You're probably right." Alex took his hand. "I would appreciate it if you helped Aaron with one more thing. He may not have told you. Gryphon kissed me."

Harold raised his eyebrows. "Explain."

"It was the last day. He wanted Moorloc to believe he'd come to take me away. I couldn't fake the hate I needed to show. So he kissed me. I shoved him off, but I let it happen."

"Not your choice. Not your fault, though I can understand why Aaron is angry."

"He is . . . though not at me. But this kiss is why he's convinced Gryphon did something to me."

"What matters is you were honest. You've hidden nothing from him, and it's time he listens to you."

"Thank you, Harold."

Harold bowed to her and held his arm out. "I'll escort you to our dining hall, and after you've eaten, you shall crack me to my Emmerich."

Despite everything, Alex snorted. "He won't enjoy being called Emmerich."

Harold smirked. "Which is precisely why I intend to call him that. If he wants to act like his father, I shall address him as such."

CHAPTER 5

AARON

Aaron gave the stable boys the list of improvements he wanted made by the time he returned. He was heading to the kitchen to grab a quick bite when he ran into Michael.

"Are you and Jessica all packed for the week of wedding nonsense my mother insists on putting us through?" Aaron asked.

Michael, who was usually jolly, looked tense. "I am, but what time did Alex and Stefan leave?"

"Early. Why?"

"I received word from Warren—they never arrived."

"They should have been there hours ago," Aaron said. Terror and rage settled into Aaron's stomach like rocks. "Megesti!"

I let her go because she needs space, but if anything happens to her, it's my fault.

"You don't have to shout," Megesti groaned.

"Can you crack me to Warren?"

"No. Alex and I are working on it, but I'm still terrible at cracking. I would probably end up putting you into a tree."

Michael asked, "What if you cracked me?" His light copper features creased with worry.

"We have to find her," Aaron said. He ran his hand through his hair, panic taking over.

"General approaching!" a guard shouted.

Michael, Aaron, and Megesti looked up and saw General Matthew Bishop, the second general of Warren, riding across the drawbridge toward them. He dismounted and handed the reins to a squire. He held a charred cloak soaked in blood.

"We found this with the mutilated bodies of Alex's and Stefan's horses. Something attacked them on the road."

Aaron took the cloak. It was Alex's. He clutched it tight. "We have to go find her. She has to be all right."

"She's safe in Warren now," someone said from the doorway.

They all turned to find Harold, dressed in his royal garb and crown. But it was the blood on his tunic that drew Aaron's attention.

"Harold, whose blood is on you?" Aaron asked.

"Alexandria's, mostly. Some is Stefan's."

"Is the princess all right?" Matthew asked.

Harold nodded. "My physician tended to her, and I wouldn't let them leave without a good meal."

"Stefan's safe too?" Michael asked.

"Yes, and I'm here to update my Emmerich."

Matthew sniggered behind Michael.

Aaron gave them both dirty looks, then asked, "Emmerich?"

Harold grinned back. "If I am your Edward, that would make you my Emmerich."

Aaron opened his mouth to argue but realized he *had* been

acting like his father lately, letting his temper get the better of him more than he should. "Harold and I will leave immediately for Warren. Matthew, could you finish preparing things with Michael and Megesti?"

"Of course, Prince Aaron," Matthew said.

As they rode toward Warren, Harold told Aaron everything that had occurred in Betruger. Soon they reached the site where the attack had taken place. It was brutal and ugly. The mutilated horses lay dead on the road, and the damage to the surrounding area stretched three wagon-lengths into the trees, some of which were still smoldering. Aaron struggled not to retch as thought after thought of what could have happened to Alex bombarded him. He scratched at the scorch marks on the road with his boot. They were at least three fingers deep. It was difficult to believe Alex and Stefan had escaped in one piece.

As they rode on, Aaron kept asking Harold about what Alex had told him. However, Harold refused to break her trust. He brought the conversation back to the plans the three of them had devised to use Alex's magic to create an easier mountain road from Datten to Betruger to make trade between the kingdoms faster. Aaron admitted that she seemed to have been struggling to control her powers more and more lately, so they'd likely have to delay the creation of the trade route.

"Have you considered bringing Gryphon back?" Harold asked as they rounded another bend.

"No."

"No, you haven't thought of it, or no, you don't want to?"

"We don't know how to get in touch with him," Aaron lied.

Harold considered this. "Uh-huh," he said after a minute,

then turned his focus toward the road ahead. "What's going on up there?"

Aaron followed his gaze and spotted a frail old woman standing beside a cart overloaded with potatoes. She was barely taller than the equally frail donkey that pulled the cart. As they rode closer, Aaron noticed a young man trying to fix the cart's wheel.

"Truthfully, Alex is all right?"

"Yes," Harold replied. "Why this insistence?"

"In a week, I'm going to be Prince of Warren. I should start acting like one."

Harold nodded his approval. "I greatly admire your endless desire to help others. It shows your Strobel side, and I believe Alex prefers that side of you."

As they arrived at the wagon, Harold and Aaron dismounted and tied their horses to a nearby tree branch.

"Please, do not trouble yourselves with us," the old woman said. "My grandson will have the wheel back on in a moment. We don't wish to keep you from your important business." She had no doubt noticed the Warren crest on Aaron's shirt, as she bowed her head.

"Nonsense," Aaron said, rolling up his sleeves. "With our help, your wagon will be fixed in mere moments!"

Harold moved to the rear of the wagon, and Aaron went to the middle. They looked at the nervous, scrawny young man between them, who couldn't be more than twenty. Aaron smiled, hoping to put him at ease. "We'll lift the wagon so you can fasten the wheel."

The young man nodded. Harold and Aaron managed to hold the wagon up despite the load of potatoes weighing it down, and the wheel was back on in a minute.

"Oh, thank you," said the old woman. She slowly hobbled toward Aaron and Harold, but she stopped at the wagon and removed a small sack of potatoes. "Please, allow me to pay you for your kindness."

Aaron held up his hand. "That isn't necessary."

"My grandmother insists," the young man said. "She won't give up until you accept."

"We appreciate your offer, and we were happy to help," Harold said. Then he whispered to Aaron, "These are *your* people now. Accept the payment."

Clenching the bag, the old woman held out her thin, shaky arms. He took the potatoes from her, then sighed as he put them back on her wagon with the others. "I'm on my way to the castle in Warren. I couldn't possibly accept payment. I have more than I need, and you should keep your goods to sell at the market."

"Then will you accept a kiss as payment?"

The young man rolled his eyes, but Aaron grinned. "I would be honored, milady." Aaron leaned down, and she grabbed his face, kissing his cheek. As Harold chuckled across the road, the old woman's cold lips sent a shiver through Aaron.

"We are indebted to your kindness," the grandson said.

"Safe travels to you both," Harold said. "Take extra care. There have been attacks on this road today."

"We certainly will. And you, travel safely as well." The old woman waved and gave them a toothy smile as Aaron and Harold continued down the road.

CHAPTER 6
ALEX

Alex and Stefan arrived in Warren. To avoid causing a panic, Alex cracked them into the spare hall. They heard shouting from inside the throne room and silently slipped in unseen through the adjoining doors.

Lord Wescott, Alex's law tutor, yelled, "Bring her home. General Bishop said she was attacked on the road, coming from that *ferflucsing* castle you let her live in. How can you let your only daughter live half a day's ride from you?"

Cameron's father, Bernhard, angrily added, "She belongs in Warren, surrounded by guards and generals. She's your only heir, Edward."

Alex and Stefan stole behind the thrones, eavesdropping.

"That's enough," Edward said. "She's my daughter. What happened during her time with Moorloc deeply affected her. She needs time to heal—away from the prying eyes of Warren nobility. And it's only a three-hour ride, not half a day."

Someone else said, "From what I've heard from my son, healing is not what she's been doing with Prince Aaron. I'm surprised they haven't had to move up the marriage due to pregnancy."

Alex set her jaw. She couldn't see who was talking, but the idea that her guards would gossip about her was painful. She looked at Stefan, and he looked even angrier than she felt. *He'll take care of that guard when we return.*

Edward said, "If they decide they're ready to fulfill their obligations of giving us an heir, I'll be thrilled. But no matter *what* they're doing, she is entitled to her privacy, so if your son says one more word about my daughter or her *activities,* he'll be out of her guard in a second."

She grinned to hear her father defending her.

"I understand your need to give her space, Edward," Bernhard said. "But she isn't just your daughter. She's the future Queen of Warren and of Datten. Once Emmerich hears about this, he'll be demanding Aaron and Alex move to Datten, where he and Jerome can properly protect her."

"No one is taking my daughter from me."

"Aaron will be," another man said. "What'll happen once they're married? What if he reconsiders and wants to go home? He may not get along with his father, but once Alexandria's pregnant, they may want to be around his mother."

"That won't happen," Edward replied.

Alex sighed. She'd heard enough, so she stepped around the thrones. "My father knows I intend to raise my children in Warren." The men gasped as they turned toward her. "I spent enough of my life away from the sea."

Lord Wescott said, "Well, princess, Verlassen Castle isn't by the sea, yet you live there."

"True, but I can be here in a few hours or crack if I choose to."

"And was that the plan today as well?" the unknown noble said.

"I'm sorry, we haven't met, Lord . . ."

"Baron Germund Vinur, Your Highness."

Alex paused. *Vinur? As in Reinhilde's family?*

Stefan broke in. "I assume you're the father of Felix, Archibald, and Henry."

"Indeed, and you are?"

Bernhard said, "Germund, that's Jerome's boy."

Alex spoke up. "The head of my personal guard and the man who will chastise your son for speaking about my personal . . . *activities*, is how I think you put it."

"Guards are under strict rules not to speak of the princess's personal matters with others, including members of the king's council," Stefan said.

The baron gulped and looked at Edward.

"Don't look at me," said the king. "Stefan's responsible for Alexandria's guards." Edward turned his attention to Alex and seemed to notice her shirt. "You went to Betruger?"

"I panicked and ended up there. Harold was very helpful. I'm thankful I managed to get away from the sorcerers—"

"Sorcerers attacked you?" Bernhard exclaimed. "We thought it was mercenaries."

Lord Wescott said, "You see, Edward? Had Randal and Matthew been there, she wouldn't have had to resort to fleeing to Betruger!"

"I'm sorry, gentlemen. That isn't true," Alex said. "No mortal is a match for a powerful sorcerer. The generals couldn't have helped. They'd have been only more people for me to protect, and honestly, I barely got away with Stefan. Had there been others, someone would have been left behind or I would have failed to escape altogether."

"What exactly are you saying, Your Highness?" Germund asked.

"I'm saying that as it currently stands, if I'm attacked by

sorcerers, there's nothing any of you can do to protect me. All I can do is retreat, so where I live doesn't make a difference."

Edward said, "Gentlemen, please excuse us. As you can see, my daughter is back." His council murmured and headed toward the door. Edward waited for them to leave before he turned and grabbed Alex into a tight hug. She winced when he squeezed her, but he let out a loud sigh that reverberated through her chest.

"Never do that to me again!" he said. "Do you have any idea how horrifying it was to learn that you didn't arrive and that we found your dead horses on the side of the road?"

"Almost as horrifying as watching it happen," Stefan said.

Edward took Alex's face in his hands. "Were you injured?"

Alex shot Stefan a warning look before glancing at her father. Fear had aged him, making his auburn skin wrinkle like a washboard, and his eyes seemed sad. "Nothing a good night's sleep won't heal."

"Does Emmerich know about the attack?" Stefan asked.

Edward shook his head.

"I cracked Harold to update Aaron and calm him down," Alex said. "I'm sure they'll arrive shortly. I could go to Datten and retrieve Emmerich."

"You shouldn't go alone," Stefan said.

"It's Datten. I'll be fine. I'd like to check Merlock's journals. The sorcerers who attacked us said they were titans, so maybe I can learn more about them. But first, I'll crack Megesti and my ladies to Warren."

"Do you want to get changed first?" Edward asked.

Alex looked down at her Betruger uniform and shrugged. She pointed to Stefan. "You certainly need to."

"I took the brunt of the attack to protect you."

Alex's reply was cut off by several sharp cracks of a whip.

This time, the sound ricocheted through the large, empty room.

"Alex?" Stefan asked.

"I'm fine."

"Are you sure?" Edward asked.

"Yes. Now I'm off to fetch my godfather."

THE DATTEN THRONE room was empty when she arrived. *That's odd. It's the middle of the afternoon.* Her soft footsteps echoed as she cautiously made her way across the hall, feeling as if the paintings were watching her. When she reached the doors to leave, guards in red tunics accosted her and drew their swords. Alex simply held up her hands and smiled.

"Apologies, Your Highness," they said, dropping to their knees as King Emmerich came around the corner with Jerome.

"Alexandria!" Emmerich's blue eyes sparkled. He held out his arms and kissed her cheek, but seeing her state, his posture changed at once. "What's the matter?"

"What gave me away?" Alex asked, stepping back from the hug.

"Well, you are wearing a bloody Betruger tunic," Jerome said.

"I've looked worse. But you're correct. I'm not here for a visit. I need to find Merlock's journals and bring you back with me to help my father with a decision."

"I believe there is much more to this story," Emmerich said, waving Jerome away.

Alex smiled weakly as they strolled to Megesti's lab. She told him about the attack and what she'd overheard from the counsel after she'd returned to Warren. "I'm worried about why these sorcerers left the Forbidden Lands. They looked older, so I'm hoping there will be something in Merlock's journals about who they are. I want to see if—" A whip cracked several times, and she stopped walking. The sound was louder and closer than ever before.

Emmerich gently touched her shoulder, making her jerk and clutch at her chest in fright.

"Alexandria?"

"Did you hear it?" she asked, wide-eyed and frantic as the sound echoed down the hall. "There it is again."

"What?"

"The whip! Did you hear it? I keep hearing a whip."

"Could you have hit your head?" Emmerich asked. His pale skin turned ashen.

"I need to figure out what's happening, both with the sorcerers and to me."

"Of course." Emmerich opened the lab door for her. Once inside, she flicked her wrist, and the fireplace roared to life, illuminating the entire room. Emmerich's golden hair and crest reflected the fire, sending lights dancing across the floor.

Megesti's lab was similar to her mother's. The main door was in the far left corner of the room, and the opposite wall was covered from floor to ceiling with bookshelves. Merlock's books were available for Megesti whenever he needed them. In the furthest corner stood the fireplace and a small table covered in pots. On the other side was an enormous wall with shelves filled with strange jars and pots. Alex loved Merlock's collection. Her mother's vessels were a mix of styles and colors, whereas Merlock's had been gifted to him by the kings he served and thus matched perfectly.

Emmerich asked, "Do you know what you're looking for?"

"I think so." She scanned the books and picked out a few journals. *It has to be here.*

"How are the memories and nightmares? Have you been trying the generals' suggestions? Do they make a difference?"

Alex glanced at Emmerich. "A little. I woke up terrified last night, and Aaron says I still talk in my sleep."

"Does having him there help?"

"Yes and no."

"So he's on his way to Warren with Harold now?"

Alex nodded. "My father wants a meeting with everyone tonight to decide what action to take."

"You should be prepared. Edward will scold Aaron when he arrives."

"This wasn't his fault."

"When your father gave Aaron permission to propose, he expected him to protect you. That's why Edward wanted you married the night you came home. Aaron failed in his duty today. He allowed you to go off on your own, and it almost cost you your life."

Alex looked down and swallowed. "I've been telling everyone the same thing. Even if he'd been there, he wouldn't have been able to do anything. He'd have been just another person for me to save."

"Your father won't see it that way."

The whip cracked again, and Alex glanced around.

"Did you hear it again?" Emmerich asked.

Alex nodded. Her lip quivered.

"Let's get you back to Warren. Tomorrow you'll return to finalize the wedding preparations for next week. We'll arrange it so you and Jerome can talk through your nightmares."

Alex exhaled. "Thank you. I appreciate that. Aaron is so proud of having saved me, but he doesn't understand how the deaths weigh on me. They were his men, but they died for me."

"Saving you brought him honor in Datten's eyes, but I understand the pain you feel all too well."

"Should we summon Jerome now?"

"No. With those sorcerers around, I want him to stay close to Guinevere," Emmerich replied.

Alex prepared to crack them to Warren but paused. "Are you feeling all right, Emmerich? You look pale."

"You're marrying my son. I feel great."

Alex blushed and cracked back into Warren's throne room. At night, the room was quiet and filled with glowing candles.

Randal said, "King Edward and King Harold are waiting in the king's suite, Your Royal Highness. Princess, you and Megesti will join them after they've discussed how far they'll go in this matter."

"However far is necessary to protect a Princess of Datten." Emmerich winked at Alex.

Alex handed Randal the journals Megesti had asked for. "Where's Aaron?"

The man glanced around, then leaned toward Alex, focusing his brown eyes on her. "I saw him heading toward your room—sulking."

Emmerich scoffed. "Sulking?"

Randal sighed before continuing. "Edward had some choice words for him after he arrived from Verlassen Castle."

"You were in the room for the scolding?" Alex asked.

"No, but as you know, your father's voice does carry."

Emmerich laughed. "I warned you. When Aaron fails *you*, Edward takes it personally. Go and be with Aaron until we summon you."

Randal added, "Edith and Jessica are off collecting the last things you'll need in Datten tomorrow."

Alex groaned and scrunched her nose. "More dresses?"

"Most likely. I'll escort you to your suite."

Emmerich said, "You were attacked this morning. Allow your father this precautionary measure."

49

Alex allowed both of them to escort her to her suite before they continued on to Edward's. When she entered her room, her stomach rumbled, and she realized she'd missed dinner.

"Aaron?"

Please don't be petulant or terrified anymore. I don't have the energy to go through it all again.

Alex leaned into the stairwell and called, a little louder, "Aaron?" There was no reply.

So either he's angry, he's hiding until he's calmed down, or he left. Alex lowered herself onto one of her green reading chairs, curled her legs under her, and sighed. A whip cracked, and she tried to ignore it by examining the Betruger crest on her shirt.

The door flew open, and Aaron trudged in with a basket full of bread, dried meat, cheese, and apples. His face told her everything. He was devastated and exhausted, and terror ran under his forced smile. He plodded across the room and set the basket on the chair beside Alex.

She swung her legs out, looking up at him. She wished she had some power to skip the next ten minutes of her life.

Aaron dropped to his knees and grabbed her hands as tears welled up in his eyes.

"Aaron . . ." Alex swallowed hard.

He opened his mouth but shut it without speaking, and they stared at each other.

She finally whispered, "Please don't be angry with me."

Aaron's eyes widened, and he shook his head. "You have nothing to apologize for. I failed you. I should have been with you . . . protecting you."

Alex leaned down and pressed her forehead to Aaron's. Gripping his shirt, she pulled him closer and kissed him. Aaron slid his arms around her waist, pulling her off the chair and into his arms.

"I'm sorry," he said. His voice cracked as he fought to get

the words out. "I should never have let you go. I've been pushing you away because of what you say in your sleep. I'm jealous of a dream, and we haven't properly talked about Gryphon, but . . . I know something happened. I've blamed you, and that's unfair. You're not responsible for everything I've imagined another man has done. What if something had happened to you?"

Alex sighed. "You sound like my father and Harold."

"They aren't wrong. Please tell me what happened. And forgive me. Finding Flash dead was more terrifying than waking up to you being gone. And this time, I knew you were all right."

Alex swallowed. *How could I just leave Flash? I'm so sorry.*

"Harold told you what we discussed?" Alex wanted to run, but she was still sitting in Aaron's lap on the floor.

Aaron looked down. "He thought it would be better for me to lose my temper with him than with you. You've been through enough today."

"I appreciate that."

Aaron wouldn't look at her. "Are you hungry?"

Alex managed a smile. *I need to feel something besides fear.* "I will be. Afterward."

Aaron finally looked back at her. Alex placed her hand on his chest and kissed him again. Wrapping his arms around her, he pulled her against his chest. The moment he let go just a little, Alex lifted her tunic over her head. Aaron raised his eyebrows.

"What about your guards? Your ladies?"

"Gone. Busy with wedding things."

A mischievous grin spread across Aaron's face as he stripped his own shirt and lay down on the rug, pulling Alex on top of him. She leaned down to kiss him. It didn't take long for their pants to join the discarded tunics and the room's silence to be filled with their moans and gasps for breath.

Later, Alex ended up in Aaron's tunic, Harold's tossed over the chair. They sat on the floor together, eating the food Aaron had brought. When Alex reached for an apple, Aaron's oversized shirt slipped, and she caught him frowning at the fresh scar on her back.

Alex took a deep breath and confessed everything she'd never told him about what had happened with Gryphon on the last day at the castle. He said nothing but took her hands in his when she wouldn't stop fidgeting. She wasn't sure he breathed once while she talked about Gryphon kissing her in front of Moorloc the evening before the battle. She even told him about the fears she had about getting her memories back.

She told him her version of what had happened when she and Stefan were attacked and how Harold had helped them. Aaron moved his arms around her waist without thinking, and her body tensed. She allowed him to gently lift her tunic. Cool air hit her skin as his fingers gently traced the new scars on her back.

"So Gryphon showed his true colors," he said. "He told them about you. How else could they know where you are?"

"The sorcerers mentioned that Lygari arrived there. He must have told them. I can't believe Gryphon would betray me."

"Well, we'll have to agree to disagree on that."

Alex scoffed.

"I have one thing to say. I know you defend your own honor, and you did that in your way." Aaron pressed his forehead to Alex's, making her feel even closer to him. "However, the honor of the Princess of Datten is the responsibility of the king or, in our case, the crown prince. If Gryphon returns, I'll defend your honor my way. Otherwise, I won't be able to live with myself."

Alex kissed him quickly. "I'll respect Datten's traditions and let you try."

"Try?" He pulled away with a wry grin. "Do you doubt my ability to defend you?"

"Against any mortal man? Never. Against a sorcerer who can vanish at will? That would be trickier."

After a while, he said, "I'm so sorry about Flash."

Alex swallowed her sorrow. "I had him for so long. I don't know how I'll ever replace him."

"Cameron will help you and Stefan find new horses. You won't be able to replace Flash, but hopefully you'll find a new horse."

Alex smiled weakly, remembering the day she got Flash and how freeing it had felt to have her own horse.

"Do you know why they came after you?" Aaron asked.

She adjusted her tunic. "It happened so fast. And when they started burning and exploding the trees . . . Gryphon worked so hard to teach me, and my control was *terrible*. But when we practiced, he never tried to hurt me." She froze, remembering when the sorceress had mentioned Gryphon, and at once, she felt Aaron's eyes on her. Since her return, he was better at sensing the subtle shifts in her emotions.

"What?"

"The sorceress who threw the fire. She said they were supposed to take me to their king. That he wanted to meet me after hearing about me from Lygari and Gryphon. But they also asked *where* Gryphon was."

"So Gryphon did tell them about you."

"That doesn't make sense," Alex said. "Why would he help me, save me, kiss me . . . all to turn me over to their king?"

"Men do stupid things," Aaron said.

Alex heard the whip crack again and jumped up from the floor. "Tell me you heard that."

Aaron glanced around before fixing his eyes on her, confused. He moved to take her hands, but she stepped back.

"His father!" Alex's eyes widened. "The current Head—the king, he's Gryphon's father."

"That means they know you're the Heart," Aaron said.

"That has to be why they came after me," Alex said. She groaned and sat back down.

"What do we do now?"

"I'm not sure. But they aren't done with me."

"Get some rest. I'll deal with our fathers and Harold."

Alex stuck out her tongue at Aaron and took a bite of bread. "I'm not letting a group of men decide what's best for me. When has that ever gone well?"

CHAPTER 7
ALEX

For hours, they argued about how best to keep her safe from yet another danger from the Forbidden Lands. *If my father had known how much trouble I'd be, would he have still wanted my mother?* Alex sat between Aaron and Harold. The kings, Warren generals, Stefan, Michael, and Megesti filled the remaining spots at Edward's meeting table, on the main floor of the king's suite.

"Is there a way for someone without magic to injure a sorcerer?" Michael asked.

"Not without you putting yourselves at risk," Megesti said. "We're dealing with titans, and they're the strongest of a line —generals, if you will. Alex and I aren't powerful enough to go after one, even together."

"But you're both titans," Harold said.

"We are," Alex said. "But Megesti is the Titan of Merlin, which means his skills are diverse, not focused. These sorcerers are each skilled in one area, making them more powerful."

"And you?"

"I'm Titan of Cassandra. We heal and have premonitions,

neither of which are directly helpful in battle. As far as being the Heart, my powers are too far out of my control, so it's risky for me to go up against that kind of power without Gr—I mean, a more powerful sorcerer to guide me." Alex avoided looking at Aaron, but he slid his hand into hers and squeezed it lovingly.

Stefan said, "So the best course of action is to keep you away from them. Protected." He glanced toward the generals and then back to the kings.

"No," Alex said.

"What?" Michael and Harold both exclaimed at once.

Alex scowled. "Stefan, don't you dare suggest it."

"It's the obvious choice," he replied.

"I don't care. No."

"We're missing something," Emmerich said.

"They always do this," Michael groaned.

"The *only* choice is—"

Alex slammed her elbow into the table and pointed at Stefan. "Catch your tongue."

Stefan stared her down and growled, "We take her to Datten."

"Because that worked so well the first time," Alex snapped before she could stop herself. Dread rushed through her as she looked over at Emmerich.

"We'd do things differently this time," he said calmly. "We have not emphasized guarding the town in the past, and yes, that's how they got to you before. You'd live in the castle, which you'd do as Princess of Datten anyhow. And we'd surround you with generals and guards."

"Except she won't stay in the castle," Aaron said. "She has a long list of people who can't keep track of her. Jerome's good, but he's not that good."

"Would you stay put for your own safety?" Edward asked.

Alex looked at Emmerich and the generals, rubbing her collarbone. "I will not be locked away again." The tower Moorloc had imprisoned her in flashed across her mind.

Aaron sighed. "They mutilated your horses."

"What?" Alex turned to him.

"We stopped at the site of the attack," Harold said. "On our way here, we stopped to see where you were attacked and to help an old woman with her cart."

Alex peeked at Aaron, trying to hide her smile. *I like when you help my people.*

He said, "There were scorch marks on the road so large I had to take five steps to get from one side to the other. All the trees are gone—no, obliterated. They looked as if something had broken out from inside them."

"We had to walk fifteen steps from your road to find anything left alive," Harold said. "What you must have gone through..."

Stefan and Alex looked across the table at each other.

"We'll go to Datten for the wedding," Edward said. "At least one general and two guards will protect Alex at all times when she's not in the main castle, and—"

"I can't live my life in fear—"

"And I will not risk your life again!" Edward slammed his fist on the table, startling everyone. He looked at Aaron as he spoke. "I made a mistake thirteen years ago, and it cost my wife her life. Others made mistakes this morning, and while all that is forgiven, if someone dares to attack you again, you *shall* be properly protected. You'll have a general with you at all times."

"But—"

"Alexandria. This is not up for discussion," Edward said.

Alex dropped her gaze to the floor. Aaron squeezed her thigh, but she refused to look at him.

Harold spoke up. "I offer Sir Macht to assist in protecting Alex. With an extra general, it will be easier to keep her protected without wearing out your men."

Alex stood, making all the men in the room jump to their feet.

"And where are you going, young lady?" Emmerich asked.

"To bed. Or do I now require permission for that too?"

Edward nodded, and Randal opened the door between the king's and queen's suites. Alex lifted her chin and marched into her room without looking back. She ascended the stairs to her changing area, undressed, and threw her clothes on the floor. She grabbed a worn tunic of Aaron's from the wardrobe and pulled it over her head before groaning loudly and slamming the wardrobe door.

"That was quite the exit."

Alex exhaled as she looked back at Michael. "I expected Aaron."

"He's being scolded again. All three kings are concerned that he let you leave alone. You should expect him to stick to you for a while."

"Stefan was with me! Michael, I won't spend my life locked away . . . hiding. Not again."

Alex missed his reply because another whip crack echoed down the stairs from her bedroom. Her heart pounded as she turned toward the stairs, hearing a second and third crack.

"Are you listening to me?" Michael shook her shoulder, and Alex jerked back. "I'm worried about you."

"I'm fine, Michael . . . I'm jumpy after this morning, and the idea of being locked up in Datten—"

"Are you sure that's all?"

"Of course. Why would I lie to you?"

THE BRIGHT MORNING sun lit up the spare hall as Alex finished cracking her ladies to Datten. They were going ahead to prepare Alex's room for her arrival. Despite the wedding excitement, Alex was tired. She'd barely slept after the meeting despite Aaron's efforts to cheer her up. *You can't comfort me if you agree with them. And I can't figure out if you actually do agree or if being yelled at by both our fathers made you exceptionally cautious.*

"Are you finished here?" Stefan asked as he joined her in the hall.

Alex forced herself not to react when another whip cracked behind her. "Yes. Although I don't know how we'll replace the horses, or why we have to do it so soon."

"Your father insisted, and Cameron offered his help."

"I know, and if we don't find horses we love, my father will summon every horse breeder to Warren after the wedding."

"Perfect." Stefan held his arm out for Alex. They arrived at the king's suite, where Edward was having a heated discussion with his soon-to-be son-in-law.

When they entered, the king said, "Stefan, would you please escort my daughter to the dining hall? I had lunch laid out." His eyes remained fixed on Aaron.

"Father?" Alex asked, reaching for Edward's arm.

"It's fine, dear," he said to her. "We just need to finish our conversation."

She shot Aaron a concerned look but let go of her father and walked through the door into the dining hall with Stefan. Glancing back, she saw pain on Aaron's face before he resumed staring at the ground.

Michael and Harold were waiting in the dining hall. "What happened?" Michael asked. "You look worried."

"It appears King Edward has more to say to Aaron

59

regarding Alex's safety," Stefan said. Alex tried to shove him but failed to move him.

"Why? Edward knows Alex doesn't obey anyone," Michael said.

"Regardless, he isn't willing to risk her again," Stefan said. "Don't be surprised if Aaron and Alex end up in Datten after their wedding."

Alex glared at Stefan and jabbed her elbow into his side. He groaned, and she took her seat at the table in regal silence. The others joined her and ate without speaking. Alex knew Stefan noticed her checking the door for Aaron.

When he finally arrived, Alex was desperate to know what happened but waited for him to join them. For some reason, he sat across from her, beside Harold.

"What was that about?" Michael asked before he stuffed more cheese into his mouth.

"Nothing," Aaron said.

"We know it was something," Stefan said.

"It's none of your concern," Aaron snapped.

"Excuse us." Alex stood, giving Aaron a significant look, but he refused to make eye contact. She held out her hand to him, but he didn't move. "Fine." Alex grabbed a piece of bread off her untouched plate and stormed away from the table. She made it into the hallway before Aaron caught up to her. "If you won't talk to me, my father will," she said.

He looked at the ground. "Your father chastised me— again. Apparently, after speaking with *my* father, he decided once wasn't enough."

"I assumed as much," Alex said. "Why not talk to me?"

Aaron grabbed her hands. "Your father has never lectured me like that. I've been repeatedly reminded how I put you in danger. The woman I love, the one your father trusted me to protect. He expected me to have learned my lesson after you sacrificed yourself for us last year, and I didn't."

"Aaron, we couldn't have known that would happen."

"I should have been there," he said.

Without a shred of anger in her voice, Alex asked, "What would you have done that Stefan didn't? You saw the area. You touched the scorched ground."

"Alex—"

"No. I will not let my father make you feel guilty for something you would have been helpless to stop."

Aaron took her hand and squeezed it. "I have been given a list of rules regarding you. The number of guards, how far to let you go alone, and so forth."

Alex huffed, but he squeezed harder. "So if you are planning to leave, I cannot let you go alone."

"You know I'm going to continue to go places with only Stefan or Michael, don't you?"

Aaron nodded. "Unfortunately, yes. But I do request you take them both, so I get scolded less."

"I'll consider it." She smiled. "I had planned to take a quick nap before visiting your dear cousin." She slid her hands up Aaron's chest. "Care to accompany me?"

"Princess," Aaron teased, "are you inviting me to your bedchamber? What would your betrothed say?"

Alex burst out laughing. "Watch yourself, Your Highness, or I might not let you leave my chambers," she said as she hurried up the stairs still laughing.

❧❧❧ ❧❧❧

DRESSED IN RIDING CLOTHES, Aaron and Alex were about to leave their suite when there was a knock. Aaron opened the door to find an empty hall. Confused, he looked at Alex, but she giggled.

"Wrong door." She opened the one connected to her father's room.

"Sorry to intrude," Edward said. "I require my daughter for a few minutes before you leave for the Strobel estate."

"Of course, Your Royal Highness," he said stiffly. "Should I accompany you?"

Alex scowled at Aaron's formal behavior toward her father.

"That won't be necessary. I'll bring her to the stables when we're finished."

Aaron bowed and kissed Alex's cheek before he left.

"Did you have to be so hard on him?" she asked.

Edward scoffed. "Me scolding your future husband is not your concern."

"Considering it was *my* choice and I picked *him*, I disagree."

"Alexandria, you just turned eighteen, and like you, Aaron is young. He's only twenty-one, and so he needed reminding that his duty to keep you safe didn't end when you came home."

"He knows that," Alex said, following her father into the main hallway. "But he also respects that I don't want to feel caged or watched all day."

"Just because he shares your bed doesn't mean he's infallible."

Alex looked around the room before focusing on her father. "How long have you known?"

"The entire time. I've allowed it because he helps calm your nightmares. But I would suggest you keep it from Guinevere. She won't be as understanding as Emmerich and I."

Emmerich knows too? Alex groaned as they turned and headed into the bowels of the castle, where Edward took a torch from the wall.

"Where are we going?"

He kissed Alex's forehead. "The treasure room. I left my favorite jewels in your chamber, but the rest are in our treasure room."

They turned down a dark tunnel, and the earthen floor made it smell musty and dank. Alex shivered and rubbed her arms. "I hate this part of the castle."

"Is that why you avoid your mother's crypt?"

"I don't want to go by my grandfather's. And . . ."

"And what?"

"There are ghosts down here."

"You're still seeing them?"

"I see more now. I'm thankful that Megesti and I were able to stop my powers from growing more until I'm older. I don't think I could handle any more."

Edward handed her a list of jewels.

"Why so many?" she asked.

"It's Guinevere's list. These are the Warren jewels she asked me to bring to Datten for you to pick from once you see your dress. She wants our kingdom represented."

Alex grinned. "Warren was her kingdom too."

"And I'm sure that's why."

Edward led Alex to a circular alcove in the darkest depths of the castle. Alex recognized it from when she and Aaron hid down there to talk after his birthday celebration was ruined by Lygari. The room had ridiculously high ceilings and was exceptionally well lit by torches. The small side path was the one she had taken with Aaron. In the opposite direction were five ancient wooden doors, each standing almost triple her height, that led to the different crypts. It surprised Alex that such a large room hadn't caved in after so many centuries buried beneath the castle.

Edward unlocked the first door. "This is the burial place of the oldest kings and queens of Warren."

Before them was a vast room with a long stone path. It was lined on both sides with white marble tombs. Attached to the outside of each was an obsidian stone etched with the faces of the buried king and queen.

"Are the kings and queens always buried together?"

"They are."

"Is that how all of them are?"

"Most. Sometimes the royal had to remarry, and then they were buried apart."

Alex cautiously stepped toward the first tomb. The moment her foot hit the path, the torches sprang to life, lighting her way. Shivering in the icy air, she forced her legs to take her forward. On either side of her rested the kings and queens of Warren. This was their eternal home after serving their kingdom for their entire lives.

The crack of a whip echoed in the room, and Alex tensed. Edward took her hand and led her on. When they reached the end of the path, he pulled out a dagger.

"Is the door locked by a blood spell?" Alex asked.

Edward raised his eyebrows at her and pricked his finger. As a drop of blood welled up, he touched the wall and whispered, "Nial the brave, Veremund the wise, Warren the true."

With a click, a door that hadn't been there a moment ago appeared, and Alex gasped. When Edward turned a key in the lock, the door swung open on its own.

"Only the descendants of the three founding houses can access the vault."

"So Randal can?"

"Edith and her sisters too."

Alex followed her father into the cavernous room. It was larger than the royal crypt they'd walked through. To the right were rows and rows of shelves, more than she could see. Some held books, and others were laden with crowns, swords, and jewelry. For a moment, she could have sworn she heard whispering from the shelves, but that was impossible. *How would my mother's books end up down here?*

A mountain of riches that nearly touched the ceiling dominated the entire back half of the room. It was piled with massive chests overflowing with gold, gems, and other treasures. Around them stood other valuable gifts: a solid gold suit of armor, a pedestal with an emerald as large as a pumpkin chiseled into the shape of a sea dragon's head, and a model ship covered with diamonds. In front of it all was a large table. An unknown force drew Alex there while Edward walked toward the jewelry.

A strange tingle spread through her body as she approached the table. It looked harmless, but when she touched it, it burned her. Alex leaped back and bumped into her father.

Edward ran his hand across the elaborately carved table. "The table base is obsidian. The top is solid gold, and the finest silks at the time were set up to hold the treasure."

Alex looked at the empty table again. "What treasure?"

"It held the scepter of the first King of Warren, in fact. But the scepter has been missing for hundreds of years. Some doubt it ever even existed." Edward's expression invited a question.

"If it never existed, why the table?"

"To carry on the legend, my dear." Edward grinned, and his eyes sparkled as he motioned for Alex to follow him to the endless shelves of crowns and jewels.

Alex went but couldn't help glancing back at the table as the pain in her hand faded. They quickly found the jewelry

Guinevere had requested. Edward kept offering Alex larger crowns, but she refused them all.

"I prefer mine. It matches Aaron's," she said.

"All right. If I can't convince you to wear a larger one, is there at least one you'd add to your set for formal events? Or perhaps a new necklace." He nodded to the place where her necklace should have been.

My crown was yours, and my necklace was my mother's. I might have lost it during the fight, but I'm not ready to replace it yet. To please her father, Alex looked around the old wooden shelves and found a simple crown decorated with rubies. She gently lifted it and brought it back to him. "Rubies are Datten's gem, aren't they?"

Edward smiled. "They are, and this crown was my mother's favorite."

Alex followed her father out, but she paused to look at the empty table one last time. Edward returned for her, resting his hand against her back, and she allowed him to guide her from their treasure room. As soon as they passed through, the door closed, locked, and vanished behind them.

CHAPTER 8
ALEX

"You two are even pickier about horses than I am." Aaron laughed as he entered the throne room to crack to Datten.

Stefan added, "Alex needs to connect with a horse. She and Flash found each other."

Alex shook her head. "None of them felt right."

"How does a horse *feel* right?" Harold asked.

"It's hard to explain. Flash sensed what I wanted to do a few seconds before I did it. I don't expect to have a connection like that with a new horse right away, but I want to feel *something*." Alex sighed, and Michael put his arm around her shoulders.

Stefan shot Aaron a look of disapproval, asking, "What are you smiling at?"

"I'm thinking about how lucky I am to be marrying the best woman in all of Torian."

"Oh?" Alex asked.

"Yes. She's brave, strong, smart, enchantingly beautiful, a

sorceress, and a princess, *and* she can talk to horses. I don't know how I got so lucky."

Alex blushed and looked away.

"You got lucky because she chose you," Edward said, walking to them.

Another whip cracked, and her eyes darted to the side of the room.

"Everything all right?" Michael whispered to Alex.

"Fine. Everyone ready?"

Without letting anyone answer, Alex smiled and cracked them all into the Datten throne room. Queen Guinevere was waiting with Jessica and Edith. All were beautifully dressed in fine Datten gowns.

"Finally." Guinevere sighed. "We have so much to do. Edward, Aaron. I'm sure you can each find your way without my company. Alexandria, come with us."

Edith and Jessica each took one of Alex's arms and whisked her into the hallway, away from Aaron and the others.

"What are you doing?" Alex asked.

"In Datten, the bride doesn't see the groom for several days before the wedding," Jessica said, brushing her red hair away from her porcelain cheek.

"But—" Alex argued.

"You'll be fine," Guinevere said as they arrived at a door across the hall from the queen's suite. Edith opened it, and Jessica pulled Alex inside.

Although the room was smaller than her usual rooms, it was exquisitely decorated. The red bedding matched Aaron's, and one corner of the chamber held beautifully carved bookcases filled with brand-new books. Alex suspected Guinevere had added them for her benefit. On the left were a large mirror, an ornate wardrobe, and a beautiful red couch with a table beside it. Jessica set to unpacking the jewelry, and when Alex turned toward her, she froze. Hanging on the wall behind the door was the most beautiful dress Alex had ever seen. She was so enamored with it that she barely heard Guinevere speaking.

"Emmerich and Edward don't know this, but I am well aware that you and Aaron have been sharing a bed at the castle. However, while we wait for the wedding, I'd like you to respect tradition."

Alex gulped and looked nervously at Guinevere. The queen merely raised her brows at Alex, making her blush, before her gaze went back to the dress. "Can I try it on?" Alex asked, and Guinevere's lips spread into a smile.

"Soon. The seamstresses should be here in an hour to fit you and handle any last-minute adjustments. We used your old measurements since we knew you were trying to regain your strength."

Alex ran her fingers over the beautiful dress. The silk was softer than anything she had ever felt in her life.

Guinevere stepped toward her. "Did you hear what I said about tradition, Alexandria?"

Alex reached for her necklace, forgetting it was missing, and turned back to her godmother. "I did. But you should know I've been having nightmares again. If you want anyone in this castle to sleep during the next week, I'll need someone nearby."

Jessica put her hand on Alex's arm. "We've seen to that. My father gave Michael and me his room next door for the week. He'll be staying with Stefan around the corner."

Edith pointed the opposite direction. "I'll be between you and Stefan. I can fetch him in a moment."

Alex let out a sigh of relief. "Then what's next?"

Guinevere explained that on the actual wedding day, at least a dozen high-ranking noblewomen would be involved in getting her ready. Sir Reinhart's wife, Wesley's mother, and several others would be there in addition to Edith and Jessica. Alex cringed at the idea of ladies fussing over her. For now, she tried to stay calm and smile at the kind royal seamstress when she arrived. Her name was Valaria, and she was delightful.

"Your Highness?" she said, looking up at Alex from her work on the hem of the wedding dress.

Alex trembled as she stood in front of the mirror. The dress was a replica of her mother's, a gift from Guinevere. *Only an hour ago, I couldn't wait to get into this dress, but now it's suffocating me. What's wrong with me? I love him. I want to marry him, but somehow everything feels wrong.*

She looked at herself in the large mirror and fought back tears. The dress was now adjusted to her measurements and looked stunning. Gold details and red trim set off the white silk to perfection, and the style even covered most of her scars from her time with Moorloc. Valaria had made it fit snugly around her waist and bust to show off her figure while the skirt flowed around her feet and ran into a long train behind her. The long, loose sleeves made her look as if she was floating when she moved. When a Torian noblewoman married a man, she would leave her family and become part of his, but everyone knew that wouldn't be the case for Alex and Aaron. Their marriage would unite Datten and Warren forever, and their carefully worded betrothal allowed them to choose where they'd live.

"Your Highness?" Valaria asked again, bringing Alex out of her thoughts. "Do you like the gold detailing with the red trim?"

Jessica and Edith exchanged a look, but Alex smiled even more widely than before, trying to show them everything was fine.

"It's exquisite. I think the red is especially lovely."

"I'm sure His Highness will like it too," Jessica said, holding up two pairs of slippers to see which would suit the dress better.

"We could ask him," Edith said.

Valaria gasped. "He can't see the dress. In Datten, it's bad luck for the groom to see the bride's dress prior to the wedding."

Edith winked at Alex. "In Warren, the groom helps pick the dress to ensure it fits their ranks."

Alex smiled. *I know who to ask if I need to see Aaron.* A clang echoed in the back of the room. Alex whipped her head around, terrified she was hearing a new phantom sound, but all she saw was Edith and Jessica picking up the crowns they'd accidentally knocked to the floor. She sighed with relief and went back to looking over the dress in the mirror when two whip cracks echoed around her. *No,* she thought. *I don't hear you.*

After Valaria finished the last adjustments, Jessica and Edith helped Alex out of the wedding dress and into her favorite red gown. Guinevere took them all to the dining hall, where the wives and daughters of Emmerich's council members were waiting to have a royal tea with the soon-to-be Princess of Datten.

Alex smiled and made polite conversation. Several of the daughters were Jessica's friends, so Alex immediately liked them. She was pleasantly surprised that Wesley's mother, Tanja, was a delightful woman. Apparently, the Rassgat women were kind and intelligent, while the men were boorish and horrible. Edith referred to them as "beauties and the beasts," making Alex giggle.

After tea, the younger noblewomen begged Alex to join them for a stroll around the city. Guinevere insisted she go and summoned Stefan as an escort. Despite Alex's insistence that she was tired, the moment Stefan arrived, the ladies giggled and started toward town.

So this walk was their excuse to get close to the handsome Sir Stefan. It had nothing to do with wanting to show me Datten or getting to know me. Alex went along but soon lost interest. The ladies were all fawning over Stefan, making it hard for him to even stay near Alex, let alone guard her. Still, she couldn't help but snicker. *You can run into battle with your sword drawn and face down sorcerers to protect me, but throw a bunch of available ladies at you, and you're petrified.*

"Are you really all right?" Jessica asked as they watched Stefan struggle to get away. "What Stefan told me about the attack—"

"Michael already asked me that."

"Just because I'm married to Michael doesn't mean I don't get to worry about you too."

Alex sighed. "I'm rattled from the attack, so I'm not in the mood to see Datten. I'd rather Aaron take me."

"Speaking of . . ." Jessica pointed up the road, and Alex spotted Aaron leaving a shop with Michael and several of the younger knights.

"Hello, Your Highness!" Edith shouted across the square.

The smile that brightened Aaron's face lifted Alex's spirits.

"Thank you, Edith." She squeezed Edith's arm and headed toward Aaron.

When she reached him, she batted her eyes, acting like the ladies fawning over Stefan before losing herself in laughter. "Would you escort me back to the castle? I seem to have lost my guard."

"Where's Stefan?" Michael asked.

Alex pointed, and Aaron stared long and hard before a mischievous smile took over his entire face. "Yes. I think he's quite occupied. I'd be happy to escort you back." Alex looped her arm through Aaron's as two whip cracks echoed around her.

Stefan was livid when he finally returned, but he calmed down once he learned Aaron and Michael had brought her back to the castle. The evening flew by, and Alex was soon dressed for bed and left looking around her unfamiliar room.

How am I going to sleep in here alone? When I have my nightmare, I'm going to wake the entire castle. She was so lost in thought that it took several knocks before she realized someone was at the door. She found Stefan standing there with a blanket and pillow in his hands.

He nodded. "Princess."

Relieved, Alex stepped back to let him enter the room. Stefan dropped his bedding on the floor at the foot of her bed and then pointed to the sheets with a stern look.

Alex climbed in as he settled on the ground. "Good night, Stefan," she said.

"Good night, Alex."

She laid her head on her pillow and was soon asleep.

Alex was back in the basement of Moorloc's castle. The air was stale and damp as she walked down the long hallway to investigate the screams she knew would come. As soon as she heard the girl, Alex found the door, which was ajar and made from a different type of wood than the others. She froze. Something felt familiar, but before she could remember what it was, the door flew open, and she came face-to-face with herself—the girl who was fleeing. Alex watched herself run from the room and stumble down the hallway. She had blood on her hands. Something had ripped her clothes. Terror swept through Alex as she slowly turned back to the door. Dreading what she would find, she pushed it open and screamed.

Stefan was shaking her. "Alex, breathe!"

Alex's eyes grew wide with pain. She felt as if someone were sitting on her chest and choking her. Panic surged through her, her body refusing to cooperate. She pushed at Stefan, but her vision went dark.

CHAPTER 9
AARON

"What in the Forbidden Lands is going on here?" Emmerich roared.

Aaron was dressed in his sleeping pants, his heart still racing after the short run from his room. He'd arrived to find Stefan violently shaking Alex. Even now, he scowled at the man, feeling the same intense rage he reserved for anyone who hurt the one he loved.

I will never forget seeing that. And I might never forgive you for it, Stefan.

Alex's breathing normalized as her blue lips returned to pink. In moments, the room filled with her ladies and guards.

"What happened?" Jerome asked.

Stefan pushed past his father to glare at Aaron. "How am I supposed to know? Ask His Highness—*he's* the one who spends every night in her bed. Does she often stop breathing during a nightmare?"

Aaron threw back his shoulders and shoved Stefan so hard he stumbled into Jerome.

"Aaron! Stefan!" Emmerich snapped, and Jerome stepped

between them. He pushed Aaron back and then grabbed Stefan, pulling him out of the room.

"She's awake." Edith's gentle voice broke through the tension, and everyone turned to Alex.

Aaron dashed to her side and helped her sit up. "Are you all right?"

Alex ran a hand across her throat. "I think so."

"Have you ever stopped breathing in a dream before?" Megesti asked. He moved between Edward and Emmerich, looking at her curiously.

"Yes, but only the first nights I was back."

"What stopped them?" Megesti asked.

Alex blushed and looked down at her quilt. She smoothed it out before she turned toward Aaron and squeezed his hand.

"I did," Aaron said. "Anytime she had one, I . . . um, brought her out of it."

"It's the reason he's never slept in his room," Alex said. "If I'm alone, I wake up half the castle."

"Then forget the ferflucsing traditions," Emmerich said. "I'm not losing sleep because my wife insists we keep you two apart until the wedding. Aaron, you're sleeping in here. Everyone else, get back to bed."

Aaron kissed Alex's forehead as everyone except Edith and Edward left the room.

"Do you need anything?" Edith asked.

Alex kept holding Aaron's hand. "I have what I need now. Thank you."

Edith curtsied and left the room.

Edward kissed the top of Alex's head and gave them both a look they knew too well. "Aaron, you are *not* to leave her."

"I won't."

Her father sighed and left the room, closing the door behind him.

"What did you dream about?" Aaron asked.

"Same as the last few nights—the basement of Moorloc's castle. But tonight, I was about to enter the room when I woke up. I couldn't breathe."

Aaron pulled her close. "Well, I'm not leaving your side until you figure this out. You're mine to protect, and finding Stefan trying to shake the life back into you is not something I ever want to do again."

"Please don't start anything with Stefan. He's as scared as you are."

Aaron leaned down, kissing her neck. "Would you rather I start something with *you*, Your Highness?"

Alex giggled as Aaron nuzzled her neck. "That's a sacrifice I am more than willing to make."

AARON AWOKE and found Alex curled up against him. When she'd first arrived back from Moorloc's, she had done it every night, but it happened less frequently now. She lay in his arms, her cheeks and lips perfectly pink as she softly breathed in and out. Aaron tucked her loose hair behind her ear and froze—her neck was bruised. He leaned closer to get a better look.

Hand marks? Did Stefan do this to you? No, he'd never. But then how did they get there?

Alex stirred and opened her eyes.

"Do you remember last night?" Aaron asked. He failed to hide the concern in his voice, and Alex immediately sat up in bed.

"The nightmare?"

"After that."

"Yes, why?"

"You have bruises on your neck like someone choked you."

76

Alex sucked in a breath when she touched the sensitive skin. "Aaron, you can't think Stefan—"

"Then where did those marks come from?"

"I don't know. Lately, I've been getting a lot of bruises."

"Alex—"

"No. You will not accuse Stefan of hurting me—not after what I've endured from the Rassgats. When it comes to Datten nobility, the Wafners—including Stefan—are above reproach."

"Fine. But I'm asking Michael to take charge of watching you until the wedding, and I won't negotiate on that."

Alex narrowed her eyes at Aaron, but he stared back, leaning forward. When his forehead met hers, she relented and kissed him in agreement. She sighed happily as he deepened the kiss, but then there was a knock on the door.

"Come in," Alex called.

Aaron groaned and turned to see his mother standing in the doorway. The moment her eyes fell on him, she was livid. *Ferflucs. Father didn't explain.*

"What is going on here?" Guinevere strode into the room as Aaron leaped from the bed. He dashed to his mother, looped his arm through hers, and led her back out into the hallway.

"You haven't spoken to Father this morning, have you?"

"Of course not. Your father is far too busy to be dealing with wedding things."

Aaron put his hands on his mother's shoulders to calm her. "Yes, he is busy, but you need to speak to him about Alex. He ordered me to stay with her last night."

"Young man, I don't believe that for a second."

Aaron saw his father coming down the hallway and smirked as his mother spotted him.

"Emmerich," she called out, "did you *order* our son to stay in Alexandria's bedroom?"

77

Aaron watched his father pale and clenched his jaw to keep himself from laughing. *This fight's yours, old man.*

"Well, dear, you need to understand . . . that is to say . . . let's discuss this in my room."

Guinevere followed Emmerich into his room, slamming the door behind her.

When Aaron returned to Alex, he found her looking in the large mirror. Her neck glowed faintly, and the bruise faded away.

"Are you healing it?" he asked.

Alex avoided looking at him. "Yes."

Aaron walked over to slip his arms around her waist. "How long have you been healing mysterious injuries?"

"A week."

"I thought we agreed on no more secrets."

"I'm training harder. I couldn't be sure the injuries weren't from that, and I didn't want to worry you."

Aaron sighed and kissed her neck. She moaned and pressed herself back into him, but he said, "None of that, Your Highness. My mother will be back any minute, and I cannot have her walking in on us."

Alex giggled and spun around. Aaron shuddered as she ran her hands down his chest. Every carnal thing he wanted to do to her ran through his mind.

"Then we'll have to save it for tonight," she said.

"Temptress."

Alex's smile spread across her entire face as she gazed up at him. Aaron playfully swatted her butt as she went to the wardrobe to pick a dress.

"I'll see you later. I'm off to finish some last-minute things," he said.

"What? Is it another Datten tradition that the men actually

help with wedding work?" Alex's eyes sparkled as she teased him.

"No, but there is a tradition where the groom gives the bride a gift."

Alex tensed, and her smile vanished. "We exchange gifts? No one told me about that."

"No." Aaron grabbed her hand. "In Datten, the royal getting married is always a prince. I buy *you* the gift. Your gifts to me and the kingdom are the children you will bear once we're married."

Alex sighed. "I'm not in any hurry for that. I still feel like a terrible princess most of the time, so how am I supposed to teach our child to be a royal?"

"It's fine with me if you want to wait. The longer it takes for us to make an heir, the longer I have you all to myself. I'm rather selfish and don't like the idea of having to share you." Aaron kissed her cheek and ran back to the door, narrowly avoiding the pillow Alex threw.

"Whelp!" Alex shouted as the door closed. Aaron laughed as he headed to his room to get dressed.

With Alex's gift in hand, Aaron took the long way back to the castle from the royal jeweler's. He knew Alex didn't want jewels, but this Datten tradition was centuries-old, and his mother had insisted. Jerome seemed to be lost in thought and not his usual self as they traveled.

Aaron broke the silence to ask, "Everything all right, Jerome? You're awfully tense."

"I can't stop thinking about Alexandria's nightmare and how we found my son shaking her."

Aaron stopped walking and looked at his father's general.

Jerome successfully hid his feelings from everyone else, but Aaron knew to look at his eyes, which were narrowed. *You're furious. Am I really going to defend Stefan now? For Alex . . . I will.*

"Stefan was trying to help," Aaron said. "They shared a room for years, and nothing inappropriate ever happened. He sees her the same way he sees Jessica. Despite what I said this morning, I trust Stefan."

When they arrived at the castle, Aaron was summoned to the library. He went reluctantly, expecting a scolding from his mother for being in Alex's room or from his father for letting his mother find out. Instead, he found Harold sitting at the large table in the middle of the room. He had a book about Betruger propped open in front of him.

Aaron said, "With how much you enjoy reading, it's obvious why you get along with Alex so well. She's always surrounded by books."

Harold smiled. "She has a curious mind. The questions she's asked about our society and people show that. She'll make an exceptional queen."

"I couldn't agree more."

"Excellent. Now let's get some horses. You and I are going off on a ride to talk things out."

Aaron tilted his head. "With or without guards?"

"Without, of course. It's more fun that way."

Aaron led Harold through the secret door from the library to the throne room, where they slipped into the dining hall through the kitchen and then into the basement. They were off before anyone even knew they had been in the stables, and then they rode for hours in the Dark Forest. Despite the refreshing activity, Aaron still wasn't feeling like himself, and he eventually confided in Harold.

When they stopped to water the horses, Harold asked, "You don't actually believe Stefan would hurt Alex, do you?"

"I don't know. She didn't have random bruises. They were hand marks. Someone strangled her." Aaron squatted beside the stream to wash his hands.

"Could someone have gotten into her room?"

"If Stefan slept through someone attacking Alex, then he's in even more trouble," Aaron said.

"She sees ghosts. Could she have developed powers to let them touch her?"

"I don't think so. But I suspect she can talk to them now. She hasn't said anything and I haven't asked, but I've caught her talking to herself."

"Perhaps it's a habit she picked up when she was alone at the castle." Harold crossed his arms and scrutinized Aaron. "You aren't trying to come up with an excuse, are you?"

"Excuse?"

"To call off your wedding."

"What? No—"

"Because after the horrors she went through to get back to you, if you changed your mind, I'd have to reconsider our truce."

Aaron ran his hand through his hair and scowled. But Harold stared at Aaron as if he could burn through him. "Are you saying if I don't marry the Princess of Warren, you'll abandon our truce?"

"Of course not." Harold's lips curved into a smirk. "I'm saying if Datten and Warren's truce broke, I'd side with Warren. I've seen what Alex is capable of, and I'm not about to get on her bad side, even for you."

Aaron laughed. "She is extraordinary, isn't she?"

"Yes. So why do you have doubts?"

"It isn't doubt, Harold. I'd have married her a hundred times already. I'm worried that she's the one reconsidering.

That she wants . . . *him*." The words got out before he could stop them.

Harold stepped toward Aaron. "That's ridiculous. She could have left with him when she was in Moorloc's castle, but she didn't. She endured more than we know to come home to you."

"Then why does she call his name every night?"

"She has nightmares about that time, and one person helped her—Gryphon. How does she call him?"

"Why does that matter?" Aaron's temper rose. He clenched his jaw and scratched at his neck.

"I'm serious," Harold said, uncrossing his arms. "Does she call his name like she calls yours? Is her breath steady or raspy? Does she tremble, whimper?"

Aaron thought hard. "It sounds like panic. She breathes short, fast breaths like when she's losing control. She does whimper."

Harold pursed his lips and patted Aaron's back. "Doesn't sound as though she's screaming his name in passion. I understand you don't want her calling another man's name, even in her sleep. But you're about to marry her. That will make her yours regardless of what she dreams about."

"Don't tell her that. She'll throw something at you."

Harold smirked as he rounded up their horses.

"I could use your help," Aaron said.

"Anything."

"I want to gift Alex her new horse. Nothing Cameron had impressed her, so I want to find her the perfect horse to replace Flash. The Betruger horses are so beautiful. I thought you might have one she'd love."

"As a wedding gift."

"I know it sounds unusual, but—"

Harold laughed. "Unusual? A Betruger groom always gives

a horse to his bride. She's given a house, a horse, and whatever other animals she likes, along with everything needed to set up a proper home. What do you usually gift?"

"Among the nobility, it's jewelry."

Harold frowned. "How do you make a home with jewelry? But I might have a horse for Alex."

"Thank you. I know she would agree with you that more jewelry is ridiculous since she already has a room full of it."

"Let's go back. I'm hungry and have been told your venison is the best in Torian."

Aaron chuckled as they mounted their horses and headed back.

WHEN THEY RETURNED to the castle, dinner was well underway. Before they had left on their ride, Harold had told everyone about the Betruger tradition where friends took the groom out for some fun before the wedding.

They arrived in the bustling dining hall to cheers from the men. While Warren reserved its head table for the royals and had longer ones for everyone else, Datten had several kinds of tables filling the room.

An enormous head table rested on a stone dais at the end of the hall and stretched almost the entire width of the room. Any of the nobility Emmerich selected could sit at it. Title, rank, and king's choice determined the seating at this table.

The generals, Alex's guards, and the lady's maids sat at a set of smaller tables in front of the head table. They faced the room, just as the nobility did behind them. Finally, long tables ran from the front to the back of the room for everyone else. There were usually four of them, but it seemed two more had been added due to the number of knights attending the wedding.

Aaron and Harold crossed the room to the head table where Emmerich and Edward waited. There was a free seat for their Betruger guest on Aaron's side of the table. On the opposite side, Emmerich sat in the middle with Edward and Guinevere beside him. Since Aaron and Harold were late, Alex sat by herself on the other side of the table.

Harold bowed to the kings. "Emmerich. Edward. Your Majesty, you look more beautiful every time I see you. Princess. I'm sorry we lost track of time."

The royals all nodded to the latecomers as they took their seats.

"I'm so sorry we're late," Aaron said as he sat beside Alex. He couldn't help noticing her plate was spotless besides a few crumbs of bread.

"You seem to be in better spirits."

Alex kissed Aaron's cheek, and the knights all cheered.

She blushed. "Do they have to do that?"

"It's worse than that. When the king kisses the queen, they have to look away. My mother won't even kiss my father in front of the men because she hates the noise the armor makes when they do it."

"They look away? Why?" Harold asked.

"Affection between the King and Queen of Datten is sacred. They will not dishonor it by bearing witness."

Alex rolled her eyes. "And yet they cheer when I kiss you."

"Ah, princess." Aaron playfully tapped her nose. "You've figured it out. They're still excited that their prince is settling down, but once we're king and queen, they won't cheer."

Harold poured three full mugs of ale.

Alex asked, "Does that make any sense to you, Harold?"

"None. In my kingdom, our knights expect affection

84

between their king and queen. They demand their royals produce heirs. If your wife is unwilling to kiss you, that outcome is unlikely."

"Are you saying Dattenites are prudes?" Aaron asked.

"Yes," the other two replied together, and both broke out laughing as Harold passed them the ale.

CHAPTER 10
ALEX

Alex lay awake while Aaron soundly slept beside her, dead to the world after Harold had whisked him away for the day, claiming it was a Betruger tradition. Alex had suspected he wanted to get Aaron away from everything going on, so she'd kept quiet. He'd been in much better spirits because of it—that, or the copious amounts of ale Harold kept pouring during dinner. Alex, on the other hand, felt like she'd never sleep again after yet another nightmare.

She sat up and heard another whip crack. She put on her training clothes, braided her hair, and crept out of her room to the west stairwell. On sleepless nights, it was usually the library that called to her, but tonight, she went to the lab. As she headed upstairs, the village bell chimed five times, echoing through the tower windows, and Alex could see the summer sun lightening the horizon.

The lab was on the third and uppermost floor of the castle. She arrived expecting to discover why she was drawn to this place, but the room was empty. Her fingers danced along the bookcase as she waited, knowing something was coming. Then the room turned cold.

"I didn't expect you," she said.

Daniel grinned at her. "You didn't think I'd miss my little brother's wedding?" She was always struck by the way his pale skin, blue eyes, and blond hair were identical to Aaron's.

"Of course not. But why the lab?"

"You're in danger, princess. If you go through with this, she believes it will destroy you."

Alex defiantly crossed her arms. "If my mother has something to say, let her tell me. I don't need you to be the messenger, Daniel. I need to finish what I started."

"Then you know where you need to go. But don't go alone. If you do, they'll never find you."

Alex gulped and headed for the door. She turned around to thank him, but he was gone.

She walked down the hall and quietly slipped into Megesti's plain room. Even the guest rooms had more charm. It was circular like Aaron's but located in the opposite tower, and it held nothing more than a bed, a wardrobe, and a few bookshelves that Megesti had magically curved to fit the wall.

His room made her uneasy because it reminded her too much of Lygari's at Moorloc's castle. She found her cousin in the darkness and poked his shoulder until he woke up.

"What?" he mumbled, rubbing his bushy chestnut brown hair.

"Ready for trouble?"

"Not you too! Aaron has gotten me into so much trouble over the years, and now you're starting?"

"I'm going to Moorloc's castle, and I need your help."

Even in the dim light, Alex could see worry written across Megesti's tanned face. "Why?"

"I can't say. Will you come?"

He nodded and tossed his blanket aside to get up.

"Thank you." Alex walked to his window and looked out at the forest while Megesti got dressed. He handed her his extra cloak, and she draped it around her shoulders.

"Are you sure about this? We were told at least one general must accompany you everywhere."

"We'll be back in a few minutes. No one will even miss us." Alex held out her hand, and when Megesti took it, she cracked them inside Moorloc's castle courtyard. Even after all the repairs, updates, and changes, it still made Alex's skin crawl. No amount of renovation would ever dispel the disturbing energy of this place. *Hopefully, I can learn not to let it bother me so I can visit our knights here without shaking like a leaf.* It was early morning, and with the royal wedding only two days away, no one noticed the two sorcerers appear in the courtyard.

Alex headed toward the main hallway with Megesti behind her. The fire rolling across the ceiling lit their way. Despite her best efforts, Alex hadn't been able to figure out how to remove it.

Megesti finally spoke up. "You know if things go bad, I can't help you, right?"

"We won't be fighting. You're here in case I can't get myself back."

"My cracking is terrible."

Alex stopped and looked at him. His emerald eyes sparkled in the firelight. "Terrible is better than none," she said. "If I went alone, they'd never find me."

"You're being rather ominous for someone who assured me this would be a quick trip," Megesti said.

"I'm a Harbinger, Megesti. Almost everything I do is ominous." She grabbed a torch off the wall, and they headed down the narrow stairs into the bowels of the castle where the enchanted fire couldn't follow. The basement had a dirt floor and arched ceilings. Despite all the changes to the castle, this part still smelled stale and muggy. Alex explained her plan to find the room from her dreams, hopeful it would lead to answers.

They wandered the maze of hallways and small rooms. Alex couldn't find the right path since so much work had been done when they converted the castle into a training school.

As she turned down another corridor, she heard a whip crack, so loud this time that her fingers flew to her cheek and found blood. She quickly wiped it away.

"Did you hear a whip?" Megesti asked.

Alex spun to face Megesti, dropping the torch. "You heard that?"

"Why wouldn't I?"

Alex gasped in relief before bringing her hand to her forehead for a second. "I've been hearing whip cracks for days, and no one else ever does. I thought I was losing my mind."

Megesti retrieved the torch and handed it back to her. "Apparently, only sorcerers can hear it. Alex, I don't like this. We should go back or at least get someone to come with us."

Alex shook her head and charged on into the maze of halls. Megesti groaned and chased after her. They walked up and down halls until Alex recognized the place from her dreams.

"It's down here." Alex exhaled sharply and rushed forward. There, she found a door that didn't match and jiggled the handle.

"It's locked. Can we leave now?" Megesti asked.

Alex glared at him. She handed him the torch, placed her hands on the lock, and whispered the spell Merlock had taught her. The door clicked. Alex swallowed hard and pushed it open, a rush of musty and heavy air meeting her as she did.

"Alex, this room feels wrong. Something *horrible* happened in there."

"I know. You don't have to come in if you don't want to."

"Why are you going in?"

"Because whatever happened here . . . happened to me."

Alex stepped through the door and looked around. The small room was used for storage, with chests and old armor tossed into one corner. Another corner held a stack of broken chairs, and old and broken bookcases sagged against the back wall. Megesti crept in behind Alex. The air became heavier, and Alex sensed pain and terror in it.

"Do you remember anything?"

"No. I thought coming here would make the memories come back."

"Try touching things. Sometimes memories attach themselves to an object."

Alex gently ran her fingers along one of the bookshelves but felt nothing. She tried the chest, the armor, and then everything else in the room.

Megesti shrugged.

Why did I think this would work?

She'd lost a night's sleep, and it was catching up with her. Alex leaned between the two broken bookcases. Instantly, her chest tightened as if it were in a vise. Megesti vanished, and brown eyes appeared in front of her. A crushing force made her feel as if she were being slammed into the wall. She tried to scream but couldn't breathe. Something struck her face so hard her ears rang. She gasped, air filling her lungs, but a hand covered her mouth. She kicked and bit and attacked the way Stefan and Michael had taught her, but she remained trapped between the wall, two bookcases, and a monster.

That was when the physical pain struck, a sensation of being ripped into pieces, and she shrieked. One after another, a jumble of memories surfaced. She felt her wrist snap. Pain shot up her back when she hit the bookcase. Her arms burned as lightning left them and struck Reinhilde, filling her nostrils with the stench of charred flesh. Then she was being strangled. Brutish fingers squeezed her neck until blood vessels burst and bruised her skin. Gryphon was there, warning her: *If the memories return, whatever you are feeling will be much, much worse. This won't fix things. Trying to run away from your problems has a way of catching up with you.* Alex now realized what he'd meant. She wasn't just getting back those lost memories; she was reliving them all at once. Her wrist was broken, and her throat hurt so badly she could barely breathe. Then the whip cracked, and she crumpled onto the floor.

"Alex! Look at me!"

She heard Megesti, but she could only see the wall in the courtyard. Kruft's men held her against the stone, and with the crack of the whip, the skin on her back ripped open. *Crack.* Bile filled her mouth from the terror raging through her. *Crack.* More bruises and pains shot through her body. Faintly, she heard Megesti's voice screaming at her to get them out of there, but she couldn't. *Crack. Crack.* Pure evil laughter drowned him out as the lashes flaying the flesh from her back came faster and harder. Blood ran down her back, pooling around her, and she fought to stay conscious. But that only brought more pain.

As the last memory faded, Megesti's face appeared in front of her. He was pale as a ghost, his eyes wide with terror.

"Alex, we have to get you back."

She vomited onto him, and her wrist burned in pain as she lurched forward. Megesti pressed his cloak onto her back, and Alex saw he was covered in her blood.

"Megesti." She held out her hand to him, and he grabbed it. They arrived in Datten, but they ended up in the courtyard. *Ferflucs!* The guards were warming up for morning drills. Someone arrived at their side in seconds.

ALICE HANOV

"Alexandria, I'm here."

Randal, Alex thought.

"I have you," he said, his voice calm and reassuring as he scooped her into his muscular arms.

"Bring her to Emmerich's room. We can't have her being carried through the castle like this," Jerome said, and he started shouting orders at his men. "Caleb, sound the alarm. We need everyone at their posts. Lucas, fetch the physician. Matthew and Avery, keep Her Majesty, Aaron, and Edward away from us. The last thing we need is them getting in the way. Megesti, go to the lab and get whatever herbs will help."

Jerome's voice faded as Randal carried her into the castle.

"Randal?" she managed.

"I already told you, Alex. I've got you now." Randal ran through the hall and kicked open the door to Emmerich's room. He placed her on the table and threw more wood on the fire. He looked around in panic and frustration. "Alex, can you make it—"

Alex didn't even let him finish his request before she made the fireplace roar to life. But she was too weak to control it, and the flames erupted, nearly burning the general. She waited for the fire to die down before letting her head fall against the table. She felt so cold and tired. As she closed her eyes, the Datten alarm bells began ringing in the distance.

Someone shook her awake. "Stay with me, Alexandria," Emmerich ordered.

There was a crash, and Megesti rushed in with his arms full of jars. A few tumbled from his arms, and the physician shouted at him to be more careful.

Emmerich looked at her gravely. "We're going to turn you over now. The bleeding isn't stopping, so we need to cauterize the wounds or you'll bleed to death. Do you understand?"

Alex nodded weakly. "Tell Aaron . . . I'm sorry."

"No last words, princess. You're going to explain yourself to both your father and Aaron. Randal?"

The general's shirt was soaked in blood. *Her* blood. Emmerich gently lifted her up and laid her on her belly. Alex heard the fabric being cut away, and then Emmerich and Randal pressed her shoulders into the table. Someone else held her hips—Jerome.

"This is going to hurt," Randal said.

"I know," Alex replied.

The physician came over with a blade that glowed like the flames in the fireplace. Flesh sizzled as he pressed it into her back, and she screamed so loud the walls shook, knocking a shield and armor to the ground. Magic flooded her as she struggled to get free, but the hardened warriors holding her down wouldn't relent. The physician continued his work until her back was burned shut and the blood ceased to flow.

As soon as the generals released her, the tears came, harder and faster than ever before in her life. She couldn't stop shaking. The physical pain was excruciating, but the pain of what she'd learned broke her soul, and she cried on the table.

He'll never forgive me.

The room fell silent as the servants grabbed the rags and pails of dirty water and left the room, leaving Alex with the king, generals, Megesti, and the physician.

"She'll need rest, Your Royal Highness," Emmerich's physician said. "I'll prepare something to help with the pain. I'll need to use your lab, Megesti."

"Of course."

Alex heard footsteps and the sound of the door closing. She tried to push herself up, but she was too weak. Her broken wrist collapsed, and she fell back on the table.

"Can you handle me touching your back long enough for

me to carry you to bed?" Randal asked, but Jerome shook his head.

"If you'll allow me, I'll take you, Alexandria. You should get out of those clothes, Randal."

The man's silver tunic was spattered brown from all the blood, and his hands were filthy.

Alex said, "I'm sorry, Randal."

"For scaring me?" he whispered, trying to mask the tremble in his voice. "Apparently, you've caught up on twelve years of missed mischief. Perhaps you could slow down."

Alex smiled weakly at him as Jerome lifted her up. She winced and clenched her jaw as he rolled her against him.

Randal nodded. "I'll send Edith and Jessica."

Emmerich moved a chair out of Jerome's way and followed them upstairs.

"But this is your room," Alex said as they arrived on the second floor.

"Right now," Emmerich said, "it's yours, princess. The king's suite is the safest place in this castle outside of Her Majesty's suite, and I insist you stay here."

Jerome set her down on the bed. There was a knock on the door, and Edith and Jessica entered.

"We'll leave you to it," Jerome said. "We need to update Their Highnesses."

Emmerich looked up. "Do you need help?" he asked the lady's maids. "We could send in one of her guards."

"We'll manage, Your Royal Highness," Jessica said. Edith was already collecting the water bucket from the corner by the fireplace. Emmerich nodded and left the room with Jerome.

"Alex?" Edith gingerly approached the bed, then stopped.

Jessica swallowed and dipped a cloth into the bucket of water. She wrung it and carefully wiped the blood from Alex's face and neck, tears streaming down her face. Her eyes equally watery, Edith bit her lip as she watched Jessica, who worked in silence until Alex was clean. Edith grabbed the fresh clothes they'd brought, and Jessica supported Alex as she tried to stand to remove her pants.

The loss of so much blood left Alex feeling as if her weak legs were made of water. She struggled to stay upright as the door opened. All of them turned to see Aaron standing there. He closed the door behind him gently, but Alex flinched anyway. She'd expected anger.

"Edith. Jessica," he said. "You may leave."

"We have to help her get changed," Edith said.

"Leave," Aaron repeated himself. He opened his clenched fists and wiped his hands on his pants. Alex could tell he was struggling to hold his temper, and she gave her ladies leave to go.

Edith glared as she walked past Aaron, but Jessica stopped and gave him the commanding stare only a Wafner could give. "Do not upset her. She requires rest." Her voice was curt.

Aaron nodded and whispered, "I have no intention of upsetting Alex. I need to see for myself that she is all right and would prefer to do so alone."

Jessica indicated she understood and followed Edith out of the room.

"Aaron—" Alex tried to take a step toward him, but her legs gave out. Aaron moved with lightning speed and caught her without touching her back.

"Megesti told me what you did. What were you thinking?" His voice wavered as he spoke, shifting from anger to terror.

"I had to know," Alex said.

"You did this to get your memories back?" Aaron set her on the bed, gently removing her blood-soaked pants before carefully helping her put on the clean pair. Alex rested her hands on his chest and looked into his eyes. They were red.

You've been crying. I'm sorry I scared you. "How long has it been?"

"Almost three hours. I woke up to the alarms ringing. When I arrived outside, Avery refused to let me, your father, or your guards into the room. But we all saw Megesti and Randal leave covered in blood. *Your* blood. Alex, I thought you were dead."

"I'm sorry."

The physician had cut Alex's shirt down the back, so Aaron only had to slide it down her arms. He sucked in his breath as he looked at her back and took in the bruises covering her body. "What in the Forbidden Lands happened to you there?" He picked up the clean shirt, realizing Edith had grabbed one of his by mistake. He smiled wanly at her as he helped her into it. It was far too big.

"I got my memories back, but when they returned, I physically had to relive all the terror, beatings, broken bones, whipping, the . . ." Alex swallowed and sobbed.

Aaron sat down, reaching for her, but then he paused. "How do I hold you without hurting you?"

Alex slid her arms around Aaron's neck, crying out in pain as the burns on her back throbbed. She clung to him like her life depended on it, and he delicately held her as tight as he dared, keeping his hands low and clear of the wounds.

"I'm so sorry," he said. "If I'd known about all of that, I never would have asked you to relive it even in summary."

"I know."

"Please don't hate me," Aaron said. He buried his face in Alex's hair, and he trembled as he cried.

"I could never hate you. I worried you'd change your mind about marrying me."

Aaron let go and cupped her face in his hands. She flinched and watched as his eyes moved to her neck, then to her face, arms, chest, and back to her face. Then he pressed his lips carefully to hers. She wanted him to kiss her more roughly, to claim her again. But he was gentle. He was always gentle with her when she needed it.

"I will never change my mind about marrying you," he said. "Mother will postpone the wedding to allow you time to heal, but if you are the least bit worried, I'll get the judge in here and marry you this minute."

Alex slid her hands into Aaron's. His blue eyes stared back at her, demanding a reply.

"The things I did. Aaron, they're unforgivable."

"Alex—"

"No." Alex's lip trembled. "I killed people, I wanted to hurt people, I . . . I kissed him." She pulled away.

Aaron took Alex's hand and rubbed it with his thumb for a long time. His breathing was ragged. She expected him to storm out any second, but he took her other hand in his. "If you want him, I'll let you go. No wars, no consequences. I want you to be happy."

"No. All I've ever wanted is you. I'm so sorry." Tears burst from her as she covered her eyes with her hands.

"Were you in your right mind when you . . . kissed him?"

"No, not at all."

"Would you kiss him now?"

"No." Violent sobs racked Alex until Aaron leaned down and kissed her forehead.

Tentatively, she asked, "Do you need me to tell you . . . ?"

"Not unless you want to. The price of you getting these memories was far too high already."

They silently looked at each other. Part of her still believed he'd leave as soon as she dropped her gaze.

He said, "Do you want me to go so you can—"

"No." Alex barely got the word out before more tears fell.

"Do you want to see your father? Or Michael? Stefan?"

Alex shook her head. "I don't want them to see me like this. Please."

"All right. I need to go tell them that then."

A whimper escaped her before she could stop it. Aaron leaned down and kissed her cheek gently.

"I give you my word I'll be right back. Then I'll stay with you as long as you need."

Alex nodded. Aaron got off the bed and helped her shift so she could lie on her side. As soon as he left, tears fell from her cheeks again. She was broken, both body and soul, and she didn't know if she'd ever recover from it. *Is there a spell to cure this?*

After he left, a breeze smelling of lavender filled the room. She looked up and saw a hooded woman wearing a long, pale green sorcerer robe standing before her. Alex yelped and tried to rise. She'd forgotten about her wrist, and pain exploded up her arm.

The woman crouched down until her face was inches from Alex's. "Please don't cry out, Alexandria. I'm here to help." When the woman pushed back her hood, Alex recognized her from the paintings in her mother's castle. She had lovely brown skin that reminded Alex of acorns and raven-black hair crowned with a wreath of leaves and flowers. Her green eyes matched the pines in the Dark Forest. She smiled softly, and Alex realized she smelled like lavender despite there being none on her wreath.

"How do you know my name?"

"I knew your mother and your grandmother, or hexa, as we say. My name is Birch. I'm here because Gryphon can't be." She straightened up and placed her hand on Alex's good one, a gesture that immediately made Alex feel calm and safe. "Your loved ones will be back soon, but I brought you something to help you sleep. As so many of our exceptionally powerful potions do, it smells terrible and tastes worse, even if you add apple blossoms. But it works like magic." She winked at Alex as she pulled a vial from of her robe and helped her sit up. She removed the cork before handing it to her.

Alex sniffed the strange, moss-colored potion. It was as thick and pungent as slug slime. "How does it work?"

"This potion is powerful enough that you'll sleep for however long your body needs to in order to heal, and when you wake up, you'll feel completely refreshed, as if you've had the best sleep of your life. You'll regain your strength so you can heal yourself emotionally. Gryphon told me he took some of your memories, but he never shared what was in them. I'm sorry for the pain you're feeling, but you are Victoria's daughter. You will pull through. Cassandras are exceptional healers. You take on the pain of others, so managing it is a critical lesson to learn."

Alex felt tears welling up in her eyes. Birch leaned down, tilted Alex's face upward with one finger, and kissed her forehead. Alex breathed deeply and felt at peace again.

"No more tears, dear. Drink up. I must be off."

Alex drank the vial in one big gulp, and everything went black.

CHAPTER 11
ALEX

Alex woke up, feeling rested and starved. She tried to push herself up, but her wrist gave out again. She winced and pushed with her elbows instead. Sitting up, she cradled her wrist and released some power into it. A golden light spread under her skin. *That never stops amazing me.*

"She's awake," Edith said, rushing to her side. "How do you feel?"

"More rested than I have in a year. But I'm stiff everywhere."

Jessica looked her over with concern. "Edith, would you go get Their Highnesses?"

"Of course. They're going to be so relieved." Edith scurried across the room and headed out the door, letting it bang shut behind her.

"How are you feeling . . . really?" Jessica asked.

"What do you—"

Before she could reply, the door flew open and Aaron ran into the room, followed by their parents.

Edward hurried past him. "Alexandria! I was so worried."

"I'm sorry." Alex stood on shaky legs and hugged her father around the neck. He embraced her so gently she hardly felt it.

"We'll be discussing this once we're home."

"Home?"

Aaron spoke up. "You need to heal properly before we hold the wedding. Despite everything that's happened, we felt Warren would be better for you to recuperate in."

"We're postponing the wedding?"

"We already did," Aaron said.

Guinevere said, "The wedding date was three days ago, dear. You've been asleep for almost a week."

"A week?" Alex sat back on the bed, unable to hide her shock. *How did I sleep for a week without waking even once?*

"It doesn't matter when we get married," Aaron said. "We'll go to Warren. You'll heal, and when you can wear your dress without worry, without pain, we'll come back here and wed."

"I'm sorry," Alex said.

"Put it out of your mind," Emmerich said. "The wedding is a banquet that lasts one day, but your marriage will last forever."

Aaron looked at his father in shock, and Alex had to laugh.

Guinevere said, "Now you see why I married him. Your father can be very romantic, Aaron." She took Emmerich's hand. "Your only job, Alexandria, is to heal. Whether we delay the wedding a week or a month, we want you whole and well. Lady Bishop and Lady Nial will remain in Datten to help me complete the new plans so your ladies can stay with you."

Edward gave her shoulders a gentle squeeze. "See? Nothing to worry about. Now you get dressed so we can send Harold home, and then we'll go back to Warren—where you will *rest*."

ALEX WAS under strict orders from both royal physicians not to exert herself, and Aaron was ready to dutifully enforce those orders. The two of them stayed in the library reading, except for during mealtimes. For most of them, Alex arrived starving. She ate two plates of food at lunch and three helpings of fish at dinner. She couldn't sleep, so Michael joined her in the library at night to let Aaron go to bed. She read and worked on her ideas for the new school at Moorloc's castle.

The first few days followed this routine, though Alex was allowed more freedom every day. She went on a walk with Aaron and a ride the next day. After discussing it with Aaron, Alex approached her father and proposed a morning walk along the pier to finally talk about what had happened. Edward wholeheartedly accepted.

When the day came, Alex leaned over to kiss Aaron, sound asleep in their bed, and left to meet her father for their morning together. They enjoyed a quiet breakfast alone. Alex even wore her father's favorite blue dress, but she was distraught when she still couldn't find her mother's necklace.

They headed out, accompanied by General Bishop and two senior guards. Two of Alex's guards, Sir Benjamin and Sir Christian, attended them as well. Alex rode Edith's horse. She missed Flash terribly, but Edith's mare was sweet and readily responded to her movements. As they neared the pier, the only sounds she heard were the horses' hooves on the cobblestones. Alex barely noticed. Her mind was full of worries. *How am I going to explain everything to you? I hope you have questions so I can just answer those.* Once they arrived, they left the horses with one of the knights stationed at the pier and began their stroll. Matthew and the other guards walked several paces behind to allow them privacy. They made small talk about wedding details before either was brave enough to approach the subject that had brought them there. Finally, Edward broke.

"What possessed you to do that, Alex? You could have died, and for what? Some terrible memories that should have stayed forgotten?" Edward's anger and disapproval pained her. It broke her heart to think she'd disappointed her father.

"Aaron and I decided together that we needed to know."

Edward shook his head. "Stupid, jealous boy."

"Father." Alex put her hand on his arm, but he pulled away.

"*No*, Alexandria. You almost lost your life because he didn't trust your word about Gryphon. I don't believe any of this was your idea, and I'm furious with Aaron for insisting you go through with it."

Alex grabbed her father's hand and squeezed it. "I told you we both agreed, and I *didn't die*. I'm safe. And I will find my way out of this pain and be stronger for it."

Her father searched her face, but then he smiled. "You will, won't you? You truly are your mother's daughter."

Alex beamed back at him. Everyone always told her she was like her mother, but it meant more when her father said it. *How do I tell you what happened at that horrible place—what I did? You'll never look at me the same way.* She looked away, watching fabric being unloaded from a ship, and a sense of déjà vu washed over her. Her smile faded as a magical tingle crept over her, and her hair stood on end.

"What's wrong?" Edward asked.

"Something's coming." Alex's breath hitched, and she started to panic. They were too far out on the pier—away from their guards, the street, and everyone. "We need to leave. *Now!* Matthew!" She grabbed her father with one hand and her skirt with the other and started to run down the pier. Matthew and her father's guards were already closing the distance between them, but Alex only made it a few steps before a tall, hooded man in a black cloak appeared out of nowhere and blocked their escape.

Alex screamed, causing the nearby merchants to drop their wares and join the guards rushing to their king's defense. The man who'd appeared raised his hand, his cloak sliding down his arm, and with a mere snap of his fingers, the merchants, Edward's guards, and General Bishop all vanished. *We're alone.* Edward tried to push Alex behind him, but she couldn't move. The tingling started to hurt as if her blood was trying to burn its way out of her veins.

The man stalked toward them. He was tall and muscular, and while he wasn't quite Jerome's size, he could certainly take on her father. He cocked his head, his golden eyes shifting from Alex to Edward and back with each step. Alex swallowed hard and reached for her father's hand. With each beat, her heart felt as if it would burst. As he neared, he removed his hood, revealing a golden bronze face. The silver streak in his raven-black hair sparkled in the morning light. It began above his left eye and ran through his hair exactly like Gryphon's streak. His gaze was so intense Alex's heart slowed, and she shivered. She barely breathed as she felt his powers reach out for hers.

"You are as stunning as your mother was. The likeness is exceptional. I suppose I can understand my son's fixation on you." When he turned his attention to Edward, Alex could breathe again. "It's been a long time, Edward. How is the man who stole *my* Victoria?"

As he moved closer to her father, Alex's heart hammered in her chest. She tried to crack her father to safety, but something was blocking her.

"I have to say, I'm still underwhelmed. She could have had me, and she picked you instead."

He was an arm's length away from Edward when Alex's

legs finally started to work again. She stumbled back, and Edward instinctively stepped in front of her, saying, "She picked me, *Garrick*, because I loved her and she loved me."

Alex had never heard such revulsion in her father's voice. Her pounding heart drowned out the waves crashing against the pier. The intensity of the power radiating from this sorcerer made her nauseous, and her head throbbed. *You're Gryphon's father. The—*

"Correct, Alexandria. I am the Head."

He read my mind.

"Garrick of the line of Mystics and Salem, Head of the generation." He bowed to her and held out his hand, but Edward pushed Alex further away from him.

"I know exactly who you are," her father said, "and of your obsession with my late wife."

"When isn't love an obsession?" Garrick asked. "Consider how that Datten boy treats your daughter."

Edward growled, "Aaron is honorable. I'd sooner die than let you or your family anywhere near my daughter."

"I can arrange that." Garrick snapped his fingers, and suddenly weakness spread through Alex. Her limbs felt as if he'd turned them into stone, and even the idea of lifting her arm to use her magic was inconceivable. Fire erupted from Garrick's hands the same way it had from Ember's during the ambush on the trail.

"Alex, run." Edward's voice was calm and firm, just like when he held court.

"I can't leave you," she whispered.

Edward turned her around. "I order you to run."

"No," Alex protested, but he shoved her down the pier.

She only made it a few feet before she couldn't move anymore for the weight in her blood. *Magic shouldn't weigh anything.*

Alex spotted her guards. Sir Christian and Sir Benjamin were sneaking up the pier, and they had almost reached her. Seeing help coming, she spun around to see her father had drawn his sword. The sorcerer's eyes flashed the same blue Gryphon's did when he opened his well. Alex tried to crack again and failed. *Gryphon, I need your help! Please!* When she blinked, she removed the lid from her well, and the surge of magic flowed through her just as Phobos appeared beside Garrick.

"See, I told you the little witch was the Titan of Cassandra now. Her eyes turn gold when she's mad." Phobos laughed, and his eyes flashed orange. He spun toward the knights, and before Alex could warn them, Phobos unleashed explosive fire at her men.

Alex grabbed the seawater but was too slow. The fireball struck the pier and blew it apart. Pieces of flaming wood and ash rained down on them. A plank bashed Sir Benjamin in the chest, and he flew backward, slamming into the wrecked pier. Another hit Sir Christian on the shoulder, and he fell back. A large piece of burning wood singed Alex's arm. One of the warning bells sounded throughout the city.

The pier beneath her lurched, and Alex stumbled, landing hard on her knees. The fire had split the pier in two, leaving her knights on the side still attached to land while she and Edward were trapped with the sorcerers. With a loud groan, the vast support beams at the end gave out, and the pier crashed into the sea.

Edward lost his balance and landed on his hands and knees, his sword skittering away. Alex slapped her palms against the wood, and instantly the sea stilled and the pier's spinning slowed.

She looked up and saw Phobos's gaze fixed on her. A flaming piece of wood stabbed the wooden dock and pinned her dress. Phobos picked up more pieces of burning wood and threw them at her with his magic.

"Phobos, I need her alive!" Garrick shouted. "Edward won't suffer enough if we kill her." Tongues of orange fire covered his body, making him glow as he stepped toward her father.

Edward regained his footing and grabbed his sword with both hands. Alex ripped her skirt free and thrust her arms toward the sorcerers. A ship-sized wall of water erupted from the sea behind her, and she sent it charging forward as someone yanked her arm hard.

The scent of burning wood flooded her senses as Gryphon held her against him, surrounding them both in a bubble of hot flames as Alex's wave roared past. The force of it pushed them along the pier as Gryphon clutched her tight, keeping them safe. He'd spun her so quickly Alex barely registered that he'd shielded her from her own wave. Another explosive fire slammed into Gryphon's bubble. It held, but Alex screamed as she saw Edward fly past. The force of Alex's tidal wave sent the pier rocking again, but Gryphon's grip held her fast. He kept her upright and shielded her against the onslaught.

Edward landed hard and cried out in pain. On the other side of the pier, Sir Benjamin still lay senseless, but Sir Christian was struggling to get up.

"Stay down!" Alex shouted at him.

Gryphon turned to face his father and Phobos. Both were soaking wet and unable to use their fire or explosive powers.

"Get my father and our men out of here. Please," Alex said, clinging to Gryphon for balance.

A second later, Edward and the knights disappeared. *Please be some place where help will come fast.* Gryphon glowed orange and stepped purposefully toward his father.

"Don't you dare, you insolent child!" Garrick yelled.

Gryphon cackled. His eyes flashed blue, and Alex realized that her tidal wave had not affected his explosive powers.

"You're welcome to stop me," he shouted to his father. Gryphon's orange glow turned a darker shade. "Give me your water power," he said to Alex.

"How?"

"Grab me. I'll do the rest."

"But—"

"*Ferflucs*, Alex. Listen to me."

She wrapped her arms around Gryphon, and his magic poured into her, making her glow orange too. It coursed through her entire body before it rushed back into Gryphon. He summoned all the water that had pooled on the pier and then sent an explosion of seawater at Garrick and Phobos, sending them both flying backward. Suddenly, Gryphon gasped.

Alex glanced at him and then knew what had happened. *He attacked his father. That means . . .*

She grabbed his arm and pushed up the cloak's sleeve, nearly gagging on the stench of burned flesh. His arm was freshly branded with the same three *x*'s she had—the betrayer mark.

Gryphon turned and surveyed the damage. Alex still felt heavy, like her well was sealed shut again. *He must be interfering with my powers.* As if he knew, Gryphon touched her cheek, and Alex felt his father's control on her magic break. Phobos and Garrick were staggering to their feet. Gryphon pulled her to his chest, sent a torrent of water back at them, and cracked himself and Alex away.

CHAPTER 12

AARON

The echo of the bells was so loud Aaron fell out of bed. Alex's side of the bed was empty. She was off with her father. He pulled on his pants, grabbed a shirt, and rushed down the stairs.

"Are those the alarm bells?" Michael asked as he ran into the suite.

"No. Those are the royal family bells," Stefan replied.

They dashed into the hallway and found knights and guards rushing in all directions.

"Sorcerers are attacking the royals at the pier!" Matthew shouted. He ran past them, hollering orders at knights as they raced after him into the courtyard. "Julius, gather the princess's guard. Randal, get the king's guard. *Everyone* to the pier now. I was cracked back here by a sorcerer along with Edward's guards before I could protect them."

"What?" Michael cried.

"Get to the horses!" Randal shouted at the young knights. "This isn't a drill. The royal family is in danger."

Shouts from inside the castle made Aaron, Michael, Stefan,

and the generals freeze. Uncertain guards milled around the hallway, and Aaron weaved between them until he could throw open the doors to the throne room, where he found a terrifying sight among a wasteland of flaming debris and smoke.

Sir Christian was screaming for help. Blood welled from a giant piece of wood protruding from his shoulder, though he held Edward with his good arm. But the king, hanging limply in his grasp, was soaked in blood. When he spotted Aaron, Sir Christian collapsed into a heap over Edward. Nearby, Sir Benjamin lay crumpled like something dragged behind a horse, his wounds a gut-wrenching sight.

"Alex," Edward gasped. "Where is she?"

Aaron dropped to the stones beside the king as Randal arrived. With no thought for himself, Sir Christian used the last of his strength to push on Edward's grievous wound, panting and puffing. Aaron gently pushed him back, and Randal took over from the knight. Edward lurched forward, screaming in pain. He grabbed Aaron's shirt and pulled his face to his.

"You cannot let Garrick take her! That boy saved us. If he hadn't come . . . I'd be dead."

A second later, the entire room shook. A gust of wind rushed in, the force pushing everyone across the floor. Burning bits of ash and wood filled the room along with a wave of icy water. Aaron glanced up to see Alex, safe. Gryphon's arms were fixed around her waist, and he held her close. Her face was buried in his chest.

Rage filled Aaron, and he couldn't have stopped himself for all the gold in Torian. He marched toward them. "You arrogant, egotistical son of a boar!"

Alex stumbled as she stepped back from Gryphon. He tightened his grip to steady her, but he never saw Aaron coming. The prince wrenched Alex from Gryphon's hold, then pivoted and punched the sorcerer right in the face.

Gryphon slipped on the water and fell to the stone floor, holding his bloody nose.

"Ares, what is wrong with you?" he shouted as he leaped to his feet and marched toward Aaron, his eyes flashing blue.

"Keep your filthy hands off my wife!" Aaron shouted back.

"Both of you, stop it!" Alex begged.

Aaron kept his eyes locked on Gryphon. *You may be a little taller than me, but I'm stronger. I took out Kruft. You don't scare me.*

"He's dead." The rattle in Alex's voice made Aaron focus on her. She was kneeling at Sir Benjamin's side. Shaking, she moved her hand to her mouth before she pushed herself up and ran for her father. After only a few steps, her strength gave out, and she fell to her knees.

Aaron rushed to her side and helped her get to Edward.

The king pushed Randal aside so he could grab Alex's arm. "You cannot go with him under any circumstances. Your mother would never forgive me."

"I'm not going anywhere," Alex said.

"Garrick . . . he's evil."

Alex looked worried, so Aaron began to rub her back, but she shook him off and focused on her father. "How do you know Garrick?"

"Your mother chose me. He couldn't have her, so now he plans to destroy everything I love." Edward groaned and fell back against Randal, unconscious.

Gryphon, rubbing his chin, glared at Aaron.

Good. Maybe now you'll keep your hands off what's mine. Then the sorcerer smirked and raised an eyebrow. It sent a shiver through Aaron. *I'll wipe that smirk off your cocky face.* Behind Gryphon, Aaron spotted Matthew and several royal guards.

Alex must have seen them too, because she stood and brushed past Aaron. "Gryphon! Where are the sorcerers?"

"Gone."

"Good." She turned to the guards. "Matthew, take my father to his bedroom and summon his physician. Sir Christian will need the physician as well. Someone needs to inform Datten and Betruger. And we'll need to inform Sir Benjamin's family." Alex examined her ripped skirt. "Randal, since my father is incapacitated, do I go to his family, or should you, as the general, be the one to tell them?"

"Sir Benjamin's father is a retired knight. He'll want to hear from you what happened. I can accompany you if you wish. Telling a family their son isn't coming home is never a straight-forward job."

"I know." Alex trembled. "But it needs to be done, and I want it done properly."

"I'll go with you," Aaron said.

"Thank you." She held out her hand to him, a small act that gave him a powerful sense of relief.

The general nodded. "I'll notify our allies after your father is settled."

"Thank you, Randal." Alex tightly squeezed Aaron's hand. "Would you wear your formal royal garb? I'd like us to dress in our official roles for this."

"Don't you need to be checked by the physician?"

"I'm fine," she said, releasing his hand.

"Alex!"

She stopped and whirled back toward him. Her face was streaked with tears. "I'm fine, thanks to Gryphon." Her eyes narrowed. "You remember Gryphon, the sorcerer you punched the second you saw him because he had to touch me to save my life."

Gryphon approached and squeezed her shoulder. "I don't think he likes me, princess."

Aaron frowned at him, and Alex shook off Gryphon's hand the same way she'd shaken him off earlier.

"You kissed my wife," Aaron said.

"Betrothed—not wife," Gryphon said. "Though, frankly, that wouldn't matter in our world."

"Either way—she's mine," Aaron growled.

Alex groaned. "You two can try to kill each other later." She slipped her hand into Aaron's. "Right now, I need your support. *Please.*"

Aaron broke his staring match with Gryphon and squeezed Alex's hand. "I'm sorry," he whispered back. "Let's go find some dry clothes."

⁂

Aaron got dressed and waited for Alex in their receiving room. Although he despised his formal royal clothes, he understood why Alex had requested he wear them. He was reading a book on the couch when Alex came down the stairs. She was wearing one of the ornate blue dresses that her ladies loved so much. The belt and trim were made from silver lace, and the belt had been embellished with added sapphires, most likely a touch made by Jessica. Edith followed her, making final adjustments to the back. Then she wished them both good luck and slipped out of the room.

Alex clutched her crown in her hands, betraying her nervousness. Aaron put down his book and joined her. She exhaled loudly as he took the crown. He tucked some hair behind her ear and then placed the crown on her head. Alex looked down as her breathing grew strained, and he wrapped his arms around her.

"It's all right. I'm here if you need to come undone."

"Later. Right now, I have to tell Sir Benjamin's parents that their son died to protect me and my father."

Aaron kissed her forehead and held her until her breathing settled into a steady rhythm. They headed to the stable to collect Thunder and another royal horse and rode to the home of Sir Benjamin's parents. Alex was an exceptional rider, but today she could hardly keep her horse in line. *I wish I could take this burden from you, Alex, but you'd never allow that, and this is going to be one of the hardest things you'll do as a princess.*

At Sir Benjamin's parents' house, Alex sat with his parents and patiently answered all their questions. Aaron was in awe of her poise despite what she'd been through only hours before. She explained how brave their son had been in trying to save her and the king from the sorcerers who attacked them. Aaron listened silently to Alex's version of what had happened. She squeezed his hand harder as she described the attack, the destruction of the pier, and how their son's distraction had given her time to call for help—help that came from another sorcerer, who had shielded her and sent them all back to the castle when her powers failed. She even apologized that she hadn't been able to use her gifts to help Sir Benjamin.

When his mother hugged Alex, both of them were crying, and his father thanked her for telling them the truth. Aaron spoke up to explain that Edward would take charge of burying the brave young knight in the royal knights' cemetery and cover the cost of the funeral. They accepted this, and Aaron and Alex left the house. As soon as they were outside, her resolve cracked.

"I'm sorry, Aaron."

"Why would you need to apologize?"

"I summoned Gryphon after I told you I'd stay away from

him. I know how you feel about him, but I did it anyway." Alex looked apologetic.

He slid his hand along her cheek and kissed her. "I just heard what happened on the pier. It's a miracle we only lost one person. Your father is going to need days to recover, and I don't know if Sir Christian will ever be able to fight again. You did the right thing." Aaron smiled weakly, but she still looked uncertain, as if she were deciding whether to tell him something.

"What did you leave out of the story?" he whispered. "Whatever it is, we'll face it together."

Alex stepped away and stiffened. Wide-eyed, she stared at him with her mouth open. Finally, she said, "I think I need Gryphon to help me control my powers."

"No. I don't trust him not to hurt you."

"He won't hurt me."

"Really? He had no problem putting his hands on you without your consent. Isn't that *hurting* you? I've seen what you do to men who touch you when you don't want to be touched. It isn't pretty."

Alex sighed. "He won't hurt me because—"

"Because he thinks he has a claim on you. But he doesn't," Aaron growled.

"Aaron . . . sorcerer legend says the next Head and Heart pair with a sorceress is destined to rule together."

Megesti had already told him this when they had gone to get Alex back from Moorloc, but hearing it from her felt like a deep betrayal. Aaron couldn't hold in his rage any longer. If he didn't get away from Alex, he'd say something he'd regret. He turned to leave.

"You said we'd face this together. That you'd listen. What happened to not running?" Alex called as she ran after him. She managed to grab his arm, and he was forced to face her.

"You promised to marry *me*," he snapped. "Until death parts us. Doesn't that matter?"

Alex let out a breath. "More than anything."

"How can you say that after what you just told me?"

"Aaron, you're mortal—I'm a sorceress. I'll live for centuries . . ."

Aaron's anger surged through him so powerfully he thought he would be sick. His vision clouded with rage as he pictured Gryphon holding Alex when they cracked back and the way she had looked in his arms.

How did you fit into his arms so perfectly? I'm not your future—not really. He is. I'm temporary. When I'm cold in the ground, he'll be—No! Not him.

"So because you live for a long time, loyalty doesn't matter?" he asked.

Alex rubbed his arm and moved closer. "It means more to me than anything. But one day, you'll want me to remarry so I don't spend the last two hundred years of my life alone. I'll stay in Warren and Datten until I'm not needed, and only then would I go to the Forbidden Lands."

"To marry him?" Aaron wrenched his arm from her fingers. Confusion and betrayal filled every part of him. His hands balled into fists and shook at his sides.

"I can't say for sure. I haven't seen anything of my life after you."

Aaron groaned and pounded the brick wall beside him. Alex flinched.

"Aaron . . . please," she whispered, stepping toward him. But he pushed her away.

"I need time, Alex. I'm not angry at you, but I don't know how I'm supposed to live knowing my actual replacement is following my wife. I'll see you at home."

Aaron grabbed Thunder and rode off without looking back. He rode through the woods he and Cameron had played in as boys, hoping it would calm him. He couldn't understand what was happening to him. The second he started to feel calmer, the image of Gryphon holding Alex would reemerge. Seeing them together made it too easy to picture the sorcerer kissing her. And the idea of his lips on hers made Aaron erupt with fury, a ferocity he'd never felt in his life. *If this is the notorious Datten temper, I don't know how my father survives it. It feels like I don't even know myself.*

Aaron rode and thought, talking aloud to Daniel. Asking for the advice he wished his brother could give him.

"I know Alex needs Gryphon's help. I've watched her struggle with her magic for months despite her attempts to hide it. There's only so much she and Megesti can teach themselves with books and no instructor. But how do I let a man who wants her stay at her side every day? Let him grow closer to her as he helps her with something I can't?" Aaron groaned, frustrated. "Alex needs help to master her powers, and soon. They're growing, and it scares her, even if she isn't willing to talk about it—with me or anyone."

It was well after lunch before he felt composed enough to face Alex. He trotted into the courtyard and found Michael and Stefan waiting for him there.

"Aaron! We were worried," Michael said as he took Thunder's reigns.

Aaron looked at them, confused.

"Where's Alex?" Stefan asked.

"We separated hours ago. I needed to clear my head, and she came back to the castle. Isn't she here?"

Both Michael and Stefan went pale before they turned and rushed through the doors into the castle. A squire came to take Thunder as Aaron ran after them.

"Do you think she went back to Verlassen?" Michael asked Stefan.

"I don't know," Stefan answered.

"Jessica said Alex has seemed out of sorts lately. Where would she go?"

"Who knows where she went now that she can crack?"

Aaron barked, "Don't talk about this as if I'm not here."

"Then *be* here," Stefan shouted as he spun around and threw his hands in the air. "This is why I didn't want Alex to marry you! Things get complicated and messy, and where are you? Not supporting her. You're off 'calming down,' and we're left having to find her. Datten raised you to expect everyone to bow to your every whim—but *she* never will. Michael, I'm going to Verlassen to find her. You stay here and babysit." Stefan stormed off to the stables.

"He knows I could have him executed for that, right?" Aaron grinned at Michael but only got a glare in response. "Michael, lighten up."

"Tell me where Alex is, and I will."

"I don't know."

"Then don't tell me to lighten up. Instead, go explain to Edward why we don't know where his daughter is. He's only been asking for her from the moment he woke up." Michael stomped off, leaving Aaron alone in the hallway outside Edward's room.

The king was distraught when Aaron entered his suite. To calm him, Aaron lied and told him Alex went to get something from Verlassen Castle. He then brought his godfather up to speed about the visit they made to Sir Benjamin's family, and he remained at his bedside as the physician looked him over. Edward had a fever, and the physician gave him something to help him sleep.

Alex will need to soothe your fever when she returns from wherever it is she went.

Edward was asleep, so Aaron went to grab some food from the kitchen. He was sitting alone in the empty dining hall with a large mug of ale when Gryphon appeared.

"You *really* don't like me," the sorcerer crowed as he sat down beside Aaron. There was still a smudge of blood on his neck.

"Yet you sit right next to me in a deserted dining hall."

"For Alex's sake, we should figure out a way to tolerate each other."

"Tolerate?" Aaron scoffed. "You could start by keeping your hands off my wife."

"I shouldn't have kissed her, but at the time, I couldn't come up with a better way to make her angry. Besides, it's the Ares in me . . . we're passionate and attracted to power. So when she called me, I came. I tell you, though, the amount of trouble that helping her has caused me isn't for the faint of heart."

"So why do it?"

"The same reason you went all that way, risked getting killed by Betruger, and fought a battle for her. Most sorcerers don't find a partner they actually care about, so when I felt her, I jumped without thinking. She's my other half."

"No, she's *my* other half . . . the better half," Aaron muttered, taking a drink. "So you can show yourself out because I'm not thrilled to have my replacement walking around."

"Replacement?" Gryphon asked. "Is that how you see me?"

"Clearly."

Gryphon snorted. "You're an even bigger idiot than I thought."

Aaron slammed down his mug. "Excuse me?"

"Never mind." Gryphon stood to leave.

"Wait." Aaron groaned. "I need your help."

"In what way? I'm sure the list is lengthy."

Aaron huffed. "I know where she went, but I can't get there."

Gryphon smirked. "Then lead the way."

CHAPTER 13

ALEX

"Princess, were we expecting you?" Macht strode across the courtyard moments after Alex cracked there.

"Not exactly." She was fighting back tears, but she managed to sound as if nothing was wrong. "I had an idea about the new trade route between Datten and Betruger. I wanted to run it by Harold before I forgot. I hope I'm not interrupting anything."

"He's holding court right now. Would you like to watch?"

"I'd like that," Alex said.

Macht smiled and showed her to the throne room. They tiptoed in to sit at the back, but Harold saw them immediately and stood. "We have a guest. The Crown Princess of Warren. She is a most honorable and righteous judge. I invite her to join me. Perhaps her gentle nature will bring some balance." He beckoned Alex forward.

She walked to the front, then curtsied deeply to Harold and accepted his outstretched hand before whispering, "You weren't supposed to see me."

"Well, I did," Harold whispered back. "Save me from these petty noble squabbles."

"I shall endeavor to be of service," Alex said, and he gestured to the throne beside him.

The two of them listened intently to all the cases. Though she wasn't as well versed in Betruger law as she was in Warren's and now Datten's, Alex helped speed things along. They got through all remaining cases in a few hours, and then Harold dismissed everyone. When the room emptied, he took Alex's arm and led her out into the yard for a stroll.

"So, princess, are you here to update me on a new wedding date or to discuss the sorcerers' attack on you and your father that happened this morning? Perhaps you want to add some Betruger men to your guard, considering these new threats?"

"My father will likely take you up on that offer," Alex said halfheartedly. "During the attack, we lost a knight." She went on to explain how Aaron had been acting.

"What did you fight about?" Harold asked.

"Nothing. Everything. Gryphon showed up. He saved us," she said, twisting her belt.

Harold looked sympathetic. "Aaron didn't take it well?"

"That's putting it mildly. He grabbed me, punched Gryphon, and later punched a wall, shouting about how he didn't want his 'replacement' around me and needed time to think. He left me alone to go clear his head. I don't understand where this is coming from or what I'm supposed to do about it, so I came here."

"How's your father?"

"I . . . don't know. After visiting Sir Benjamin's family, I didn't go to see him. I'm a terrible daughter." Alex flushed with guilt and embarrassment. *Why did I let Aaron make me feel so small?*

"You aren't a terrible anything." Harold patted her arm.

"Your father loves you and only wants you to be safe. He'll be furious at Aaron for leaving you alone again after everything that's happened. You have a deep bond with your father, and nothing will change that. Especially not Aaron."

"Thank you."

"You're always welcome in Betruger, Alex."

"I'm glad, because I have something I need your help with."

"Oh?" Harold said, intrigued.

Alex explained her plan to him as they strolled through the garden.

***

WHEN IT GREW LATE, Harold offered Alex the queen's suite for the night, should she wish to avoid Aaron a little longer. It was the safest room in the castle. They were well entrenched in the library, spending hours debating the best routes for the trade paths from Datten.

After everything that had happened in the last few days, Alex was happy to be away from both Datten and Warren. Spending time with Harold felt normal and comfortable, the same way being around Stefan and Michael did.

"Lady Edith sends her regards. She looks forward to seeing you at the wedding." Alex winked.

"Message heard, Your Highness." Harold looked away, but Alex caught the blush that crept onto his bronzed cheeks.

After they had a few trade route options mapped out, Alex took advantage of the opportunity to poke around the library. She loved reading what Betruger had written about Warren. Harold regaled her with stories of the biggest and fastest ships Warren had ever constructed. Soon they had the ship plans on the table, laughing over some really terrible ship designs her kingdom had tested out a century before.

"Warren actually built ships with stones attached to the outside for strength?" Alex asked.

"Yes, but they all sank since they never added enough buoyancy to account for the stones' weight." Alex and Harold laughed until Macht arrived at the door.

"Sorry to interrupt, Your Highnesses, but we have company."

"Company?" Harold asked, glancing at Alex.

"Prince Aaron and that cocky sorcerer," Macht said.

"Will you fight or flee?" Harold asked Alex.

"Fight. Warren women aren't cowards." She sighed, and he patted her shoulder.

"Enter," Harold said, standing to greet them while Alex stayed in her chair and continued looking at the maps.

She heard Aaron's voice first. "Hello, Harold."

"Welcome, Aaron. Gryphon," said the king.

He turned to her, but Alex immediately looked back down at the maps.

"Please come in," Harold finished.

Alex swallowed her frustrations and put on her proper princess face. "Welcome," she said flatly. "We were working on the trade route paths. Care to take a look?"

Aaron's expression said he didn't believe her, but he remained silent as he strode across the room and moved to kiss her. Alex moved back and crossed her arms.

He leaned down, but Alex turned to the maps and whispered through clenched teeth, "Did you come to see Harold, or do you not trust me around any men?" Her face twisted into a scowl. "Are my guards next? Or maybe the generals?"

Aaron shot a halfhearted smile at Harold and Gryphon before he whispered, "I came to apologize."

Alex, still staring at the maps, spoke a little too loudly as she said, "I prefer the slightly less direct route. The mountains I need to break through are smaller."

Aaron sighed and turned toward the pile of papers, placing both fists onto the table to steady himself. Alex looked him over carefully. *Bags under his eyes, shoulders tense, and jaw clenched.* She uncrossed her arms and slid her hand under one of Aaron's. He opened it, and Alex interlocked her fingers with his, though she still refused to meet his gaze.

Harold brought Sir Macht to join Aaron and Alex in deciding which route made the most sense, but she struggled to focus on what was being said as Gryphon walked around browsing the library. Having Aaron and Gryphon in the same room together gave her so much anxiety that she caught herself chewing on her cheek three times. At one point, she caught the sorcerer watching her.

"I should go," he said suddenly.

"You're welcome to stay," Harold said.

"Long day. I'm tired and late for dinner. Not to mention there will be consequences after what happened today. But don't worry, princeling, if you need me, just have your princess summon me. She seems to have gotten very good at it." He winked and cracked away.

"That was odd," Harold said.

"*He's* odd," Aaron said.

Alex stood. "I'm going to bed. Harold, thank you for the hospitality, but if you'll excuse me, it has been an exhausting day." *Actually, it's been a very tiring week.*

Harold stood and bowed. As she turned her back to leave, she could sense him and Aaron gesturing wildly behind her.

Aaron finally cleared his throat. "May I join you?"

Without a word, Alex held out her hand, and he took it. She led them to their room, and he closed the door.

I hate fighting with you. Why can't things be easy for us?

Before she could say a word, Aaron wrapped his arms around her, hugging her to his chest. He tucked her hair behind her ear and pushed the rest aside so he could kiss her neck.

"I'm so sorry," he whispered. "I behaved terribly today, and I will spend the rest of my life proving I am better than my Datten temper."

Outrage at his behavior rushed through her. With tears pooled in her eyes, Alex turned to face him. She wrapped her arms around his neck and kissed him. Then he looked down at her, and she slapped him hard across the face.

Aaron stumbled back, furious. She watched his usually contained temper roar to life. Tears streamed down Alex's face, and her eyes burned with anger.

"You know me. So either you trust me, or you go back home to Datten. I'm finished with letting you pretend my feelings don't matter. I was supposed to become your wife this week. One day, I'll be your queen. That means you trust me unconditionally. The only man I want is you—but not if you keep disrespecting me this way."

Aaron closed the space between them, grabbed her face, and kissed her. The possessiveness driving him alarmed Alex, but as her tears stopped, she kissed him back. She kissed with desperation, and she could feel his heart pounding against her chest as he pressed her against the door.

"I hear you, and I will respect you the way my queen deserves."

Brown eyes flashed across her mind, and she shuddered. Fighting to push aside the memories, she tried to focus on Aaron, but he gripped her with a strength he rarely used on her. She couldn't stop herself from trembling at his touch as more memories came to her. *I can't do this.*

She pushed him away, and he stopped.

"Can we go to sleep? I'm exhausted," she said.

Aaron eyed her suspiciously but then nodded. "Of course."

ALEX WOKE up in the early morning hours. She sighed as Aaron caressed her bare back with his fingers. He avoided her fresh scars, though his touch made her shiver when he stopped on the unusual birthmark on her shoulder.

Alex tried to look at it. "They didn't damage my arrow mark, did they?"

"The birthmark that looks like a sword through a pumpkin? It's fine."

She groaned. "It's an arrow, not a sword."

"If you say so." Aaron stared at her. "Alex . . . I love you."

"I know you do. Despite everything, I don't doubt that." She rolled over, buried her face in his chest, and inhaled deeply.

"I convinced myself he would take you away from me—that he'd replace me, and you'd forget about me."

"Aaron . . ." Alex began softly, but he pulled her closer.

"But our friends made me realize that isn't the case. You chose *me*. You could have left with Gryphon many times, but you didn't. I hate knowing you'll have another husband after me, that I'm temporary. But I can't imagine the pain you'll go through burying me. I know how much it would destroy me to lose you. I'm sorry you'll have to bear that burden."

Alex rested her head on Aaron's chest, feeling his deep breaths. His heart pounded so fast it sounded like a drum in her ear. She knew being so honest scared him.

"I doubt I'll ever be happy to have him around," he continued. "He loves you, and not in the way Stefan and

Michael do, but in the way I do. Probably more because you aren't his."

"I only care how *you* feel about me."

"I know, but when he touches you, my blood boils, and I get crazy. But I realize now . . . you need him. I can't protect you from his father, and you can't learn to use your more volatile powers without him, at least not safely. Even though I know and understand all of this, it doesn't hurt less. I have to watch another man who loves you help you with something I can't."

Alex sat up and cradled Aaron's face. "He may marry me one day, but you will *always* hold my heart. I can only give that away once." She nuzzled back into his arms and soon fell into a deep, peaceful sleep.

CHAPTER 14

GRYPHON

Gryphon arrived in the darkest part of the Forbidden Lands—the Celtics forest. The Celtics territory was nothing but wilderness; still, Gryphon felt more at home here than anywhere else. *I wonder if Warren will eventually become home? If the princeling lets me stay near Alex, it might.*

Gryphon crept down the hidden stone path toward Birch's rustic cottage. He dodged her beloved plants and tried not to hurt the birds and butterflies that fluttered around him. At the edge of her immense garden, the path became impossible to discern. Birch let her plants grow how they wanted and only pruned them when they asked, leaving everything else overgrown. Gryphon knew the way by heart and jumped over a wide bush, landing on the last section of stone path that led to the front door.

Countless flowers, herbs, and bushes filled the garden. Gryphon knew to ignore them. Birch kept certain plants as pets, and if you paid attention to them, you'd be outside for ages petting them. The large, multihued butterfly bush had always been his favorite. True to its name, butterflies completely covered the bush, and the ones following Gryphon soon left to join their friends.

As soon as his foot hit the doormat, he was filled with an overwhelming sense of peace. A man-sized Venus fly trap looked interested, but Gryphon shook his head and opened the door. The cottage looked deserted, though he knew better. As he crossed the threshold, feelings of love engulfed him. No matter what happened outside, the cottage was calming and permeated with the scents of lavender and baking bread.

Gryphon strolled into the small kitchen, which was also the sitting room, and found a mug of hot green liquid waiting for him on the small table. He lifted the beaten old mug, sniffed it, and made a disgusted face.

"Drink it," Birch's gentle voice ordered from the bedroom behind the kitchen.

"It smells like feet."

"Drink it anyway. I will not have your family tracking you here."

Gryphon sighed and drank the entire cup in two gulps. "This one doesn't taste nearly as bad as it smells. You should know Echidna is begging for food. I think he's hungry again."

"You need to stop feeding him so he remembers how to feed himself." Birch stepped out of her room and leaned on the door frame. She wasn't curvy like his mother or skeletal like his grandmother. She just was, and everything about her and around her seemed right. Gryphon smiled at his aunt and set his mug on the table.

"How was your very long adventure in the mortal lands?" she asked.

"I was gone a day," Gryphon replied.

"A day was enough. Haven't I told you you're my favorite nephew?"

"I'm your only nephew." Gryphon dropped into a chair and winced.

Birch raised an eyebrow. "True. But even if I had a hundred nephews, after today, you'd be my favorite forever." She grabbed something out of a kitchen cupboard and strolled across the room. She sat in the chair across from him and folded her hands in her lap, hiding what she'd fetched. Gryphon couldn't help but grin at her again. The feelings of peace and calm she carried with her were the greatest gifts he'd ever known. The chair she was sitting on had several birds resting on the top, and butterflies fluttered around the flower wreath atop her head.

Gryphon smirked. "You say that because I went after my father."

"Yes, you did," Birch said. Her sheepish grin was enough to make Gryphon flush with embarrassment. She held out her hand, a tin of peppermint ointment in her palm.

His good humor waning somewhat, he plucked it from her, then peeled off his shirt and rubbed the ointment onto his wrists and shoulder. His wounds still burned even though it had been weeks since they'd broken him out of the dungeons.

"How do you know? Did my mother tell you?"

"Your mother hasn't spoken to me in years, and this won't change that. Everyone knows what you did. We can all feel the battles between the current and future Head. Such a disruption is not something even I could hide. Use the cream on your betrayer mark too. It won't take it away, but it will ease the sting."

He leaned forward and put his head in his hands. "What are we going to do now?"

"Gryphon, your father is a terrible sorcerer. I've always said that . . . much to the dismay of my mother and sister."

"It's just . . ."

Birch scooted her chair closer to Gryphon. "What do you mean, Sprout?"

"He attacked Alex and her father."

"He's wanted revenge on Edward since the day he failed to retrieve Victoria."

"He was draining her. I attacked him to protect her."

"Are you sure you're an Ares? Protecting someone doesn't sound typical of a sorcerer from the line prone to explosive tempers and literal chaos."

Gryphon rolled his eyes. "Hilarious."

Birch rested her hand on his knee. "That's odd. I thought you exploded."

"I did. At my father. That's how I got my betrayer mark."

Birch looked confused. "But that's impossible," she said. "Whenever you use your explosive powers, your magic is chaotic afterward, and I have to use my Celtics gifts to balance you. But . . . you're *already* at peace."

"I feel fine."

She skeptically eyed Gryphon. "She touched you, didn't she?"

He nodded.

"You and Victoria's daughter. She told me decades ago, but I wouldn't believe her. The very idea of an Ares and a Cassandra. You two were as likely to destroy each other as you were to find something more."

"She looks like her mother."

Birch dropped her hands into her lap and sighed. "I miss Victoria. She was such a kind sorceress. If only she'd never met your father."

"That's not how destiny works. At least I don't have to pretend to listen to my father anymore." Gryphon sighed, rubbing the mark on his forearm.

"Well, stay as long as you like. Just make sure you drink

that *sludge*, as you call it, every day so Garrick can't read your thoughts and find you." Birch stood and kissed Gryphon's cheek. "I'm going to turn in. You should too."

"Thank you, favorite aunt."

"My home is open to all my favorite nephews." Birch laughed as she walked through the kitchen to her bedroom. Gryphon grabbed his shirt and took it into his room.

Soon he was sitting on his bed. Birch had crafted it from a growing tree, so it resembled a nest more than a bed. She took exceptional care of her trees, so his bed was always soft from the feather lining and warm from the animal pelt blanket draped over it. Despite the tranquility all around him, he couldn't stop picturing his father's face when he'd gone after him, combining Alex's water powers with his Ares.

What was Garrick thinking now? Birch's drink made it impossible for his father to hear or track him so long as he also stayed out of his father's head. *Is it worth the risk of getting caught to hear what they are planning? See what they know about Alex and if they figured out anything about her friends? Or worse, how little she can control her powers?*

Gryphon closed his eyes and concentrated on his mother instead. She was a strong sorceress, but she didn't have the raw power his father and hexa possessed. In spite of Imelda's demands, her father had gifted her the powers of Tiere rather than those of Ares. When Eris found out what her husband had done, she had killed him.

In a moment, Gryphon found himself in the Head's lab, looking at his father and hexa through his mother's eyes.

"Garrick, put an end to this. I want that little witch here as much as you do, but what if you had hurt Gryphon? He's our son."

"*He* attacked *me*, Imelda."

"It wasn't him. It was the witch—she's worse than her

mother," Eris said.

Imelda said, "Something about Cassandra sorceresses makes it so that Ares sorcerers can't help themselves. He's the first Ares to actually get a Cassandra to consider him."

"Their bond is already forming," Garrick said. "I sensed it the instant he arrived. The more time they spend together, the stronger it'll become."

"We have to make sure he's influencing her. She needs to be controlled and reminded of her place," Imelda said.

"And where exactly is that, dear?" Eris asked.

"With her level of power? Here! Learning how to use her powers for our benefit," Imelda said.

"Or in our son's bed." Garrick laughed. "She's powerful enough that they could easily have several children. We should lock them up until she births a brood of sorcerers. Even a third-born son of a Head and Heart would possess unimaginable power."

"Especially if he inherited Ares and Merlin," Eris added.

"Now we only need to convince Gryphon to follow his true nature and claim what's his. Failing that, we take *her*, and he'll come after her," Garrick said.

Eris chuckled. "Still have it out for Edward, do we?"

Garrick smirked. "Taking her from him is an added bonus. Let him know how it feels to lose what you love most."

"We need their bond to set. Once it does, nature will take over, and they won't be able to resist each other. This isn't a contract bond. They're the next Tabitha and Grindal; nature bonds bring about evolutions in sorcerers," Imelda said.

Gryphon stopped listening and returned to his bedroom. *I can't do this alone, and she doesn't have the control she needs. I need to come up with a plan to help her.* He slumped and fell asleep remembering how, even among the chaos, Alex had smelled of sea air and flowers when he'd held her at the pier.

CHAPTER 15
ALEX

Alex was up with the sun. Leaving Aaron asleep, she put on her dress and strolled around the halls until she found a young Betruger girl, who told her Harold started his days in the stable. She found him tending to one of his horses and crept in silently.

"Good morning, Harold!"

"Alex!" He jumped at her greeting, then recovered and bowed, which made her giggle. "You startled me."

"So much for Betruger's reputation of never being caught unawares."

"I've never been caught unawares by a *mortal*." Harold laughed. "What brings you out so early?"

"I'm always up early. I wanted to ask when that certain project would be ready. I need to go back to Warren with Aaron today and come back for them later." On instinct, Alex picked up a brush and began currying the horse Harold had been tending to.

"A few more days. My blacksmith is rushing them as a favor."

"Thank you." She continued grooming the horse.

"Did you and Aaron talk things out?" Harold asked.

"Apparently, you and Stefan knocked some sense into him. But we'll see how he reacts the next time Gryphon shows up."

"At least he's trying."

"I wish Aaron would realize that no matter what Gryphon and I might share in the far, *far* future, that will never change the love I have for him. Aaron's my soulmate."

"How he could need reminding of that is beyond me. It's pretty obvious to everyone else." Harold laughed.

Alex turned her attention to the horse to hide her blush. He was beautiful, nearly all white except for some scattered black specks down his nose. The colt stomped and shook his mane, but Alex rubbed his neck and soothed him. Harold raised an eyebrow.

"Would you like to ride him? This colt's as stubborn as I've ever seen."

She continued stroking the horse's neck. "This sweet boy? He's as still as fresh snow in the forest, though I *do* have quite the effect on stubborn males."

Harold held up a saddle. "Let's see how he rides."

Alex led the horse to the yard and climbed into the saddle as Aaron arrived in the courtyard with Macht. She gripped the reins, and Harold released the lead line. The powerful horse was the perfect size for Alex. Aaron waved at her as she cantered around the perimeter.

After a few laps, Alex noticed both men were watching her. Harold cupped his mouth with his hands and asked, "How's he doing?"

Alex trotted the horse over to them and dismounted. "I can't understand what you're saying, Harold, but this is a magnificent horse."

"Well, he's yours, princess," Harold said.

Alex gaped. "What?"

"A wedding present from your groom."

Alex looked at the colt. He nuzzled her shoulder, reminding her of the way Flash had picked her. *It seems you've made up your mind too.* Swallowing the memory that threatened to overwhelm her, she kissed Aaron on the cheek. "Thank you—he's perfect. And thank you, Harold. This means more to me than you'll ever know."

Harold bowed. "I'm sure you want to head back to check on your father."

Alex gave him a suspicious look. "Why do I feel you're trying to get rid of us?"

"He probably wants an excuse to visit Warren," Aaron said.

"You're always welcome in Warren, Harold."

Aaron took the reins from her. "Is there anything you need before we head back home?"

Alex strode to Harold and hugged him. "Thank you, and not just for the horse."

Harold spoke to her softly so Aaron couldn't hear. "It's going to be all right. Give him time."

"I'm all set," she said to Aaron. He was holding the horse's bridle, so she reached over and gently stroked the horse's face, whispering softly to it. Once the horse was calm, she cracked them back to Warren.

Alex brought them to the royal stable. Her new horse had handled traveling exceptionally well. She stroked him again and brought him inside. Nathaniel was there, and she asked him to brush the horse, call the farrier to have him shoed, and have Cameron fit a new saddle.

"I'm going to go see my father," Alex told Aaron.

"What can I do?" he asked.

"I'd like my healing books from Verlassen Castle. I can crack you there, and you can ride back with them. I want to allow my father time to recover, but that means we'll have to stay here in Warren."

A corner of Aaron's mouth quirked up as he stepped toward Alex. Firmly, he ran his arms around her waist and pulled her against him, enveloping her in the scent of pine. "Are you asking me to play king with you, Alexandria?"

Alex nodded and put her hands on his chest. His heart was pounding as she looked into his eyes. "As crown princess, I will have to act the part of queen, but you may choose either prince or king, depending on how much you'd like to take on."

"Whatever you need, I'm at your disposal, Your Highness."

STEFAN ESCORTED ALEX WITHOUT A WORD. She spotted the scowl on his lips and the seething rage in his eyes with just a glance. "Say what's on your mind, Stefan. Your silence is deafening."

"I'm furious with your spoiled, pompous, useless—"

"Obviously."

Stefan took Alex down a small side hallway that led to the guardrooms. "He left you. After Kruft, Moorloc, the attack on us, and the pier yesterday . . . what in the Forbidden Lands is wrong with him? I wouldn't have let you out of my sight, and he *leaves* you whenever he feels like it."

Alex exhaled, trying to mask the pain she felt. "He's trying to respect my wishes to have freedom."

"There's a difference between giving you space and risking your life."

"It's hard for him, especially with Gryphon in the picture. He's realized I *need* Gryphon, and he hates it."

"Alex—"

"Enough! Your anger with Aaron is not my priority right

now, Stefan. My father is." She turned and headed down the hall toward her father's room, leaving Stefan behind.

Sir Nial nodded to her as she entered her father's room. "Princess."

Before the door even closed, she overheard Randal ask Stefan in low tones, "Is everything all right with Her Highness? I recognize that look from Edith."

Alex climbed the stairs to her father's bedroom and found a healer preparing a cold rag.

"Let me." Alex took the rag and smoothed it across her father's forehead.

After an hour, he stirred. "Alexandria?"

"How are you feeling?" She moved to the edge of his bed.

"You're unharmed!" Edward winced in pain as he sat up, but he still hugged her tighter than he should have.

"I'm fine, and I've updated Harold. You rest up, and I'll take care of everything." Alex moved to touch her father, but when she tried to heal him, her hands wouldn't glow.

"You don't have to do all that, dear. I'm fine." Edward tried to move, but Alex pushed him back down with a stern look.

"You're staying in bed, and I'm staying in Warren. Aaron and Michael will get our things, and we'll stay until you are well enough to return to your duties. Now I'm going to get you something to eat and bring you a book."

Edward kissed Alex's cheek. She got up and headed down the stairs to his meeting room, where Aaron was waiting.

"How is he?"

"He still has a fever. I tried to heal him, but I think I'm too drained."

Aaron kissed the top of her head. "Are you sure you want to crack us? We could ride to the castle instead."

"It's just Michael, you, and your horses."

Aaron leaned down. Alex flinched as he gently kissed her,

and she cracked them all to Verlassen Castle. He seemed himself now, but she couldn't stop seeing the flash of anger he'd had in his eyes before.

Alex grabbed some books as well as food and drink and brought them to her father. When she arrived, he was asleep again. She set the tray of food on his side table and crawled into her father's gigantic bed. She snuggled beside him with the book on Warren funeral ceremonies she was using to plan the service for Sir Benjamin.

She woke up to the feeling of someone moving her hair out of her face. "Aaron?" she asked sleepily. Alex glanced out to her father's balcony and realized it was dark outside. "How long have I been asleep?"

"Since late afternoon," Aaron replied. "Stefan found you sound asleep here, so he gathered your notes before you could scatter them everywhere. I came to bring you to our bed, but you're welcome to stay here."

She examined his face. There was no sign of the rage from before. "I'd like to go with you," Alex said and slid her legs off the side of the bed, but Aaron snatched her up.

She held onto his neck, and he quickly kissed her. "I'll ask the nurse to come back."

Aaron carried her to their room. Then, standing beside their bed, he loosened her corset with a gentleness that made her sigh. *That's the Aaron I know.* Removing her dress, she watched him disappear down the stairs and climbed into their bed.

❧❧❧❧ ❧❧❧❧

BLOOD SPLATTERED ACROSS HER FACE. *A crack sounded as Doyle dropped to the ground. Another swing, and Tristan followed. The smell of burning flesh hit Alex, and she looked down to see Reinhilde in flames.*

Alex sat up in bed, covering her mouth with both hands to hold in her screams. Her heart pounded painfully in her chest. Beside her, Aaron groaned and rolled over, sound asleep. She slipped out of bed and hurried down to her wardrobe to change. She rubbed her arms as she snuck into the hallway. Once she found the door she was looking for, she knocked once, and it opened.

"Alexandria, come in." Randal ushered her in, then closed the door. Alex looked up to find Matthew seated in front of Randal's desk. On the table sat a pitcher of ale and two mugs.

"Is everything all right?" Matthew asked softly. She could feel his eyes searching for any outward sign of injury.

Alex rubbed her arm and looked down at the stone floor. She blinked back tears as she whispered, "Pine needles."

In an instant, both generals were at her side. "Whenever you're ready," Matthew said as Randal patted her shoulder.

Alex took a deep breath and cracked them to Datten's library. Matthew was out the door in seconds, and Randal led Alex to the corner and sat her down on the couches Emmerich had made for her. He took a seat beside her and offered his hand. She squeezed it while they waited.

After what felt like an eternity, Matthew returned with Jerome in uniform and Emmerich in his sleeping clothes.

"I'm sorry I woke you," Alex said, her voice softening with each word.

Emmerich strutted across the room and sat opposite her. "None of that. I gave you those words to use if you needed us, day or night, and I meant it. What do you need?"

Alex looked up at the generals and back to Emmerich. "How do you live with the knowledge that you've done something so horrible, you're unforgivable? That you took a life?"

Matthew sat on Alex's other side while Jerome remained standing beside Emmerich.

Jerome asked, "Are you talking about the men who died to free you or about dealing with your uncle yourself?"

"Neither." Alex tucked her hands between her knees. "I got my missing memories back. And I did unspeakable things."

"We've all done horrible things, Alexandria," Emmerich said. "As king, I'm responsible for the deaths of thousands of soldiers and citizens through the courts. We'll understand anything you did, and we'll help you bear it. But you need to tell us, since we can only help you with what we understand."

"You'll hate me."

"We could never hate you," Randal said. "You've dealt with more in your young life than most of us will in a lifetime. We believe it will make you a fair and honorable queen, when your time comes. Please, let us help you."

Alex exhaled and told them about losing control in the basement, murdering Tristan and Doyle, and causing the accident that killed Reinhilde.

"That all happened in one day?" Matthew asked.

Randal shook his head. "How did you survive it?"

"I almost didn't." Alex confessed what had happened at the beach and how Gryphon was the only reason she was still here to speak with them. As she spoke, Emmerich reached over and squeezed her hands tightly.

"You are *not* a monster," he said when she finished. "You are redeemable. Aaron, Stefan, Michael, your father—all of them would love you and forgive you for all of this."

"No—they can never know. They wouldn't understand."

"What we speak of here never leaves this room," Jerome said. "Not unless you give us permission."

"How can we help?" Randal asked.

"I can't sleep. I see things, hear things. I hear the cracking of the whip that did this to my back, a punishment I obviously deserved."

"No. What they did to you was not a proper sentence," Emmerich said. "In Warren and Datten, if a case like yours came to my court, you would not be whipped for your past actions. We would deem killing the men self-defense, and for Reinhilde"—Alex gasped at the name—"you would need to make a payment of retribution."

She stared at Emmerich. "How do you put a price on a life?"

"Sometimes we have to," Matthew said. "Accidents happen, and the consequences exist to ensure the family is taken care of."

"Do you know her family name?" Emmerich asked.

"Vinur."

"As in the Warren Vinurs?" Randal asked.

"I think so."

"I'll look into the family records and find out for you," Matthew said.

"She was my friend, and I killed her because I let myself get angry at Lygari. How do I live with that?" *Maybe that's why Aaron is so angry now. It's my ongoing punishment for this crime.*

Emmerich gripped her hands again. "It will take time. The pain is raw, like a fresh wound, but in time, you'll learn to live with it and eventually make amends in your own way."

"What if I can't?"

"You have to. Because if you don't, the guilt will eat you alive," Emmerich said.

The town bell tolled four. Alex sighed and looked up at the seasoned men around her. "We should go back. I don't want Aaron to wake up and find me gone again."

"Are you going to tell him about our chats?" Emmerich asked.

"I don't know. I worry he won't understand." She wiped the tears off her face and dried her hands on her pants.

Jerome gave her the same look Stefan and Jessica had. "He worries because he doesn't know you have support. I suspect he'd feel better knowing you do."

"I'll consider it," Alex said, reaching for Randal and Matthew.

❧❧❧ ❦❦❦

THE NEXT WEEK felt like an eternity. Alex was so exhausted she felt nauseated and barely ate. She spent all her early mornings and evenings at her father's side, but he hadn't woken up in days. His fever worsened, and every effort she made to heal him failed.

Her days were spent ruling the kingdom: meeting with the merchant council, trading supplies with the other kingdoms, deciding disputes between nobility, presiding over the court, and making all the little decisions she'd never noticed her father tending to. The little free time she had was spent in her library searching for clues about why her healing powers weren't working. Several times, Edith brought her food only to find Alex asleep facedown on a book. Aaron and Michael tried to drag her to the dining room to eat, but she refused. Sleep was better.

After a week of watching her struggle, her loved ones had enough. When the royal physician came to check on Edward, they demanded he examine Alex too. She frowned and ordered everyone out of the room.

"What? Even me?" Aaron asked, flabbergasted.

"Get out," she ordered. "You made me see the physician, but I didn't agree to anyone else being here."

"But I'm acting king."

"You're a foreign prince, and I'm acting queen with birthright. I outrank you."

Aaron shook his head and left the room.

It only took a quick conversation for the physician to figure out Alex's issue. "Shall I inform His Highness?" the man asked.

"No. My *delicate state* requires rest, but my father is ill with a terrible fever because a crazed sorcerer tried to kill us. Rest is not a luxury I have."

"If you don't take it easy, you will lose this baby."

"I know," Alex said darkly. "And that's why Aaron can't know. He can't grieve what he doesn't know he lost."

"As you wish, princess."

Aaron rushed into the room with Jessica as the physician left. "What did he say?"

"I'm overexerting myself. I'm supposed to eat and sleep more."

"Are you going to listen to him?" Aaron demanded.

"Tell Matthew to inform the merchant council that we'll suspend meetings until my father is better. That's all I'm giving up."

Aaron and Jessica looked at one another. "I'll take what you give me," Aaron replied, then left to inform Matthew.

"You're not telling him about the baby?" Jessica asked.

"How did you . . . ? My bedding." Alex looked at Jessica, who was holding her stomach. A small smile spread across her lips. "Are you pregnant too?"

Jessica nodded, and Alex rushed to hug her. "Congratulations." She rubbed Jessica's belly, making her laugh.

"Why aren't you telling Aaron? He'd be thrilled!"

Alex sighed. "We both know how risky a pregnancy is when it starts under such distress. I don't want to hurt him if I lose it."

"Are you ordering me not to tell him?" Jessica asked.

"No. I don't order you or Edith to do things. I'm asking you as my friend."

Jessica tightly hugged Alex. "I'll keep your secret, but I'm also going to look out for you the same way Aaron would if he knew."

"I'd expect nothing less."

CHAPTER 16
ΛLEX

Λ lex was exhausted and tried her best to sleep, but anytime she was in bed curled up in Aaron's arms, she'd remember Gryphon's kiss. Then the guilt would seep in, adding to the growing dread that she wouldn't be able to heal her father. She hadn't figured out if it was because she took so long to get to him, if her powers were weakened from the attack, or if the pregnancy interfered with them. Maybe it was all three. Aaron murmured and rolled over, so Alex took advantage, climbing out of the covers and heading down to her wardrobe. She dropped her nightgown, put on her training clothes, and stopped. For the first time in months, they fit properly. She was finally getting back the muscle she'd lost. Alex looked at herself in the mirror and exhaled. *My clothes might fit better, but my scars aren't going away.*

She willed the visions and memories to stay buried and slipped into her father's room to check on him. He was pale and clammy. The nurse excused herself to get a drink while Alex stayed with him. Alex wandered around his room, and when she adjusted his crown on the bedside table, something fell to the ground. It was a set of keys. When she examined them, one key glistened, and she remembered their visit to the treasure room. The nurse returned, and Alex quickly stuffed the keys into her pocket. She kissed her father's cheek and headed down to his meeting room. She was so lost in thought that she nearly shrieked when she heard a voice ask, "How is he?"

Alex spun around, her heart in her throat, and found General Bishop.

"I didn't mean to scare you, Alexandria. I'm sorry."

Breathing deeply to calm herself, she smiled. "It's fine, Matthew. I was distracted. He's still unconscious. I'm worried."

Matthew strode to her and took her hands. "Your father is strong and determined, and with you finally home, he has everything worth fighting for. He'll pull through."

His kind words brought Alex relief. "Thank you. I should get something to eat."

"I'll escort you."

"That's not necessary. I'll grab some food and head to the library to prepare for court. When I saw how many legal books Warren had, I mistakenly assumed most were historical. I now understand why my father hates that part of his job."

"And your memory's better." Matthew chuckled. "Are you sure you don't need an escort?"

"Send Stefan and Michael to the library when they wake up. I'd rather you sit with my father and update him when he wakes than watch me choose a loaf of bread in the kitchen."

Matthew reluctantly nodded, and Alex headed toward the kitchen. The cooks had started breakfast and were happy to give her a large sunflower seed bun stuffed with herbed sheep cheese. By the time Alex left the kitchen, she'd eaten half of it.

When she rounded the corner to the library, an icy chill surrounded her.

She swallowed hard. *Please don't be Grandfather.*

Slowly, she turned and was startled to find her mother. After everything that had occurred at Moorloc's castle, Alex had expected to see her mother and Merlock often, but she saw their ghosts least of all. Daniel usually accompanied her when she was out with Aaron. He loved to tease and mimic his brother, trying to make Alex laugh. Aaron quickly figured out what was going on, and now, as soon as the chill arrived, he'd smirk. But it had been ages since she'd seen her mother.

Victoria nodded toward the stairs and glided down them. Alex rushed after her without a second thought. The top of the stairs was illuminated, but as they descended deeper into the castle, darkness closed in around her. When they reached the bottom, Alex realized she'd left her breakfast somewhere, but as her mother floated down the hallway, she had to dash to keep up. Torches roared to life in front of her but snuffed out behind her as she ran, lighting only the space she was occupying.

At the end of the hall, Alex's heart pounded as she realized they were standing in the circular room with the doors that led to the crypts. Victoria passed through the first one. Alex rushed after her, but the door was locked. Frustration surged through Alex, and she pounded on the door with her fists. When she threw herself back, an unfamiliar rattle caught her ear. She turned, but the room was empty. She spun in a circle and heard it again.

"The keys!"

Alex pulled her father's keys out of her pocket. She chose the large brass one, and it clicked when she placed it into the keyhole. She swung open the door and hurried into the crypt, but she couldn't see her mother. Alex edged along the ancient path, and the torches burst to life as she walked through the room.

"Mother?"

When she reached the end of the path, she looked at the keys in her hand. There were two she hadn't used: a gold one and a smaller key made of a metal Alex didn't recognize. She heard a whisper and spun around, her heart racing. But there was nothing behind her. She ran her fingers over the wall, searching for a hidden door, then yelped. She pulled her finger back from the jagged stone that had cut her, intending to suck on it, but then she saw the blood bead on her finger. She pressed it against the wall and whispered, "Nial the brave. Veremund the wise. Warren the true."

With a rumble, the door appeared. Alex put the gold key in the lock and stepped into the vault. The large door swung shut behind her. Clutching the keys, she looked around. *Why did you bring me here?*

The room was as they'd left it. She glanced at the table where her father had told her the scepter of the first king should be. Once again, the table drew her forward, and then the whispers started. Alex froze and glanced back at the shelves of trinkets, jewels, and books. Only one thing had ever whispered to her like that. She inhaled sharply and went to the shelves.

She trailed her fingers along them, trying to take in everything as she listened for the whispers. There were crowns, swords, jewels, vases, statues, and gems the size of her hand, some even larger than her head. There were books of all sorts, but none of them whispered.

When she rounded the last of the shelves, she noticed artwork leaning against the wall. There were paintings of noble families, royals, castles, ships, and all manner of things Alex had never considered good subjects. *Who would paint a picture of a feast but only the food?* She noticed a painting near the back that depicted a woman with emerald eyes, but as she started moving other paintings out of the way to get to it, a different one caught her attention.

The family was familiar; a handsome man stood proudly in a black Warren tunic, which confirmed he was Warren nobility. The Warren crest matched his gray eyes and black hair perfectly. The woman at his side had a soft, eerily familiar smile, and her blue eyes almost sparkled on the canvas. Her flowing auburn hair fell past her shoulders and matched her complexion. Her dress was a beautiful green shade in the style Alex preferred to wear. The boy in the picture made Alex laugh. His smile took up his entire face. He bore his father's black hair and warm tan skin but his mother's blue eyes. He, too, wore the black Warren tunic with an embroidered letter in the corner.

Alex was leaning closer to examine the letter when the hairs on the back of her neck stood up. She rushed past the art and heard the whispers again. Moving aside the paintings as quickly and carefully as she could, she slipped behind the last one and found the thin outline of a door. She reached into her pocket. *One last key on the ring.* It was small and had a strange feel to it. She ran her finger over it and then touched the door. *They're the same stone. But what is it?*

She took a deep breath, shoved the key into the keyhole, and turned it. Nothing happened, but the key wiggled, so Alex continued turning it. After a full rotation, it clicked and fell out of the lock. Alex picked it up, then placed her hand just above the keyhole and pushed.

The entire door swung away from her, like the one that took her and Aaron from the courtyard into the bowels of the castle. She stepped through it into a tunnel carved out of the earth, which felt the same as the secret passages she used to avoid her guards. She rubbed her hands together, producing a small fire orb, and floated it before her as she followed the whispers deeper into the tunnel.

She walked for what felt like forever, and the walls drew closer together as she went, but the whispers continued. When she finally stumbled into a larger space, she was shocked to find an actual room. The tunnel continued on ahead of her, but the room lit up, so Alex stayed to explore the long and narrow space.

A bookshelf carved into the stone took up the entire wall at the end. In the middle was a large brown chair. Alex looked around for the source of the light and heard a crackle. Above her head, the ceiling burned with enchanted fire, just like at Moorloc's castle.

Where am I?

The rug was an animal pelt, complete with head and paws splayed. It looked like a wolf, but it was much larger than any she'd ever seen. She shivered, remembering the wolf that had attacked the camp she'd lived in when she was young and her powers came in.

"I'm going to pretend you're the wolf that attacked me, because if there are other wolves as large as you, I don't want to know about them."

A painting of her grandmother adorned the wall. Elizabeth had truly been beautiful. Her smile was kind, and Alex recognized the crown on her head as the one she'd chosen to wear for her wedding. She sighed. *My father grew up without his mother too. He understands my pain. How has that never occurred to me?*

Along the opposite wall were a huge wooden desk and a pedestal with a velvet cloth on it. She trailed her fingers along the desk and felt the room chill as she stepped up to the pedestal. Lifting the velvet, Alex found a pearl underneath.

This one was cobalt with flecks of other colors swirling through it. She thought back to her studies, but she had learned of only three pearls: white, black, and clear. Nowhere had she read about a blue one. While leaning down to get a closer look, Alex heard her name being called.

"Princess? Alexandria, are you in here? We've been looking for you for over an hour now."

Alex dropped the cloth back over the pearl and checked her pocket for the keys as she hurried down the dark tunnel toward the treasure room. She leaped through the door, stuffed the key into the lock, and turned it the opposite way. The door slid back into place, and Alex replaced a painting before rushing down the stacks to the family painting she'd been looking at. Standing there, she forced her breathing to slow.

"Alexandria!" Randal was angry now. "Only two people have keys to this room, and your father is in bed. I know you're in here."

"I'm over here! In the painting area," she shouted back, squatting to make it look as though she were examining the painting.

The footsteps grew louder, bringing her father's general around the corner. "Alexandria, what are you doing here? You nearly gave Matthew a heart attack."

"How'd I do that?"

"You promised you'd go to the library after getting breakfast, and then he and Stefan found your half-eaten bread on the stairs. We thought someone had kidnapped you."

Alex shot up. "I'm sorry. I had planned to go to the library, but ..."

"But what?" Randal crossed his arms with a frown.

"I don't know why, but my mother's ghost led me here. Do you know who this family is?"

Randal sighed and stepped closer to examine the art. "It's the Veremund family. Matthias was your father's cousin."

Alex swallowed hard. "They're the family Arthur killed around the anniversary of my mother's death?"

"Yes. Growing up, I was close with Matthias, Edward, and Cameron's father, Bernhard."

"I'm sorry for your loss."

Randal looked sadly at the painting. "Matthias and Catherine knew the risks when they offered to help Matthew hunt for your mother's killer. They even sent their son Percival to his grandmother in Datten as a safety precaution, but he never arrived. I wish they'd have told me what they were planning. I'd have sent knights to escort him."

"Why Datten?"

"I'll explain on the way to the library." As they walked, Randal explained that Matthias's mother had been a noblewoman from Datten. After her husband's death, she moved home to Datten since her son and family visited often with Edward. Catherine was friends with Victoria, and even though Alex had been too young to remember, Percival had often come and played with her at the castle.

When they arrived at the library, Alex paused on the threshold. "I'm sorry I frightened everyone. I didn't intend to go down there. To be honest, I hate it there."

"I do too. I'll send Stefan to fetch you when it's time to go to court."

"Thank you," Alex said and headed into the library.

CHAPTER 17

ALEX

O n the morning of the tenth day since the attack, Alex arrived at Edward's room to the sight of her father sitting up in bed. His fever had broken. The moment he turned to her, she lost all composure and ran across the room to throw her arms around his neck, bursting into tears. A minute later, Aaron charged into the room, pale as a ghost.

The king chuckled. "Good morning, Aaron. Did we wake you?"

"No," Aaron replied, letting out a loud sigh of relief. Alex turned to him, her cheeks streaked with tears. He came over to the bed and kissed her, then turned back to the king. "How are you feeling?"

"Tired. And weak. I still can't fathom that I've been out for ten days. Have you two been running things the whole time?"

"Yes. We split your duties," Aaron said.

"I assume you took the courts and the castle matters, Alex," Edward said. "Leaving Aaron with the guard and port duties?"

Alex nodded, unable to take her eyes off her father.

"You must be starving. I'll get you both something to eat," Aaron said.

"Yes, please," Edward said.

Alex managed to say, "Don't go in your nightclothes."

Aaron looked down and laughed at himself. "Why? Worried the maidens will be unable to resist me?"

She laughed until Aaron kissed her again and left the room.

Alex slipped into bed beside her father, and he put his arm around her. Aaron, fully dressed, returned with Stefan and Michael. They'd amassed a feast, and it took all three of them to bring it into the bedroom. Together they all ate and informed Edward about everything he'd missed. No one could contain their excitement that he'd made it through the fever. When Alex had to leave to attend an important court case, she made Aaron and Michael promise to have the physician check her father before he went anywhere. She and Stefan headed toward the spare hall, and she relayed the same instructions to Randal when they found him.

While Alex was in the middle of the case, she spotted her father, Aaron, and Michael sneaking into the room through the back door. Alex motioned to Stefan, and he moved to join them.

Warren only held royal court when needed. Simple matters were handled by rotating judges at the port, but the larger issues and crimes went to the royal court to be decided by the ruling royal. For these cases, they converted the spare hall into a courtroom of sorts, and the presiding royal sat on the throne on the opposite side of the room, facing the door. Before the throne were two tables for the two sides arguing the case, and behind them were benches for their families and supporters. No one other than the royal, the two parties, and their barristers could speak.

Alex sat on her father's throne with her law tutor, Reilly, on her right, and as soon as Stefan moved away, General Bishop took the place he'd vacated on her left. They had provided her with a small table to hold the specific legal texts and documents for the case being discussed. Alex sighed as she looked up from the evidence. Before her stood a knight charged with treason, one of the most challenging crimes to come before any royal.

"I demand to know who accuses me!" the knight shouted.

Alex said, "You were seen by four knights on four separate occasions. They are all honorable men, which is more than can be said about you, Sir Sawyer. Do you have an explanation for your actions, or shall I dispense my justice?"

He spat at her, but before Randal or Matthew could react, she lifted her hand. "Sir Sawyer of Warren, the punishment for stealing from the king is death; however, you have a family and your death would impoverish them, so instead I will strip you of your title. You shall work in the stables of the castle, cleaning up after the king's pigs. I will see to it that your payment goes directly to your wife. If you fail to perform your new duties, you will be held accountable with your life. Do not waste the opportunity I grant you."

He muttered to himself and removed his knight's crest, throwing it on the floor. A young boy ran up to him to say something, and the man shoved him down. "Get lost, you rat."

In a second, Alex was out of her chair and darting toward them. "Is this your son?"

"This good-for-nothing boy is mine."

Alex tried to hide her scowl as she lowered herself to meet the boy eye-to-eye. "What's your name?" His eyes were as blue as Aaron's and his black hair just as messy.

"Samuel, princess."

"Well, Samuel, how old are you?"

"I'm ten. Makes me a man now." He smiled proudly.

"What do you wish to be one day, Samuel?"

"I wanted to be a knight like my father." He looked down at the ground.

Matthew leaned down to whisper that the son of a disgraced knight would never be able to become one without help.

Alex put on a smile as she looked at the scruffy boy. "What kind of knight do you wish to become?"

"I'm really good with a bow since I'm too small to use a sword well."

"I had the same problem when I was ten, and Sir Michael taught me to use a bow very well." She looked at Michael, and he grinned. "Well then, you shall become a royal archer, Samuel."

The boy looked at her with his mouth open and hope in his eyes.

"You shall study under Sir Michael, and if you do well, we'll send you to Datten to study with the Reinharts. Can you work hard?"

He nodded excitedly. "I can, Your Highness!"

"And do you promise to follow our honor code, regardless of your father's actions?"

"I do."

"Then I welcome you as a squire of Warren." Alex ruffled the boy's hair, took his hand, and walked him over to Randal before she turned back to the room. "Let it be known today that the sins of the father will no longer carry on to the son. In Warren, each citizen will be held accountable only to their king and themselves."

Randal took the boy's hand as Matthew escorted the disgraced knight out of the room. Alex dismissed the court and glanced at her father, trying to read his face. *I hope you aren't upset with me.*

"I've always wanted to see you in court," Aaron said. "You were even more impressive than I've heard." He kissed her cheek.

"Thank you, though I didn't intend to set new laws today."

"Well, I'm thrilled you did," Edward replied. "That old law dates back to my great-grandfather's time. It needed an update." He held his arms out, and Alex hugged him.

"We were hoping you'd join us for dinner," Aaron said.

"Sounds lovely." Alex took Aaron's and her father's arms as they headed toward the dining hall.

After a few more days, Edward was healed, giving Aaron and Alex more time together. The first day Edward was back to his duties, Alex knew she needed to face the pier. She dressed for the excursion, but as she stood at her door, she couldn't make herself open it.

Sweat ran down her back, and her hand trembled above the door handle. *Just open it. Stop being a coward. Remember the throne room: the longer you wait, the worse it will be. Nothing is going to happen this time.*

But memories of her time with Moorloc and the recent attacks swirled in her mind. All of them had happened while she'd simply been living her life—riding to Warren, strolling the pier with her father, even attending her birthday party last year. Alex's heart raced as she stepped back from the door. A pair of arms gripped her, and she screamed.

Aaron let go as quickly as he'd embraced her. "I'm sorry!"

"I'm fine." Alex tried to retreat, but he was too fast, leaping in front of her.

"Please talk to me."

Alex gulped. "I need to go to the pier. Would you accompany me?"

He stared at her. "You never ask for an escort."

She stepped back, worried Aaron would see her tremble or

hear her ragged breaths. "It's fine. Forget it. I'll ask Stefan and Michael."

Alex turned, but Aaron blocked her again. "I didn't say I wouldn't come."

"Didn't we agree that I'd be more careful?" Alex forced a playful smile.

"We did. I'm just surprised you're doing it."

Alex crossed her arms and shot him an icy glare. Anger was the easiest way for her to hide her fear. With a teasing smile, Aaron went to knock on Stefan's door. Alex asked Jessica to come too, and they all headed down to the stables.

Alex's horse was the first one ready. As she walked him out of his pen, she caught her friends whispering. She couldn't make out what they were saying, but their faces made it clear they were talking about her.

"I can hear you busybodies," Alex said, glaring at them over the back of her horse.

Stefan and Michael hushed and looked at her. As she settled into the saddle, the chatting began again, though Michael walked toward her. Rage replaced fear. *I do not need my friends talking about me behind my back.*

"The next person to speak about me as if I'm not here is being left behind . . . or set on fire. You can all ride in the carriage. Michael will escort me since he's the only one smart enough to keep his mouth shut when asked." Alex pulled the reins of her horse and looked down at him.

"Right away, princess." Michael jumped on his horse as soon as it was ready, and the two of them headed out. "You were harsh back there."

"Don't start with me."

"Fine. New topic. Have you named your horse?"

"Snow," Alex said, patting her new horse's neck. His white coat almost glistened in the sunlight.

Michael watched her in silence for a few minutes. "We're worried about you."

"I know, but I need people to stop treating me like I'm broken."

"We don't think you're broken, Alex. We need to know you're dealing with things because if you bottle it all up, you'll explode."

"I refuse to let Aaron or anyone dictate *how* I heal."

"That's fair. I know you'll get through this. You need time." He reached across and squeezed her hand. "Speaking of getting through things, I have a favor to ask."

"Anything."

"I want to find my family."

Alex smiled. "Because of the baby?"

"Jessica told you?"

"Yes."

Michael chuckled and shook his head softly. "Since I'm starting my own family, I'd like to know where I came from. I feel safe now."

"Meaning?"

"Meaning if they aren't what I hoped, I have the perfect family already."

"Stefan and I have ideas. We've just been waiting on you."

He beamed. "Thanks. Maybe we can try to figure it out after your wedding."

They purposely took the long way down to allow the carriage to get there at the same time. When they arrived, Aaron ran to join them. The group strolled along the piers and visited the bakery, bookstore, flower shop, and every other shop that stretched along the road near the damaged pier. Alex purchased a few books and some other things. She avoided looking at where it happened until the smell of burnt wood from the nearby blacksmith filled her nose.

Aaron came up behind her, gently running his fingers down her arm.

"What's on your mind?" he asked, caressing her lower back in a way that blanketed her with calm.

"I need to go on the pier," Alex whispered. "But I'm scared, just like I was in the throne room." Heat crept to her cheeks, and she turned to hide her face from him.

"Don't be embarrassed," Aaron whispered. "We're here for you."

She squeezed his hand and stepped onto the pier. As the group walked along its length, Alex smiled nervously at the men busy rebuilding it. Aaron's eyes widened and his mouth hung open when he saw how much damage the sorcerers had caused.

I understand. I'm just as horrified by what they did.

As usual, Michael broke the tense silence. "How did you walk away from this?"

Jessica held his arm, her face pale as she took in the mangled pier in front of them.

Alex sighed and carefully stepped onto the unfinished expansion. "Here is where my father ordered me to run, but I couldn't. It was as if they stripped my powers and free will from me. That's where Sir Benjamin was hit, and here is where I stood when I could finally fight back." Her words softened as she spoke.

"And where did Gryphon arrive to help you?" Stefan shifted from brother to head guard, collecting information he would need to assess future attacks.

"I want to leave." Alex tried to turn, but Aaron interlocked their fingers. He reached up and tucked her loose hair behind her ear.

"He saved you, Alex. We need to know."

She searched his eyes, but there was no anger or jealousy in them, only love and concern. *I'll let you in, but if you use this against me, I'll never trust you again.* Alex pointed to where she stood.

"I screamed for him to help us. He arrived over there as I was pulling up the sea to throw at the sorcerers. When they fought back, Gryphon pushed me behind him and engulfed us in a ball of flames. He blocked me completely, taking the full force of their onslaught himself. None of their fire touched us. I don't know if it was my sea that protected him or his own fire powers."

"So he used himself as a shield?" Stefan asked.

Alex nodded.

"Well, thank goodness he's so much taller than you," Michael said, making Alex laugh.

Aaron wrapped his arms around her and held her close.

She hid her face in his chest until her strength returned. *I want to feel safe again. I'm still scared from that day, and I hate feeling this way.* When she looked up at him, Aaron smiled, and she kissed him so passionately he nearly stumbled backward in surprise.

"Thank you, Aaron. I'm ready to go back now."

WHEN THEY RETURNED, King Edward was in the courtyard observing the knights' exercises. Alex stood silently watching him for a long time before she headed inside, her heart full of relief that he was all right.

She excused her guards and went to the library to review her mother's journals, hoping to find out why her powers had abandoned her. After reading for some time, she learned that terror, trauma, hormonal changes from pregnancy, or overuse could disrupt her powers, and only rest could settle them.

Three times now, my powers have failed me. When I wanted to heal my father, when I needed to protect us at the pier, and when I tried to save Stefan and Flash on the road.

Alex flipped through the ledger and recognized a name: E. Strobel. *Could that be Elfrieda, Cameron's mother?* She flipped back a few pages and found her name listed under "fertility issues." She read further.

Elfrieda Strobel
Health good—inability to conceive a child naturally

Herbs—herbs for strength
Spell—Fertility spell to ensure conception of a son

Payment 10 gold coins
Successful

No wonder Cameron's *parents loved my mother so much.* Alex scanned the other names: Rassgat, Veremund, Bishop, Wescott, Vinur. The list went on. *So many sons were born over the decades thanks to my mother.*

Alex slammed the ledger shut, feeling anger course through her. *It's not fair. She helped so many people have their families, but she couldn't be part of ours.* She closed her eyes and took a deep breath to calm herself. But when she opened them, she saw her hands were glowing orange. She heard footsteps on the stairs and groaned, hiding her hands in her skirt.

"You're still here? You missed dinner," Michael said.

"I'm not hungry."

His eyes narrowed. "What's going on?"

"Nothing."

He snorted and crossed his arms. "What are you hiding?"

Alex sighed and placed her hands on the table.

"Orange is new." Michael walked over for a closer look.

"Not exactly—this happens when I'm furious. It's my Ares powers."

"Isn't that Gryphon's power?"

"Yes. We have weak versions of each other's strongest powers. His water skills are adorable."

Michael held out his hands. "Let's see if I can help with orange as well as gold." She let him hold her arms. "Close your eyes and breathe."

Alex obeyed, and a few moments later, the orange disappeared. She sighed. "I don't know why that works, but thank you."

"It never works when Stefan does it, so clearly, I'm the favorite brother."

"Have you seen Aaron?"

"Hoping to help nurse his wounds from all the scoldings?"

"Michael!"

"What? Many people are very upset with him right now, and you are a healing sorceress and his soon-to-be wife."

Alex stood and pushed him. "Getting married made you lose your mind."

"Jessica would probably agree with you. Aaron's in your room. I'll start my rounds and come guard you after you've had some alone time."

Alex walked back to their room and, sure enough, found Aaron sitting in the chair on the first floor, reading. She summoned her courage as she marched up to him.

"I can't fight with you anymore about childish reactions,"

she said. "I won't live like this." She had intended to use her proper princess voice, but it came out in a whisper.

Aaron closed his book and stood. "I'm sorry. I know you're exhausted and scared, and I need to be patient. Is there anything I can do to help?"

"I don't know. I'm tired of being scared and angry. My father got hurt, and I couldn't heal him, and I think it's because I'm drained." *Or it's the pregnancy.* Alex sighed as she slipped her arms around Aaron's waist. "Today on the pier, when you held me, I felt safer than I have in a long time."

Aaron smiled at her. "I'm glad. All I want is to take care of you. I promise you . . . once you and your father have healed up, we'll get married. And I will make *you* my priority. Nothing will be more important to me than you."

"And the jealousy?" Alex's voice was barely audible.

"I'll work on it."

"Thank you."

CHAPTER 18
ALEX

Alex was ecstatic; her father had recovered enough that life in Warren could return to normal. In the mornings, she'd walk in the garden with her father. He never once suggested they go riding. *Is it that obvious that I'm scared to? Or did Aaron tell you? Nosy prince!*

One morning, they finished their walk and headed to the hall for their quiet breakfast to find Aaron already waiting for them at the head table.

"Have you come to join us for breakfast?" Edward asked as the servants brought out the meal.

"Yes, but I also have news." Aaron handed Edward a letter with Datten's seal before he kissed Alex's cheek and stole the bit of cheese she'd put on her plate. He sat beside her and began filling both their plates.

"What does Emmerich say?" she asked, sneaking the bits she didn't like onto Aaron's plate.

"Guinevere has everything prepared. You're to be married tomorrow," Edward said.

Alex choked on her bread. Aaron slapped her back until she coughed. It took a full minute for her to regain herself.

"Tomorrow?" she managed. "As in *tomorrow* tomorrow?"

Aaron and Edward exchanged looks of concern.

"Are you having doubts?" Edward asked.

The fear that spread across Aaron's face made Alex's heart hurt. She put her hands on his face and kissed him. "No, it's just unexpected," she said.

Aaron took a bite of his food and watched her more intently than usual. "I wrote to my parents once Edward was well. I suspect they started preparations immediately."

"Stop looking at me like that," Alex told him. "I want to marry you." She laughed, and the mischievous smile that so naturally took over Aaron's face reappeared. "I love you. I honestly have been so distracted by everything that . . . well, I forgot. Don't tell Jessica. She'd be furious!"

"Tell my wife what?"

Stefan and Michael had entered unnoticed.

"Oh, nothing," said Aaron. "Just that my bride seems to have forgotten she has to actually marry me to be my wife."

Stefan chuckled. "You *forgot* about your *wedding*?" His deep laughter echoed through the empty hall. "You're right—if Jessica finds out, you're in big trouble."

Alex narrowed her eyes. "Then I order you to catch your tongues." She stuck out her own tongue to finish the order. Stefan frowned at the childish act, but Aaron and Michael laughed.

"I should get started then," Alex said. "I have to fetch Harold and the Betruger guests, the men from our castle—"

"No, we agreed our men would come to the Warren wedding," Aaron reminded her.

"Oh . . . you're right."

"Don't worry, Alex. I have the list." Jessica's voice came from the hall's entrance. She'd arrived with Edith.

"We made it since we figured you'd forget after everything that has happened in the last two weeks," Edith said.

"As soon as we get you into something appropriate, we'll have everything accomplished in no time," Jessica said.

Alex looked at Aaron, though she didn't have the words to tell him what she felt. *Fighting for me changed you, and your anger scares me. I want my kind Aaron back. But I broke you, so now I have to fix you.* She kissed his cheek and scurried over to her ladies.

She spent the morning cracking all over Torian to bring Aaron, her father, the Strobels, and the Nials to Datten. Other important personages would attend the royal wedding in Warren. Next she went to Betruger to fetch Harold, Macht, and a few members of the nobility. She was delighted to meet the high-ranking men who would be helping to run the training school at Moorloc's castle. Once they were all in Datten, she was exhausted. Nevertheless, she smiled at everyone and hid it well, except from Jessica, who stole her away so she could rest and had Jerome refuse entry to everyone, even the royal families.

Before dinner, the judge walked them through the entire ceremony. Emmerich arranged for him to come to the royal hall as a precaution.

The rehearsal dinner was a typical Datten feast, and after the main part of the meal had concluded, Emmerich pulled Alex aside. "Would you come with me? I have a gift for you."

As the banquet continued in the dining hall, Alex followed him into his suite. On his table, she noticed a crown so beautiful it took her breath away. Like hers, it was decorated with etchings rather than jewels.

"It was my mother's," Emmerich explained. "I never gave it

to Guinevere because it was too soon after my mother's passing, and then she picked one she loved. But now, I'd like for you to have this one, if you wish."

Alex looked up at Emmerich and saw the glimmer of a tear in his eye. "I'd be honored. Should I wait for my coronation, or may I wear it tomorrow?"

Emmerich gave her the boyish grin Aaron had inherited. "You may wear it tomorrow." As she picked up the crown to examine it up close, she could feel him watching her. Finally, he asked, "How are you holding up?"

Alex sighed. "I see their faces every time I close my eyes, and if I close my eyes when I'm sparring, I'm transported right back there. The sounds, the smells . . . all of it haunts me."

"That's common."

"I know. Jerome reminds me every time we train."

"Are the breathing exercises helping?"

"No. I have to close my eyes to do them, and then everything is worse."

"Have you spoken to Aaron or your friends yet?"

Alex shook her head.

Emmerich sat at his table and motioned for her to sit too. From her seat, she could see the dark stain on the table where she had almost bled to death. She turned away from it to face her godfather, saying, "Aaron, Stefan, and Michael—they all fought to get me back. What they did to get me back . . . there's honor in that. But what I did—"

"You did to survive," Emmerich interrupted. "Alexandria, I know those deaths haunt you the same way mine do. You feel guilty for those lost lives, but hear me. They are not your fault. We didn't force any knights to join us, and the men who held you hostage, who hurt you—they got what they deserved."

Reinhilde didn't. "Deserved or not, that doesn't wash the blood from my hands."

"That this weighs so heavily on you only proves your worthiness as a future queen all the more. Many rulers become monsters because they lack a conscience. The only time Aaron ever fought in battle, it was to get you back, and you both feel the guilt of those actions. You two will never allow a senseless war to occur. But you're going to have to tell him that it haunts you and that you talk to the generals and me about it. I promise he'll understand eventually."

They continued to talk until Alex was too tired to stay awake. She hugged Emmerich, took her new crown, and headed to her room, where Jessica and Edith were waiting to help her prepare for bed.

"It's the night before your wedding, and you look so sad," Jessica said as Edith finished with Alex's hair.

"Why should she be nervous *or* excited? She already knows what she's getting tomorrow night." Her other lady's maid giggled.

"Edith!" Jessica scolded, playfully whacking her with the hairbrush, and Edith burst into full laughter.

"Enough. Everyone to bed. We're up early tomorrow." Alex shooed them both from the room. She leaned on the closed door to catch her breath, then moved to the mirror. She ran her hand along her belly. It looked like she had eaten a little too much at dinner, but she knew the truth.

"I'm sorry I'll fail you," she whispered. The door suddenly opened, and she jumped to attention.

"Fail who?" Stefan asked.

"No one."

"You look like you're going to run," Stefan said. He tilted his head, asking her without words if he should be nervous.

Alex smirked at him. "A little late for that, wouldn't you say?"

"I came to say that . . ." Stefan awkwardly rubbed his hands on his pants. "I'm sorry."

"For what exactly?" Alex asked, crossing her arms and holding her chin high.

He grimaced. "For all the bad things I said about him. Ignoring your feelings for him. Needing to be more important in your life. The doubts I may have put in your mind."

"You'll always be important to me, Stefan. We may not be blood, but I love you. You're not going anywhere. And you didn't express any doubts I didn't already have."

After closing the door, Stefan leaned against it. "Have you figured out what's going on with Aaron? He's been acting odd."

"No. Harold doesn't know either. It started after the sorcerers attacked us. He's become jealous and angry all the time."

"Maybe because the wedding kept getting pushed back?"

"I don't think so. But it makes me question how much I really know him."

"You could still run."

"Stefan!" Alex gave him her best impression of the Wafner glare.

He laughed. "I'll behave."

"You'd better. Are you in here or guarding tonight?"

"After what happened last time? I'm staying in the hall-way." Stefan held his arms out to Alex, and after a big hug, he headed out.

As the door closed, she turned toward the mirror. In the corner stood a silver-haired woman with black eyes. Alex shrieked and spun around as Stefan came rushing into the room.

"What's wrong?"

Trying to calm her breathing, Alex shook her head. "Nothing. I saw a shadow and scared myself."

Stefan looked around the room and spoke into the empty air. "Ghosts, Her Highness is marrying the crown prince tomorrow. It would be nice if you allowed her to sleep."

Alex couldn't help but laugh. "Thank you."

Stefan nodded and returned to the hallway.

ALEX WOKE up in a cold sweat, feeling like she was going to be sick. She remembered glimpses of Datten from her dream. The castle. The royals. Everyone was crying except Guinevere—she was screaming. Knowing she wouldn't be sleeping any more that night, Alex threw on her training clothes and headed outside for some fresh air. She opened the door to her room and found Jerome standing there.

"Planning to run, princess?" he asked.

"Nightmares," Alex admitted. Honesty worked best with Jerome.

"Of the castle?"

"I don't know. I only remember blood . . . and wailing."

Jerome motioned for her to follow him. As they walked, he told her some tricks he'd picked up over the years to still his mind at night. When they reached the kitchen to get Alex a snack, they found Aaron sneaking some of the banquet food. He came over to Alex and put his arm around her.

"Isn't it bad luck to see me before the wedding?" Alex asked.

"I believe that only applies to Datten brides. You're Warren," Aaron said loudly before whispering, "Everything worth seeing, I've already seen."

She gave him a teasing shove. The bells tolled six, and Jerome asked Aaron to escort Alex back so he could supervise the guard's rotations. Together, they strolled toward her room. When they reached her door, he kissed her and headed off.

Edith and Jessica ambushed her the second she entered her room. Despite the early hour, the room was full of Datten noblewomen who had all arrived to help her get ready. She was nervous, but whether that was due to the number of people or the wedding itself, she couldn't say. Aaron had been living with her at Verlassen Castle since they returned from Moorloc's. In so many ways, being married to him wouldn't change anything, but for some reason, having the final gold touches put on her wedding dress terrified her.

She looked at herself in the large mirror. The dress was identical to her mother's, and Guinevere had ordered it to be made from the finest Torian silks from the southern kingdom of Bearen. The gown was white with real gold detail and red trim. They'd adjusted it since the first fitting, and it looked stunning. The seamstress had replaced the stiff panel at the back with one of the softest velvet. The rest of the dress grazed every curve and flowed around her legs before running behind her in a long train. The one change Guinevere had made was raising the neckline after noticing how nervous Alex was in the old version. She was grateful to be properly covered for once in a formal gown.

Alex stood on a small platform as the noblewomen fussed over her. She hated having so many people there, especially since the older women outranked Edith and Jessica and took advantage of it to push them aside to get close to the future queen. Alex's patience was evaporating.

There was a knock at the door, and before Alex could give permission, Stefan entered, wearing his formal Datten uniform. Guinevere had provided all the members of Alex's guard with dark uniform tunics for the day, in their birth kingdom's color. Edward had granted the Wafners this privilege after all their years of loyal service to both Datten and Warren. The dark red shirt beneath Stefan's formal black guard tunic made him resemble his father.

"Sir Stefan, what can we do for you?" Duchess Rassgat asked. She shared Wesley's blond hair but, thankfully, not his personality. Yet at this point, even kindness was wearing on Alex. She turned to give Stefan a *save me* look, but he had tears in his eyes as he stared open-mouthed at her.

"Stefan, you're crying worse than you did at Jessica and Michael's wedding," Alex said.

"Sorry. You look so beautiful." He came closer and handed her a small box wrapped with an ornate golden bow.

"What's this?" Alex accepted the box, and all the ladies crowded around her.

"Your wedding gift from Aar—I mean, the crown prince. He asked me to deliver it."

She ran her hand along the velvet-lined box and then looked at Stefan. He nodded to someone across the room.

"I think we should give Her Highness a minute," Jessica said.

"Nonsense. Open it," another noblewoman demanded.

"I think Lady Jessica is right," Edith said. "Her Highness could use a minute."

"We did not ask your opinion, dear. Warren's ideals do not belong in Datten," Duchess Rassgat said, looking down at her.

Alex turned on the noblewoman. "Of course they do. Get out," she snapped.

"Your Highness, it's the expectation that—"

Alex's back straightened as her courage returned to help her defend Edith. "Regardless of what you expect, you all know that I'm not what you expected in a princess. Any lady without a connection to *Warren* by birth or marriage, leave—*now*."

The Datten noblewomen looked to the queen, who politely

motioned for Stefan to open the door. They scoffed and grumbled as they stormed out of the room, leaving only Guinevere, Stefan, Edith, and Jessica.

Finally at ease, Alex removed the ribbon and opened the box. Inside was a gold necklace with three raindrop-shaped stones strung in a line. From left to right hung a ruby, a sapphire, and finally the black stone from her mother's necklace. *I didn't lose it.* Running her fingers over it, she suspected the ruby and the sapphire had stories behind them as well.

"The ruby is from Daniel's sword," Guinevere said. "Aaron had it removed for this necklace and a new stone put in its place. Emmerich doesn't know."

Edith explained, "My father said the sapphire is from a brooch your grandmother loved. Your father keeps it in his room, and he allowed Aaron to swap a stone."

Gazing at the gift, Alex felt tears slip down her cheeks. "So it has a piece of Datten, Warren, and the Forbidden Lands?" She looked at Guinevere, failing to hold back the emotions escaping her.

"Stefan, please summon my son," said the queen.

He nodded and left. Edith and Jessica hugged Alex before they left the room to go to the carriages.

"Your mother would be—no, *is* so proud of you," Guinevere said.

"Thank you." Alex cried softly against Guinevere's shoulder as her mother and Merlock watched from the corner.

There was a soft knock at the door, and Guinevere went to open it. She whispered, stepped into the hallway and then Aaron came in.

Alex had never seen him look more handsome. His tunic was gold, and she wondered if he wasn't wearing a shirt made of actual gold. The black Datten-crested tunic was identical to Stefan's, though Aaron's sparkled more. Alex threw her arms around his neck and cried. Aaron held her in silence as she released all her pain and fear.

"I'm sorry," Alex said when she finally got control of herself.

"What in Torian for?" he asked as he cupped her face and wiped away her tears.

"For making you come here, the nightmares, missing the first wedding, keeping things from you—"

Aaron cut her off with a soft and loving kiss. When he finally let her go, Alex held up the box.

He said, "I didn't mean to make you to cry so much." He kissed her forehead, picked up the necklace, and fastened it around her neck.

"Then you should have given me a normal piece of jewelry."

Aaron's smug smile spread across his lips. "I'm not really the 'normal gift' sort of prince."

Alex sighed.

"Are you all right?" he asked. "You keep rubbing your stomach."

"Yes—no," she said, quickly running her hands up Aaron's muscular chest. "But I will be."

"You haven't been yourself for some time now. We have time if you want to talk about it. They can't start without us."

She smiled up at him. "Let's get through today. Before anything else delays our wedding. All I want is to become your wife. The rest can wait."

"It's true. Once we're married, we'll have a lifetime—or at least, my lifetime—to figure things out. Before we go, can I tell you how beautiful you look? I've never seen anyone as enchanting as you."

Alex blushed. "Thank you."

"I especially like the red trim, though, if I'm being

completely honest . . ." Aaron stepped against her, slid his arms around her waist, and leaned down to whisper, "I'm most excited about getting you *out* of that dress."

Before Alex could reply, there was a loud knock.

Harold peeked around the door. "Time to go, you two."

"Figures they'd send a king," Aaron said. He squeezed Alex's hand, and they headed to the carriages.

THE CEREMONIAL HALL was the grandest in all of Datten, built by Emmerich's great-great-grandfather for his wife. The outside was simple and elegant, but the inside was exquisite. The long aisle led to an obsidian stone dais at the front, a gift from an old Warren king. Rows of benches flanked the aisle, and the hall was lined with ornate stained glass windows. Some panels showed legends of Torian while others depicted the former kings and queens of Datten. The domed ceiling high above was painted with tales from history and portraits of the king and queen who'd commissioned the ceremonial hall. The large window at the back spilled rays of colored light down the aisle as Alex entered.

They finished the last touches in a small room usually used by judges preparing for court cases. The ride to the hall had tousled Alex's hair, and Jessica worked on it a long time before she was happy with it again. She brushed, braided, and twisted everything until not a hair was out of place. Alex looked at herself in the mirror, smiling when she noticed Jessica tearing up. Suddenly, a dark shape appeared over her shoulder. Alex turned to look at it, but nothing was there. Shaking it off, she looked back at herself. Somehow, instead of the dazzling dress, this time she couldn't help but notice all her scars, the damage that hadn't healed since she had come home.

Guinevere arrived to help. "What's wrong, Alexandria?" she asked.

"It's nothing," Alex said. "Just a lot on my mind."

"So I heard. Ladies, would you give us a minute?"

Jessica and Edith curtsied and left the room. Guinevere took Alex's hands. "You're so much like your mother in so many ways, some wonderful and some . . . not as much. But I know for certain she'd be so proud of the amazing woman you're becoming. I know it's hard not to have her around . . . I lost my mother shortly after Daniel was born. I'm not Victoria, but I love you all the same. I'm always here if you need advice, Alex." Guinevere hugged her, making Alex burst into tears. "And for the record, you are *not* weaker because you suffered at the hands of someone else."

Alex trembled as she looked at Guinevere.

"You aren't the first princess to have been used to punish a Datten royal. Unfortunately, it is a risk we take when we marry these Datten men."

There was a gentle knock on the door.

"Come in," Alex said, wiping away the last few tears as Jessica and Edith slipped back into the room.

Jessica handed Guinevere Alex's veil so she could tuck it into the bride's hair. Then Alex bowed slightly, allowing Edith to set the crown in place.

"You look stunning," Guinevere said. "I especially like you in Datten colors."

"I do prefer red to blue," Alex said.

Edith nodded with satisfaction. "Perfect."

"Lady Edith, please go tell Sirs Michael and Stefan it's time," Guinevere said. "They should be next door in the other suite."

Edith nodded and headed downstairs.

"Should we give you a minute?" Jessica asked as Alex looked in the mirror again.

"No. I'll be fine," Alex said. *It's stupid, but I'm scared my heart will beat out of my chest at any moment if you leave me alone.* She heard male voices growing louder. A smile broke across her face as she turned toward the door. Michael and Stefan looked extra handsome in their formal attire. They wore Datten crests to honor the Wafner name.

Michael whistled. "You look amazing. You're almost as beautiful as Jessica was!"

Alex laughed. "Nice catch, Michael."

"It's a complete lie. Alexandria is much more beautiful than I was," Jessica said. "A princess is always more beautiful than a lady's maid."

"But true beauty is in the beholder's eye," Alex said. "So I certainly would hope that in your husband's eyes, you were the most beautiful."

Michael blushed and took Jessica's hand. Alex beamed; she always knew how to say the right thing with Jessica and Michael. Then she spotted Jessica unconsciously rubbing her belly, and her smile drooped.

Stefan held out his hand, and she took it. "Princess, you are the most beautiful bride I have ever seen," he said.

Alex was finally ready, and the guests were seated. As Alex's friends positioned themselves at the back of the hall, Emmerich kissed Alex's cheek and complimented her before he escorted Guinevere inside. In Datten weddings, the marrying royal stood alone. Edward would escort Alex to the front and formally give her to Aaron and to Datten. From that day forward, her Datten title would take precedence over any Warren title as long as she was on their land. At last, Warren and Datten would be united through more than friendship.

Alex peeked into the packed hall. Noble families were

standing at the back and along the sides. Outside, she heard rowdy voices. Guinevere had warned her that the route from the ceremonial hall to the castle would be lined with the people of Datten, all of them waiting to glimpse their new royal couple.

Her father gently kissed her hand. Dressed in his finest Warren attire, he looked every bit the king of a prosperous, forward-thinking kingdom. His formal tunic was black, and the Warren crest was larger than normal. The velvet cape he wore was blue and lined with silver. But it was the love and pride filling his face that made Alex smile.

"You are captivating," Edward said, slipping his arm through hers.

Her heart pounded so loudly it almost drowned out the cheering outside. She nodded, and they positioned themselves behind the now closed doors leading into the hall. She fidgeted, but Edward smiled and squeezed her arm.

"Focus on Aaron," Jessica said as Edith handed Alex her bouquet of lilies. Then her friends slipped into the hall.

Alex sighed loudly, trembling with nerves.

"Are you ready?" Edward asked, joyfully beaming at her.

"I am," she said, swallowing hard.

"Then let's get you married." Edward led her up the doors. He rapped on the door once, and the guards opened them from the inside. The royal musicians on the balcony above them started to play, the music flowing as Edward stood tall and swept Alex down the aisle.

As the pair slowly passed by, Alex smiled at the nobility of Datten and the royalty of the southern kingdoms. Waiting at the end of the aisle was Aaron. Grinning, he winked at her, and Alex's nervousness melted away. Despite standing alone in front of so many royals of Torian, he looked nothing but excited. His eyes never left her as she approached.

Do you even see any of the guests here?

The musicians softened their playing as Edward and Alex neared the front. From here, she could see all the people she loved. The Wafners and Nials were near the front on the left, and Harold sat beside Edith. Aaron's parents sat with other royal families on the right.

When they reached him, Aaron stepped off the dais to meet them. He bowed low to her father, and when he straightened, the two men stared at one another for what felt like hours.

"I, King Edward of Warren, am here to give you, Crown Prince Aaron Edward Johnathon Arthur, my daughter, Crown Princess Elizabeth Katrina Alexandria, to take as your wife. She has chosen you out of all the men in Torian, and I have deemed you worthy of her hand. I give her to you freely so that Warren and Datten may finally be united, but I do so expecting you will honor and treasure her until your dying breath. Do you agree with my terms?" Edward's eyes glittered with tears as he waited for the groom's response.

Looking intently serious, Aaron bowed to him again. "I accept your terms. I will protect her and our future children with my life, and I will love her until my last breath. As long as I may live, there will never be another."

Alex smiled, blushing and crying at the same time. Edward took her hand, gripping it with tender affection, and gave her to the groom before retreating to his seat beside the Nial family. Aaron nodded to Alex and gently led her onto the dais toward the judge.

"Thank you, Your Royal Highness," the judge said as the bride and groom turned toward each other. Aaron gently lifted her veil over her head. This was another tradition from old Datten, to ensure that the bride was actually the maiden chosen to marry the royal. Alex beamed at him so brightly her cheeks hurt, and Aaron grinned back at her. He took her hands in his, and they both faced the judge.

Datten marriage ceremonies were short. Alex tried not to stress about the eyes on her and kept hers fixed on Aaron as the judge performed the ceremony.

Aaron didn't present a ring because Alex had decided to wear only the one he had carried through battle to get her back. But now she gave Aaron his ring. It was gold and had been gifted to the first King of Warren by his queen. As she placed the ring on his finger, his lips curled into a mischievous smile. She could almost read his thoughts. *Yes, I claim you, Aaron, just as you claimed me.* Alex exhaled loudly when they were declared husband and wife, the words finally making their union official in the eyes of their kingdoms and families, and they shared their first kiss as husband and wife.

Aaron squeezed Alex's hand as they made their way down the aisle of the ceremonial hall. The knights opened the doors, and the moment they stepped outside, the people of Datten greeted them with boisterous cheers. The new couple stopped for a moment to wave. Aaron slid his arm around Alex's waist and pulled her closer, so she gave him a big kiss, which the Dattenites responded to with raucous applause. Both of them accepted congratulations and well-wishes as they made their way to the coach. Aaron rushed ahead to open the door for Alex and helped her into the coach before climbing in after her. They had barely begun the trip when Alex's heart stopped. In the crowd of people seeing them off, she spotted Gryphon, and his last words came rushing back to her.

I thought you'd be sick of me by now, princess, but I promise you'll see me again.

CHAPTER 19

ΛARON

The moment they arrived at the castle, Aaron and Alex were summoned to the library to sit for their official wedding portrait. They couldn't help but laugh at each other, feeling the ridiculousness of the whole thing. Once they settled in their seats, Aaron couldn't stop staring at her. *You're perfect. With you as my wife, my life is going to be a never-ending adventure.*

"Your Highness, you must not move," the royal painter scolded. Alex couldn't stop squirming. "Your dress has lovely details, and I need you to hold still so I can capture them."

Alex groaned, and Aaron snickered.

"What?" she asked.

"You seem to be struggling to sit still."

She raised an eyebrow, but his grin only grew.

"Are you impatient for our celebration or our wedding night?" he asked.

She frowned. Apparently, she didn't like him flirting in front of the painter, and the expression the man gave Alex made her try to hide her flushed cheeks. Aaron grabbed her hand and squeezed it. "Just a little longer. We only have to sit for the first painting, and then they'll make the rest from this one."

"The rest?"

"Princess—*please* stay still."

Alex rolled her eyes and glared at Aaron.

"Yes, the rest. We're the heirs of Datten and Warren. Each castle will need one, and I assumed you'd want one in Verlassen Castle."

Alex turned bright red and looked down.

"Don't be embarrassed," Aaron said. "You left Kirsh a little over a year ago. It's understandable that you've forgotten about these things."

"That isn't it," Alex said. She interlocked their fingers and looked away.

"Then what is it? Please, talk to me."

"I feel silly for not realizing how much this matters to everyone. I think of weddings as a banquet, and the ceremony seems to be the most important part. But our marriage ties Warren and Datten together for the next hundred years or more. I thought all the fuss was for the wedding day, but it isn't. I should have realized that sooner."

Aaron smiled. "Well, in your defense, the wedding and banquet are all anyone has talked about for nine months. We barely celebrated our birthdays after the announcement."

The painter had nearly reached the end of his patience. "Your Highnesses, I must insist that you both hold still!"

Aaron sighed and stood.

"Prince Aaron!"

"I'm sorry, Karl, but we're finished for today. We're going to our wedding celebration, and tomorrow morning, I will make sure someone brings you both my tunic and my wife's dress. You can keep them for as long as you need to paint our outfits, and we can come back for shorter sittings so you can finish our faces if needed. Will that suffice?"

Alex looked from Aaron to Karl hopefully.

"I can manage that."

Aaron turned around and offered Alex his hand. "Ready for our wedding feast?"

She beamed and grabbed his hand.

Before they headed into the hall, Aaron wrapped his arms around his wife and kissed her. "Thank you for picking me out of all the men in Torian," he said, giving her his best Edward impression from the ceremony, and Alex tried to stifle a giggle.

"I can't imagine finding anyone as amazing as you if I looked for a thousand years."

She put her hand to Aaron's cheek, and he noticed a sadness in her eyes. *Is it your mother and Daniel not being here? Is it because Gryphon showed up outside the ceremony? You're mine now. Not for me to own, as Datten believes, but for me to love and protect. I'll spend the rest of my life making sure you're happy.*

Inside the hall, banners of gold and red hung from the ceilings. However, the two at the far end were different. Datten used banners for both decoration and history, so every king had his own, complete with images depicting his life and accomplishments. Emmerich's bore a sword and shield to represent all his victories in battle, and now it held a dove beside a boar as a symbol of the peace brought by Aaron's alliance and friendship with Harold. Aaron's own banner followed his father's, a striking red and gold banner with a strip of silver and blue woven into the middle. It wouldn't be embroidered until he became king, but for now, everyone would know he was also a Prince of Warren.

The royal musicians were playing a traditional Datten wedding song. When Aaron and Alex arrived, the royal announcer bellowed the presence of the Crown Prince and Crown Princess of Datten and Warren.

Expansive tables ran the entire length of the dining hall, laden with food from all over Torian. There were three whole roasted venison, several boars, and a half dozen Warren swordfish covered in the traditional dill cream sauce. Beside these dishes sat heaping bowls of every vegetable Datten and Warren grew, including pickled beets, garlic roasted potatoes, peppers stuffed with ground venison, and fresh tomatoes in seasoned vinegar. Thanks to Aaron's mother planning the meal, there wasn't a single carrot in sight. After all these platters stood eleven barrels overflowing with every kind of bread that Alex loved. Aaron saw countless barrels of Warren wine and Datten ale, and the last few tables were covered with every dessert Warren and Datten could make. Jessica had instructed the cooks to use apples for flavoring whenever possible as a surprise for Alex.

To officially begin the feast, the musicians began playing the Warren waltz. Not only was it the dance Alex knew the best, it was also Guinevere's favorite. Jessica and Edith had suggested this song to make Alex comfortable and provide a bit of Warren flavor to the party. As usual, Aaron flawlessly led them through the dance. After months of intimacy, they could anticipate one another's moves and danced beautifully together. After they finished, the room applauded. The wedding feast officially began.

Alex kissed Aaron and then went to see her father. Aaron grabbed an ale and joined Cameron and Harold.

"I thought *you* were beloved in Datten," Cameron teased.

"It seems your wife has stolen your people's hearts," Harold said.

Aaron watched Alex float about the room in her enchanting dress. She hadn't smiled and enjoyed herself this much since before her time at Moorloc's castle. She spoke to noble children and their parents, danced with Edward and Emmerich, and greeted every visiting royal. The instant she was alone, her friends surrounded her. Stefan brought her wine, Michael a roll, and Edith chocolate. Alex laughed with them.

I hope I can keep you this happy every day, Aaron thought to himself. *Thankfully, I have your friends to help me.*

When Jessica dragged Michael off to dance with her, Aaron suggested Harold take Edith, and Cameron asked Alex to dance. It had taken months, but Cameron, Aaron, and Alex had settled into a comfortable friendship. Nevertheless, the prince knew the bond he'd shared with Cameron would never be the same as it had been before Alex chose Aaron. They all knew that one day Cameron would become an earl and sit on her council, and he'd likely end up being a Datten ambassador for Warren, so they'd worked hard to make peace.

As Alex danced with Cameron, Aaron felt a sting in his palm. His hand had curled into a tight fist. It happened again when she danced with Harold and Michael. *It's fine. It doesn't bother me. She's mine now.* But he couldn't stop feeling tense.

The celebrations carried on well into the night. Aaron struggled to take his eyes off Alex, and whenever he looked at her for too long, she would glance over at him. *My wife. I love the way that sounds. The way you laugh and smile makes me feel whole.* After watching her smile at everyone else, he needed to be with her. He'd had enough of mingling with Datten and Warren nobility, so Aaron pushed through the crowd of well-wishers toward Alex, feeling he'd go crazy if kept from her a moment longer. With his arrival, the group of noble ladies surrounding her scattered.

"Thank you," she whispered. "I cannot keep talking about what it's like to be married to you. It really isn't as exciting as people seem to think."

Aaron slipped an arm around her waist and began slowly dancing her away from the party. "It's the rumors. I'm known as a quiet royal, especially for Datten, so everyone thinks I'm different in private."

"A lot of them want to know if you've changed since you stormed Moorloc's castle . . ."

"People ask you about that?" It appalled Aaron that the Datten nobility would make his wife revisit that terrible time just to gossip about him.

Alex nodded. "Constantly."

"I'm sorry. They should realize you had as much to do in freeing yourself from Moorloc as I did. You got yourself out. I was only there to provide support."

"You were more than support, Aaron."

"I suppose I handled Kruft."

She flinched and looked away. "People are watching. We shouldn't talk about this here."

"Talk about what?" Aaron raised his voice. "About all the mischief I get into when people aren't looking?"

A playful grin spread across Alex's face. "We both know I'm worse."

"According to who?"

"Jerome and Stefan compared notes, and it seems I'm *significantly* more work than you."

"When did you talk to Jerome about me?"

"I talk to him often. I simply meant when all this is over and they're not keeping such a close eye on us, it may surprise you how much mischief I can get into. Although, I remember a promise you made regarding our wedding." Alex rested her hands on his chest.

"I remember it too," Aaron said. He pulled her tight against him and spoke softly into her ear. "When we're done here, you're taking us home."

"Home?"

"To our home. I've arranged for our usual guards to have the next two weeks off. It'll be you and me. We'll have Julius, a sparse group of guards, and help. I have to make sure you're fed, after all, and I've been warned you're a terrible cook."

Alex giggled, a sound that was music to Aaron's ears. Her emerald eyes sparkled in the candlelight as she stared up at him. Elation and love made her radiant.

"How did I get lucky enough to be worthy of you?" Aaron kissed her and felt Alex grip his shirt. When he let her go, she gasped for breath.

"I'm ready to leave," she said, glancing around quickly. "I want that wedding night you promised me."

"Then we should say goodbye to our parents." Aaron interlocked his fingers with Alex's.

AARON SCOOPED Alex up and carried her through Verlassen Castle to their bedroom. She argued it wasn't necessary, but he insisted. Aaron paused at the bookcase that led to their bedroom so Alex could open it, then carried her in. He gently set her down and stood back to behold her.

Finally, you're my wife.

With a Datten crown on her head and his colors on her dress, she was even more enchanting. Now she was officially a Princess of Datten as much as Warren. When he looked at her, it took his breath away. *Because she's mine. And no one else, mortal or sorcerer, can claim her. Until my last breath, she's mine, because* she *chose me.*

Aaron leaned against the bed to watch her. She set her crown on the table, then gave him a coquettish glance over her shoulder. But Aaron caught a flash of something else in her eyes—something she was trying to hide. *Fear? Why are you afraid? Oh.* Aaron realized they hadn't been intimate since her memories had returned. First her wounds had kept them apart, and then the exhaustion from ruling Warren had hindered them.

"You don't have to try so hard," he told her.

Alex's expression turned to confusion, but Aaron swaggered to her and took her hands in his.

"I know you're nervous and that your memories haunt you. I won't make you talk about it, but I need you to understand I won't blame you for anything that happened there." He pulled her into his arms, feeling her trembling against him. "And I will only do what makes you feel safe. I would like to consummate our marriage tonight, but we'll go at your pace."

Alex tugged on his tunic to bring him closer. He slowly kissed her cheek and made his way down her neck until he hit his favorite spot, and on cue, she moaned. Her hands gripped his back, hard, as he kissed her again. Aaron slid his hands along her back until he found the ribbons from her dress's corset. As gently as possible, he untied the ribbons to loosen her bodice. Having done it so many times before, he didn't need to look. He smiled down at her, and she looked away shyly.

Aaron sat on the edge of their bed. "What do you need?" he asked.

Alex opened her mouth to reply, but she said nothing. She closed her eyes and tugged on the necklace he'd given her. Aaron reached for her cheek and waited for her to look at him.

"You lead," he said. "Before the incident, you were the dominant one in the bedroom, but you've taken a submissive role recently. Tonight I *need* you to lead so I know you feel safe. I married a strong and brave princess—I'd like her back. And not just in my bed."

When he dropped his hand, Alex crossed her arms. Aaron shrugged and leaned back on the bed. Alex slid her dress off her shoulder. Aaron tried to sit still but flinched. She smiled mischievously at him, moving at a snail's pace as she slipped her other shoulder out of her dress, exposing the burn scar she'd brought back from Moorloc's castle. Aaron felt himself go hard just from the look she was giving him. His body's reaction reminded him just how long it had been since they'd made love. With everything that had happened, he'd lost track.

Alex was now holding the dress up with her hands, hiding her supple breasts. He could tell from her intent stare that she knew he was quickly losing control over himself. She was having far too much fun torturing him. She stepped back out of his reach and released her dress, which collapsed into a white puddle on the stone floor. The gold accents reflected the firelight, sending golden sparkles dancing around the ceiling.

Alex now stood naked before him, her head held high with as much pride as when she had walked through the nobility. Slowly she sashayed up to him, then lowered herself and slid her hands down his chest. She stared into his eyes, every blink like the beat of butterfly wings as she continued her journey down his pants. Aaron closed his eyes, and his head lolled back as Alex's soft hand stroked him. A deep, guttural moan escaped him as she slipped her hand out of his pants. She grabbed his crested shirt and tunic and lifted them over his head.

Aaron's self-control snapped. He grabbed her hips and pulled her onto his lap. She straddled him and kissed him before he could say anything. Aaron held her tight against him. She moaned into his mouth as she ground against him. *Clearly, you've missed me as much as I've missed you.* He kissed her neck and collarbone and then her mouth, thrusting his tongue inside. *Forever mine.*

"Aar—please."

Aaron smiled. She couldn't even say his name.

"Please what?" he asked, just to be sure.

"I want us to."

He felt her body shiver against his. Her skin flushed, and warmth covered him. He grabbed her waist and flipped her onto the bed. Leisurely he ran his hand down her chest, stroking her perfectly peaked nipple with his thumb, and grinned. Harold had shared with Aaron details of his experiences with women, and the prince had saved the best suggestion for their wedding night.

He knelt on the bed and lifted Alex's bottom up slightly. Before she could move, he lowered his mouth to her swollen area and flicked it with his tongue. Alex's entire body jerked, and she caught herself mid-scream.

Harold was right.

Aaron locked his arms around her thighs and used his thumbs to spread her before him. Gently he moved forward and pulled the swollen bud lightly with his lips. Alex moaned and thrashed, but he kept his mouth locked onto her and continued sucking and licking. After several minutes, he heard Alex's moans switch to the little high-pitched gasps she made whenever he made her come. In a second, he felt her thighs tremble around him before they went limp. From between her legs, he could hear her gasping for breath.

He threw his pants aside and slowly kissed his way up her body. She quivered as he moved up to her face and kissed her lips. "I promised you by the end of our honeymoon I'd know every part of your body and that I'd know how to give you more pleasure than you ever imagined."

"Achieved," Alex whispered, kissing him deeply.

Aaron nibbled that sensitive spot on her neck as he gently pushed himself inside her. Alex cried out and dug her fingers into his back. It didn't take long before her moans went high-pitched again. Aaron felt Alex's body shudder around him as he came. She clung to him as if her life depended on it, and he kissed her to give her the connection he knew she needed.

"I love you," she whispered between kissing and panting for breath. And then the tears came as she clung to him.

Whatever is torturing you, get it out now where you know you're safe and loved.

After she'd finished crying, Aaron kissed her gently to see if she was all right, but she growled playfully. Aaron's mischievous grin spread across his lips as Alex slipped away from him. Before he could react, she'd taken over and was straddling him again. Gripping her hips, he let her use him however she needed.

AARON WOKE up feeling sore but amazing. Alex was sound asleep on his chest, and he smiled, running his hand along her bare back. He counted the thirty lash marks. Somehow, they had stayed through the cauterizing scars. Even her funny pumpkin-with-a-sword birthmark survived, though the pumpkin was distorted now.

It amazed him how deeply he loved her, no matter how many scars her body bore. He looked at his own arrow scars, thinking of the times Alex begged him to let her heal them. He always refused. *You marked me as yours with those arrows. They'll come to the grave with me.*

She whimpered and almost rolled off him, but he held onto her, not ready to let go. She was having nightmares again. *What's making you struggle every night? Even on our wedding night, these nightmares plague you.*

They'd talked about her time at Moorloc's castle and how she was struggling to work through it. Now, she was stronger and could defend herself, but her powers were failing more than people knew. Until the sorcerers arrived, everyone had believed she could get away if needed. The emotional toll of the deaths still weighed on her heart, but at least she was working with his father and the generals.

They had kept her secret well. Aaron only found out accidentally one night when he couldn't sleep. He had been trying to find Jerome to ask if he'd seen Alex and discovered her confiding in his father. *I'm glad you have someone who understands the pain you carry. I want you whole again and talking to someone. It doesn't have to be me, though I wish you would let me in, even just a little.*

Alex jerked awake, gasping for breath. Her hair cascaded over her shoulders, and her eyes widened in panic until she found Aaron, at which point relief flooded them.

"You're safe," he said. She was always skittish when she woke up from a nightmare. He gently tucked her hair behind her ear, and she rested her hand on his chest, curling up against him and burying her face in his neck.

"Do you remember this one?" Aaron kissed her head, and Alex nodded. She rarely remembered them. He was about to ask her about it when he felt her kiss his neck.

"We could talk about it," he suggested, but she kissed him harder and slid her hand down his chest and grabbed his penis. An involuntary moan escaped his lips.

"You can't keep using sex to distract me. We have two weeks alone. While I intend to keep you in this bed as much as possible, we're going to talk about what's going on with you."

Alex roughly kissed his lips to silence him, and she looked into his eyes as she stroked him. Aaron's resolve shattered, and he pushed her to the bed beneath him.

CHAPTER 20

ALEX

A lex woke up in the middle of the night feeling tender, chilled, and starving. She couldn't even remember the last time they'd left the bed long enough to eat a proper meal. The morning after their wedding, Aaron had teased that he intended to make an heir, but she didn't realize he would keep her in bed for a week straight. *Or has it been longer?* Alex's healing powers had come in handy, and it felt as if they'd been making love for days straight.

Aaron had kept his promise—they had explored, played with, and memorized every part of each other. She snorted, realizing the guards probably knew they were alive simply from the amount of noise coming from their bedroom. After the third night, Alex hadn't been able to keep quiet anymore. *By now, probably the entire castle has heard me scream.* She brushed her thigh, and her healing magic went to work, banishing the tenderness. She risked waking the ravenous beast as she moved Aaron's arm. He groaned and rolled over.

Once out of bed, she tiptoed toward her wardrobe and dressed. Aaron was asleep facedown, and she could see his sculpted back among the blankets. Alex ran her hand across her belly and wondered if she shouldn't tell him. But then her stomach grumbled, and she remembered why she'd gotten up. She headed toward the kitchen. Along the way, she spotted a couple of the younger guards. They both blushed when they saw her and scurried off. Alex laughed, suspecting Julius would shortly learn she was up, and their burning cheeks confirmed what Alex had already guessed.

In the kitchen, she collected bread, hard cheese, and smoked venison. It wasn't her beloved fish, but she was so hungry she didn't care. She stood at the small workbench and ate while she filled a platter with food for Aaron. As she turned to leave the kitchen, a sharp pain struck her head, and she dropped the tray. A vision of Daniel at Emmerich's side flashed before her, and she heard strange bells.

She shook her head and tried to stop trembling. She raised her hands but froze when she saw they were covered in blood. Daniel appeared in the kitchen, his lips pursed and his eyes sorrowful. She knew that expression from Aaron—pity.

"It's his time, isn't it?" she whispered. "That's what I keep dreaming about? What I keep seeing?"

Daniel didn't answer, but he maintained the serious scowl he shared with his brother.

"Is he ready?" she asked softly.

"He'll have to be."

"That soon?"

Daniel nodded, and Alex sighed.

"I'm still dealing with my time with Moorloc. We're barely married. *I'm* not ready for this. Please," she begged, though she knew he couldn't do anything to stop it. Alex left the mess on the floor and cracked to Warren.

"ALEX, I DON'T UNDERSTAND," Edward grumbled. She had dragged him out of bed at three o'clock and was throwing things into a chest.

"I've been having premonitions in dreams for a while. Bits and pieces. But today, I got a vision while I was awake. You need to go to Datten, Father. You need to be with Emmerich. He doesn't have long."

"If you know, then we can stop it."

"That isn't how it works." Tears slipped down Alex's face. "If it were, my mother would be here."

"Alexandria, you are as skilled as any physician. Healing is what you do." Edward reached out for her hands.

"No. If we try to change things, we'll lose more." Her breath caught. "Fate won't be interfered with."

"He's my dearest friend," Edward entreated.

"I know."

"Alexandria, won't you try?"

She shook her head. "I *can't*! Don't ask me again."

Edward dropped her hands and embraced her as she cried.

"We'll go to Datten," he said. "Spend the time he has left with him . . . ensure he tells Aaron all those things he'd always planned to and makes peace."

Alex nodded.

"Are you sure *you* need to tell Aaron?"

"I'm his wife. He deserves to hear it from me," she whispered.

Edward nodded. "I'll gather the guards from Datten and bring them with us. Your guards and ladies are still in Datten. Harold is there as well since he's been spending time with Edith. There are others who worked in Datten before coming here. I'll ask Matthew to make a list." He kissed Alex's head. "Are you up for this?"

"I have to be."

She cracked back to Verlassen Castle and stood in the bedroom she shared with Aaron. It was almost dawn now, and Aaron was still sleeping exactly how she'd left him, one arm dangling off the bed. He looked so peaceful. *I have to tell him. It has to come from me.*

Alex leaned down and kissed his cheek. He groaned and turned away. She gently ran her fingers down his back, and Aaron twitched as she tickled him.

He moaned through a stretch and opened his eyes. He grabbed her around the waist and playfully threw her in bed beside him. "Morning, my love," he said. Before she could get out a word, his lips were on hers, and his hand slipped under her shirt to fondle her breast.

"Aaron, stop."

He yanked his hand back and sat up at once. His eyes widened as he examined her face and puffy eyes.

"What is it? Another nightmare?"

"No."

"Then what?"

Alex picked up his hand, held it, and took a deep breath. "We have to go to Datten." Aaron frowned, clearly annoyed at being woken for this, but Alex remained determined. "Your father is dying. He doesn't know it yet, but he won't survive the week. We need to go so you can say goodbye and make your peace."

Aaron looked at her, confused. "How do you—I mean, are you sure?" He rubbed his neck with his free hand and let out a breath.

Nodding, Alex pursed her lips.

"Can't you do anything?"

"No. If we tried to affect this, it would put you and your mother at risk."

"But if my father passes, that means . . ." He trailed off, looking at their hands.

"That you'll become King of Datten."

"And you'll be queen."

"I know."

"But I promised nothing would come before you," Aaron whispered.

"You're going to have to break that promise."

He looked at her, his face a mixture of dread and love. "Are we ready?"

"We don't have a choice, Aaron."

He leaped out of bed and hurried to the wardrobe. Alex left to find Julius. She told him what was happening, and he agreed to remain in charge of the castle while they were gone. As soon as they were ready, Alex cracked them to Warren. The throne room bustled with activity, though it was only seven in the morning.

"You're back." Edward hurried over and kissed Alex's cheek.

As the knights of Datten made their way through the throne room, Alex sent every one of them home. Soon the only people who remained were Aaron, Edward, and herself. Matthew would stay in Warren to handle things.

The general looked at her with a worried expression. "Do you need to rest? You've been at this all morning, princess."

"I'll be all right. I'll go to bed early tonight."

"I'll make preparations to initiate the official mourning period once the king passes, Your Royal Highness."

"Thank you, Matthew," Edward said.

"Ready?" Aaron held out his hand to her. Taking it, Alex cracked them to Datten.

Emmerich and Guinevere were waiting for them on their thrones. The king stood up immediately. "Why are half your knights here, Edward? You'd never leave Warren without a significant reason. What's going on?"

Aaron said, "Father, we need to speak with you. In private. Where's Megesti?"

Jerome went to fetch the sorcerer while they all gathered in Emmerich's meeting room. Alex explained what she'd seen.

"It can't be," Guinevere argued. "Emmerich is as healthy as he's ever been. It must have been a nightmare. You have a lot of those."

"It wasn't a nightmare," Alex said.

"Everyone makes mistakes, dear. It's fine," the queen said, her tone on the edge of scolding.

Alex sighed.

"It might be the curse of Cassandra," Megesti informed them as he entered the room. "She could see the future, but no one believed her."

"It's not a curse. The princess is wrong," Guinevere replied.

The princess? When did I stop being Alexandria?

"I'm not trying to upset you," Alex said, her eyes blurred with tears. "The last thing I want to do is bring you pain, but I know what I saw."

"Then stop it. Stop this from happening," Guinevere demanded.

"I can't," she snapped.

"Then what good are you and your magical powers?"

Alex felt as if her heart were being ripped in two.

"Dear . . ." Emmerich reached for her hand, but Guinevere pulled away.

"If you can't stop it, then why did you even tell us?"

"She told us so we could all say goodbye," said Aaron. "Her speaking up brought everyone here and provides Father a chance to give me the advice he always thought he should tell me. To have a last ale with Edward. How can you think *knowing* is a bad thing?"

"Because I'm not ready to lose him!" Guinevere shouted back.

Alex flinched. She'd never heard the queen raise her voice at anyone, let alone her son. But Aaron didn't back down.

Guinevere huffed and looked back at Alex. "You're upsetting everyone. Now do your job and stop this."

Tears flooded Alex's vision, but as she gripped her shirt, she said, "I'm sorry, but I can't stop this from coming. All I could do was give you a chance to say goodbye. I would have given anything to say goodbye to my mother." She fled the room.

In the hallway, her mind raced, and she instinctively headed toward the tower that held Aaron's room. Emmerich caught up with her.

"Alexandria—wait, please."

She stopped and turned around, tears streaming down her face.

"I'm sorry," she sobbed. "I didn't want to upset Guinevere or snap at her, but I needed everyone to know so you could say goodbye." Daniel appeared beside his father, but his presence only made everything feel worse, and she cried harder.

Emmerich held her as she wept. "I haven't felt like myself lately. I was going to summon my physician, but . . . how long do I have?"

"Two days."

The king squeezed her as Aaron came out into the hallway. "Two days. I can do a lot of good with that. And I'm glad I got to see you make an honest man out of my son."

Aaron joined them. "You should go to Mother."

Emmerich nodded, patting Aaron's shoulder. "Tomorrow

you and I will have a lot to discuss, son. But your wife needs you now."

The second she lifted her face to look at Aaron, Alex broke out into sobs.

Aaron came over and wrapped his arms around her. "It's all right."

"No, it's not. I'm supposed to be strong for you right now."

Aaron held her tight and kissed her forehead softly. "All I need is you here. You being by my side gives me more strength than you could imagine. But you should rest before dinner. It's been a hard day for you."

CHAPTER 21
ALEX

"Wake up, Princess of Datten. Dinner is being served, and you're late."

"I'm not hungry." Alex rolled over and pulled a blanket over her head to block out Stefan's voice.

"You can't stop eating every time you're upset. Besides, Aaron needs you. In a few days, your formerly cowardly husband is going to be king. That makes you queen, and everything will change—*forever*."

Alex lowered the blanket to reveal one eye and whispered, "I know."

"I'm here for you." Stefan held out his hands to Alex, and she let him pull her to standing. He slid his arm around her shoulders and guided her to the hall.

Only select citizens of Datten had been made aware of Alex's premonition, yet dinner was still a massive feast with nearly as much variety as their wedding banquet. Emmerich had ordered all his favorites and sat happily in the middle of the head table eating and drinking with his closest friends.

Edward and Guinevere were on his left while Aaron sat on the other side with Jerome. Alex had offered Jerome her place. Just because she was a Princess of Datten now didn't make her friendship with Emmerich more important than the general's.

Alex still wasn't hungry, and she excused herself the moment Michael and Stefan were distracted. Megesti followed her out into the hallway.

"Are you all right?" he asked. "I know your premonition powers are . . . challenging. Your mother was certainly upset by hers more than once."

Alex stopped. "I never realized how painful knowing things like this would be."

"Her Majesty will come around. It's a lot for anyone to learn that the love of their life will die soon."

"I didn't choose this, Megesti."

"I know. Emmerich is fifty. War and being crowned at thirteen made his life hard. He's ruled for thirty-seven years. That's longer than most Kings of Datten."

"I hope he'll have enough time to . . . finish things."

"Because of *you*, he has that opportunity."

Alex whimpered, glancing at the third, silent person in the conversation. "Please tell *him* to go away."

Megesti sighed and looked at the empty space between them. "Daniel, you're upsetting her."

Alex watched the ghost frown and vanish. "Thank you."

"He's waiting for Emmerich?"

"I think so. But I can't handle everyone's pain and expectations right now."

"That's fair. Go rest. I'll let Stefan and Aaron know where you went."

She nodded and watched Megesti head back into the hall before she walked back to the tower. In Aaron's room, she stood at the window overlooking the kingdom of Datten. The city was compact compared to Warren, and the double walls provided a stronger defense. Alex missed the sea air and lost herself in her thoughts until she felt strong arms squeeze her around the middle.

"How are you doing?" Aaron asked.

"I should ask you that." His body was warm against hers, taking away the chill of the night air. She turned and wrapped herself around him for warmth.

"I'll be fine. I have you, and I get to say goodbye. That's all anyone can ask for."

ALEX WOKE in the morning with Aaron's arms still wrapped around her, and she could feel his slow, steady heartbeat. He was sound asleep. She crawled out of bed, dressed, and headed off to find Emmerich. He was in the dining hall eating breakfast.

"Alexandria. Just the person I was hoping to see. Considering how late Aaron went to bed, he must still be sleeping." He motioned for her to sit down. "I have some questions for you. Some things I wanted to know but obviously won't be here for." She settled across from him, and he set a plate in front of her before passing her the platter of smoked meats and cheeses.

"I can try to answer them," Alex said, grabbing bread from the basket between them.

"Will he be a good king?"

"He'll be a great king. If everything works out, he'll rule for longer than you."

"So he'll live a long and happy life?" Emmerich asked, and Alex nodded.

"You'll be good to him?"

"As long as he's good to me."

Emmerich laughed. "That's fair. And what about my grandchildren?"

Alex detailed all she'd seen of their future children, and Emmerich beamed with pride.

"And what about you? What will become of you?" he asked.

"That's the strange thing about seeing the future. I rarely see myself."

Emmerich put his hand on hers. "How are you holding up with all . . . this?"

Alex allowed her face to fall. "More death? It's hard. I'm concerned Guinevere will blame me afterward."

"Do you actually know that?"

She shook her head. "Call it women's intuition."

"She'll come around. I need to thank you, Alexandria."

"For what?"

"For saving my son. I know you've always believed that you were responsible for what happened to Daniel, but that couldn't be further from the truth. He was exactly like me— brave, stubborn, and headstrong to a fault. He wouldn't have listened to anyone."

"Sounds like someone else I know."

"Oh? So there is some of me in Aaron. Losing Daniel left Datten in a dark place, and Aaron was never the same. But when you returned to us, you brought back the sweet boy we lost when we lost Daniel. His bitterness is gone, his anger is tempered. It would be even better if you stopped hiding things from him since he believes it's his responsibility to protect you."

Alex rolled her eyes before she could stop herself.

Emmerich folded her hands inside one of his enormous palms. "I know you're strong, but Datten men are very protective of their wives. If any harm comes to you, he'll take our men to war in a heartbeat. You know that already. For years, he believed nothing was worth going to war over, and then he found love. I can leave knowing my kingdom, my legacy, will thrive with Aaron."

Alex let out a breath. Her eyes stung.

Emmerich continued. "I need you to promise me you won't run away from everything after I go. Keep working with our generals. They've lived through the pain you're fighting. One day, the burden you carry will get lighter, but only if you keep lifting it." He cradled her cheek. "Your mother would be so proud of the woman you've become."

Alex's tears poured down her face.

Aaron appeared at the entryway. "Am I interrupting? What are you two busy plotting?" He sat on the bench behind Alex and ran his arms around her waist. Emmerich released her hand so she could hug Aaron back. Her husband tenderly wiped the tears from her cheeks and kissed her forehead. "It'll be all right. We'll be fine."

"I know," she said as she stood and rubbed Aaron's shoulder. "Your turn. Stefan and Michael?"

"In the courtyard."

She nodded and walked toward the doors of the dining hall. When she glanced back, both men were watching her. She exhaled to still her tears and headed toward the courtyard.

Harold, Michael, and Stefan were watching Jerome train his men while they discussed ideas for expanding her guard. Harold was pointing out the similarities between Datten and Betruger training methods.

She joined them silently so as not to interrupt. When the conversation came to a natural close, Michael finally looked at her and asked, "Do you remember anything from when you were here as a little girl?"

Alex grinned at him. "I remember pushing Aaron into the dirt a lot. And I think someone fell into the moat."

Stefan laughed. "They didn't just fall. *You* pushed Aaron into the moat too. Daniel encouraged it."

Michael nodded and whistled. "You and water."

Alex shrugged. She watched Jerome leap to avoid an opponent's slash and then counter with an attack of his own. "Can we try that, Stefan?"

Stefan watched his father move and strike out at the guard. "Um . . . no."

"Why not?" Alex demanded.

"You're not ready for it."

Frustration ripped through her. "Thank you for your concern, but I am perfectly capable of trying new forms of training."

Stefan stepped up to Alex.

"Stefan—" Michael stepped forward, but Stefan shot his arm out to hold him back.

"I will not take chances with your safety, not with everything going on."

"The people of Betruger train through everything," Harold said. "Our women even train while pregnant. Being sick won't save you from an attack."

Alex crossed her arms, but Stefan said, "No."

She stormed past him and headed straight for Jerome. He'd finished his demonstration and now stood fixed with his arms folded as he watched the young knights practice. Seeing her, he nodded toward the training ring. Alex hurried toward the supplies and returned with a pair of staves. She handed one to Jerome.

"Stefan, Michael—supervise the guards." Jerome didn't even look back as he motioned for Alex to head toward the largest sparring ring.

"There'll be no sparring today." Jessica's voice carried across the field, making all the men turn toward her and Edith. "We are going to take you on a proper tour of Datten, Your Highness."

"Who's we?" Stefan asked.

"Why, the entire Wafner family, dear brother."

"King Harold, it would be delightful if you were to join us too," Edith said, curtsying to him.

"I'd love to, Lady Edith. I'll have Macht come too."

Edith smiled as Harold joined her and Jessica. Stefan and Michael looked at Alex. She glanced down at the staff in her hands. *A proper tour would be nice. I am going to be the queen shortly.*

"Will Aaron join us?" Michael asked.

Alex shook her head. "No. He's with his father."

Stefan offered her his arm. "Then I will have to suffice."

"Thank you," she whispered, taking it.

"It's still early. We'll start with the market," Jerome said.

⁂

Alex was in awe of Datten's market. It seemed like everyone in the kingdom was packed into the square at the center of town. She hadn't realized how large it was back when Aaron brought her during their secret visit after she'd first come home. There were as many, if not more, people milling about as she'd ever seen at the pier in Warren. Wooden booths were piled high with amazing things for sale: fruits, vegetables, fabrics, flowers, plants, books, treats, and so much more.

"Have you ever had chocolate?" Jessica asked. "It's made from a bean discovered in Oreane."

Alex glanced at Jerome before shaking her head.

"You have to try it," Edith said. "Jessica got me a piece

210

yesterday, and it is to die for." As she realized what she'd said, her hand shot to her mouth, and she turned bright red.

Alex smiled kindly. "Then I certainly can't say no."

"Take me to this chocolate. I'll buy everyone some," Harold said. Alex's lady's maids led him toward the stand with Michael and Macht in tow, leaving Alex with Stefan and Jerome.

"How are you holding up?" Jerome asked.

Alex looked from him to Stefan.

"He means with adding another death to your conscience," Stefan clarified.

Alex scowled, looking from Jerome to Stefan.

Stefan turned to her. "Don't blame him. When you wouldn't talk to us for months, we were worried. I went to ask for my father's advice and stumbled upon one of your meetings with him and His Royal Highness."

"When?"

"Three months ago."

"You knew for three months and never said a word?"

"I didn't even tell Michael. I knew you'd tell us when you were ready. I didn't expect it to take this long, but I know you, and pushing doesn't work. As long as you were talking to someone, I let you be."

Alex squeezed Stefan's hand. "I feel like I'm failing everyone because I can't stop this."

Jerome put his hand on her shoulder. "You gave the king time to advise Aaron and say his goodbyes. That is one of the greatest gifts you could give anyone."

Alex's heart hurt, and her breath caught in her throat as she watched her friends laugh and smile at the chocolate stand. Heat hit her belly, and she looked down to see she was rubbing it without thinking.

"Hello, princess."

A young voice brought her out of her thoughts, and she saw a little girl staring at her. Alex glanced at her guards. The girl's boldness startled Stefan, but Jerome merely raised an eyebrow.

"Hello. Who might you be?" Alex asked, smiling at the precocious youngster. She had fine blonde hair and pine-green eyes, and she wore a lovely red gown. It reminded Alex of the style Jessica preferred.

"I'm Ruby Avery. My father is King Emmerich's head archer, and my brother is—"

"Caleb. One of the guards who watches over me and Aaron."

The girl nodded proudly.

"I've heard many stories about you, Ruby. Any time Prince Aaron catches me getting into mischief, your brother insists on telling us about you. Apparently, you and I get into a lot of trouble." Alex winked at her, and the girl giggled.

"Is it true you're going to live in Datten soon?"

"Possibly. Would you like that?"

"Very much. We've had enough boys in charge for a while. We need a smart girl to teach them a few things."

As Alex and Stefan chuckled, Jerome cleared his throat.

"You sound a lot like Her Highness when she was ten," Stefan said.

"That's how old I am!" Ruby beamed with pride. "You're Sir Stefan, aren't you? My brother talks about you a lot. He says he'd have been the princess's head guard if you hadn't been around."

"Does he now?" Stefan asked, and Alex tried to disguise her laughter with a cough.

Someone called across the market, and Ruby turned. "I have to go, but it was lovely to meet you, princess." She curtsied to Alex and hurried into the crowd.

"She reminds me of Edith," Stefan said. "A little too wild and boyish for her station."

"A curse of many daughters of generals. We treat them very much the same way we do our sons. I was fortunate that Her Majesty helped guide Jessica," Jerome said.

"I don't think Jessica has a wild bone in her body," said Alex. "The Wafners are too serious for that." She smirked at Stefan's frown.

Their friends returned with the chocolate, and Alex had to admit it was delicious. They split up and strolled through the market, looking at the booths. The last booth had various trinkets for sale. Alex took her time examining them with Stefan. She was almost ready to leave when a box glistened and caught her attention.

"It plays music too, though no one around here knows the tune," said the old woman working the stall.

Alex examined the box. The mother-of-pearl covering refracted the sunlight into a myriad of beautiful pastel colors. She opened it, admiring the rich cobalt velvet lining, and the song started to play.

"See? Peculiar tune," the shopkeeper said.

Alex stiffened. "I know this song."

Stefan examined the box in her hand. "Isn't that the tune you and Michael hummed as children when we lived in the woods?"

Alex nodded. "I thought we made it up. Stefan, could Michael be from Warren?"

"Maybe. How else would you both know this song?"

"How much for the music box?" she asked.

"Take it as a wedding gift, Your Highness."

"I couldn't," Alex said.

"I insist, princess."

"Thank you." She clutched the box as Stefan led her back to their friends.

"You look tired," Michael said when Alex and Stefan joined them. Jessica elbowed him, making Harold and Edith laugh. "It's not rude when I tell my friend she looks tired," Michael argued, but Jessica elbowed him again. "Wafners," he grumbled.

"I am tired," Alex admitted. "Could we head back? I'd like to see if I can find Aaron."

THEY ARRIVED BACK at the castle in time for dinner. Alex hurried to find Aaron but spotted her father leaving the library.

"Hello, Father." She kissed him on the cheek. "Did you have a good afternoon with Emmerich?"

"I did. Were you looking for Aaron?"

"Yes."

"He went in to speak with his father again. I suspect they'll be there for a while."

Alex exhaled. "How's Guinevere holding up?"

"Not well. She still thinks this is somehow a mistake and he'll be fine."

"I'm worried she'll blame me," Alex said.

"She might."

Alex looked at her father, horrified.

"I know that isn't what you wanted to hear, but grief does terrible things to people."

She closed her eyes and sighed. "I need some air."

"Take someone with you."

"I'll be fine."

"Alexandria," he replied sternly.

"I won't leave the castle. I just need to cool down." She squeezed her father's hand and headed down the hall.

Alex strolled around the outside of the fortress, thinking about Datten, her day in town, and how everything would change soon. *How will Aaron handle being king? Will he be scared or overwhelmed or angry? His temper has been worse lately. What will life in Datten be like? Will we be good for the kingdom? Will I be good for it?* It was getting late, so Alex turned to head back. Then the hairs on the back of her neck bristled.

Am I being watched?

Out of the corner of her eye, she thought she saw a dark shadow, but when she looked, there was nothing there. *It's just ghosts.*

Still, she slowed her pace and listened to the noises around her, just as she had done as a little girl when something scared her. Her heart beat like a drum in her ears. Satisfied, she turned to go back inside. Alex hurried around a corner without paying attention and ran into a woman, accidentally knocking her down.

"I'm so sorry." She reached down to help the woman up, and the instant their hands touched, a chill ripped through her. Fear poured from her well, and Alex fought to keep her power under control.

The woman smiled kindly, but Alex couldn't shake a feeling of dread. She was short and very curvy, with flowing strawberry blonde hair and soft, pinkish skin. Alex couldn't make out the color of her eyes in the dark, but they didn't feel kind to her. She felt as if the woman were trying to see through her.

"I'm the one who's sorry, princess." She took Alex's hand and kissed it.

Alex nodded but took her hand back.

"You should be more careful walking alone at night. A

princess must always be among her guard, even in Datten. What would your husband say if someone were to snatch you away?"

Alex stepped back. The woman laughed and continued on her way. Alex rushed back to the castle, and only once she was inside did her feelings of unease disappear. She pushed the woman from her mind and headed to bed.

CHAPTER 22
AARON

Aaron spent the day learning from his father. Emmerich allowed him to ask anything and everything he'd ever wondered about being king. Nothing was off-limits. Aaron questioned Emmerich's past choices, many of them made when Aaron was growing up, and his father answered with patience even when his son disagreed with how he'd handled things. As the king explained his decisions, Aaron understood what had led him to make those choices. Emmerich was openly shocked at how much his son had noticed as a boy. When they broke for lunch, Emmerich gave Aaron a king's journal—Aaron's first. Aaron spent the afternoon writing down additional questions in the book. He paused for a quick dinner and then rushed to talk to his father again. They finished when Jerome arrived with ale.

Aaron excused himself to check on Alex but ran into Jessica and Michael first.

"How are the meetings going?" Jessica asked.

"Well. I think Jerome's with him now."

"Did you get to ask all your questions?" Michael asked.

"All the ones I had and dozens more. I keep worrying that I'm forgetting something obvious and will regret it later."

"You'll have Harold and Edward to help you too," Jessica said.

"What did you do with Alex today?"

"Jessica insisted we all get a proper tour of Datten, courtesy of the Wafners," Michael said.

"Did you show them that new chocolate stand?" Aaron asked.

"Yes." Jessica laughed. "Harold insisted on treating us all to as much as we wanted, and I think Edith ate half the stand."

"I prefer cheese," Michael said. "Alex tried some. She liked it but didn't indulge the way Edith did."

"How was she?" Aaron asked.

"Still distant," Jessica said. "She stayed between my brother and father for most of the tour."

Michael added, "She was quiet, and Alex isn't quiet."

"I wish I knew what was bothering her," said Aaron. "It's more than this vision. She's been withdrawn for weeks now."

"Aaron, she's been different ever since we got her back from Moorloc," Michael said. "She was fearless before, and now she's frightened of . . . everything."

"How do we help her? She's already training constantly, and she's gotten physically stronger in addition to developing her powers. What more can we do?" Aaron asked.

Jessica sighed and pursed her lips.

"What?" Michael asked, but she shook her head.

"Jessica—you know you can speak honestly with me. You always have," Aaron said.

"You won't like it."

"Tell me anyway."

"Bring Gryphon here."

Michael's eyes grew wide. "Jessica—"

"He insisted." She brought out the Wafner scowl and glare, crossing her arms for good measure.

Aaron clenched his jaw, his hands balling into fists.

"Keep talking before he changes his mind about you being honest," Michael said.

"Alex feels powerless. Yes, you train her, and she's stronger, but the memories of that time haunt her. She and Megesti are working with books, but they have no idea how to make these spells work. It would be the same if you gave squires books on fighting and expected them to become knights."

Aaron's mouth fell open. *That actually makes sense.*

"The last time she wielded her powers with complete control was right after she returned from Moorloc's. Gryphon had taught her how," Jessica finished.

Aaron said, "The fact that he wants to be around her is enough reason to say no."

"And there's the actual issue," Michael interjected. "You don't trust her. Some part of you doubts her devotion to you. She almost died getting her memories, and you worry she'll leave you for him."

"I trust her. It's him I don't trust."

"No," Michael snapped. "This hypocrisy ends now. If you *trust* her, you trust her with *him*. You know what she did to the suitors who were too forward. She left a lot of men with bruised faces and egos."

"And one soaked prince." Jessica giggled.

"Stefan and I taught her how to handle herself," Michael continued. "She went after Kruft, and you're worried about some arrogant sorcerer. If he ever tried to touch her inappropriately, she'd probably set him on fire."

Aaron looked at his friends. *There has to be another way. I trust her, but I can't have* him *around my wife all day. He touches her, but she's mine—not his.* "I'll think about it," he said.

After checking the kitchen and stables for Alex, Aaron headed to his room. As he walked up the stairs to the tower, he felt a chill and stopped. He was outside Daniel's room, so he stepped onto the threshold. "If you're here, Daniel," he said hesitantly, "take care of him. I'll try to make you both proud."

The room grew noticeably colder, and Aaron felt an uncontrollable urge to find Alex. He ran up the stairs to his bedroom and found her leaning out his window, watching the town. She was wearing his favorite red dress and had the dagger she'd found in her mother's castle belted at her side. After the first attack, he'd asked her to keep it on her, so he was happy to see she'd listened. Her locks danced softly in the breeze, but she looked lost in her thoughts.

How many times have I done exactly that? Aaron smiled, but Jessica's words rushed back to him as he gazed at his wife. She was paler than usual, and her hand rested on her stomach.

"Did you eat something at the market that didn't agree with you?"

Alex turned, dropping her hands, and sniffled. Aaron tensed. Her eyes were red, her cheeks glistened in the setting sun, and Aaron knew at once why Daniel had chased him up here. He rushed over and wrapped his arms around her.

"Alex, you're cold as ice."

"Am I? I didn't notice." She glanced down at where her hands rested on his chest.

What is going on with you? Aaron let go and tucked some loose hair behind her ear. She looked at him and opened her mouth but closed it again.

"Let's get you something to eat," Aaron said. "Don't tell me you've lost your appetite again."

Alex took his hand in hers. "I'm starving."

"Then come with me." He led her down the stairs into the kitchen and snuck her into the larder. He ripped apart a loaf of bread, piled cheese and venison in it, and handed it to her. "Being married to the prince has to have some benefits!" Aaron took her hand again, and they headed to the dining hall to eat.

"How was your day?"

"Enlightening. I spent most of it exploring Datten, and then I went for a walk tonight."

"Alone?"

"I stayed inside the walls. I needed some quiet and fresh air."

"As long as you're being safe."

They were eating when Edward came into the room. "Aaron, join us for an ale before bed," he said.

Aaron looked between them, but Alex stood. "Stay. I want to go to bed." She kissed Edward's cheek and headed out of the hall as Emmerich arrived.

"You realize how fortunate you are to have won her heart, right?" his father asked.

Aaron looked smug, but his face flushed a little as he ate the last piece of venison off the tray. "Every day, I ask myself how I got so lucky."

"Did she eat?" Edward asked.

"A little." Aaron sighed, glancing at her mostly untouched sandwich.

"Is she ill?" Emmerich asked.

Aaron shook his head. "When she's upset, she doesn't eat, and I think being the bearer of this bad news is harder on her than she lets on. Lately I feel as though I'm always saying the wrong thing. She's unhappy, and I don't know what to do."

Emmerich beamed with pride at his son.

"What?" Aaron asked.

"I'm astonished at the man you've become," Emmerich said.

Aaron bit into Alex's sandwich.

"Your father is right, Aaron," Edward said. "Worrying about how to make Alex happy is a tremendous step for you as a man and a husband."

"I worry I'm going to fail her. How am I supposed to balance being a husband and a king?"

"Wait until you have children," Emmerich added. "Then you'll have to balance being a king and a husband *and* a father."

Aaron groaned and held his head in his hands. The table shook as a mug of ale crashed down in front of him, and Harold dropped onto the bench next to him. Jerome took the other side, fortifying them with two giant pitchers.

"Well, one advantage you'll have is that you won't spend your entire reign fighting me." Harold held out his mug, waiting for Aaron to bump it in a toast.

"Ruling a peaceful kingdom is easier than ruling one at war," Edward said.

"Your biggest job will be getting our people to listen to your plans to make Datten more like Warren," Emmerich said.

Aaron said, "It'll take time, years maybe, but I believe we'll get there."

"So do I," Emmerich said, smiling at his son. "You're going to be an amazing king, Aaron."

CHAPTER 23

ALEX

The bed shook worse than a raft at sea. Alex's eyes snapped open. Aaron had collapsed into bed beside her, his arm strewn haphazardly across her. She smelled the ale on his breath as he started to snore, and she brushed his hair back from his face

Unable to sleep, she dressed and went to Emmerich's room. He was standing on his balcony, gazing down at the courtyard.

"Hello, princess," he said without turning around.

"Your Royal Highness." Alex stood beside him.

"Care for one last walk with your godfather?"

"It would be my honor," Alex said, taking Emmerich's arm.

They strolled through the silent streets and visited Emmerich's favorite spots. She let him lead and listened intently as he shared stories of Aaron's and Daniel's childhoods with her. She tried to commit them all to memory so she could share them with her children one day. As they arrived at the castle walls, Alex's magic tingled. Emmerich must have sensed something as well because he pushed her behind him as he drew his sword.

Alex shivered.

"Stay behind me," Emmerich said.

"What if this is it? What if my presence here causes your death?" Alex whispered.

Someone else answered. "Then you'd have even more blood on your hands, *witchling*."

Emmerich and Alex spun around but saw no one.

"Over here, mortals."

A large wolf with blue eyes padded out of the shadow of the castle walls. Gasping, Alex grabbed Emmerich's arm. She tried to crack them away but couldn't. The wolf slowly stalked toward them and snarled. Alex looked into its eyes, and her breath came fast and sharp.

"It can't be," she whispered.

A green fog surrounded the wolf, and in a moment, the blonde woman from earlier stood before them. Her simple dress was gone, replaced by a dark green cloak. The sleeves were pushed up to her elbows, showing off a large scar that ran from her thumb up along her left arm.

Alex swallowed hard. *A titan cloak.*

"How nice to see a family that gets along." The woman slowly applauded as she swaggered toward them. Emmerich stood ready with his sword out while he held Alex behind him. "But it took a long time to get to this happy little family. You struggled with your own wild son, didn't you, Emmerich? And how will you feel tomorrow, princess, when your husband becomes king and forgets you in place of his new duties? Will you abandon him and follow my son back to your rightful home? Or will I be forced to encourage you?"

"Datten is her home," Emmerich rumbled.

The sorceress crossed her arms and glared at him. "She's a sorceress. The Forbidden Lands are where she belongs."

Alex held her chin high and stepped out from behind Emmerich. "Whoever you are, leave now and I won't hurt you."

Laughter erupted from the woman. "I'm not afraid of you, girl. I helped get rid of your mother, and now I get to torture you. Such a sad excuse for a sorceress. You can barely keep those powers tucked away. Nightmares, scars, and—" She sniffed the air, and her eyes locked onto Alex's stomach. "That explains everything. I'm surprised you haven't done damage yet. Most sorceresses in your condition lose control."

Emmerich's lips pursed, and he gripped his sword tightly. "What did you have to do with Victoria?" He tried to pull Alex back behind him again.

"I got rid of the competition. Garrick only had eyes for Victoria. What is it with Heads and Cassandras? Seems they can't think with their proper head when your line is around, only the little one. But she's long dead now, and my new problem is her offspring. You and your irritating influence over my son."

Alex's eyes widened with realization. "You're Gryphon's mother."

"Correct. Imelda of the line of Tiere and Ares. I'll admit, I expected better for my son, the second choice of a half mortal. I didn't care who your parents were because a Cassandra would never be enough for him. But the *Heart*? That I can live with. So I'm here to talk to you, woman-to-woman as you'd say, and convince you to come home with me and choose my son."

"And if I don't?"

"Then I'll finish what Lygari started twelve years ago. No charming Prince of Datten, no reason to stay here."

Imelda flashed her ice-blue eyes to green, and her skin glowed the same way Gryphon's did when he summoned the water on the pier. Alex tried to grab her water or plant powers but instead brought the wind. She heard a growl behind them and whirled to find a pair of imposing gray wolves stalking toward them.

"Gryphon!" Alex cried, but Imelda laughed.

"He can't hear you, *witchling*. I've seen to that. His father and hexa may not know where to find him, but I do. He always goes to stay with my troublesome little sister, so I shielded her house to ensure he can't hear you."

Emmerich grabbed Alex and pulled her toward the wall. He shouted a strange rhyme, and a door swung open, almost hitting them. Alex saw it was one of the secret doors Aaron had shown her when they'd snuck to Datten.

"Fun, a chase," Imelda said. She snarled, and the wolves rushed at them.

Emmerich shoved Alex inside and screamed as the wolves sprang. Alex heard a loud snap, and the beasts clamped onto Emmerich, dragging him away.

"Run!" he shouted, still trying to close the door.

I can't leave him. Rage erupted inside Alex, and her skin ignited, illuminating the tunnel with orange light. She caught the door and threw it open. Emmerich was holding his own against the two snarling creatures, despite their size. Alex unsheathed her dagger and ran to his side.

"I told you to run!" he shouted.

"I won't leave you."

Alex threw wind at the wolves, shoving them back, and Emmerich charged Imelda with his blade. She cracked but not fast enough, and he sliced her left arm. When she reappeared, she examined her bleeding arm. The gash ran parallel to her old scar.

She narrowed her glowing eyes at Emmerich, then started

laughing. "Mortal blades can't hurt us," she said, summoning static from the air as she shifted her gaze to Alex. "Last chance, princess. Come willingly, or I'll take you by force."

"Never." Alex shook her head and stood proudly beside her godfather.

Imelda shot orange lightning into the ground before them. Rocks and dirt exploded, but Emmerich grabbed Alex and shielded her with his body, protecting her from the debris. The wolves yelped in pain as they were struck.

Alex saw the glowing strands of lightning crackle over Emmerich's body, and Imelda screamed in rage.

"Emmerich, what did you do?" Alex whispered.

"My final act. My kingdom's new queen . . . safe."

Alex managed to summon a wind strong enough to throw Imelda and the wolves far enough away for a brief respite. Emmerich wheezed as patches of blood appeared on his shirt.

I need to get you inside before this gets worse. Alex prepared to crack, but Imelda was faster. Her explosive power hit them, violently throwing Alex to the ground and sending her dagger skidding out of reach. She struggled to push herself up. Each attempt flooded her body with pain. She was defenseless, and the snarls were getting closer.

Imelda cracked over to her and looked down, hands on her hips. "I'm through playing. You're coming with me, witch." The sorceress tugged on the collar of Alex's dress as if to drag her, but then she screamed and let go. Emmerich stood behind Imelda holding Alex's dagger, which was dripping with blood.

Imelda screeched and clutched her side. "Why does it burn?"

"It's red steel," Alex said.

The woman's eyes flashed with anger. "You little witch! You're just like your mother!" She waved her hand and cracked away, taking the wolves with her.

Emmerich collapsed. His arm was bent in the wrong direction, though his fingers still clutched the bloody dagger.

He broke his arm. He must be in so much pain. Alex forced herself to her feet, swallowing the cry of pain that threatened to escape her.

"I'll heal you," she said and dropped to her knees beside Emmerich.

"We both know this is the end for me. Save your strength, and only heal the outside. Hide the wounds." He coughed. "I don't want Guinevere to see me like this. Take me back, and we'll hide the evidence."

Alex's eyes filled with tears as she agreed. She was shaking so badly it took her three tries to crack them to Emmerich's room. She laid out his nightshirt and threw his bloody clothes into the fireplace, letting fire destroy the evidence. She carefully healed Emmerich's external wounds. As he lay down, she healed her own wounds to hide what had happened. She avoided healing too much or too deep, knowing that she was exhausted.

"Thank you for saving my life," Alex whispered. She felt utterly drained as Emmerich took her hand.

"One day, tell Aaron about tonight."

She kissed Emmerich's cheek and sat beside the bed, holding his hand until he fell asleep. Daniel appeared beside her to rest a chilly hand on her shoulder.

"You gave him a chance to make things right with Aaron and to die a hero," he said.

"Thank you, Alex," Emmerich said, but his voice wasn't coming from the bed. She looked up to see her godfather smiling at her as he stood by Daniel. "I couldn't have asked for a better wife for my son."

Alex couldn't speak without sobbing, so she said nothing. She rose and went to the ancient bell tower. She trudged up the stairs until she reached the top and pulled the rope. The royal bell rang out in Datten. Guards and knights stopped and dropped to their knees in homage to their fallen royal. This bell only had one meaning.

Her task complete, Alex collapsed onto the floor of the tower and wept. She cried over the heartbreak she knew all of Datten was also feeling, the pain surging through her half-healed wounds, and the guilt of knowing when these tragic events would happen but having no power to stop them. She sobbed, knowing nothing would ever be the same for her and Aaron.

A short while later, she heard footsteps, and a tuft of black hair appeared in the stairwell.

"Stefan said I'd find you here," Michael said. "Are you all right?"

"No," she whimpered and burst into tears again. Michael sat beside her on the tear-soaked floor and held her while she cried.

"They're with him. The queen, Aaron, and the Wafners." He gently stroked her hair. "Do I want to know why you look like you just left a battlefield?"

"I don't want to talk about it."

Michael squeezed her close. "We'll stay here until you're ready. Then we'll get you changed and go be with them."

"I have to be strong for them."

"We both do."

"I don't know if I can."

"I know you can, but right now, you can be a mess, and I'll be strong for you." Then, just as he had done her whole life, he settled his arms around her and let her be.

ALEX CHANGED into a black dress she found in the wardrobe of their royal suite. Aaron still preferred to sleep in his old room, but now all of that would change.

She walked into Emmerich's bedroom with Michael at her side. Stefan was comforting Jessica while Edward and Jerome hovered beside the physician, who was examining the king's body. Emmerich's and Daniel's ghosts stood behind Aaron and Guinevere, watching them hold each other.

"He died peacefully in his sleep. It's what we all would ask for," the physician said.

"We'll have to begin the funeral preparations," Jerome said.

"Stefan and I can help with that," Michael said. "Alex told me where his plans are."

"Thank you," Jerome said.

"We'll need to plan the coronation too," added Jessica.

"Let me and my father handle that," Alex said. "Aaron can be crowned later. For now, Datten needs to grieve."

Guinevere nodded and went to hug Alex, crying. Edward came over and rubbed Alex's back before gathering the sobbing queen into his arms.

Aaron looked at Alex and mouthed, *Thank you.* She saw his father and brother watching him proudly, and when Aaron saw her fresh tears, he came and held her.

"He's here, isn't he?" he asked.

Alex nodded.

"Both of them?" Another nod, and Aaron's eyes filled with tears. "I'm not ready," he whispered.

"They say you are," Alex said, one more tear streaking down her cheek as she clung to him.

Jerome gently said to Aaron, "Your Royal Highness, you'll need to address the knights."

"Now?"

"Yes. They must swear their loyalty to you as king."

"Can't we wait until morning?" Aaron asked.

"No. King Aaron, my last duty as your father's general is to ensure we fulfill our traditions as we crown you. That starts with the men giving you their oath of loyalty. Have you given thought to who you want as your general?"

"You. I have no intention of changing everything all at once."

"I'm honored to remain, but you'll need to think of who you want to promote to second as my replacement one day."

Aaron was about to leave with Jerome when Alex stopped him. She walked to Emmerich's bedside table, and Aaron gasped when she turned to him with the king's crown in her hands. Trembling, he took a knee before her, and Alex placed the crown of Datten on his head.

"Thank you, my queen." Aaron rose, gently kissed her cheek, and followed Jerome to summon the guards.

"I'm sorry I didn't believe you," said Guinevere, her eyes red and puffy. "I so badly wanted you to be wrong!"

Alex hugged her. "I didn't want to be right."

Edward came over and held them both. "It'll be all right."

Alex nodded.

"Aaron and Jerome need you now, Edward," Guinevere said.

Edward said, "Go to him, Alex. Aaron wants his queen to have responsibilities, so anything as significant as this should include you."

Michael and Stefan escorted Alex out. They quickly caught up with Aaron and Jerome, and together, they walked the rest of the way.

"Are you ready for this?" Michael whispered to Aaron.

"I don't think I ever could be." The new king took a breath and walked toward his father's men. He looked solemn and serious with his father's crown on his head, but Alex noticed the tremor in his hand. He glanced at her when she curled her fingers around his, and his shoulders relaxed before he addressed the men.

"Armies of Datten, knights and guards of the king. You all heard the bell and know why I am standing before you in the middle of the night, wearing my father's crown. It is with a heavy heart that I inform you of the passing of King Emmerich Gordon Otto Daniel. As the laws of Datten dictate, I, Crown Prince Aaron, stand before you, asking you to swear to me the same oath that you swore to my father years ago. Any man who doesn't wish to follow me as king may leave. But I hope you'll stay. Datten is my home, and I plan to make you all—and my father—proud."

All the knights and guards of Datten pledged their loyalty to Aaron as the new king. Then he walked among them, receiving their condolences on Emmerich's death and many compliments on his peace with Betruger.

Alex's visions had told her that he'd become a great king—*if* she were at his side. So she didn't leave him once. In fact, she intended to be at his side however and whenever possible.

After dismissing the guards, Jerome suggested they get a bit of rest since the next few days would be taxing. Alex led Aaron back to their room and sat with him in silence on the bed for some time.

I wish I knew how to help you. I was so young when my mother died. I don't know what to say.

Aaron was restless, and her heart ached for him. He tried to sleep, but it wouldn't come. He let her hold him for a bit, but then he got up to pace the room. Finally, he leaned against his window and looked out into Datten.

"What can I do?" Alex asked, wrapping her arms around him and leaning against his back. "Do you want me to go get

Harold? Do you want to go for a ride? I'll do anything. Tell me how to help you."

Aaron turned around and weakly said, "Nothing."

Alex's heart sank, but he gently caressed her face. "What I mean is, there isn't anything you can do. Just be here with me."

She breathed him in, but then she caught sight of Emmerich and Daniel watching them from an empty corner of the room. They spoke softly to her, and she gently released Aaron.

Following her stare, he looked into the corner, aware of what was happening.

Alex slipped her hand into his and said, "Come with me."

CHAPTER 24
AARON

Alex took him down the stairs and along the hall to the king's suite. His father's body had already been removed and the room he'd known his entire life stripped bare. Aaron gulped.

They're going to expect me to pick decorations for it. It's my room now. No, our room.

Alex gazed around the empty room, her face full of sadness and confusion. A group of maids came up the stairs, curtsying to Aaron before continuing with their work. Two carried his formal clothes and began putting them away into the wardrobe while a third remade the bed.

Alex crossed the room to Emmerich's small bookshelf, one of the few pieces of furniture left, and picked up an enormous tome of the king's horses that Aaron had always thought was useless. Opening it, she took a smaller book out of the hollow volume and handed it to Aaron. He recognized his father's handwriting, then his grandfather's and great-grandfather's, all scrawled across the pages. The back of the book was filled with empty pages.

Alex said, "Emmerich says this book accompanies the king's journals. They write about their accomplishments and struggles in their journals, but all their doubts and fears from their first year as king are in this book." She grabbed Aaron's free hand, squeezed it, then briefly glanced behind him. "He says you aren't alone and never will be."

Aaron stared at her. *I wish I could see him too, if only to take that burden off you. Speaking for him is going to wear on you very quickly.*

"He says to use Harold or keep my father here for a while. Having an experienced king around makes your transition easier."

Aaron finally broke down, and the maids scurried out of the room while Alex held him as he cried.

After what felt like an eternity, he finally let go, and she suggested they get something to eat so the maids could finish. Breakfast was waiting in the dining hall. They sat in front of the food, but neither ate. Aaron's mind was too busy. *I'll have to reestablish alliances with the southern kingdoms. Will the old families bow to me? Will the southern lords?*

"You should eat something." Alex's voice brought him out of his head. Rubbing his thigh, she rested her head on his shoulder.

"I will if you do," Aaron said, pushing his full plate at her before grabbing another.

Michael and Stefan arrived, soon followed by Jerome and Megesti. As the general approached, Aaron asked, "What do I need to do next?"

"All the men took an oath to follow you, but now we need to assess whether you want to assign new, younger men to lead. You may, of course, consult with anyone else you deem worthy. I'll wait for you in the library. Come when you're ready." Jerome bowed and headed out of the room.

"Should I fetch Harold or my father?" Alex asked.

"No. I have everyone I need. Jerome, Michael, and you."

"Me?" Alex and Michael asked in unison.

"Of course. Michael, you were my second-in-command the entire journey to retrieve Alex, so you're clearly qualified. As for you, my wife, you're a brilliant strategist. I intend to do things differently, starting today." Aaron pressed his forehead against Alex's and kissed her, the loud clang of the knights turning to look away from their new king and queen echoing through the room.

Alex sighed. "Can we do anything about that?"

"Probably not." He stood up. "Michael, are you ready?"

Michael gulped. "Yes, my king," he said as he rose and straightened his tunic.

King. Aaron paused, letting that word sink in. Then he held out his hand to Alex. "Ready, Your Royal Highness?"

Alex glared back and tightened her lips, but he spotted the slightest curl of a smile. Stefan stood to accompany them, but Aaron motioned for him to stay. He pulled Alex close as they headed to the library, with Michael flanking her other side.

As he'd said, Jerome was expecting them. They went through every single castle guard, and Aaron had to decide who would retain their current positions, move to new roles, or receive promotions, and who they suspected were ready to retire. It took hours, but in the end, Aaron was pleased with their choices. He even surprised Michael by asking him to be the head of the king's guard, just as Stefan was for Alex. Though Michael was nervous at the prospect, Jerome said that he had every confidence in him and that he'd given the young man the Wafner name because he was worthy.

"Where are we with the funeral?" Aaron asked Jerome.

"We have his plans," Jerome said. "We'll begin preparations for both the funeral and the coronation since they occur on the same day."

Puzzled, Alex asked, "The same day? Doesn't the kingdom have a mourning period?"

"It's tradition. We bury the old king at the same time that we welcome the new one," Aaron said.

"Datten is not to be without a king," Jerome added.

Alex groaned softly and rubbed her face.

You look exhausted. We should finish up so you can get some food and rest.

"I've only had time to read about the funeral," she said. "What does the coronation involve?"

Jerome explained Datten's coronation traditions. Since Guinevere was still alive, they would offer her the honor of crowning Aaron. If she declined, then the duty would fall to Edward.

There was a knock on the door. "Come in," Aaron called.

"I'm sorry to disturb you," Stefan said. "But Harold would like to return home tonight to attend to some matters."

"What time is it?" Alex asked.

"It's almost eight," Stefan replied.

"We've been in here all day?" Alex said as she jumped up and rushed toward the door. "I have to start the funeral preparations. Where's Harold?"

Stefan opened his mouth to reply, but Alex brushed past him. He sighed and started to follow after her.

"I think this is enough for tonight," Aaron said. When he stood up to stretch, Michael and Jerome both leaped to their feet. "Dispense with the formalities when it's us. You know I hate them."

"All right, Aaron," Michael said.

Jerome shook his head. "I don't know if I can, Your Royal Highness."

"I'm still me, Jerome. It doesn't matter if I have a bigger crown now." More softly, he added, "There won't be a day my father comes home for it." He sighed. "You're both excused."

"I'm going to go find Jessica." Michael bowed and left.

The general remained. "How are you doing?"

"After our wedding, I promised Alex I'd make her my priority—my only priority—and here I am, King of Datten, responsible for an entire kingdom. Knights, guards, people, all of them rely on me . . . need me. And I can't even figure out what's bothering her."

"This will be an adjustment for both of you. But you'll manage." Jerome patted Aaron's shoulder. "Your suite has been prepared."

"My suite . . . ?"

"The king's suite is now yours, Your Royal Highness. I'm not sure if your mother will have left hers yet, but we will, of course, make sure she has comfortable chambers."

"No," Aaron ordered. "As long as my mother lives, the queen's suite is hers."

"Where will Her Royal Highness sleep?"

"We've shared a bed almost every night since she returned from Moorloc's, and I have no intention of sleeping away from Alex. Not tonight, and not ever."

"As you wish." Jerome bowed and turned down the hallway.

We're going to have that talk soon, Alex. I know I said I'd give you time, but I need to know what is going on. I can't protect you from what I don't know, and you haven't told me everything you remember. You don't lie as well as you think you do. You're mine, and if he did something to you, I'll use my entire army to hunt him down and make him pay for it tenfold—a hundredfold.

Aaron went to their new room and walked out to the

balcony overlooking the courtyard. He waited for what felt like years before the door opened and delicate footsteps padded across the room toward him.

"I lost track of time," Alex said, "and then I went to the wrong room, and—"

Aaron interrupted her with a kiss. Pulling his right arm around her waist, she pressed herself against him. He buried his other hand in her hair as she draped her arms around his neck. She kissed him until she had to pause for breath, and he stepped back.

"I hate keeping things from you," she said. "When you're ready, I'll tell you everything from Moorloc's."

"Thank you. But we've been through enough today."

Tears spilled out of her eyes. Her mouth worked, but then she closed it and glanced away.

Aaron turned her face so she looked at him. "*Nothing* that happened to you there will change how I feel about you. You know that, right?"

She whimpered and tried to turn away again, but he gently cupped her cheek. "Alex, I mean it. Nothing will ever stop me from loving you."

Her watery emerald eyes looked up at him, and Aaron wiped tears from her cheeks with his thumb. Then he slid his hand into hers, and they left the balcony.

The enormous four-poster bed was fitted with luxurious red sheets rather than the gold ones that had been there before. The candles on the wall gave the room a warm glow. Alex walked to the wardrobe on the right and found it full of only Aaron's clothes.

"No one believed you intended to stay in my suite with me," he said. "We'll have another wardrobe brought in tomorrow."

Alex went to the bookshelf and walked her fingers along the spines before pausing on one. The moment she picked it up, Aaron recognized the plant book the Kirsh boy had given him during his honor rite so many years ago. He kissed Alex's neck, distracting her long enough to snatch the book away.

"Not this one, you little book thief. This book is special," he told her.

"Wasn't it in your room in Warren?"

"It was. I took it when I went to find you, and it ended up coming back here with my other things."

"What's special about it?" She seemed to be fighting back a smile, but Aaron wasn't sure why.

"This book saved my life, so hands off. Books vanish around you."

"I merely put them in *my* library where they have friends."

"Well, this book likes it here." Aaron put the plant book back, giving Alex a firm look. Her eyes sparkled in the candlelight, but her expression grew serious.

"What is it?" She caressed his face.

Aaron sighed. "I know you're feeling sad, overwhelmed, and lost right now. So am I. But . . ." he swallowed hard. "I need it to stop, even if only for a short time. Please."

Alex peeled off his crested shirt and whispered, "I want that distraction too."

Aaron kissed her and roughly untied her dress. It fell on the floor, and he broke away to tear off his own clothes. Then he grabbed her, and she locked her legs around his waist as he carried her to their new bed so they could both have some time without pain or fear.

AARON COULDN'T SLEEP despite Alex's best efforts to relax him. She was dozing when he put on his pants and went out to the balcony. *What will it be like to lead this army? Will they respect me as they did my father? Now it's even more important to produce an heir. Why isn't Alex pregnant? Am I doing something wrong? Is it because I'm human and she's a sorceress? Did something happen to her at the castle, or is she not fully healed? Is that what she wants to tell me? What if we can't have children? No, that's foolish, she's seen them. Even if we can't, she's mine, and I won't ever let her go.*

"Aaron?" Alex called from the bed. She sounded frightened.

"I'm here." He dashed inside, reaching her in a flash.

"I'm sorry. I forgot where I was."

He let her pull him back into bed. She shivered as the cool night air hit her bare skin, and Aaron wrapped his arms around her, feeling her heart pounding in her chest. He still had not forgiven himself for the last few weeks and needed her close.

As if she were reading his mind, Alex whispered, "I forgive you."

"For what?"

"Being a pigheaded Prince of Datten. Acting jealous and overprotective, hiding your feelings from me, and not letting me in when I needed you to. All these things that make me crazy will make you a truly amazing king."

Aaron ran his hands down her back, making her shudder even more. Her scars reminded him of how badly he'd failed her. *I'll never fail you like this again.* "You think I'm pigheaded and jealous?"

"Only when it comes to Gryphon."

"Well, I outrank him now. He's only the future Head. I'm already a king. And one day, I'll be a king of two kingdoms."

"That seems a little extreme, even for you." Alex smiled sleepily.

"I'd go to the underworld and back for you if I had to. You

are the most important thing in this world to me. I don't want you near Gryphon, but if you're ever in trouble and need his help, call him. I need you to be protected more than I need him to stay away from you."

Aaron waited for a reply but realized Alex was asleep. Squeezing her tighter, he fell asleep, assured she was safe.

CHAPTER 25

ALEX

Aloud knock startled Alex and Aaron awake. They had barely sat up when Michael barged into the room, followed by Jessica, several maids, guards, and noblemen.

"Good morning, Your Royal Highnesses," Michael said.

Jessica rushed toward Alex, carrying a bundle. She held open a beautiful golden robe, and Alex slipped out of the bed, blushing as Jessica tried to conceal her naked body from everyone in the room.

"Thank you," Alex whispered as she tied the robe shut.

Jessica asked, "Should I find you some lovely new night-dresses, my queen?"

"Does this happen every morning?"

"I'm told so," replied her lady's maid. "I think I understand why the queen has her own room."

"Then yes to the nightdresses."

Aaron leaned across the bed to add, "Or let them see. I think you look amazing." He winked at Alex.

"Your Royal Highness, don't." Jessica scowled at Aaron.

Aaron's eyes were still fixed on Alex, and his impish grin and raised eyebrows were like a dare.

"I won't embarrass my lady," Alex said.

Aaron pouted for a moment before he shrugged and turned toward the group. "Everyone out."

"Your Royal Highness?" a nobleman asked.

"My father enjoyed being woken up with fanfare and updates and *whatever* it is you all do. I don't. From now on, *your queen* will be in my suite, and as you can see, she's uncomfortable with the size of this audience. From now on, only the queen's ladies and the Wafner men may enter this room before my wife has left it."

"But Your Royal Highness—"

"This isn't a request. I'm giving you an order. Everyone out." Aaron got out of the bed and pulled on his pants.

"But—"

"Out!" he shouted, and both the maids and the guards hurried away, leaving only Jessica and Michael.

Aaron smirked. "Is that better?"

"Thank you," Alex said, still flushed and clutching her robe.

Jessica smiled weakly back at her. *The last thing I need is the maids starting rumors about my belly looking swollen.*

Michael laughed. "I finally understand why queens have their own suites."

Alex was happy to laugh with him. "Jessica just said that. Where are my dresses, by the way?"

"I'm not sure. None of the maids would believe me when I told them you planned to stay with Aaron," Jessica said. "I'll fetch one of the queen's old ones. Your Royal Highness, what should we call your mother now?"

"Her Majesty," Aaron replied. "As a royal-born queen, Alex will be addressed as Her Royal Highness, the same as me. My mother keeps her title."

The lady's maid bowed, but the new king held up his hand.

"Jessica. When it's just us—and that includes Megesti, your husband, your father, and your brother—I'm still Aaron. I have a new crown and title, but I'm still me."

"All right, *Aaron*." She smiled and hurried out of the room.

"Do you think the yelling worked?" Alex asked, pulling on her robe's tie. "I think I'm going to have to wear a nightgown to bed again."

"Don't you dare," Aaron said. "Well, do whatever you want, but for the record, I love what you sleep in."

Alex felt her blush return as Aaron crossed the room and kissed her gently.

"All right, enough of that, you two," Michael said. "You have a kingdom to run."

"Michael, let me enjoy what's left of my honeymoon," Alex said.

Jessica came back, holding a Datten mourning gown. "We found something appropriate," she said.

Alex scrunched up her nose, and Aaron snorted as she said, "It's . . . so poofy."

"Guinevere picked it. She insisted you wear her Datten mourning gowns until we can have some made for you. They're the only dresses we don't already have for you."

Jessica held the dress out. Alex sighed, but she dropped her robe to step into it.

"Ugh!" Michael cried, spinning away. "Warn me next time."

"It's not as if you've never seen me naked, Michael," Alex said.

"When did he see you naked?" Aaron asked, and she caught the glare that he gave Michael.

"Many times at the camp, over the years."

Michael said, "It's like seeing your sister naked. Gak."

Alex snickered, but Aaron still looked annoyed.

"You're their guard," Jessica said as she did up the dress. "How are you not used to this yet?"

"Because I prefer to see only my wife naked," Michael replied.

Alex and Jessica exchanged a look, and then Jessica said, "We'll warn you next time, love."

"Why the gown?" Aaron asked Alex.

"Your mother doesn't seem to want my help for your father's funeral, so I'm having Jessica assist her. I'm going to Betruger to see Harold and Macht."

"Why are you visiting Harold?" Aaron asked. "You brought him home, and the funeral isn't for a few days."

Alex paused before answering. "He needed to take care of something last night and asked me to come back today to get him."

"Are you up to it? You look tired," Michael said.

"I'm fine. Besides, it's Harold and Macht. I'll rest there before I bring them back, all right?"

While Jessica fussed with her hair, Aaron had gotten dressed. Alex smoothed wrinkles from her skirt, but she couldn't help staring at his new tunic. She didn't think it was possible, but the crest sparkled more than any other tunic he'd worn. Somehow, a king's tunic always looked regal and formal. Aaron caught her staring and winked.

"Wait," Alex said. She picked up the crown of Datten from the small table, and Aaron bowed so she could place it on his head.

"Are you taking Stefan?" Aaron asked.

"No. I'm going to Betruger. You know Harold won't let anything happen to me."

Aaron pursed his lips, but she merely crossed her arms until he sighed. "All right."

Alex vanished with a wink, cracking to the throne room of Betruger Castle. The room was empty except for Harold.

He stood to greet her, immediately discarding formality to give her a sympathetic smile. "How are you all holding up?"

His casual manner put Alex at ease. *I'm so glad you haven't changed how you look at me.* "I wish I knew what to say to help Aaron, but I don't."

"There isn't anything you can do to make this better. It'll take time," Harold said.

Alex smoothed her skirt again. *I feel so silly in this formal gown. Why did I let Jessica make me wear it?*

Clearly sensing her discomfort, Harold spoke. "Are you ready to pick up Aaron's sword, or would you like to meet the men who will be training your guards?"

Alex shrugged and looked at Harold with half a smile. "Your choice."

Harold held out his arm. "Swords it is. The fresh sea air will do you some good. After that, we can eat. Let you have some fish that I'm sure you're missing in Datten."

Alex laughed. "Only a royal who lives on the sea would understand." She suddenly realized someone important was missing. "Macht should accompany us. If Aaron found out I went anywhere without a general, he'd be furious."

"We'll collect him on the way."

She took Harold's arm, and they headed out of the castle and into the town. Alex took her time walking along the dirt roads through the Betruger kingdom. The king and his general walked at her pace, allowing her to take in everything. She was entranced by Betruger's unique buildings. *How did they learn to build their homes into the rocks? What if one falls?*

"You look lost in thought," Harold remarked.

"I'm fascinated by your architecture. In Warren, our houses

are just as intricate, but yours are so strong. Do you get a lot of storms here?"

"We do," Harold said. "In a hurricane, our sea rises significantly, so we build our houses to be sturdy in case of floods. In older areas, some have been standing for hundreds of years."

"Really? Are those the styles you told our builders about for Verlassen Castle?"

"They are. I figured if they lasted centuries here, they would survive for most of your lifetime."

Alex laughed, slipping back into comfortable old habits. "Are you sure you don't mind coming to Datten for a bit to help Aaron get settled? I don't want to take you away from anything important here."

"Macht has agreed to remain in Betruger and watch things," Harold said. "Aaron is our ally, and you only become king once. If I can help him somehow, I want to."

"Thank you, but you are wrong about one thing." Alex smirked. "Aaron will become king twice. He'll become King of Warren one day too."

"I forgot about that!" Harold laughed. "Well, by then he should understand his job well enough not to need my help again."

They arrived at a simple-looking building, and it was clear to Alex what it was. Smoke rose out of the oversized chimney, and heat poured out of the blacksmith. She marveled at how the main entrance slid open like a barn door.

Harold gestured for Alex to enter ahead of him while Macht stood guard outside. Inside the building, the air was hot and thick. Alex immediately regretted wearing such a heavy dress and fanned herself with her hand. Soon, a robust man with copper skin, black hair, and rich brown eyes met them. Harold introduced him as Schwert, and he looked up at them as he took off his gloves and shoved them into the front pockets of a thick leather apron that covered most of his chest and legs. He greeted Harold using his first name, and Alex relaxed despite the suffocating heat.

"Is this your Lady of Warren, the one you're so smitten with?" Schwert asked.

Harold's eyes went wide. Schwert winked at Alex, and she tried to hold back a giggle.

"No, Schwert," the king said, wiping his forehead with his sleeve. He was clearly sweating, and Alex suspected it wasn't from the heat. "This is Alexandria, Queen of Datten and Crown Princess of Warren. She is here to pick up her red steel swords."

"Your Royal Highness!" Schwert kneeled before her. "Please, I beg you to forgive my appearance and impertinence."

"There is nothing to forgive, Schwert. I've heard great things about your skills, and I would never expect a master blacksmith to keep his apron spotless just in case a queen dropped by unexpectedly. You seem far too dedicated to your craft not to make the most of the time you have to create your pieces."

Schwert smiled at Harold.

"He approves of you," Harold said.

"I'm glad. I hope you have considered my request to have you come to the stronghold and help us teach the new blacksmiths," Alex said.

"I have, Your Royal Highness, and we've decided to come. This opportunity will be good for my family."

"That's wonderful," Alex said as she patted her mother's dagger, which was sheathed to her belt. "I recently learned a cut from red steel hurts a sorcerer. So I suspect your blades will be worth more than their weight in gold in the future."

"I'm pleased my work will help you, Your Royal Highness. Allow me to fetch them." Schwert bowed and hurried into the back of his shop, leaving Alex and Harold alone.

"Were you attacked again?" Harold asked, touching her arm.

She nodded quickly before she fumbled with her bag of gold coins.

"Is that a third time now?"

"Let's not talk about it here," Alex whispered.

Alex stepped away from Harold as Schwert came out carrying a thick bundle. "Here are your swords, Your Royal Highness."

He beamed as he took out each piece, one at a time. He'd created three swords and three arrowheads. The sword grips were crafted from gold, and each was decorated with a different gem: rubies, obsidian, and sapphires respectively. The last pieces he showed Alex were small loops with long pins. "His Royal Highness requested I make a set of penannular brooches for your ladies." He held one out to her. The brooch, which was covered in gems, took up his entire palm.

"They're beautiful." Alex took it from him and examined the exquisite detail. The metal between the gems sparkled with gold.

Harold added, "I asked him to cover the bases in gold so no one would know their true nature."

"Thank you. Schwert, you have most certainly gone above my expectations." Alex reached into her bag to pay, but the blacksmith waved away her money.

"King Harold has already taken care of everything, Your Royal Highness. Please enjoy your new weapons. I hope they serve you well."

Alex and Harold headed outside. Adjusting the sword bundle in her hands, Alex closed her eyes, concentrated, and successfully cracked the bundle back to Aaron's old room in Datten.

As they began their walk back to the castle, Harold

gestured to Macht, and the man hung back to give them more space.

"So what about this third attack?" He scrutinized her expression and asked, "Aaron doesn't even know, does he?"

"No."

"Any reason you're keeping it from him?"

"I couldn't tell him yet."

"It seems like something he deserves to know."

"I know, and I will tell him, but Aaron has had enough to deal with lately without also worrying that his wife isn't even safe in his kingdom. Since then, I haven't gone anywhere without Jerome at my side. And I have you and Macht now."

"You were attacked in *Datten*?"

"I was walking with Emmerich the night he died. We were attacked by a crazed sorceress who sent wolves after us."

"Have you told Stefan or Gryphon?"

"If I told Stefan, he'd never leave my side again, and I haven't seen Gryphon since he was here last. Aaron believes he's failing to protect me, and it's making him possessive. If Gryphon is even brought up . . ." Alex swallowed.

"I've noticed that. I didn't take him as a jealous man."

"He isn't . . . or wasn't. Gryphon seems to bring it out in him. Which is another reason I'm hesitant to tell Aaron about this attack—the sorceress was Gryphon's mother. I don't know how badly Emmerich hurt her. And what if he killed her? I don't know how I'd tell Gryphon. Aaron may not like him, but he's my friend."

"That's an awful lot for you to bear."

"I'm used to it. I've always carried secrets. When I was little, the enchanted necklace from my mother hid that I was a girl. It was a secret that I had powers, that I was in love with Aaron. I secretly made that deal with Moorloc. Now the memories I have from the castle and all those attacks are secrets too."

"Aren't you supposed to share burdens with your husband?"

Alex sighed. "I try to, but he doesn't take bad news well, and now he's too busy."

Harold sighed. "I'm going to have a conversation with your husband about things he doesn't know but should. Now that he's king, he needs to know everything going on with you, even if you think he doesn't."

"And why is that?"

"Because otherwise he's going to be worrying about what he doesn't know. If he worries about you, he'll never be able to focus on his duties as king."

"Do you know how much he doesn't know on any given day, Harold? Women are complicated."

Harold laughed. "That I believe!"

"Thank you for the swords. I really do feel like I should pay—"

He shook his head. "They're my coronation gift for Datten's new king and queen. With that sword, Aaron can act if you're in danger, and that will be worth more than all the gold in Torian to him."

When they arrived at the castle, they went inside to have lunch. The guards had finished eating, so the room was mostly empty and they could continue their private conversation. Afterward, they decided to walk down to the beach for some fresh sea air, but as they left the castle, Alex's head started pounding, and the world spun.

Then she blinked and looked around, finding Harold holding her up. He and Macht were both ashen and wide-eyed. "I feel tired suddenly. What happened?"

"You muttered terrifying things and nearly passed out," Macht said.

"The words were likely a premonition. What did I say?"

Harold repeated:

"Your kingdom's end is near. You'll go back to the sea with him,
Or you'll sink into your fear and wish you'd learned to swim."

"Ominous and confusing. That would be a vision," Alex said.

"I think we should go back inside so you can rest before we leave," Harold said.

"Thank you, but no. The water helps me. Poseidon sorcerers take strength from the sea."

"Come. This way to our beach." He supported Alex, leading her to the path. They cautiously descended the steps carved into the cliff down to the beach. Macht stayed at the base of the steps while Harold took Alex to the water.

She gazed at a beach much like the one where she'd learned her Poseidon skills with Gryphon. In Warren, the sand was a rich gold; at Moorloc's castle it was brassy, but here it was a deep auburn color. Harold explained that the color was a result of the mountain runoff mixing with the sea.

She threw her shoes aside, lifted her heavy black dress to her knees, and waded out into the sea. Some distance away along the coast, she could see the Betruger port, with its ships bobbing in the water. Feeling at peace for the first time in weeks, Alex breathed in the salty air and filled her lungs.

"Feel better?" Harold asked, taking off his own shoes.

"Much." She relaxed and kicked the water. "Aaron doesn't understand the calm that the sea gives me."

"The sea is like a wild horse. You have to hold on and accept its ride. Those who don't will quickly learn." Harold joined her in the water.

Alex smiled. "Tell that to Aaron. I think he'd understand my love of the water better if you put it that way."

A gust of wind tousled her hair, and as she combed it away

from her face, she turned to Harold, a sense of unease washing over her.

"What's wrong?" he asked. "I've been told winds come when you're scared."

"It wasn't me," she replied.

At the base of the steps, Macht was talking to a blond man. When they spotted Alex glancing their direction, both men waved.

"Looks like Aaron came to visit too," Harold smiled.

But how? Megesti can't crack.

The surrounding wind grew stronger, and she lost her grip on her dress. The skirt sank into the water, soaking through in seconds. Harold was going to wave back, but Alex pulled his arm down.

"Alex, what are you—"

"That's not Aaron."

CHAPTER 26
ALEX

Harold looked back toward Macht and the newcomer. "Of course it is. I recognize that golden blond from here."

"He looks like Aaron. But that's not him."

"How can you be sure?" he asked, dropping his arm and focusing on Alex.

"Because Megesti can't crack well. He wouldn't send Aaron."

"There must be an emergency."

Her heart pounded as Macht and the false Aaron crossed the sand to join them. "If there were," Alex whispered, "do you think he'd look so calm? Besides, Megesti would come himself. He'd never risk Aaron's life, especially now that he's king."

By all accounts, it was her husband marching toward them, but Alex knew better.

"Hello, darling," the false Aaron said.

Even the voice is right, but he's never called me darling.

"You aren't Aaron, so who are you?" Harold demanded.

The other Aaron snarled at him and cracked. He reappeared

in front of Harold and punched him in the face, sending the king into the water as Macht charged. Alex screamed when Harold hit the waves, and the false Aaron dove for her.

"They weren't kidding when they said you were a smart little witch, but let's see how strong your powers are!"

He grabbed her wrists and yanked her to him. Despite the weight of her soaked dress, Alex kneed him in the groin as hard as she could and bit the hand holding her.

"You little witch." He released Alex and hit her with a back-handed blow to the face, sending her crashing into the waves. Her mouth filled with blood, and black spots burned her vision. Harold and Macht were calling her name and trying to reach her when a sorceress appeared.

She was tall and slim, and her skin was so pale it was nearly translucent. Visible beneath her ash-blonde hair was a single line mark of two waves on her neck. Her titan robe was sea blue. Her eyes changed to a darker shade of blue, and her whole body glowed. She threw one arm up, and both Betruger men went flying toward the cliff, leaving Alex alone with the sorcerers.

"I'm ready when you are, Ridge," the sorceress said to the false Aaron.

Ridge turned toward Harold and Macht, and the beach rumbled as he raised his hand. In an instant, the sand rose beneath their feet and sent them tumbling against the cliff. Rocks broke off and pinned them against the stone like chains.

The sorceress turned toward the Oreean Sea. Alex managed to get to her knees as a torrent of water surged around her, threatening to pull her out to sea. She looked up in alarm as an enormous tidal wave rose in the middle of the sea and rushed toward them.

Ridge laughed, cracked his neck and knuckles, and began glowing with a faint brown light as he turned to face the town.

Alex glimpsed the mountain marking on his neck. He held his arms over his head, and the ground rumbled louder and convulsed. The castle and the entire Betruger town began to sink toward the sea.

No! I won't let you ruin this peaceful place.

Alex pushed herself to her feet and thrust both hands toward the water as hard as she could. Her force knocked back the tidal wave, making the sea calm as glass. In the stillness, she heard panicked screams and twisted around. The sorcerers had trapped the Betruger people in the town.

No, no, no. No more innocent blood on my hands!

As the screams grew louder, Alex released the sea and slammed her hands into the water to punch the sand below. The bonds holding Harold and Macht in place cracked, and they freed themselves.

"Alex, run!" Harold shouted.

"No. Get your people out!" she yelled. "I don't know how long I can hold them!"

Alex threw both hands at the castle, and the rumbling stopped. Ridge stalked toward her, but a rock struck the side of his head, and blood trickled down Aaron's face. His eyes turned brown and filled with a fury she'd never seen. He ducked out of the way as Macht threw another stone.

"Macht, get our people," Harold commanded. He grabbed another rock and threw it at Ridge, getting his attention. Alex stopped holding up the castle and rushed the sorcerer, slamming her shoulder into his gut. She knocked Ridge off his feet into the murky water, but a moment later, she couldn't find him.

"Look out!" Harold hollered as Alex was struck from behind. She fell forward into the water, and Ridge grabbed her around the neck and squeezed, choking her. She fought him but couldn't reach his face. She felt the water rushing past her ankles and managed to glance out toward the sea. The tidal wave was back.

No, this can't be the end. I can't be killed by someone masquerading as Aaron.

Struggling to breathe, Alex desperately clawed at his arm. When he let go, she dropped like a stone. Icy water washed over her, and she struggled to get upright. Alex got her head above water long enough to fill her lungs, and she saw Harold fighting the sorcerer. His eyes briefly met hers. That distraction was disaster, and the sorcerer sent him flying back against the cliff face. The man with Aaron's bloody face turned back toward her and smirked.

"No," Alex pleaded as he approached, his hands reaching for her.

Water and sand exploded in front of her. The force knocked Alex backward, and when she rolled over in the waves, she saw a vast crater filling with water.

What is going on? How am I not dead? A flash of orange caught her attention.

The sorceress shouted, "Your father and hexa are going to be furious!"

Gryphon's face was fixed in a scowl. His eyes shone blue, but his hands blazed with orange. Without taking his eyes off the sorceress, he marched up to Alex and held out his hand. As soon as she accepted it, she was on her feet, and Gryphon's arm held her upright. He looked her over, taking in the injuries Ridge had given her.

"Are you all right?" he asked.

The ground rumbled beneath them, and Alex instinctively grabbed him for support despite him holding her tight. "We have to get the Betruger people out."

The sorceress cackled. "The next Head being ordered around by a little girl. What a joke."

"Catch your tongue, Pearl!" Gryphon shouted at her. He narrowed his gaze as she held up her hands. Giggling, she cracked herself to the beach, where Harold was. With each passing second, the sea grew rougher, and the tidal wave rushed faster and faster.

Alex had to shout over the roar. "They're trying to wipe out the kingdom. We have to help those people. Gryphon, *please*."

"I won't leave you." He turned to the castle. "Show your face, Ridge. We know you're not the princeling!"

Ridge shook his head, and his bushy blond hair darkened to brown while his skin shifted to a shade that reminded Alex of the brownish peat moss she used in her garden.

Gryphon braced himself in the wet sand and aimed his hands at the castle. He groaned and strained against Ridge's powers, but he managed to stop the castle and town from sinking further.

Alex demanded, "Get the people out, Gryphon. I'm not worth the lives of an entire kingdom."

"You're worth all the mortals in Torian!" he shouted back.

Alex looked behind her and watched the tidal wave barrel toward them. She felt her well erupt inside her, so she braced herself and threw her arms out. But it wasn't enough. The force of her power rushed out of her as a massive wind sent her sliding backward into Gryphon.

Why is this so hard?

Because you aren't used to it and you're drained. Lean against me. I'll hold us both up.

Steadying herself against Gryphon's back, Alex made a shield of wind and pushed it across the sea. She couldn't stop the tidal wave, but she slowed it down.

Gryphon had to shout into the wind to be heard. "If I leave you now, you won't be able to slow the water with your wind, and I have to hold the castle or Ridge will sink it."

"Then what do we do?"

"BIRCH!" Gryphon shouted.

"Leave that witch out of this!" Ridge yelled. His brown light intensified, and he grunted, pushing harder. The castle began to sink again.

"Or what?"

Alex whirled and found the beautiful raven-haired sorceress right beside her.

"You're the one who brought me the sleeping potion."

"I am."

"Save the people. Please!" Alex begged.

"Take the women and children to Moorloc's or Victoria's castle," Gryphon ordered. "Take the men to Datten."

The sorceress nodded and vanished.

Alex felt her power waver. She wasn't at full strength, and Gryphon was losing against Ridge. Despite his best efforts, the mountain on which the castle stood had disappeared into the earth, and the castle itself was now at sea level. Alex whimpered in pain.

Birch returned. "Everyone is safe. Now what?"

"Get the king and his general to Datten. Tell them what is happening here!" Gryphon ordered.

"As you wish."

"Wait! Come back!" Alex implored, and Birch reappeared.

"Save the books in the library. Please!"

Birch nodded and cracked Macht away with her, leaving Alex and Gryphon fighting the two unnatural disasters.

"Alex!" Harold shouted. "It's just a castle. My kingdom is our people, and you saved them! Let them take our buildings. We'll rebuild."

"Gryphon, send Harold to Datten!" Alex shouted.

The rest happened so fast. Gryphon stopped fighting the sinking castle and let go. Alex's powers gave out, and she collapsed into the water as her shield of wind gave way. Harold vanished an instant before the tidal wave reached them. It slammed into Gryphon and Alex with more force than Alex had ever experienced in her life. Sharp pain exploded everywhere as they slammed into the cliff face. The air left her lungs, her ribs cracked, and the icy cold water entombed her before everything went dark.

CHAPTER 27
AARON

There is something soothing about the sound of metal on metal.

Aaron crossed his arms as he watched his knights spar. Jerome suggested he make an appearance at least once a day for the first month to boost morale and to remind the men that their king was watching. Michael, Stefan, and Jerome had joined him, and they were finalizing compensation for the knights they would be promoting when a Betruger guard cracked into the courtyard.

Within a minute, the entire yard was filled with Betruger men, and alarm bells rang in the castle. Aaron spotted a guard who was usually with Macht.

"Sir Kampf," Aaron greeted him. "Where are Harold and Macht?"

"I'm sorry, Your Royal Highness. We don't know. A woman in a green robe appeared, and then we were here."

"Did you see the queen?" Michael asked, unable to mask the fear in his voice.

"He means Alexandria," Stefan said.

"She was with King Harold, Sir Macht, and you, Your Royal Highness, on our beach."

"I haven't left Datten the entire day. I couldn't have been in Betruger with Alex."

"We saw you with our own eyes," the guard said.

"We assure you, the King of Datten has not left the castle today," Jerome said.

Suddenly Macht appeared in front of them.

"Macht, what is happening?" Aaron demanded.

In return, Macht asked, "Where's Harold? A sorceress was supposed to bring him here after she moved our people."

"What sorceress?" Stefan asked.

Aaron rubbed his neck. "Inside. Alex always comes to the throne room." He ran into the castle, with the others behind him. They had just reached the hall when a deafening crack shook the entire castle, and a cry of pain echoed out of the throne room.

"Harold!" Stefan shouted as he and Aaron rushed inside.

The Betruger king looked as if someone had thrown him from one side of the hall to the other. He was soaking wet and gasping for breath as he struggled to his feet. Macht ran to his king's side.

"Where's Alex?" Aaron asked, catching up with Macht. He reached down to help Harold, but the king threw up his hands.

"No! I know it wasn't you, but he looked so real."

"What are you talking about?" Aaron asked.

"I'm sorry. I failed you." Harold shook uncontrollably. "But you—he—it sank my castle. Everything's gone! We did everything, but even we couldn't protect her. We failed! I'm sorry."

Before they could make sense of his ramblings, a sorceress in a light green robe appeared.

"Where are they?" she asked, looking at the perplexed men. "My nephew and the prince—" She paused when she saw

Aaron and tilted her head to the side. "The crown of Datten. The queen. Where are Gryphon and the queen?"

"We don't know," Michael said.

Megesti blew into the throne room, asking, "Aaron, what in Torian is going on?"

Hearing Megesti's voice, the sorceress spun around, a look of shock and elation on her face.

"We don't know," Aaron said.

Suddenly Megesti's eyes flashed violet. "Brace yourselves!" he shouted.

As the words left his mouth, a crack louder than any they had ever heard before split the air, and the entire castle and town shook. A torrent of seawater burst into the throne room and flung everyone to the ground. A mass arrived with the water and slammed into the back wall hard enough to send a large painting teetering on its hooks.

Gryphon hauled Alex against him as the Wafner family portrait crashed to the ground. The wooden frame shattered, sending wooden shards flying through the hall. Birch and Megesti struggled to their feet, but Aaron was up first and rushed to Alex.

Gryphon leaned back against the wall, blood running down the side of his face. He was shivering violently and gasping for breath while Alex lay in a crumpled heap next to him. He was gripping her dress so tightly his knuckles were pure white.

"What happened?" Birch asked. When she touched Gryphon's shoulder, he winced in pain. She placed her other hand on Alex's cheek. "Oh, Celtics, you're like ice!"

"She couldn't hold the wind anymore, and I couldn't fight, help her, and crack Harold all at the same time. It was Pearl and Ridge. They destroyed Betruger."

Gryphon slumped over and lost consciousness.

Birch stood and turned to the group. "We need two hot baths—*now*. As hot as you can make them." She turned to Aaron. "Your Royal Highness, we'll need men for assistance. Choose those you can stomach seeing your wife undressed."

Aaron looked at Megesti, Stefan, and Michael. All of them nodded.

Birch turned to Megesti. "I'll need the ingredients for my sleeping spell so they can rest and recover. Do you know how the spell is made?"

The sorcerer stared at Gryphon and Alex.

"Megesti!" she snapped at him.

He jumped, startled. "How do you know my name?"

Her face softened. "We can talk about that later. Right now, we need to get them warmed up. Gryphon is a fire sorcerer, so cold weakens him considerably. Alexandria exhausted all her magic to save the Betruger people. She's completely drained. We'll need to give her some power to keep her alive."

"I don't have much power," Megesti said weakly.

"You have no idea *what* you are, do you?"

"What I am?"

A smile spread across Birch's face. "You are in for a big surprise tonight, sapling." She turned to the rest of the group and shouted, "Get to work!"

Megesti and Michael raced off to retrieve the ingredients Birch requested. Jerome went with Macht to calm their men and figure out what to do with the Betruger knights until they knew more. Stefan had bathtubs brought into the throne room. When the tubs were filled and heated, both Reinhart knights stood guard at the entrances.

Following Birch's orders, Aaron and Stefan stripped Alex down to her underclothes and lowered her into the first bath. Megesti and Michael did the same for Gryphon, placing him into the other tub. Pulling off everything but his pants, Aaron climbed in with Alex to hold her face out of the water. Her skin was freezing, her lips blue. Gryphon was in no better shape. Even his bronze skin looked pale. Everyone stood at the edge of the baths, still as the death they feared was hovering. A short while later, Jessica and Edith arrived with fresh clothes and kept vigil off to the side with Harold.

They waited for what felt like an eternity, but Alex remained frozen. Aaron glanced at Gryphon. His color had returned, and he looked completely normal. When Birch reached in, his eyes shot open and flashed blue, and he sat up in a burst of water.

"Water! Everywhere!" Gryphon started glowing orange as the blue in his eyes deepened.

Birch leaped over the tub's edge, grabbed his shoulders, and shook him. "Gryphon, calm down!"

Everyone gasped as his glow intensified to a darker orange and his hands clenched into fists that shook with rage.

"Gryphon," Birch pleaded, "she needs you. You didn't break your mother's spell on my home to let them win. Release your chaos—do not let it engulf you."

When Birch rested her hands on top of his head, he let out a breath, and the glow dissipated.

"How did you do that?" Megesti asked.

Birch smiled. Her green eyes had lightened, glowing softly. "I'm the Titan of the Celtics. We control plants, commune with nature, and bring about peace and balance. I've spent a large part of my nephew's life helping him handle his explosive tendencies."

Gryphon stood and climbed out of the tub. Jessica held out a pair of pants. He purred at her, stripped off his wet pair, and accepted the dry ones.

"Thank you, milady." Gryphon winked at her, but Jessica was already blushing when she looked away.

Michael put himself between Gryphon and his wife, scowling at the sorcerer, but Birch was faster. She smacked her nephew across the back of the head. "Manners."

Rubbing the injury, Gryphon gave Birch a look of indignation.

"I'll do it again," she said. "Don't think I don't know what you already pulled with Alexandria. Manners, and hands to yourself, Sprout."

Gryphon walked toward Alex's tub, but he stopped a few paces away and waited until Aaron nodded. Only then did he venture closer, though he stayed between Stefan and Harold.

"Why hasn't she woken up yet?" he asked Birch, and everyone turned to look at her.

"I'm not sure." She looked down at Aaron cradling Alex in the water. "Your Royal Highness, may I?"

Aaron got out of the tub and allowed Birch to take his place. She closed her eyes and held Alex's face in her hands. Aaron found himself staring at Gryphon, and as he did, his jaw clenched and his hands gripped the tub so hard his knuckles turned white.

"She's still in there. She's struggling to come back."

"Why?" Jessica asked, putting her hands on the edge of the tub.

Birch looked from Gryphon to Aaron. "She's exhausted and afraid. Tired from fighting and losing control of her powers, and she hasn't recovered from her last fight. But the fear—her fear is dangerous."

"How is fear dangerous?" Michael asked.

"Her powers are deep, and her fear runs just as deep. She's afraid of what she'll find at the bottom of her well. She's afraid to face you, Your Royal Highness, and confess everything that happened at Moorloc's."

Aaron looked at Birch, concerned. "She can tell me anything."

"Not everything, princeling," Gryphon said, earning a glare from Aaron.

"If you had left her memories alone, she wouldn't have had to go through what she did to get them back."

"If I'd left them with her, she'd be dead!" Gryphon shouted back.

The group stared at the sorcerer in disbelief, but he assured them it was true, though he refused to reveal Alex's secrets.

"Enough," Birch snapped. "This isn't helping."

Aaron watched Birch run her fingers along Alex's temples. A faint green light moved from her fingers into Alex, and she stopped. Her head dropped briefly before she looked up at Aaron.

"I'm so sorry. She's lost the baby," Birch whispered. "Her magic couldn't heal them both."

Aaron froze. "Baby? She's pregnant?"

"Was," Birch said softly.

The room began to close in on Aaron. He shook. *Her exhaustion, mood, strange behavior, refusal to eat . . . that explains everything. Why didn't she tell me?* "How do we keep her fighting?" Aaron felt tears fill his eyes. "I can't do this without her."

Birch put her hand on Aaron's. "To help her, I need all of you to leave for a few minutes. Gryphon, Megesti, you stay with me. She's weakened to the point of being unable to heal herself. Her body is giving up, so we have to help her regain enough strength so that her magic can replenish itself. It will be extremely painful for us, but it's even more dangerous for you if you remain."

Megesti encouraged Aaron with a nod.

Aaron stepped back and followed their loyal friends to the doors. Before he left, he saw Gryphon and Birch lift Alex out of the tub. Then Birch wiggled her fingers, putting Alex in a golden titan robe. Harold squeezed Aaron's shoulder and led him out of the room.

Not long after, the new king was pacing outside the closed throne room doors.

"What did Moorloc do to her?" Jessica asked.

"Whippings, beatings, enough to break her," Michael said, embracing his wife and kissing her forehead.

"Aaron, you cannot overreact to whatever we learn," Harold said.

Aaron stopped pacing and looked at his friends. "I need her to be all right. As long as she survives, I don't care what happened there. If he kissed her or she kissed him or more, I don't care." He ran both hands through his hair and breathed deeply to control the tears he wouldn't be able to stop. "She's losing *our* baby. A baby she never even told me about. How much have I failed as a husband that my wife wouldn't tell me she was with child?"

A loud bang came from the throne room, and bright light flashed under the door. Everyone stiffened until they heard Alex scream.

Aaron burst through the door and spotted her. She was pale as death, but at least she was sitting up. He rushed across the room to her. *You're still cold as ice.* He cupped her face, and when she looked up at him, he burst into tears. She grabbed him and kissed him.

"You promised you wouldn't scare me like that again," Aaron said.

"I'm sorry."

"Let her catch her breath before you move her," Birch said.

Gryphon rubbed his arm and winced. A red line ran from his palm up the entire length of his arm. The mark spread out like a tree branch and emitted a faint red glow. Birch and

Megesti had the same mark. Aaron noticed that Gryphon's ran through another scar. *You have a betrayer mark. The same three x's as Alex. When did you get that?*

"The scar will fade in time, but it will always be there," Birch whispered. "Transference of power marks you permanently. It will forever remind you of what you did to save her."

"What am I?" Megesti asked softly, running his finger down the long red mark on his arm. "Everyone keeps hinting at something."

"He doesn't know," Gryphon said to Birch.

"He's only ever been around one sorcerer, so how would he?" Birch replied before turning to Megesti. "You're what we call a Usurper. You take on the powers of the sorcerers surrounding you."

"Merlock taught me they come from only one family," Alex said.

Birch smiled. "That's right. They are exceptionally rare."

"Even more than a Head or Heart," Gryphon said. "There is only one Usurper alive at a time. One is born every two or three generations."

"It can't be me," Megesti said. "There is no mention of a Usurper in any of our journals, and those records go back to Merlin and Cassandra themselves. Nobody in our family was one."

"Not on your father's side," Gryphon corrected.

"My mother was a mortal."

"He never told you?" Birch stared at Megesti, completely shocked.

"Told me what?"

"Your mother isn't a mortal, Megesti," Birch said. "*I'm* your mother, and the last Usurper was my father."

Megesti's mouth dropped open. Aaron wanted to go to his friend, but Alex was struggling to even stand up, and he couldn't leave her. Megesti reacted exactly as Alex would have —he turned and bolted from the room. Aaron knew he'd hide in his lab and stay there for at least a day. *I'll find you as soon as Alex is asleep.*

"Can we move her?" Aaron asked. Birch was looking toward the door Megesti had just left through and merely nodded.

"Aaron, don't you dare." Alex gave Aaron a warning look, which he ignored as he lifted her into his arms. She clung to him and didn't protest any further.

"Michael, Stefan, we need to warm her up. Start the fire in our room. Ladies, fetch some hot food and drink, please," Aaron said.

Harold walked ahead and opened doors while Aaron carried Alex to their suite. On the way, Aaron ordered some maids to get more blankets, and when he got Alex to the second floor of their rooms, he placed her beside the bed. Michael and Stefan prepared the fire.

Once she was dressed in her warmest nightgown, Aaron tried to tuck her in, but she grabbed his shirt. "You have to go," she said.

He sat on the edge of their bed. "Alex, what happened in there . . . you need me."

"No. Our people need you," she said firmly. "The whole Betruger kingdom has just been cracked onto the castle grounds. Families were sent to Moorloc's and Verlassen Castle. They must be terrified." She gestured across the room. "You, *King* Aaron, will help *King* Harold settle his people into our kingdom, because as of this afternoon, they don't have one anymore. Take Jerome, Michael, and Macht with you." She glanced at the others. "You know Stefan and my ladies won't let anything happen to me. They're almost as annoying as you are."

"I will remain also," said Birch. Everyone looked at the opposite side of the bed where she'd suddenly appeared. She turned to Aaron. "You'll need a sorcerer to help you. I'm told Megesti isn't capable, and clearly Alexandria is unable, so I offer you my nephew." She snapped her fingers, and Gryphon appeared beside her with his arms crossed and a scowl on his face.

"At least he's clothed now," Michael said, loudly enough that Harold snorted.

Alex asked, "Where did you put the books, Birch?"

"Your mother's castle."

Alex asked Gryphon, "Could you please tell Megesti to handle the Betruger library? He's the only one I trust with books."

"Of course, princess."

Alex glared at him, and Gryphon abruptly smirked.

"Thank you," she said and turned her attention back to Aaron.

Aaron clenched his fist. *I don't know what happened there with that intense look between you two, but I'm not happy about it.* Even as Alex spoke to someone else, Aaron kept watching Gryphon. The sorcerer's eyes never left his wife.

"Aaron?"

"Sorry?" He realized she'd been speaking to him and he'd missed it.

Alex grabbed his tunic and kissed him. "You can't stay. Today will be the first of many hard days for you as king. I know you want to stay with me and let someone else handle this, but the reason I'm in this bed is that I put all of Harold's people before myself. Now please go finish that job for me. Be the king I know you are."

Aaron sighed. "All right. Stefan—apart from relieving herself, she doesn't leave this bed. Understood?"

"Completely."

"You're the queen's guard, Stefan," Alex said. "I have the last word around here."

Stefan and Aaron glanced at one another.

"That may be true in Warren. But in Datten . . ."

Alex scrunched up her nose. "You answer to the king now, don't you?"

He nodded.

"More of that protecting my honor nonsense, isn't it?" Alex asked. After Stefan nodded, she shot another look at Aaron. "When this crisis is over, we're changing that law." She called for Megesti, and Birch stepped out of sight behind Gryphon. A moment later, a confused Megesti appeared.

"Alex?" He looked around nervously, his body stiff as a sword.

"Megesti, I need you to sort through the books from the Betruger library. Decide which books go to which kingdom."

"Of course," Megesti said, letting his shoulders relax.

"Thank you. Gryphon, would you—" But the sorcerer cracked Megesti away before Alex could finish, and then grinned at her.

The door creaked open, and Edith and Jessica arrived with a large tray. It held a teapot, a heaping basket of bread, and a giant bowl of steaming stew. Aaron smiled in relief. *They will take care of what matters most to me.* Alex's ladies sat on opposite sides of the bed.

"Peppermint tea and rabbit stew," Jessica said, handing her a spoon.

"And a basket of fresh bread." Edith handed a loaf to Alex.

"Go," Jessica said. "We have her."

Aaron finally stepped back, and Jessica settled more comfortably onto his side of the bed, rubbing Alex's hand. Edith was already offering to go get some chocolate if she needed it, and Alex smiled weakly at her ladies fussing over her.

"I promise I'll protect her," Stefan said.

"Where are we off to?" Gryphon asked.

Aaron ordered, "Take me and Macht to the courtyard, but send Harold and Michael to the Betruger people. *You* will stay with me."

"As you wish, *kingling*," Gryphon said and cracked them away.

CHAPTER 28
GRYPHON

Mortals are so boring.

Gryphon yawned again as Aaron and Macht organized all of the newcomers. It took a long time, but they eventually figured out which men were supposed to be going to Moorloc's old castle for training. They gathered these men in the courtyard and asked Generals Avery and Wafner to find accommodations for the remaining men. When everything was settled, Gryphon cracked the men due for training to what Aaron called the Oreean Stronghold.

Call it what you want, use it however you want . . . but Moorloc's castle will never be anything but the place that broke Alex so badly nothing will ever fully put her back together again. Megesti was right. You should have burned it to the ground.

The sun was setting when they arrived, so Gryphon raised a boulder from the earth and perched on top, judging the mortals.

I'll start with Michael. Scrawny, but cleverer than anyone believes. You're by far the most observant of everyone. Yes, you joke, but you watch everything. It's no wonder you can read Alex like a book. If you were a sorcerer, you'd be Mystics and Celtics.

Harold and Macht—you two are as strong among the men as titans among sorcerers. Your men obey without hesitation, and you have a presence to you that amuses me. Others cower before your might, and I can smell the fear on them. You would both be Ares sorcerers, and oh, the fun we'd have. Macht, you'd be a Mire since you love the earth so much, and Harold, you'd be Poseidon. Like Alex, you seem to be drawn to the sea and its power. Yet you allied yourself with him.

Princeling—kingling now—your temper would make you an Ares or Salem, and your obsession with your horse screams Tiere. Hmm. Now I think Little Wafner would be the Ares. You'd be Salem. It would be ironic for you to have the power that killed your brother, and it would put you at odds with our princess, though she'd claim you balanced each other. Yes, Little Wafner would be Ares and Merlin. He's hard to pin down and seems to have a strange set of skills I wouldn't expect to find together.

Dusk had arrived by the time Michael and Harold found accommodations for most of the families, but now they were talking with Aaron and Macht about how it wouldn't be enough. They couldn't decide between taking the rest to Warren or Datten. Gryphon's patience ran out. Though he was drained and his scars still burned, he would do this—for Alex.

"What are you doing?" Macht asked suspiciously as he stepped forward.

"I didn't think it was possible, kingling, but this one likes me even less than you do." Gryphon smirked at Aaron. He brushed dirt off his black pants and adjusted his burnt orange tunic. It bore the Ares line mark of an ax, with the Head's mark of a crown above it.

"Do you think Alex will like it? I had a tunic made for her too. Luckily, she looks stunning in gold."

Aaron's mouth turned down with a frown. Michael put a hand on his shoulder and shook his head.

I was right—definitely Celtics.

Gryphon stepped forward and rolled up his sleeves. Pain rushed through his arm, but he refused to show weakness in front of Aaron. He pushed out his hands, threw the lid off his well, and felt his raw power burst out. Everyone gasped as the ground beneath them began to rumble, and the castle rose off the ground.

Birch instantly appeared beside Gryphon with her arms crossed. "What are you doing? You don't have the power for this," she scolded.

"They need more room for these people, so either help or leave."

Birch glowered but closed her eyes and thrust her hands toward the woods Alex had grown during her time at the castle. There was a popping sound, and the mortals staggered back as trees levitated from the ground with their roots intact and flew through the air toward the castle. Together, Birch and Gryphon worked to turn the two-story castle into a three-story castle.

An older, black-haired sorcerous wearing a gray nightgown arrived beside the mortals, causing Michael to yelp in surprise.

"*Hades*," Kharon groaned. "Stop infuriating the dead, Gryphon. I'm trying to sleep."

Gryphon chuckled and ignored his friend's complaints. He focused all his attention on the task before him, but the sorcerous wouldn't be put off. Kharon stormed toward Gryphon but stopped when they spotted Birch. After taking a moment to watch what the two were doing, they rolled up their nightgown sleeves, thrust their arms upward, and helped. Stones flew toward the castle and began affixing themselves to the walls.

"Go back to your grave!" Kharon shouted at the empty space beside them. "I am *not* saying that to him, you nasty old goat."

Gryphon grinned mischievously as he watched Kharon shout at ghosts the mortals couldn't see.

"Tell Moorloc hello from me." Gryphon laughed, but the others' jaws dropped in a mixture of awe and terror.

"Don't antagonize the dead," Kharon grumbled at Gryphon.

A faint giggle spilled out of nowhere, and a gorgeous young sorceress appeared. Her dark green robe made her sandy-colored skin and dirty blonde hair sparkle as she sauntered toward the men, swaying her hips. She only looked a few years older than Alex, but her dark brown eyes were filled with wisdom.

She laughed when she reached Gryphon and Birch. "What are you two doing?"

"Playing in the dirt," Gryphon said, making her shake her head.

"You could help, Lynx," Birch said.

"Fine." She exhaled loudly and threw out her hands to help Birch bring the trees to the castle. With the four of them working, it only took a few minutes to finish adding the third story.

"Is that enough space, kingling?"

"Who are these sorcerers?" Macht asked, eyeing Kharon and Lynx, but Harold scolded him for his tone.

"It's all right," Birch said. "This is Kharon. They're a sorcerous, the Titan of Hades."

"Sorcer-*ous*?" Michael asked.

"I don't identify as male or female."

"Oh, well, nice to meet you," Michael said.

"Pleasure, Michael, Macht, Harold, and Aaron."

They all warily regarded the sorcerous.

"Ignore Kharon," said the beautiful sorceress. "They enjoy the looks on people's faces when they seem to know all. They talk to the dead, and the ghosts told them your names. I'm Lynx—Titan of Tiere."

"She controls and communicates with animals," Gryphon added.

"We're also on Gryphon's side in this whole mess," Lynx said.

Gryphon grinned. "Then what took you so long?"

"We broke you out of the dungeon. Or have you already forgotten?" she asked.

"Dungeon?" Aaron asked.

"He refused to tell his parents anything about what happened here or about any of you," Lynx said. "His parents threw him in the dungeon while they tried to extract the information by force."

"Lynx," Gryphon warned.

Birch stepped between them. "How did you find us? Only Mystics can crack so far without a proper guide point."

"We sensed Gryphon," Kharon said.

Gryphon turned to the Oreean Sea. "You could sense me?"

"Yes," Lynx said.

Gryphon turned to Birch. "The potion wore off sooner than expected. If Lynx could find me, that means *he* could find *her*."

"Not tonight," Birch said. "I added something to the sleeping draft."

"Oh, thank Ares." Gryphon ran his hands down his face.

His aunt said, "As soon as the princess wakes, we're going to have to look for a protection spell to put on the castles, whether or not she's strong enough."

"What princess?" Lynx asked.

"Victoria's daughter. Her father's a mortal king," Kharon said.

Lynx gasped. "What title doesn't this Heart have? No wonder Garrick is so angry! Gryphon, your family has completely lost their minds. Your father's started turning on our own."

"What do you mean?" Gryphon asked.

"He's imprisoning anyone he thinks will be on your side," Kharon said.

"How'd you manage to evade him?"

"We'll have enough time for questions when we return to Datten," Birch said. "I need to get back to that lab to make another large batch of potions to keep Garrick from reading our minds and cracking to us like he did at the pier. For now, Gryphon, you need to get these people settled and then come back to the castle. Lynx and Kharon, you need to go back to the Forbidden Lands before they realize you've left."

"It's too late for that," Lynx said.

"Garrick has set up all sorts of enchantments," Kharon said. "No one who leaves will be able to get back undetected. You know firsthand what happens when you set him off, Birch." They looked annoyed and turned aside. "I'm *not* telling them that, Moorloc, so just go away!"

"Still holding his grudge against me?" Birch asked.

"Yes."

Aaron spoke up, saying, "I don't know who you are, but if you mean my wife and my kingdom no harm, you're welcome to stay in Datten."

"And who are you?" Lynx asked, wrinkling her nose.

"King Aaron of Datten," Gryphon replied. "Alexandria's husband."

Lynx's eyes grew large. "She married a mortal? How does that work? He'll be dead in a decade. And why him? I mean, look at that one." She winked at Macht. "Do they know the

Head and Heart will rule together? What you two are destined to do?"

"Lynx! Go to Datten," Gryphon growled.

"It's a legitimate question."

He snapped his fingers, and all three of the other sorcerers were gone.

Aaron smirked. "Nice to see that you actually have friends. Maybe I *can* trust you around my wife with all these chaperones."

"I suggest we finish this task, or else I might forget to bring you back with me," Gryphon grumbled.

By the time they returned to Datten, it was almost morning, and Caleb escorted Harold and Macht to their rooms.

Gryphon looked at Aaron and exhaled loudly. "I'd like to see how Alex is, if that's all right with you."

When Aaron nodded, Gryphon followed him to the king's suite where Alex was still asleep. There was a small box on the bedside table, covered in mother-of-pearl. Gryphon picked it up and examined it, trying to summon the courage to look at her.

I failed you when you needed me. I'm so sorry.

The bed groaned when Aaron sat down. Gryphon's stomach churned as he finally looked at Alex. Bruises were forming on her face and neck, and she was terribly pale. Her face twitched, and she let out a moan.

"May I?" Gryphon asked Aaron, holding his hand over Alex's head.

"What are you going to do?"

"Read her mind," Birch said. "It's rude to read someone's mind without consent." She held out a mug to Gryphon.

He took it, sniffed, and made a face. "Alex is asleep. I would only need to peek at her dreams. She has nightmares of whatever is torturing her."

"How do you know she has nightmares?" Aaron asked.

"She told me when she was at Moorloc's."

"So you can see our dreams and read our minds?" Aaron asked.

"Those of mortals and other sorcerers? Easily, but not hers. Not anymore. She's only the second sorcerer who's managed to keep me out."

"Drink it," Birch prompted. "We don't want your father or his friends tracking you here."

Gryphon plugged his nose and chugged the whole potion before setting it on the table beside Alex, shaking his head and groaning. Then he looked at Aaron.

"Do it," Aaron said.

Gryphon briefly glanced at Birch. "Are you sure?"

"She rarely remembers her nightmares," Aaron said. "If we know what she dreamed, we might be able to help."

Gryphon agreed and placed his hands on Alex's temples.

"She's reliving the battle in Betruger and the moment when the sea hit her. It gets cold and dark." Gryphon removed his hand.

"Does she seem stronger?" Birch asked.

"She does."

Birch turned to Aaron. "What does she have to do today?"

"Nothing, but within the next week, we will have the funeral and the coronation. I'll need her at both," Aaron said.

"We'll make sure she's strong enough," Birch said. "Gryphon, go get some rest. If you want her safe, we'll need you at full strength. You shouldn't have moved that castle. No more showing off until you've recovered."

"If you can lift a castle, why not bring back Betruger's?" Aaron asked.

"Only Alex has Poseidon powers, and that kingdom is at the bottom of the Oreean Sea," the sorcerer snapped.

"Gryphon, rest."

"Yes, Birch." He left the room but stopped outside, leaning against the wall to listen.

"Thank you," Aaron said to Birch.

"I know he's cocky, but he's got a kind heart once you get through those walls. He had it rough with his father. Garrick is a psychopath."

"I'll try to remember that," Aaron griped.

"You may ask, Your Royal Highness."

"She'll be all right, won't she?"

"Physically she'll heal quickly, but a heart is harder to mend. You'll need to help her with that."

Gryphon lowered his head. Without a sound, he headed down the hall to find his room.

CHAPTER 29
ALEX

"Let go, you brute."

Alex sat up in time to see Stefan struggling with a woman. She scratched his neck, and when he cursed, she shoved him off her and rushed to the end of the bed.

"Get out of here!" Stefan demanded as Gryphon cracked into the room between him and the woman.

"Lynx is my friend, and if I catch you putting your hands on her again, you'll have me to contend with, *little Wafner*."

"Who exactly are *you*?" Lynx purred at Stefan as she cocked her head to the side.

"I'm Alex's head guard."

"More like an annoying lifelong big brother," Alex complained, swinging her legs out of bed. With the blanket wrapped around her, she stood to break up the fight that had woken her up. "Stand down, you maniac."

"He's your brother?" Lynx sounded confused.

"Not by blood," Stefan said, marching across the room to Alex without taking his eyes off Lynx and Gryphon. "But I've been taking care of her since she was four, so we've accepted the inevitability that we'll always consider each other siblings." He frowned at Alex. And though she didn't want him to, he gently turned her face to the side and examined her bruises. "When I meet the man who did this to you, he's going to regret it."

She swatted him away. "I'm fine. It'll heal."

Stefan took a step back to look at all of her now. "Are you naked again? You're married to a king. Can't he buy you clothes?"

"I'm wearing a nightgown. Leave me alone and go bother Jessica."

Lynx laughed. "They sound like us." She elbowed Gryphon until he groaned and rolled his eyes at her. "What? Are you afraid your precious Heart will find out you are actually a sweet little kitten?"

"Lynx!"

"You know better than to growl at me. When you play animals with me, butterfly, you always lose."

"What are you talking about?" Alex asked.

Lynx winked at her. "Garrick says a Head has no friends. Only subjects, servants, and enemies, and all of them must fear him. But Gryphon wasn't always so good at the whole tall, dark, and brooding thing."

"I'm menacing."

"I'd say insufferable," said Stefan. "Either way, get out."

"Stefan!" Alex prodded him. "I want to know about this butterfly thing."

He said, "I meant so you can get dressed, Your Royal Highness. If you want to learn about these sorcerers, I'd rather you did it clothed and in the royal library, not half-naked in your bedroom."

"Fair enough. Is Jessica around?"

"I can help," Lynx piped up. "I am capable of tying strings and fastening buttons."

"All right," Alex said. "Men, out!"

Stefan pushed Gryphon toward the door, but the sorcerer cracked away, causing him to stumble.

"You're not supposed to use your powers unnecessarily!" Lynx hollered.

Alex found her favorite red dress, and Lynx helped get it over her head before she went to work on fastening it.

"You know you're covered in bruises, right? And your bed is—"

Alex cut her off. "I know. I'll get the maids to change the bed."

"Are you all right?"

"I'm fine."

"But the bed . . ." Lynx motioned.

Alex snapped, "I don't want to talk about it."

Lynx sniffed the air, and her eyes widened. "I'm so sorry."

Alex opened her mouth but closed it and twisted her hands into her skirt. "You can tell by smell?"

She nodded. "Tiere sorcerers can."

Alex covered her mouth, staring at Lynx for a long time before deciding to trust her. "Are we going out to where Gryphon and Stefan are waiting, or shall we escape?"

Lynx raised her eyebrows and smiled. "I think we're going to get along fine, Your Royal Highness."

"Call me Alex. I hate my titles, and I know sorcerers don't use them."

Lynx said, "It's a deal, Alex."

The two of them went downstairs to the main floor and snuck out of the king's room.

"Where are we going?" the sorceress whispered.

"To the dining hall for food and then off to the library to wait for Aaron."

"How do you know he'll go there?"

"He always ends up there. He hates the meeting table in our suite because of the stain."

"The stain?"

"I almost bled to death on that table when I got my memories back."

"Couldn't you replace the table?" Lynx asked.

"It's centuries old, and . . . you know, tradition." After grabbing some bread and cheese from the dining hall, they entered the library and stopped dead in their tracks. It wasn't Aaron they found but Gryphon, reading a book with his feet up on the table while Stefan stood beside him.

Gryphon closed his book. "Queen Alex."

"How did you find us?" Lynx asked as she and Alex sat down opposite the men, who exchanged a significant look.

"I know you," Stefan said.

Alex was annoyed at being so predictable, but then a sudden, excruciating cramp struck her. *Ferflucs. I have to get out of here.*

Stefan must have noticed the slight twitch in her face because he cocked his head. She leaped up from her chair and fled the room, bolting down the hall until she remembered she could crack. Immediately she was in their bedroom. She locked the door and collapsed onto the ground, holding her stomach as the sharp pain intensified.

Eventually she heard footsteps and a knock at the door.

"Alex." Stefan's voice was gentle. It was the tone he had used whenever she had been frightened as a little girl.

"Go away," she whimpered.

"Can I get you anything?"

"No."

"Jessica or Her Majesty?"

"No," Alex snapped. "I need some rags and water."

She looked down at the blood that had pooled on the floor. *I couldn't even protect my baby. How am I supposed to protect a kingdom?*

"Alex . . . you have people for that."

"No. This is not a *people* job," she said, tears streaming down her face.

"What's going on?"

Aaron's voice, mumbling to Stefan in the hallway, made her pull her knees up to her chest. Then two sets of footsteps walked away. She exhaled and dropped her head.

They're gone. I'm alone, just as I deserve to be. The tears came harder and brought sobs, but the door from the queen's room creaked. Alex looked up as the bookcase door opened, and Aaron came in with a bucket and rags in his hand. Before she could say anything, he kneeled down beside her and kissed the top of her head before he set to work wiping the floor.

"Aaron, I'm sorry . . ."

"No," he said firmly, looking at her. "*You* didn't lose this baby. *We* did. And I'm not letting you suffer alone, even if that's what you planned. Whatever you need, I'll support you. If you want to heal yourself or you want me to postpone the coronation and the funeral, I will. My father is gone. He won't care when we bury him."

Alex took Aaron's hands off the rags. When he sat on the ground beside her, she sighed and put her head on his shoulder.

"When you're ready, we can try again," he said.

"All right."

"Why didn't you tell me?"

"I knew I'd lose it. I didn't want you to hurt any more than you already were."

"I'm hurt you didn't feel that you could share this with me."

She fought back her tears, but they won and poured down her face again.

"Alex?"

"There are so many horrible things I'm keeping from you, Aaron. This is honestly the least of them."

"So . . . tell me."

"Aaron . . ."

"You don't get to ask me for honesty and not give it in return."

"You'll leave me."

"No, I won't. Trust me to listen and be fair."

"Because that worked so well the last time." Alex regretted her words the instant she said them, but the pain of him leaving when she needed him was still too raw.

Aaron sucked in his breath. "I deserve that. Alex, you saved the entire Betruger kingdom yesterday. The least I can do is listen."

Alex finally told him about the worst of her time at the castle. The abuse from Moorloc and Kruft, the violence she had received at the hands of his men, the night her Ares powers came in and she killed Kruft's men, how she threw herself at Gryphon, and then the death of Reinhilde, which had led to her trying to drown herself on the beach.

"He told the truth."

"What do you mean?"

"While you were unconscious, we . . . fought, and he told me if he hadn't taken your memories, you wouldn't have made it home."

Tears streaked Alex's face. "So leave."

"What?"

"I betrayed you exactly how you thought I did, killed an

innocent woman, and couldn't protect our child. I'm worthless. You can leave—I won't stop you."

Aaron stood and walked out the door.

I deserve this. No one deserves to suffer from being with me. Alex tightly clutched her knees to her chest and was sobbing when Aaron walked back into the room.

"Your bath is ready."

"My what?"

"I assumed you'd want to get cleaned up too, not just the suite." He held out his hand to her. "Will you let me help?"

Alex nodded and took his hand. Aaron embraced her and kissed her. Alex locked her arms around him and kissed him with everything she had as he scooped her up and carried her to their bathing chamber.

"I have a few questions now. The rest can wait. All right?"

Alex swallowed hard and nodded as Aaron set her on her feet. The maids had filled a large copper tub with steaming hot water.

"Were you in your right mind at any time at the castle?"

"At the start. But not by the time Gryphon arrived."

"Do you still *want* Gryphon?"

"No. I don't even know if I wanted him then. There was a pull to him—it's hard to explain. I wasn't in control of my body. Our magic is connected, and if he's around, my powers are different. Sometimes better and sometimes more chaotic."

Aaron gently loosened her corset until her dress slipped off, and then he lovingly kissed her neck and shoulder. "Now we have no more secrets between us. I will forgive everything if you can forgive my mistakes, *but* you're not to be alone with him."

"Aaron . . ." She turned to look at him.

"That's where I'm drawing my line, Alex. I can live with

what happened, knowing everything you went through there, but I can't have him alone with you again. I can't."

"I was going to say that's fair." She swallowed and looked up at him. He leaned down and kissed her again before he helped her into the tub.

CHAPTER 30
AARON

Breathe slowly. Don't let her see how ferflucsing furious you are. Not at her—never at her. She had to find friendship to survive that place. Michael said that. Just one friend, and she would get through. But he *abused that friendship for his own purposes. He's been trying to wedge himself between us since the day he met her. He can try to deny it, but the way he's been antagonizing me shows his true motives.*

"Aaron?"

Alex's voice snapped him out of his spiraling thoughts. The back of her dress was open, exposing the mess of scars from her whipping. Aaron gently ran his fingers over them, and Alex shivered. He tugged at the corset ribbons.

"You'll never be alone, Alex, not anymore. I meant it when I said you were my priority, so come with me and sign new peace treaties with Harold and your father. I would hate for you to have to go to war with yourself." Her green eyes sparkled as her hand slipped into his, but though she held her shoulders back, he could still feel her trembling.

"You're sore, and I don't blame you for doubting me, but I

will show you I mean it—with my actions and not just my words."

They headed toward the library in silence. After Aaron ushered Alex into the room, he stopped a maid and whispered a request to her. She curtsied and scurried off to clean their room.

As they entered, the library fell silent. Aaron led Alex to the closest bench and sat beside her. Guinevere and Edward sat beside them. Edward reached over and squeezed his daughter's hand, but she looked down at her lap, avoiding everyone. Harold, Macht, and Gryphon arrived and took their seats. Michael and Jerome stood nearby.

News travels much too quickly here. She deserved privacy with this whole situation.

Jerome brought over the Datten and Warren peace treaty, but Edward held his hand up.

"I don't think Alexandria needs to sign a treaty with herself. So long as Aaron treats my daughter with respect, there won't be any issues."

Aaron looked at the aged parchment before him. His father's signature was below a long line of kings—all the Kings of Datten who had protected Warren for centuries.

"Agreed," Aaron said, and Jerome rolled up the treaty.

Next, Macht brought the truce between Datten, Warren, and Betruger. Harold smiled as he signed his name. One by one, Edward, Alex, and Aaron added their signatures.

Gryphon snapped his fingers, and Lynx appeared beside him. She handed Aaron a parchment.

"A truce between the Forbidden Lands and Datten?" Aaron asked.

"With Datten *and* Warren," Alex read aloud.

"I don't speak for my father," Gryphon said, "but the day I become Head, not one sorcerer will harm a son or daughter of

Datten or Warren." Gryphon's words were directed at Aaron, but his eyes were on Alex.

Aaron clenched his fist. "I don't understand what this is," he said softly.

"He's protecting our children," Alex whispered. "The mortal children and grandchildren of a Heart will be a tempting target."

"And with this truce, I'll have the power to stop any sorcerer before they get any ideas."

Harold handed Gryphon the quill, and he signed for the Forbidden Lands. Aaron watched his loopy signature and noted that the surname was Ares—his line, just as Aaron's was Datten. Aaron took the quill next and signed before he handed it to Alex. She looked between the two signatures, then signed the treaty three times: as the Heart, as the Queen of Datten, and as Crown Princess and future Queen of Warren.

Gryphon snapped his fingers, and the parchment vanished.

Aaron pinched the bridge of his nose. Anger was still raging through him, and being in the same room with Gryphon was exhausting. "What's next, Michael?" he asked.

"Nothing for the moment," Michael said. He regarded Alex sympathetically, but she shot back a warning look.

That's my fierce queen.

"We'll leave you then," Guinevere said. She stood and hugged Alex before tugging on Edward's arm. "We have a coronation and a funeral to finish planning."

"I'll see you later, darling." Edward kissed Alex's cheek and followed Guinevere and Jerome out of the room.

"We should go too," Lynx said to Gryphon, but the doors slammed shut, and a strong wind blew through the room, sending loose papers swirling around them. Lynx turned around slowly, stared at Alex, and gulped.

Alex's golden eyes were fixed on Gryphon, but he didn't

blink as he stared back at her. There was too much going on in that look, and it sent another rush of frustration surging through Aaron's heart.

"Sit," Alex commanded. Lynx immediately obeyed.

Alex snapped her fingers, bringing Stefan, Birch, and Megesti into the room. Gryphon rolled his eyes and snapped his fingers to summon Kharon too.

Birch said, "Your Royal Highness, you shouldn't be using your powers like this. You're too weak and should use your energy to heal your—" She cut herself off as soon as she saw Alex's expression, and she sat down without another word.

Alex started to glow gold all over. Michael didn't budge from his place behind her.

"You don't want to make her angry when she's like this," Stefan said, settling in beside Macht as everyone else found a seat at the table.

Alex rubbed her eyes. Michael moved and squeezed her shoulder. Immediately, the glow vanished. Gryphon and Birch glanced at one another in disbelief. When Alex finally looked back at the group, her eyes were green again, but she was pale.

"No one leaves until Megesti and I get answers about our parents and what's happening in the Forbidden Lands." She spoke with such authority Aaron couldn't help but grin. *The fiercest queen Datten has seen in centuries.*

Lynx, Birch, and Kharon looked at Gryphon, who threw up his hands in surrender. "You heard the Heart."

"Very well," Birch said. "Who goes first?"

CHAPTER 31

ALEX

Alex tried to calm her breathing. Her ploy had worked. Aaron squeezed her clenched fist until she opened her hand and released the tightness in her chest.

"I'm Gryphon's aunt by adoption," Birch began. "My father and mother were gifted Celtics and incredibly talented, kind, and loving. But my father was also a Usurper. He took the powers from a formidable Ares sorcerer one day and got himself and my mother killed. I was only six when they died, so my father's friend Griffin adopted me and brought me home, much to his wife's disdain. Eris was the Titan of Ares. Their daughter, Imelda, got her mother's power-hungry nature and the Ares desire for violence. She married Garrick."

Gryphon shrugged. "And had me."

"Yes. Thanks to my adoptive sister, we have the stubborn, temperamental future Head who sits before us. We sorcerers split our children into two schools: one for those with dangerous powers and one for the others. As an Ares, Imelda went to the first school. Ares, Salem, Mire, Hades, and Poseidon all train together. You need the water sorcerers to keep the fire ones under control. I went to the other school, and it was there that I was introduced to the twins."

"In our world, twins born outside of the line of Tiere are unheard of," Lynx explained. "The level of power needed for a sorceress to successfully carry twins is rare. Tiere sorcerers have an easier time because of our connection with animals."

"As you can see, Merlock and Moorloc were an anomaly," Birch continued. "But after a few years, it became obvious that Moorloc was the stronger twin as the firstborn, so he began to train at the school for sorcerers with dangerous powers, where my sister went. Years later, when Victoria started at the safer school, she proved herself. She was not only incredibly talented but also kind. Everyone tried to move her to the other school, where her healing powers would be helpful, but her father, Hermes, refused. Their mother, Alexandria, had always been adamant Victoria not go there. When their father died too, Merlock and Moorloc fought over where she should study. Victoria finally agreed to try Moorloc's school, and she hated it. But while she was there, she caught Garrick's eye, and this whole mess began."

"How so?" Michael asked.

"My father became obsessed with Victoria," Gryphon said.

"Everyone knew Garrick would be the next Head, and so sorceresses threw themselves at him, Imelda especially," Birch said. "My dear sister wanted power, and it was obvious she'd become Titan of Ares or Tiere. As the daughter of the house of Ares, she was the ideal wife for a future Head, at least according to Garrick's father, Aeron. But Garrick wanted Victoria, the only daughter of the Merlin, so he pursued her. Imelda's brothers didn't get along, but even they agreed Garrick wasn't good enough for Victoria."

"Why were they fighting?" Megesti asked.

Birch looked down. "Because of me. Merlock and I bonded to each other, and Moorloc was furious."

"Bonded?" Aaron asked.

"Like marriage," Kharon explained.

"With a big difference," Lynx said. "A sorceress cannot bear a child with anyone other than the sorcerer she is bonded to. So if one of them dies, the other can find new relationships but will never again bond fully. It also gives sorcerers the opportunity to play without fear of repercussions."

If that's true, thought Alex, *how did Aaron and I get pregnant?*

Birch explained how sorcerers rarely bonded younger than seventy and waited a long time to have a child because of the power they passed on to their progeny. Lynx added that when preparing to have a child, most sorcerers performed a complicated ritual that allowed them to determine its powers and gender instead of leaving it up to chance the messy mortal way.

"When I discovered Garrick had planned to abduct Victoria and force her to bond with him, I told Imelda and Merlock. My sister was furious he hadn't picked her, and Merlock panicked. Your family left that night, but I couldn't because it would cast suspicion on my sister."

"Garrick was furious and sought vengeance on the person who had caused him to lose Victoria," Kharon said.

"Eventually he gave into the titans' wishes and married my sister, who immediately told him I had helped Victoria escape. He banished me. So I came to Datten to find Merlock. King Daniel had taken the throne and welcomed me. I visited Victoria at her castle, spent time in Datten . . . Merlock and I were happy, and then eight years later, we had you, Megesti. Your father gifted you the powers of Merlin, and I gifted you my family's tradition of the Usurper."

Megesti crossed his arms and glared at his mother. "Why'd you leave?"

"When you were five, I learned my sister was pregnant after Victoria had a horrible premonition. She told us if I didn't return to the Forbidden Lands, the next Head would not only murder both our children but also burn the mortal world to the ground."

Everyone turned to Gryphon, who remained unusually stoic and silent. Lynx reached over and gripped his hand.

"Victoria explained that the only way to save everyone was for me to return home and ensure my nephew felt loved."

Gryphon spoke up, saying, "I'm descended from monsters, but a piece of Griffin's kindness transferred to me, and Birch has nurtured that since I was an infant."

"First while watching him and then in secret after Garrick discovered his kindness."

"How did he find out?" Alex asked.

"A butterfly," Gryphon said.

"A butterfly?" Aaron echoed.

"We call him 'butterfly' because he has a birthmark shaped like one on his—"

"Lynx!" Gryphon screamed at her and covered her mouth.

Kharon added, "Griffin says it's on his butt. Left cheek."

Aaron and Harold burst out laughing. Alex tried very hard to hold her composure but ended up snickering with Michael.

Gryphon grumbled under his breath and grimaced as he rubbed his shoulder.

"I met Birch through Imelda," Lynx explained. "She was too important to be Titan of Tiere, so as her strongest pupil, I received the title. Tiere and Celtics have always been close, so the day I met Birch, we became dear friends, and I became an older sister of sorts to our butterfly."

"Despite his arrogance," Birch said, "Gryphon is the kindest Ares you'll ever meet."

"My father forbade me from seeing Birch, but I disobeyed. She taught me I didn't have to be a monster if I didn't want to," Gryphon said.

Kharon added that many sorcerers had doubted the existence of this generation's Heart, and Gryphon recounted finding the other two pearls, the white one that showed the present and the black one that told the future. He had held the black one, and it had sparked his recurring dream of a beach and a sorceress with a face he couldn't forget.

Alex glanced at Aaron. His jaw clenched, and his back was rigid.

Maybe being honest with you right now wasn't the best idea.

He squeezed her thigh a little harder than usual.

Gryphon said, "I realized the legend of another Tabitha and Grindal was real and my Heart would be a sorceress. I spent years searching, and then one day, I heard a voice I had never heard before."

"You heard a voice?" Stefan asked, his tone skeptical.

"In his head," Kharon explained. "Mystics can read minds."

Gryphon sighed. "Yes. I can read everyone's minds, except my father's or, on occasion, Alex's. She either locks me out or shouts at me. Yes, Harold, it gets very loud, especially in the mortal world."

Startled, the Betruger king jerked in his seat as Gryphon returned to his story.

"This voice begged for help, so I answered and ended up on that beach, and the rest you know. The person asking for help was a beautiful sorceress, hidden from my father's cruelty among mortals."

"We only know Alex's side of the story," Aaron said. "Perhaps you'll enlighten us with your side."

Alex squirmed, and Gryphon glared at him.

"If you're kind, why were you so aggressive toward us?" Stefan asked.

"Especially since we all wanted the same thing—Alex back home safe," Aaron added.

Gryphon scratched his chin, giving away his nervousness. His eyes dashed from one person to the next before he looked at Alex, and then his eyes flashed blue. *Do we really have to have this conversation in front of everyone?* he asked.

She remained firm. *Yes.*

"What is happening right now?" Michael asked.

Lynx sighed. "Gryphon's being rude and having a conversation with Alex in his head."

"I thought he could only *read* minds," Stefan said.

"Does Alexandria have Mystics powers too?" Kharon asked.

"She does," Gryphon said, winking at her.

"I choose not to use them," Alex said. "You can answer in front of Aaron or not at all. I won't have secrets." She squeezed Aaron's hand.

Seemingly emboldened by her support, he snapped at Gryphon, "There have been enough secrets where you're concerned."

Gryphon pushed away from the table and turned to the books. "I was raised by a father who believed the Head should take what he wants and answer to no one." He picked a book off the shelf and flipped through it. "Part of me believed his way was easier—to become the monster everyone assumed I was. To stop playing the part . . . but then I met Alex. And it became obvious that being who my father wanted me to be would never work." Gryphon sighed, putting the book back. He turned to face the group and looked up at Alex. *Because if I became what he wanted me to be, I'd never be worthy of you.*

Alex's cheeks grew hot, and she avoided looking at Aaron.

"You seem to have a gift for bringing out hidden potential in those around you, Your Royal Highness," Harold said, lightening the mood.

Alex tried to hide her flushed face again.

"How do you fit in?" Aaron asked Kharon.

"I was Gryphon's teacher at school," the sorcerous explained. "While he never had much in the way of Hades powers, he tried hard, and I felt bad for him. I had studied with his father and knew how awful he was. So I helped Gryphon any way I could, though he is still a terrible Hades."

"Are the Head and the Heart together supposed to exhibit powers from all the houses?" Alex asked.

"They can manage a few or all of them. It depends on the particular Head," Birch said. "Why?"

"I can talk to the dead," Alex said.

Kharon's eyes grew larger. "Can you really?"

Alex nodded and sighed. "Prince Daniel, King Daniel, Emmerich, Merlock, King Johnathon, have you greeted our guest?"

"Oh my Hades!" Kharon was amazed. "You can *talk* to all these people."

"I've seen ghosts since I was nine, but I couldn't talk to any until I became twice Returned, and even now, I'm limited to talking to people I've met or who are in our families."

Kharon and Alex suddenly burst out laughing.

"What?" Aaron asked.

Alex covered her face and shook her head.

Kharon, however, wasn't shy about letting everyone in on the joke. "Your grandfather says your wife is the prettiest Queen of Datten in centuries. Your brother says to stop being jealous of Gryphon because it makes you look petty, and your father says your crown is on backward." Then Kharon turned to Birch and Megesti. "Merlock says hello." They smiled at

Birch, holding out a hand, then grabbed Megesti's hand before he could get away.

"This is what makes a Titan of Hades," Gryphon said.

As Kharon touched Birch and Megesti, their eyes grew wide. A few moments later, Kharon looked over at Aaron and held out their hands to him. He looked to Alex, and when she nodded, he reached across the table. As soon as he took Kharon's hand, Aaron gasped, and his mouth dropped open.

"You can see them now, can't you?" Alex asked, squeezing his leg.

Aaron nodded. Daniel and Emmerich stood there, grinning.

"Fix that crown," Emmerich said, and Alex adjusted it for him.

Harold and Macht stood. "We'll leave you all to your family."

Michael and Stefan rose too. Alex kissed Aaron on the cheek and headed out of the room so he could have a minute with his father and brother, a gift she couldn't give him. Lynx skipped behind her and looped her arm through Alex's. "Tell me more about these handsome knights of yours, Sir Macht and Sir Stefan specifically. There isn't any old history with you, is there?"

"Ew!" Alex replied. "Stefan's like my brother."

"Good," Lynx said. She bit her lip, eyeing him and grinning. "I don't like how he treats my butterfly, but he's pleasant to look at."

"Down, Lynx," Gryphon said, arriving behind them. "He wouldn't know what to do with you."

"You're no fun," Lynx retorted as she headed down the hall toward Stefan. She slapped his backside and cracked away, giggling.

He turned around, bright red, and Alex burst out laughing. "I think you have an admirer, Stefan."

"Ferflucs," Stefan grumbled, Michael laughing beside him.

You should warn him. Lynx tends to get what she wants. Gryphon's voice came into Alex's mind.

Absolutely not. I'm going to enjoy watching him squirm for a change. She smirked as Stefan rounded the corner.

I'm sorry if I embarrassed you. You can't say things in front of Aaron that he can't hear. I know you won't do anything, but he doesn't trust you, and I need to think of my husband and make sure he's comfortable with all this.

"I understand. If our roles were reversed, I wouldn't leave you alone with him for even a minute."

"You wouldn't trust me either?" Alex turned toward Gryphon but sucked in her breath. She hadn't realized how close they were standing. Gryphon took a step back.

"It's not that," Gryphon said. "It's the effect you have on us —Aaron and me, specifically. Harold wasn't far off with his jest." He looked down at the ground. Alex wasn't sure if it was to avoid looking at her or to hide something.

"What are we going to do about your father?" Alex whispered.

"I don't know yet," he said as they started walking down the hall toward his room in the west tower.

"Where will you all go?"

"We can't go home," Gryphon replied. "Lynx said my father burned down Birch's cottage and started going after sorcerers he thought would help me."

"So you're exiled?" Alex asked.

"Essentially." Gryphon rolled up his sleeve and rubbed the betrayer mark, which hadn't fully healed yet.

Alex sighed and was about to speak when Aaron spoke up behind them. "You're welcome to stay here. I owe you a great debt for saving my wife twice now. Or is it three times? Do we count helping you get away from Moorloc?" he asked Alex.

"We do," Alex whispered back as Aaron slid his arm around her hips.

"So," he continued, "you have saved the King and Princess of Warren once, the Princess of Datten, and now the Queen of Datten, and the entire Betruger kingdom. I'd say we owe you a great deal, Gryphon. You and your friends are all welcome to stay as long as you wish."

"Thank you. I'd save her again if it was required of me."

Alex watched Aaron scrutinize Gryphon. He looked like himself, but there was a darkness in his eyes. He clearly didn't trust the sorcerer and was only doing this for her and Megesti. *I hope we don't live to regret this.*

"You probably *will* have to save her again. Alex has quite a knack for getting herself into trouble." Aaron kissed the top of Alex's head. "If you'll excuse me, I have to go convince my mother to change several things that my father's apparently not happy about regarding his funeral."

"I could have told you about them," Alex said with a grin.

"You would have had to be awake to do that," Aaron teased.

Alex wrinkled her nose as Aaron disappeared into his mother's room.

Do you often get into trouble?

I don't mean to. Alex and Gryphon kept walking down the main hall. *Trouble seems to find me.*

"It's not your fault. It's the nature of who we are." Gryphon said. "Being as powerful as we are, the Head and Heart draw imbalances to them, at least until . . ."

Until what? Alex was afraid to ask out loud.

Until we find each other.

She felt slightly uncomfortable, but before she could say anything, Gryphon spoke aloud, saying, "You should rest." He pointed at her door.

"Gryphon—" Alex began.

"I'll have Birch make you something to help you sleep." He turned to leave.

Alex watched him go, confused, then crossed the threshold to her room as a painful cramp hit her. *"Ferflucs!"*

You all right? Gryphon's voice broke through her thoughts.

You knew, didn't you?

Tieres can sense these things.

Sense and smell them.

Birch will be there with your tea in a bit. It's going to smell horrible and taste worse, but it'll work. Get to bed.

Alex was settled in when Birch cracked in, carrying a mug. "This will help with the pain so you can sleep."

"How much sleep, precisely?" she asked as she took the potion.

"Just for tonight. It'll allow you to sleep deeply so you can heal yourself."

Alex sniffed it.

"I'm sure Gryphon warned you it will probably taste like dirt—"

Alex chugged the entire cup and slammed it down on her table. "Thank you."

Birch stared, looking surprised and impressed.

"I may be a queen now, but I grew up in the woods with boys."

"Now that is a story I'd love to hear, especially considering how much Gryphon told me about your exceptional Celtics powers."

"I don't know if he mentioned it, but Aaron and I invited you all to stay, if you wish. Though my mother's castle is available, if you prefer quiet."

"We appreciate your generosity. I'll remain in Datten. I

have fond memories here, and I want to be near Megesti while he adjusts."

"Have you spoken to him?"

"I'm trying to give him space to sort out his feelings. If he takes after Merlock, he'll need time."

"I'll talk to him for you," Alex said. Then the drink kicked in, and sleep overtook her.

CHAPTER 32
ALEX

Alex woke to a loud bang. Jumping up in bed, she found Edith picking up the bucket she'd dropped.

"I'm sorry, Alex. I didn't mean to wake you. Aaron insisted we let you sleep."

"What time is it?"

"Early afternoon," Edith said. "That older sorceress, Beach, said you needed to heal."

"It's Birch, like the tree. Where's Aaron?"

"He's with his advisors. They want to visit the southern lords and get their oaths before the coronation."

"Oh. I wonder how long that will take."

Edith shrugged. "Sorry, I don't understand Datten politics. Dress or sparring clothes?"

"Pants."

"Of course." Edith descended to the first floor and returned with Alex's clothes. As Alex dressed in her black pants and golden tunic, Edith made the bed.

"That trinket box is lovely, Alex. Is that what you found at the market?"

Alex looked back to see Edith examining the box. "It is. If you open the lid, it plays a song."

"What does it play?" She opened the lid.

"The woman who gave it to me couldn't say. Some strange song she didn't—" Alex stared at Edith, who was humming along with the tune. "*Edith*—do you know the song?"

"I've heard it but don't know where. Try asking my father. If I recognize it, there's a good chance that it's an old Warren song." Edith snapped the lid shut and put down the box. "What are we doing today?"

"I need to check on Megesti, and after that, Stefan will insist I get some training in. Could you ask him to meet me in the courtyard in an hour?"

"Of course."

Once in the hallway, they went their separate ways. Alex climbed the steps of the west tower to the third floor and entered the sorcerer's lab without knocking.

Megesti looked up from his book. "Hello, cousin. Is this a social call, or do you need the lab?"

"Social."

"Ah." He tapped the book, and it flipped shut on the table. "So you and Aaron are ganging up on me now?"

"I don't understand," Alex said as she took the stool beside him.

Megesti frowned. "You're here to talk to me about Birch, correct?"

"Yes."

"Aaron did the same thing this morning."

"That shouldn't surprise you," Alex said. "We both love you, Megesti. But I just woke up, and he's in a meeting, so I didn't know."

"How are *you* doing?" Megesti asked.

Alex tugged on her shirt hem. "Trying to change the subject?"

"No. I just love you too."

Alex smiled. "I'll be fine . . . in time. You?"

"It's weird. I've lived my entire life thinking my mother was a mortal who died. I have no memories of Birch, and part of me is furious my father never told me about her."

Alex leaned against her cousin.

He smiled weakly. "So many of us have lost parents. I should be excited to have her back."

"Megesti," Alex said. "You're allowed to feel whatever you're feeling right now. We all heal in our own ways."

He leaned closer. "That goes for you too. All of it— Betruger, the trauma from what Moorloc put you through, Gryphon's arrival, and the baby."

Megesti fell silent as Alex wiped her tears. His saying it out loud reminded her of how much she'd been through. His kind words broke her dam, and she poured out her heart to him. They talked until the bells chimed, and Alex sucked in her breath.

"Training?" Megesti asked with a smile.

"If Stefan lets me." Alex sighed. "I need something to be the same." She slid off the stool and walked toward the door.

"Good luck," Megesti called out.

ALEX'S LEGS shook as she balanced on one foot on the log over the moat, and her arms wobbled as she held a staff. Stefan and Michael stood on either side, critiquing her.

She cut into their remarks, saying, "Why am I doing this? I feel ridiculous."

"You insisted on training after I said no, so it was this or nothing," Stefan said.

Alex huffed. "Why are running and sparring off the table?"

Stefan and Michael looked at each other with pursed lips and avoided her gaze. "You know why," Stefan finally said.

Enough. Alex threw away the staff and swung her arms up, sending moat water to soak Stefan and Michael. While she was laughing at them, she slipped and fell forward, slamming onto the log. The force knocked the wind out of her. Pain flooded her abdomen, and she whimpered.

"Alex!" Michael rushed forward, but Alex cracked herself away.

Why is everything so exhausting?

Michael spun until he found her again. "Are you all right? We should probably—"

"Catch your tongues." Alex pointed at her pseudo brothers. "You do not get to decide what is enough for me, understood? I am more than capable of knowing my limits. If you keep trying to protect me like I'm made of glass, I'll—I'll . . . I'll put snakes in your beds!"

Michael snorted.

Stefan heaved a sigh. "You haven't done *that* since you were thirteen."

"Treat me like a child, and I'll act like one," Alex said.

"We're sorry," Michael said. "Jessica warned us not to treat you differently, to watch for signs we pushed too hard. But we ignored her."

"We know you," said Stefan. "You don't cry for mercy, and you don't show weakness or pain. We didn't want to put you in that situation."

"I understand, but you can't force me to heal. I need to feel normal, and being treated like this doesn't help. Next time, ask me what I need. Or else."

"More threats? When did you get so vicious?" Stefan teased.

Alex looked up at him. "When I had to in order to survive. Now go inside and get changed for dinner. I'm going to check on Snow, and then I'll be right in."

She walked through the courtyard to the stable and strolled down the stalls, checking the horses. When she reached Snow, she smiled.

"Hey, boy." She gently stroked his head and thought of Flash. *Another innocent life I couldn't protect.*

"What is it with you and horses?"

"Gryphon?" Alex looked around the stable but didn't see him.

Look up, princess.

Alex heard laughter. She crossed her arms and turned around. Gryphon was up in the rafters, leaning on the stable wall.

She shook her head and went back to Snow.

"I thought your horse was black," Gryphon said. He dropped down beside her and petted the horse beside Snow.

"Flash was. He died in the first attack."

"The pier wasn't the first?"

"No." Alex told Gryphon how she and Stefan had been attacked on the road.

"That explains Ember's rage." He looked at her, but she didn't look back. "Did they hurt you?"

Alex nodded. Her magic rushed around her as Gryphon growled, clenching his hands and setting his jaw.

"Gryphon—" She put her hand on his shoulder, and he flinched and drew in a quick breath. "What was that?"

"Nothing."

When Alex grabbed his hand to stop him from leaving, he cried out.

"What's wrong with your arm?" She pushed up his sleeve. "Your betrayer's mark shouldn't hurt anymore. What's this dark red line?"

"That's from when I gave you some of my power. Megesti and Birch have it too. It'll fade in time."

"Does it hurt? Where does it go? Let me see." She tugged on Gryphon's shirt.

"No."

"Gryphon, I'm a Cassandra. I'm not asking." But she released his shirt.

"You're drained. You don't need to help me with a minor ache."

Alex stepped in front of him and frowned. "Shirt off."

"You're a bossy queen."

She didn't move, and Gryphon grunted as he lifted his shirt over his head. Alex gasped and covered her mouth.

"It looks worse than it is."

"Liar." She carefully examined him. His shoulder had a sprawling burn shaped like a hand. *That looks as bad as the one I got at Moorloc's castle, which means it hurts immensely.* His entire left side was a giant bruise of black, purple, and blue. "May I?" she asked.

Gryphon nodded. He lifted his arm and winced as she ran her fingers over the bruise, gently pushing on it. He tensed and sucked in a breath.

"Your ribs are cracked. What happened to you?" Alex asked. She rubbed her hands together to warm them.

"I wouldn't tell them," Gryphon answered without looking at her.

"Tell who what?"

Alex placed her hands on his side, and a trickle of magic flowed down her arms, making her hands glow gold. Slowly the golden light moved into Gryphon, and he stiffened as it spread.

"I wouldn't tell my parents or hexa about you. About your friends or your weaknesses. They tried various methods to get the information out of me but failed. Everything my father learned, he took by force from my mind." Gryphon inhaled deeply.

Alex's hands kept glowing, and the bruise faded. His breathing slowed, so she shifted her left hand to his shoulder.

"Alex, stop," he said. "You're too weak to do this."

"Catch your tongue, Sunset."

He twisted around and grabbed her hands, but the golden light didn't stop. Once it had healed his ribs and shoulder, it flowed down his arms and wrists before returning to her.

Alex smiled as his bruises completely vanished. *I helped someone. Maybe I'm not useless.*

"The last thing you'll ever be is useless," Gryphon whispered.

As soon as Gryphon let go of her, she saw spots and stumbled.

"Alex?"

Gryphon grabbed her waist to steady her. Alex closed her eyes, leaning against his chest as she waited for the dizziness to pass. She smelled burning wood—Gryphon's scent.

"What in the Forbidden Lands is going on here?"

Oh no. Aaron!

CHAPTER 33
ALEX

lex turned. Aaron was standing at the entrance to the stable. *Don't look guilty. You did nothing wrong. You healed a friend and got dizzy.*

Gryphon stepped back from her. "I had an injury from the fight. Alex demanded to heal it, even though I told her not to. You know how stubborn she is."

"I'm not stubborn," Alex said, and the sorcerer snorted.

"She used too much magic and stumbled, so I caught her. If you prefer, *kingling*, I'll let her fall next time." Gryphon leaned against the horse stall behind him with a shrug.

Aaron shifted his stance to the one he used whenever he'd spar with Jerome, all his force and strength on display. Alex gulped and stepped backward. She heard Gryphon in her head.

Did you flinch from the princeling? Are you afraid of him?

Gryphon's eyes shot toward her for an instant before they returned to Aaron. Aaron's mouth turned into a scowl. The tension between them crackled. Gryphon stared at him, challenging Aaron with a raised eyebrow.

Please don't start anything, Alex pleaded. *I'm not frightened of him. I'm scared of what he'll do. He already hates you, and I don't need you adding fuel to that fire.*

That fire is already raging, princess. Nothing I do will change it. I can feel his hatred from here.

Alex sighed and walked toward Aaron, keeping her gaze set on him. But within a few steps, her dizziness returned, and she staggered.

Aaron was there in an instant. As soon as she was in his arms, Alex felt his anger.

Told you, princess.

"You should crack less," Aaron teased as she embraced him.

Aaron's fury dissipated as she held him, and she realized her hands were glowing gold. She smiled at him, and the playful sparkle in his eyes returned.

"I'm sorry," she whispered.

"We'll talk later." He looked at Gryphon. "What will help her recover?"

"Food and more sleep."

"That's perfect then." Aaron spoke to her softly, saying, "I ran into Stefan and Michael as they came in. I sent them to tell the kitchen to make all your favorites from the camp."

"Rabbit stew with bread and cheese?"

"And lots of chocolate. Edith can't get enough of it, and Harold insisted. I was hoping you'd feel up to eating with us. I had a smaller table set up in the throne room so it would only be people you're comfortable around."

Alex kissed Aaron. "I'd love that."

His good humor faded as he addressed Gryphon. "Will you be joining us?"

"No. I have things to take care of."

What things?

Nothing. I just think if you and I are together any longer, your king might combust. Birch will know a place to eat.

Aaron took her hand, and they headed to the throne room for their dinner. The two of them sat in the open space at the table, with their friends around them.

Two pots of rabbit stew sat steaming in the middle of the table, one with carrots and one without. Four baskets overflowed with various kinds of bread, and two platters of cheese rested on opposite sides of the table. Everyone's mugs were filled with the finest ale Datten offered, and full pitchers were within easy reach on a smaller side table. Somehow the platter of chocolates ended up in front of Edith before the meal had even begun.

After they discussed the day and the plans for the upcoming visit to the southern lords, the conversation moved to the topic of the recent attacks.

"Isn't there anything that can be used against sorcerers?" Edith asked.

"Red steel is poisonous to us," Alex said.

"If only we could get enough to make swords," Aaron said, finishing another mug of ale. He'd already downed significantly more than he usually drank.

Alex smiled at Harold. When they gifted Aaron his coronation gift in a few days, he'd finally be able to protect her.

"What if we asked Gryphon to stay and teach you to use your powers?" Jessica asked.

"If he's staying in Datten, he may as well be useful," Stefan said.

Alex tensed, afraid of what Aaron's reaction would be.

"I'm considering it," Aaron snapped.

"Don't you mean you *and* your queen are considering it?" Harold said with an edge in his voice.

"Of course." Aaron turned to Alex and smiled, but the brightness didn't reach his eyes. He glanced at her plate. "Have some more bread. Michael told the kitchen your favorites."

"Sunflower or buckwheat?" Michael asked, holding up the two baskets.

"Even I know the answer to that." Megesti laughed and pointed at the sunflower loaf.

"He's not wrong." Alex grabbed another two slices and dipped one into her stew.

"Why does mine not have carrots?" Edith asked, looking from her bowl to Harold's.

Jessica snickered. "Aaron doesn't *eat* carrots. Never has."

"You don't eat carrots?" Harold asked.

"He says they're horse food," Alex explained. She scooped all the carrots she could onto her spoon and stared at Aaron as she stuffed it into her mouth.

"You'll need to wash out your mouth with ale if you expect to kiss me tonight," Aaron said, refilling her mug and his own.

Whether I kiss you depends on which Aaron shows up tonight.

The group discussed ideas for keeping sorcerers away, and soon, having eaten two large bowls of rabbit stew, Alex was full and sleepy. She gently ran her hand along Aaron's thigh. "I'm ready for bed, but you can stay if you want. Stefan can escort me back to our room."

"No, I'll take you." Aaron stood and slipped his hand into hers. They wished their friends a good night and headed to the door.

They walked in silence. Alex sighed as they entered their bedroom. *Are you still upset about the stable, or is it what we learned?*

Shutting the door, Aaron strode to her. "How are you really?" He gently cupped her cheek, and Alex reached for him.

"I'm sad and weak. I tried so hard to remind myself I'd lose the baby, but part of me hoped I wouldn't, and now I still feel drained from saving the Betruger people."

"How does this keep happening? What can we do to protect you?" Aaron asked.

"Jessica and Stefan were right at dinner. Gryphon's been a big help. I think we have to seriously consider asking him to tutor me." The hairs on Alex's neck stood up as the same tension she'd felt in the stable filled their room. Aaron dropped his hand. His eyes were focused on her, somehow seeming darker.

"He touched you again, didn't he?"

"Aaron, he saved me. And without him, the Betruger people would be gone."

"You didn't answer my question." Aaron's icy stare remained intent.

Alex frowned. "Of course he touched me. How else was he supposed to help me?" She made to push past him, but Aaron grabbed her and jerked her back.

"Aaron, you're hurting me. Let go."

"Where?"

"My arm. Where do you think?"

He stepped toward her, backing her up to the wall. "*Where* did he touch you?" The scowl that crossed his lips wasn't like him at all.

"Why does that matter?"

What is wrong with you? You reek of ale, and you're scaring me. When did you become so controlling?

"It matters because you're *mine*. I gave you my terms. Don't be alone with him."

"Aaron—" Alex pushed against his chest, but he slammed his hands against the wall, caging her with his arms.

"Where?" He almost shouted the question.

She gulped. "My back and waist." *Is this your Datten temper coming out or stress from your grief? You've never raised your voice at me.*

319

Aaron slowly looked down her body, an uncanny reminder of how Wesley had looked at her, and it made her stomach churn. She turned away, waiting for him to stop, but she felt him staring, so she returned his gaze. His pupils were huge, the ring of deep blue around them barely visible.

What is happening to you?

"Aaron . . ." She said his name like a plea.

Without breaking his stare, he grabbed her tunic with one hand. He yanked it up and grabbed her waist, hard enough to make her flinch.

"Here?" he asked.

"You're hurting me. Let go." Panic rushed through her, and her arms trembled. Aaron shoved her against the wall again, and she cried out in pain and fear at his forceful touch.

He leaned down so close she smelled the ale on his breath as he growled, "You're welcome to try to make me."

You're drunk. That must be it. If this is what you're like drunk, you're never drinking again.

Alex redoubled her efforts to shove him away, but he was too close and too strong.

"Aaron, don't make me hurt you!" she snapped.

He laughed in her face. "Are you going to hit me? I'm not scared of you or your magic."

Alex swallowed back the threat of her stomach bringing up dinner. There was no love or kindness in his face, only rage. Exhaling, Alex reached for her magic and flattened her hands against Aaron's chest. It didn't take much of her wind power to get him off her. She dashed toward the bookcase that held the secret door to the queen's suite, but Aaron was too fast.

He grabbed her hand and wrenched her back toward him. Pain ripped through her shoulder as it twisted too far. She shrieked, but Aaron ignored it and threw her onto their bed. Before she could even think, he straddled her and pinned her down, the way he had when she'd visited him in his bedroom while they were secretly courting. But this was anything but fun.

"Is that where he touched you?" Aaron's face was feral. The only time Alex had ever seen so much hatred was on her grandfather's face when he killed her mother. "Or was it further down?"

"Aaron! Stop!" Alex screamed, surprised by her own sudden tears.

His weight shifted, and he clamped both of her wrists together in one hand. He held them so tightly her fingers tingled with numbness. Then he shoved up her tunic, twisting her so hard it would leave bruises. He searched every inch of her body.

"What do you think you're going to find? He doesn't leave a mark when he touches me." Alex immediately realized she'd said the wrong thing.

Aaron smirked at her. "Then I'll leave marks so it's clear who you belong to."

She tried to push away from him, but his legs were too strong, and he kept her locked beneath him.

"Aaron, let me up now. I order you!" Alex screamed at him, but Aaron laughed.

"You don't order me around, witch."

He grabbed her tunic again and yanked it. Pain shot up her back as the fabric raked across her scars before it ripped at the front where Aaron clutched it.

"You know how he looks at you. All the *ferflucsing* time, he's watching you. You love it, don't you? Love to tease him, have him watch you—want you. He wants you so badly, but you're mine, and it's time *you* remembered that."

Alex stiffened. "How drunk are you? I'd never be unfaithful to you. You are the one I want." Her voice faded to a whisper.

Aaron leaned down and narrowed his dark eyes. "What about at the castle, princess? You let him touch more than your waist there."

I tell you the truth, and you throw it back in my face? Anger and hurt replaced her fear. She ripped her hand free and struck Aaron in the face as hard as she could. He loosened his grip, and she shoved him off and ran for the door.

"Alex? When did we get to our bedroom?"

Hearing his question, Alex froze at the door, her heart pounding, her whole body shaking like a leaf. She turned around to see Aaron climbing off the bed, rubbing his face with both hands. His nose was bleeding, but when he looked up at her, Alex saw that his eyes were sky blue again. Her throat went bone-dry.

"What happened to you? Why is your shirt ripped? Are those bruises?" Aaron hurried toward her.

Alex looked down at the red hand-shaped marks already forming on her arms. "Stay away from me."

"What happened? Why does my head hurt?" His voice was gentle, but it didn't matter.

"I don't have time for this act. Go visit the southern lords. We'll talk once you return, but if you *ever* touch me like that again, I'll let Stefan loose on you before I take care of you myself."

"Alex, wait!"

Struggling to slow her pounding heart, Alex threw open the door and ran from their suite. Fighting back tears, she had only made it to the corner when she almost ran into Jessica and Edith.

"Alex, what are you doing out here? We thought you went to bed," Jessica said.

When Edith asked what was wrong, Alex said, "Nothing.

I'm fine." She glanced back at the door of her suite. She tried to push past her ladies to get away, but they blocked her.

"Where did these bruises come from?" Jessica asked.

"You're shaking," Edith said.

"I said I'm *fine*," Alex snapped as a door slammed behind her.

"Alex, wait," Aaron called.

She pushed Edith out of the way and ran down the long hallway, unable to control her tears, and slammed into Jerome.

"Your Royal Highness?" he asked.

"Alex!" Aaron rounded the corner, and Alex tensed.

Jerome touched her shoulder, and Alex flinched from the pain and wordlessly pleaded with him. He frowned as Aaron hurried over.

"Stefan, take her," Jerome said.

Stefan was standing behind Jerome, and the look on his face confirmed he understood the situation. He didn't hide the fury in his glare, but he obeyed and led her away.

"Your Royal Highness, there you are," said Jerome, sounding farther and farther away. "I was coming to find you. We need to decide the order in which you will visit the southern lords."

Alex closed her eyes and tried to slow her breathing as she pushed past Stefan and hurried down the hallway and out of the castle. Silent, Stefan followed close behind. Alex strode with purpose, barely able to breathe, until they arrived at the stables. Inside, she put her head against Snow's, then Thunder's, and let her heart calm down.

"Are we going to talk about it?" Stefan asked.

"Not here."

"Then take us somewhere we can." Stefan held out his hand. Alex took it and cracked them to the strange alcove with the five wooden doors in the bowels of Warren's castle.

"Do you want me to come with you or wait outside for a minute?" Stefan had the same loving smile he always used with her when she was sad.

Alex squeezed his hand. "I need you with me. To scare the monsters away." She led them to the middle door, touched the handle, and pushed the door open.

Before them was a giant room with a long dirt path. It was nearly identical to the older room a few doors down, except this one didn't smell stale. The first third of the path was lined on both sides with white marble statues. Behind each one was a stone tomb containing one of Alex's ancestors. These were the most recent kings and queens, and she suspected they were the ghosts she saw the most.

She dropped Stefan's hand and crept inside the ice-cold room. The moment her foot hit the path, torches sprang to life, illuminating crypts, and she forced herself down the path. When she spotted her mother's statue, she stopped to catch her breath and calm her racing heart. The statue stared down at her. It was eerie to look at a face so nearly identical to her own. When she touched it, she felt tears spring to her eyes.

"So much death to protect me," she said. Stefan rubbed her back, and Alex sighed. To her mother's left was a statue of her father. *Already prepared for the inevitable.* The two statues' hands were entwined. Alex backed away to get a better view and bumped into the statue belonging to the crypt behind her. When she turned, her shriek pierced the darkness.

Her grandfather's statue was as intimidating as the man himself. She stared into the carved face of the man who, even in death, tormented her. While he hadn't visited her in months, he still stalked her dreams, and she could feel his eyes boring into her soul. She quivered with fear until Stefan's arms wrapped around her, and she knew deep in her core she was safe. But even with that reassurance, she had to bite her lip to stop the trembling.

Stefan gently led her away from Arthur back to her mother. Standing before a statue that looked so much like her in a crypt was unnerving, but Alex needed to confess. She wanted to leave everything bothering her buried in the bowels of her home. Stefan started to pull away, but Alex kept him with her. As he strengthened his grip, she closed her eyes and focused on the pressure of his embrace. Despite everything, she wasn't alone.

Tears streamed down her face as she stood in the dark looking at her mother's statue. Behind it lay the body of the woman who had brought her into the world and given up everything to protect her. Alex began to whisper.

Stefan didn't move or make a sound while she poured out everything broken inside of her to that statue. All her trauma from her time with Moorloc, the pain she'd confessed to the generals, the attack on her and Emmerich, her regrets and fears and dreams. Then she told her mother and Stefan how much Aaron had changed and how it scared her. When she told them what had just happened in their bedroom and how he hurt her, she felt Stefan's fingers tense, but his grip on her stayed gentle.

When she finished, the only thing keeping her standing was Stefan. Alex brushed Stefan's sleeve, and she realized she'd soaked it in tears. He loosened his hold on her, allowing her to turn around. She closed her eyes and nuzzled into his chest, content to be engulfed in his arms.

"Feel better?" Stefan whispered.

"I feel lighter," Alex said.

"Kruft and Moorloc are lucky they're dead, or I'd rip them apart."

"Aaron said something similar."

"I'm ready to rip *him* apart after today."

"I don't know what's wrong with him or what I did to make him act like that."

"You are not responsible for his behavior. Only he is."

"I know, but I can't help it."

Stefan grabbed her shoulders. "You are *not* responsible. Never say that again. If he ever lays another hand on you, I will personally make him pay for every time he hurt you, even if gets me thrown in the dungeon."

Alex stared up at Stefan.

"Maybe Megesti, Harold, or my father knows something about why he's acting this way. I'll ask them," he said.

"Thank you."

Stefan kissed the top of her head. "You need sleep, so we're staying in Warren tonight. It's better if you and Aaron have a night apart to calm down, think things through, and—"

"Sober up."

"Exactly. Tomorrow, we'll head back to Datten, and you can consider your options."

CHAPTER 34

ALEX

Alex jerked awake in the King of Datten's suite. Aaron's side of the bed was as cold and empty as it had been for the past two nights. She stood and straightened the bed. It would spare the maids from having to air her out and remake the bed. Visions of her nightmare from her time at Moorloc's lingered in her mind. Randal's and Jerome's suggestions had stopped working ever since the missing memories had returned.

Maybe I should ask Birch for help. I hope Aaron isn't taking longer than necessary with the southern lords because of what happened with us. I need him home so we can talk. If we can't work through this, I'm not sure what I'm going to do.

She threw open her wardrobe. She'd finally received her Datten dresses. She chose a red gown, appreciating that it fit loosely and let her move around freely, and she hoped the style would help her fit in more.

Alex went in search of someone who'd have news about Aaron. Sir Avery Reinhart, head of the archers, and his son Caleb, who'd been promoted to member of the king's guard, had both stayed in Datten. The king's guard was responsible not only for the king but also for any future royal children. Since Jerome, Michael, Harold, and Macht had accompanied the delegation to the southern lords, Caleb was left to help Stefan keep an eye on Alex.

"Good morning, Your Royal Highness," he said.

"Any word from Aaron?"

"Nothing since yesterday. I can bring you the update when it arrives today."

"Thank you, Caleb. I'd appreciate that."

It was too early to visit Jessica or Edith, so she went to the library. When she got there, it took her a moment to comprehend what she saw. The room was in shambles. Someone had removed her books from the shelves and strewn them around. This was supposed to be her home. Her heart pounded, and her hands grew slick. The last time she'd seen a library in such disarray was after Moorloc had taken the books from her mother's lab. The hairs on the back of her neck tingled. She gulped and slid her foot back through the doorway, prepared to run.

"I wasn't expecting company."

Gryphon was leaning on the ladder in the corner. He jumped off the last rung and landed gracefully on his feet.

Alex sighed. "Sorry. I'm not sleeping well."

His eyes darted to the bruises on her forearm as he approached her. "I see why. Has Aaron ever actually protected you?"

"Gryphon!" Alex grabbed a book from the floor and smacked him on the arm.

"It's a fair question," he snapped. "He can't stop sorcerers, couldn't stop Kruft, leaves you when you quarrel, and now he's *rough* with you?" Gryphon leaned so close to Alex she could hear him breathe.

"He was drunk."

"That doesn't excuse it."

"What happens between Aaron and me isn't your concern."

Gryphon locked eyes with her. "It is when he hurts you."

Alex stepped back. "We're done discussing this." She glanced around the room. "What are you doing? I don't like people reorganizing my library."

"*Your* library!" Gryphon laughed.

"Yes, *my* library. Or did I sleep so long that someone else became Queen of Datten?"

The sorcerer shook his head. "No, Your Royal Highness, you're still queen. How's your control coming along?"

"I'm getting there." Alex twisted her wrist in the air and sent every book flying back to its place on the bookshelves.

"No!" Gryphon exclaimed. "I've been at this all day."

"It's barely breakfast. How have you been at this all day?"

"If it's already breakfast again, I've been at it for more than a day."

"What are you looking for?" Alex put the last book back in its spot.

"Spell books."

Alex groaned.

"Sorry. I forget how frustrating it is being kept in the dark," Gryphon said. "There's been a shift in our powers. Something is happening in the Forbidden Lands. I don't know if my father is killing the sorcerers or if someone powerful was hurt. But something bad is rumbling. I can't go back to our library, and Birch lost her family's books when my parents burned down her home. I'm looking for a protection spell we can try."

"A protection spell?"

"Something to stop unwelcome sorcerers from cracking into your homes . . . of which you have an awful lot."

"And you're looking here?"

"This *is* the library."

"But it's the Datten library," Alex said.

Gryphon stared at her.

"We don't keep spell books in libraries."

"Then where would I find Merlock's books?"

"In his—or rather, Megesti's lab."

"Why didn't Aaron say that when I asked where the books were?"

"You asked the king for *books*. The books are here, but magic books are in our labs."

"Would you show me to the lab?" Gryphon asked. He shook his head as they left the room. "Aaron did that on purpose, didn't he?"

Alex laughed. "Probably."

Megesti's lab was dark and quiet. Gryphon flicked a finger, igniting the torches. He examined the lab with an unimpressed expression on his face.

"What?"

"It's so small."

"It was just Merlock and Megesti," Alex said.

"I know, but a son of Merlin deserved more."

Alex sighed as she looked around. *He was another victim.*

"Victim of what?"

Alex snapped toward him, furious. "Don't read my mind."

"Then don't yell thoughts at me."

She relaxed a little, telling herself that his voice sounded sincere. Gryphon marched toward the books on the shelf and perused them.

"You can help if you want." Gryphon held out a book to her.

Alex glanced back at the open lab door. *If the door's open, we're not technically alone.* She took the book and flipped

330

through it. Together, they looked through every book on the shelves.

Gryphon slammed down the last book, frustrated. "Where is that spell?"

"What makes you so sure he even has one?" Alex asked, putting the books back.

"This castle is protected, compared to Warren. I can feel it. It's not as powerful as we need, but it's something. I hoped if we found the spell, I could strengthen it." Defeated, he plopped down at the table.

"But Merlock didn't protect the castle. My mother did."

Gryphon looked hopeful. "You don't have her journals, do you?"

Alex playfully grinned. "I can do better than that." She walked to the shelf and grabbed a small red vial. Then she turned around and held out her hand to Gryphon. "I just have to tell Edith where we're going."

ALEX CRACKED them into the main hall of Verlassen Castle. Sunlight shone into the hall, and she felt at home.

"I feel like I'm being watched," Gryphon said.

"That's because you are," Alex said, making him start and look around.

Two knights came into the room from the courtyard, where they'd been watching.

"Good morning, Sir Colten. Sir Christian, how's your shoulder doing?" Alex asked.

"Healing well, princess. Thank you for asking," he replied.

"Do we address you as *princess* or *queen* now?" Sir Colten asked.

"According to my father, my title of crown princess takes

priority when I'm in Warren. Please let Julius know I'm here. We'll be in the lab."

The knights bowed and left the room to continue their duties.

"So they're watching me?" Gryphon asked.

Alex turned to him, amused. "This was my home and Aaron's. Every knight, guard, and servant will watch you like a hawk, and there's also my mother. She visits me more here than anywhere else."

Gryphon chuckled uncomfortably as Alex turned and picked up a torch from the collection that now filled the wall beside the entrance to the basement. After she'd ripped the painting from that wall during her vortex a year ago, she'd decided not to replace it.

"Could we go, please? She's looking at me."

"Who?" Alex asked, smirking.

"Your mother," he whispered as he took the torch and shook the wood to light it.

"I told you."

"Does she watch Aaron like this?"

Alex laughed. "Of course not. She loves him."

"Even lately?" Gryphon pointed to the bruise on her arm.

Alex's smile became a scowl. She grabbed the lit torch from Gryphon and stomped through the opening. Neither said a word as they descended the giant staircase leading deep into the pit of the castle. When Alex reached the bottom, Gryphon lit a pair of floating spheres of fire. The spheres meandered in front of them to light their way as they headed down the path toward the ancient wooden door. Alex took out the vial from Megesti's lab and used her teeth to remove the cork. As she poured the blood on the ground, they heard a soft click.

"What are you doing?" Gryphon asked.

Alex ignored him and grabbed a dagger from the wall

beside the door. When she slit her palm open, Gryphon lunged at her.

"Merlin's beard! What are you doing?" he asked.

Alex, deadpan, stared at him as she squeezed her hand into a fist and let the blood drip on the floor. A second click echoed around them. She opened the door and motioned for Gryphon to go in first. He set the torches alight as they walked down the narrow hall to the room. Their hands brushed, and Alex shuddered.

When they entered the lab, she sighed happily at the wall of books in front of them.

"So what is this?" Gryphon asked, looking dubious.

"The books of Merlin, Cassandra, and every sorcerer in my lineage."

Gryphon's jaw dropped. "The lost books of Merlin and Cassandra," he whispered as he walked toward the bookshelf. Alex set down the vial she'd brought on the table and healed her palm.

Gryphon's fingers touched a damaged part of the shelf, and he turned back to Alex. "Moorloc?" he asked.

Alex nodded and joined him at the books. "Cassandra's line is on the left, Merlin's on the right. The rest are on the bottom shelf."

"All right, daughter of Cassandra. Shall we make a wager as to who finds a spell first?"

"Yes. If I win, you wear a Datten tunic for a month."

"And if I win?" Gryphon stepped toward her, and Alex swallowed.

"What do you want?"

Gryphon stood close enough to her that her heart skipped a beat, and she could feel her magic stirring deep inside her. He took a long look at the bruise on her arm.

"If I win, I teach you again."

"Deal." Alex grabbed the first book off the shelf and sat down at the table. She realized the dim light would make reading difficult, but before she could say anything, Gryphon clapped his hands over his head. The small orbs of fire were replaced by a large orb of bright light that floated above them.

"I told you not to read my mind," Alex scolded.

"Then stop me," Gryphon teased, sitting down.

They opened their spell books. Gryphon wound up with a blank one, and Alex chuckled. He held it out to her and asked her to tell it to work for him, explaining that if she told the books she needed his help, he'd see the words.

"Your books have even more protection on them than my father's. Makes me wonder what exactly we're going to find."

CHAPTER 35
ALEX

Hours passed as Gryphon and Alex researched. The books of Merlin and Cassandra held vastly different spells, and they had to check all the books for protection spells. On top of that, they would eventually need to test each one to see which held up the best. At some point, Sir Colten brought them food. Alex thanked him without looking up, and only after the knight left did she realize they had read almost every book in her line.

"Have we been down here all day?" Alex asked, looking at the tray of bread and smoked fish.

"You have an impressive number of books, princess."

"You played a big part in helping me get them back."

Gryphon grinned and shrugged. "You should send word to your princeling. He's likely to throw a temper tantrum if he arrives home and you aren't there to greet him."

Alex glared and stuck her tongue at him, but she knew he was right. She wrote Aaron a note and asked Gryphon to crack it to Stefan.

"How many spells have we found so far?"

"Five," Alex said, counting the books. "And we still have to finish my mother's and grandfather's books."

"Some of these dates don't line up. I think you're missing a few."

Alex walked to Gryphon's side. There were gaps. In a few places, a decade was missing, and in one case, almost thirty years were absent.

"They must be lost. With all the traveling these books have done, I wouldn't be surprised," she said.

"We still haven't found your mother's spell. I want to see how the other protection spells compare to hers. The one protecting Datten is excellent."

"She says thank you." Alex grinned at Gryphon, but he was looking at her mother. "And no, she doesn't remember what book the spell is in."

"I heard her. I wish her face would agree with her words."

"Give her time. She'll leave eventually. Daniel did."

"She's here because of who my father is, isn't she?" he asked, and Alex pushed a new book into his hands.

"Yes."

"I'm not my father's son," Gryphon said out loud. "You have Birch to thank for that."

"Yes, Mother. Birch thinks he's trustworthy." Alex chuckled and shook her head.

"What now?" he asked, looking around.

"She left. Apparently, all we needed was for Birch to vouch for you."

"They were best friends," Gryphon said. "Are you all right? You look upset."

"I'm fine." Alex shrugged, but even she didn't believe that.

He stopped playing with the books and watched her as she sat down. "We could talk about it, like friends."

"It's stupid. I'm jealous of Megesti. He spent all these years thinking he lost his mother, and now here she is. It's terrible she had to leave him, and I understand he's conflicted, but he got her back. I'd give anything to be able to hold my mother. Especially now." She spun the book before her. "I don't know why Aaron's acting the way he is or what to do about it. Is it a mortal thing, a male thing, a Datten thing, or . . . is it me?"

Gryphon reached across the table and grabbed Alex's hands. "We'll come back to the princeling. But hear this— Aaron's issues are not *your* fault."

Alex swallowed and sniffled.

"You're allowed to feel sad or jealous about Megesti getting his mother back, and that doesn't lessen your loss. You have the queen and now Birch. Both were your mother's dear friends and can offer you motherly advice. I know it isn't the same, but you had a loving mother who sacrificed herself to protect you. You could've had *my* mother—a calculating, conniving, horrible witch."

"Gryphon, I have to talk to you about her. There's something I haven't even had the time to tell Aaron yet."

"I thought you two were done with secrets." He smirked, but when Alex bit her lip and trembled, he dropped it.

Alex told him about the night Emmerich died and how Gryphon's mother had attacked them. Then she told him how Emmerich had stabbed Imelda with red steel.

"You have red steel?" Gryphon asked.

Alex removed her dagger from her belt and set it on the table. "My grandfather had it first. I don't know how he got it, but I remember the sword he used to kill my mother. It had the same red blade, and I always thought that was so peculiar, but it explains why that blade still haunts my dreams to this day."

Gryphon looked horrified. "You can't carry that around. Didn't your uncles teach you what it can do to us? We destroyed all of ours centuries ago so we could never use it again."

"I know it can kill us. What else can it do?"

"A single prick will weaken you for a year or more. A cut, for decades. A deep wound is a death sentence. There was only ever one way to heal an injury from red steel, and we can't use it anymore."

"Why not?"

Gryphon grabbed one of the Cassandra books from a pile and flipped through the pages before handing it to Alex. "It requires a plant we can't get."

"It's extinct?" she asked, confused.

"Oh, it exists, but it only grows in the mortal underworld. It's called dragon's tear. It's a bush that looks like a bleeding heart but with flowers of sapphire blue."

"Why can't you get it?" Alex asked.

"Only mortals may enter the underworld. Any sorcerer who does can never leave," he explained.

"And mortals can? It's the underworld, Gryphon. They can't just leave when they've had enough."

"If a mortal enters while alive, has selfless intentions, and is pure of heart, they can."

"So what's the issue?"

Gryphon chuckled as he stood. "You say that as if *all* sorcerers have an army of mortals who would die for them in a heartbeat."

"What will happen to your mother?"

"She'll die," he said matter-of-factly. "How long ago was she hurt?"

"Five days," Alex said and sighed. "How has it only been five days? I feel like it's been a lifetime already."

"She has another week if she's lucky. A wound of that size

should take about seven to twelve days, and my mother is strong."

"I'm sorry that I'm responsible for your mother's death."

"I'm not upset about her death. Both my parents deserve what they get. I'm worried about what my father and hexa will do. If they know you have red steel . . ."

Alex's eyes suddenly widened. "Could that be why they went after Betruger? Harold made swords for me."

"I think we need to try some of these spells. Are you up for it, or do you need to rest first?"

Rest, but I'm not going back to Datten. I'm not ready to face Aaron yet.

"Some rest would help," she said out loud. "I'll go see what rooms are available for you and meet you in the hall in a few minutes. Could you bring the books?"

"Of course."

"Try not to scorch them. I'm quite attached to those," Alex said as she left.

She found Sir Colten and made the necessary arrangements. Then she found Gryphon waiting for her in the hall with a pile of spell books.

"You'll be staying in my father's room," she said.

"Let me guess. Farthest away from you and surrounded by knights?"

"Farthest away, yes, but next to the kitchen. I'm next to the knights."

"Of course."

They made their way to the library, and Gryphon put the books on the table. He looked around. "Where is your room? I half expected to find a bed in here!"

Alex laughed. "Only a door away." She pointed to one that led from her library to her bedroom.

Sir Colten arrived to escort Gryphon to his room. Alex went to her bedroom and put on her nightgown. When she slipped into bed, she clutched Aaron's pillow, breathing in the scent of pine and dew as she cried herself to sleep.

CHAPTER 36
AARON

Aron and his entourage arrived back at Datten Castle in the evening. Jerome had sent a scout ahead to warn the kitchens, so a hot meal was waiting for them. Everyone was excited as they made their way to the hall. They'd spent nearly four days traveling to the homes of the various southern lords, but the trip had been a great success. All the lords had sworn allegiance to Aaron and agreed to attend the coronation. Lynx had joined them in case they ran into trouble and was thrilled with every animal they'd come across. She asked a million questions of the knights and then talked off Birch's and Megesti's ears about how these animals compared to those in the Forbidden Lands.

He'd racked his brain every day since he'd left, but Aaron still couldn't remember what he'd said that upset Alex. Lately, his head throbbed almost constantly, and he was always forgetting things. He couldn't even remember what had happened to give him his black eye. *My forgetfulness is probably from the stress, but I still need to find her and make things right.*

At dinner, Harold commended Aaron for how he'd handled

the long-standing rivalry between two of the older lord families. As they ate, Jessica greeted them and then went to inform Alex of their return.

After days of traveling, the rolls, roasted meats, cheeses, and fish were delicious. Alex's favorites were there too, but they remained untouched. Aaron pushed thoughts of her aside for now. He'd focus on her after the meal because he needed to pay attention to his men, who talked excitedly as they ate their late dinner and drank pitcher after pitcher of ale. They were interrupted when Jessica charged back into the hall in a fright, Caleb right behind her.

"We can't find Alex," she panted, her face pale.

"Did you check the library?" Aaron asked, trying not to panic right away.

"Yes," Jessica said. "We checked everywhere."

"Megesti's lab?"

She nodded.

"The stables?" Alarm spiked in Aaron.

"Snow is still there," Caleb said.

"Where are Edith and Stefan?" Aaron asked.

"Kharon!" Birch stood.

The sorcerous cracked into the room in their nightdress. "Couldn't this have waited until morning?"

"Where is the Heart? In this castle, someone is always watching."

Kharon sighed and rubbed their temples. A second later, their eyes turned gray, and they glanced around the room. "Someone tell me where Alexandria went. We don't have all night."

Aaron leaned toward Megesti. "Is Kharon all right?"

"I think so," he replied.

The sorcerous blinked, and their eyes went back to blue. "Your brother said to ask Stefan, but some cranky old man said she and Gryphon were discussing spell books in the lab. She took a vial, and they vanished."

"A vial?" Birch asked. Aaron and Megesti looked at each other.

"They went to Verlassen Castle," Megesti said, and he explained how to access Victoria's lab.

"What are they looking for?" Harold asked.

"I'm going back to bed." Kharon cracked away.

"I asked Gryphon to search for protection spells," Birch said. "We need the spell that protects your towers. It gives us a starting point to protect the castles themselves from sorcerers."

"Don't you have better resources for that kind of magic?" Jessica asked.

"My books were destroyed, and Gryphon can't risk going to his father's library, not after he attacked Garrick to protect Alex and Edward," Birch said.

"How were your books destroyed?" Harold asked.

Birch sighed. "Garrick burned down my house when he found out I was helping Gryphon."

"Kharon and I fled at night so our families wouldn't know, but it's obvious now," Lynx added, looking down sadly. "Kharon doesn't have really have any close relatives, and my father has been a close supporter of Garrick for over a century. He'll be safe."

Aaron was only half listening. *They're alone at the castle after I explicitly told her I didn't want her to be alone with him.* He stood without saying goodbye and marched to his room, but Michael and Harold held the door before it could swing shut.

"You are *not* running to Verlassen Castle," Michael said.

"I'm the king here," Aaron growled. "And her husband. I don't trust Gryphon, and I made it clear she wasn't to be alone with him."

Harold stepped up to Aaron. "Enough. You can't have this both ways, Aaron. If you trust her, that means trusting them together. What has gotten into you lately?"

"She handled herself before, but she's weaker now," Aaron said.

"If you think Alex isn't strong enough to overcome everything that's happened, you don't know your wife half as well as you claim to," Michael countered.

"She kissed him when she was at Moorloc's, Michael!" Aaron shouted. "Did you know that? Not the other way around —*she* kissed *him*. What if something worse than a kiss happens? There are things I won't forgive."

Harold and Michael looked at each other, but before either could reply, Stefan entered the room. "Considering what happened in this suite before you left, you should be careful what you call unforgivable."

"Nothing happened. She was clearly emotional from everything."

Stefan crossed his arms, crumpling a paper in his hand, and scoffed at Aaron. Fueled with ale, Aaron didn't flinch. The king moved into Stefan's space and stared him down as if he were nothing.

Go ahead and glare at me. As King of Datten, I don't have to keep you around. I could even throw you in the dungeon for treason.

"What did Alex say happened?" Michael asked.

"He struck her," said Stefan.

Harold gasped. Aaron froze. He couldn't believe what he was hearing.

"Not so high and mighty now, are you? You have that black eye because she did what Michael and I taught her to do—she fought back."

Michael's mouth hung open. "You hit Alex?"

Did she tell him that? No, she wouldn't have lied to her men.

344

Aaron tried to laugh it off. "Of course not. Stefan's lying. He's hated me ever since Alex chose me."

Harold narrowed his eyes. "Aaron, I can't believe Stefan would lie about something this serious."

"You were really drunk," Michael said.

"She's covered in the bruises that prove what you did," Stefan said.

Michael started, "How do you—"

"Ask her ladies if you don't believe me. Since Aaron left, Alex has been avoiding Jessica and Edith to keep what he did a secret."

"So you have no poof." Aaron felt the ale taking effect. "Proof."

"You want proof? The only thing keeping me from pounding you right now is Alex ordering me not to." Stefan's fists trembled at his sides. "But if you ever lay a finger on her again, her orders won't stop me."

"Lay a finger on me, and your father will be throwing you in the dungeon."

Michael stepped between them. "Aaron, what is the matter with you? I fought by your side to get Alex back, and for what? So you could mistreat and abuse her? If that's the kind of king you want to be, then I refuse to be your guard."

"You're quitting over a lie?"

"No one is quitting," Harold said.

"So you believe me," Aaron said smugly, grinning at Stefan.

Harold replied, "I refrain from passing judgment until I've spoken to Alexandria myself. Stefan, you are as honorable a knight as they come, but you do have issues with Aaron."

"I was with her when she cried her heart out to her mother's tomb over what happened," Stefan said, looking at Michael. "Do you believe she'd lie to her mother?"

Michael's hands clenched. "I agree with Harold. I need to

talk to Alex before I condemn Aaron. We'll ask Birch or Lynx to visit Verlassen Castle to make sure Alex is safe, then get some rest. It's been a long week."

"Exactly. My fadder is dead five days, and my whif is off doing research with some fire pumpkin," Aaron slurred.

"You obviously had too much ale with dinner . . . again. Seems to be becoming a habit. Like father, like son," Stefan said.

Aaron stared at Stefan, his Datten temper on the verge of breaking loose completely. He took a deep breath. *Michael's right. It's been a long week, and maybe I'm being sensitive tonight, but I didn't hurt her.*

Stefan rubbed his chin and held out the crumpled paper he'd been clutching to Harold. "Here. You read her letter."

AARON,

I lost track of time searching for a spell that Birch requested. We still aren't finished, and it's late, so we've decided to stay at Verlassen Castle for the night so we can finish testing the spells in the morning. I'll be back tomorrow.

All my love,

Alex

ALL MY LOVE. As she twists the knife into my heart. I only asked of her one thing. She promised me. Aaron looked up at their friends, who all gave him a knowing look. He rolled his eyes at them all. *They know nothing of my pain.*

"I'm going to bed," he grumbled. He stomped up the stairs to his bed. Once he heard the door close, he stepped out onto the balcony to get some air. Rubbing his face, he couldn't stop picturing Alex with Gryphon in the stable.

346

Where is this jealousy coming from? It didn't even bother me this much when she was courting Cameron. But now she's my wife, and every time I turn around, Gryphon has his hands all over her.

Aaron headed back inside and stripped off his traveling clothes. Looking in the wardrobe for sleeping pants, he spotted a shirt stuffed into the bottom corner. He picked it up and realized it was one of Alex's tunics, but it was ripped up the front and had blood on the back. Holding it, he remembered the feel of fabric ripping in his hand and heard echoes of Alex begging him to stop. The room began to swirl. He dropped the shirt and stepped back, panting.

What is going on with me? I can't remember doing that. How am I supposed to ask forgiveness for a crime I don't remember committing?

When he caught his breath again, he knew what had happened. The evidence lay in a heap in front of him. He couldn't deny it any longer.

She made it up to have something against me. If that's the case, I'll be forced to remind her who is in charge of this marriage. And if I catch her alone with him again, she'll pay for that betrayal.

He kicked the bloodstained tunic into the fire and turned in for the night.

CHAPTER 37
GRYPHON

ryphon fell out of his bed as the silence was shattered by a bloodcurdling scream that echoed through the castle. He barely had time to process what he'd heard when he heard it again. He scrambled from the floor and tried to hear Alex's thoughts but couldn't. He cracked into the library and started throwing books off the shelf until the secret door opened. He dashed into Alex's bedroom and found Sir Colten there already, ashen and trembling.

"Princess! Princess!" he called, gently shaking an unconscious Alex. "You're having a nightmare. Please wake up."

"What do we do?" Gryphon asked. His entire body tensed as he watched the knight's fruitless efforts to rouse Alex.

"I don't know," Sir Colten said. He looked as if he were going to be sick. "Only His Royal Highness, Stefan, and Michael can calm her down."

"May I try?" Gryphon knew he would anyway, but he'd learned asking mortals for permission spared him a lot of grief.

"Please," the knight begged as Alex screamed again.

She was sweating, shivering, and thrashing. It almost looked as if she were fighting someone.

She would hate for me to see her like this.

Gryphon climbed onto Aaron's side of the bed and shook her the way Sir Colten had, but nothing happened. Swallowing hard, he shook her harder, and this time, she flailed violently, making the knight jump back. Gryphon grabbed her hands to stop her from hitting him and shouted, "Alex, stop it. Wake up!"

She sat up in bed, her wavy brown hair flying over her shoulders. Her eyes flashed open, dazzling white.

"Alex?" he whispered, but she didn't acknowledge him.

When she spoke, her voice was low and unlike her own.

"There is a debt to be paid, and the price shall be steep.

Their plans have been set and shall be paid with blood.

A son for the son, a father for the father.

If he fails to protect her, Warren shall fall.

If she fails to save him, the sorcerer will fall.

If they fail to unite, then everything will fall.

Chaos will spread across the lands and fill the rivers with blood."

Sir Colten feverishly wrote down what she'd said. Then Alex's eyes switched back to green, and she collapsed into Gryphon's arms.

"Is this normal?" he asked.

"It's a premonition," Sir Colten replied. "We're all taught about them in case she gets one while we're on duty. We're to write down what she said and report back to Prince Aaron or Sir Stefan, but I'm not sure how to do that. She's in no state to crack us."

"I can do it," Gryphon replied. "Do you have your report?"

Sir Colten nodded. "I will inform Julius we're departing and return right away."

Gryphon gently lay Alex back against her pillow and

hurried around to her side of the bed. He took a deep breath before removing her blanket. *Thank you for wearing a full nightdress.* He reached under her knees and shoulders and lifted her up just as Sir Colten returned and said he was ready to go.

"Then let's go see Aaron," Gryphon said, carefully keeping the nerves out of his voice. To avoid suspicion, he cracked them straight into Aaron's bedroom, but he was so quiet that Aaron didn't stir.

"Wake up, kingling." Gryphon half spoke and half shouted. He felt cold and realized he was still in his undergarments.

This is going to look terrible.

CHAPTER 38
AARON

aron heard someone shouting and groaned. His head throbbed as he sat up. There was Gryphon, standing half-naked at the foot of his bed and holding Alex.

What in the Forbidden Lands? Aaron flew out of his bed, rage thundering through him.

"She had a premonition, Your Royal Highness," said Sir Colten, standing beside the sorcerer. "I didn't know what else to do."

Aaron's anger lessened, but the adrenaline remained. He took Alex from Gryphon, and without a word, he walked back to the bed and gently placed her in it.

"What did she say, Sir Colten?" he asked.

"I wrote down what I could, but I only got the last half." He handed Aaron the paper.

"That's understandable. Thank you," Aaron said.

"Should I return to my post?"

"Gryphon, would you mind taking him?" he asked.

"Anything I can do to help." Gryphon nodded to the knight and cracked them back to the castle.

Aaron turned back to Alex and looked her over. The sleeves of her nightgown had ridden up from being carried. *Where did you get those bruises on your arm?* He brushed her hair away from her face, and she whimpered.

The image of a half-naked Gryphon holding her was now seared into his mind. He remembered when they had arrived in the throne room after the pier attack. The sorcerer's arms had been around her then too.

And the stable. So many accidental touches and innocent moments. Lying to me that there isn't something between you two. His temper ignited once more and filled every fiber of his being. *I don't believe for a second they were innocent. Time to face your punishment.*

Aaron leaned down and shook Alex.

She startled awake. "What happened? How did I get here?" She gazed up at him, confused and frightened.

You should be frightened.

"Get dressed."

CHAPTER 39
ALEX

Alex stood and looked Aaron over. *Something's wrong. You look exhausted and are dressed in the middle of the night. The southern lords wouldn't have made the visit easy. I'll do anything I can to support you.*

Aaron handed her his favorite red dress, and she slipped it over her head. He tightened the ribbons more roughly than usual, but Alex stayed silent. When he held out his hand, she took it.

Where are we going?

Emmerich appeared behind him. The late king was shaking his head adamantly at her. But when Aaron pulled her out of the room, his father's ghost didn't follow. It wasn't until they were down the stairs and in the main hallway that Alex realized Aaron was pulling her instead of walking with her like he usually did. A moment later, they arrived in the throne room.

It was the middle of the night, so the room was deserted, though still illuminated by the giant candelabras. Aaron dropped her hand and crossed the giant hall to close the main doors. She waited, twisting her belt.

"Aaron? We need to discuss what happened the other night and how you're feeling after what I told you about Moorloc's castle. We've both had time to think, and clearly, we've both made mistakes, but I love you and—"

Alex turned and almost screamed. Aaron had snuck up on her and was directly behind her. He hadn't done that since she first arrived in Warren and almost sent him flying down the hallway.

"You scared me," she said.

He stared at her. The air in the room turned icy, but he showed no sign of being cold. For the first time in her life, being so close to Aaron sent a different kind of shiver through Alex. *I broke him, so I have to fix him. He's my husband . . . the love of my life . . . I won't give up on him. Warren women are not quitters.*

"Aaron—" She reached toward him, but he grabbed her wrist and violently yanked her forward.

"Just admit it," he growled at her.

"Admit what?" Her voice quavered.

He thrust his finger at his brother's painting. "Admit it in front of all the people who died so you could become Queen of Datten. Admit you took him to bed. Did you think I wouldn't find out?"

Fury flared through her, and she ripped her hand from his grasp. "I know you're jealous of Gryphon, but you can't honestly believe I would give myself to another man after I made a vow to you." She turned to leave, but he grabbed her again. Alex broke his grip.

"Every time I look around, you're in his arms," he said, "and someone's missing clothing."

"He helped me after I risked my life so you'd survive *my* mistake. How dare you doubt my loyalty!" Alex's heart pounded in her chest. "All I ever wanted was to get back to you.

You're the only man I've ever wanted." She stood before him, but something about his eyes was wrong. They looked darker, colder.

"You seemed to want Cameron just fine before me. How would I know what you were getting up to when you were gone? You were in a castle surrounded by men, after all. You're always surrounded by men." He stepped closer, bearing down on her.

This wasn't her Aaron. But it wasn't an impostor either. He felt right, smelled right. Even his voice was right, but the tone and eyes were wrong. His hands felt cold, and the way he touched her made her stomach churn. Alex tried to step back, but Aaron pursued.

Adrenaline flooded her, and she dashed away from him. He raced after her. His face was stony and calculating, the way her grandfather's had been on the day he'd killed her mother. Aaron leaped to grab her, but Alex spun away from him as he'd taught her in all their dances. In an instant, her hands held fire, and she whirled to face him.

"Threatening to burn your husband for asking a few simple questions? That only proves your guilt."

"What happened to Datten honor? What would your father have said about you manhandling your wife for healing someone in pain?"

"You didn't heal someone—you healed *him*! Besides, you have a tiny bruise on your forearm while I have a black eye. I took the damage in our *discussion*. Now stop running. If you accept your punishment, I'll forgive you, and we'll move on from this so long as you learn your place."

"No." Alex glared at him. "You're not my Aaron. He's in there somewhere, but you aren't him."

Aaron smirked at her, and his hand moved to his side. Daniel's sword had become such a normal part of his attire that Alex hadn't noticed it. "Now your guilt has you making up lies to justify your behavior."

In an instant, his sword was unsheathed. Alex screamed as loud as she could to raise the alarm. She jumped back from Aaron, rushed to a large candelabra, and struggled to grab it, sending candles tumbling to the ground. Aaron swung at her again, but she blocked his attack with the iron fixture. His sword struck, stopping mere inches from her.

Do I use my magic to defend myself? What if I hurt him? If I crack away, will he hurt someone else? He was confused after I hit him in our room. That had to be the real Aaron, so then who is this? How do I get my Aaron back?

Aaron grunted as he pulled his sword back, his dark blue eyes glowering in the dying candlelight. He snarled and stalked around her. Alex held the candelabra the way Jerome and Stefan had taught her to hold a staff. Every time Aaron lunged, she countered to avoid him. They'd trained and sparred so much since she came home that Alex knew every one of his tells.

"Hold still, you little whore!"

"No." Alex quickly looked around for anything that could help her. She only saw the doors, thrones, tapestries, and paintings. She waited for Aaron to attack her again, but this time, she used his own momentum against him. As soon as his sword hit the iron, she slammed it down, and he stumbled forward. Alex spun the candelabra into his back, knocking him down onto the stones.

She ran to the doors and used her free hand to summon a strong wind. It threw open the heavy doors and sent the suits of armor around the entrance flying to the ground. The crash echoed through the throne room and down the hallway.

Alex slipped on a candle, and when she caught herself,

Aaron ripped the candelabra from her grasp and threw it aside. Tears burned her eyes as she watched him.

"Aaron, please." She backed away, holding her hands up, but his eyes were locked on her as he scowled.

Footsteps pounded behind them, and voices echoed down the hallway. Michael's voice rang out, demanding, "What is going on here?"

"Michael, get Stefan and Jerome," Alex shouted without taking her eyes off Aaron.

"Aaron, what's going on?" Harold had joined Michael.

Alex gulped. *What if he goes after them too? I can't let him hurt them.*

"A lesson," Aaron said coldly, cocking his head. He lifted his sword and pointed it at her.

"Aaron's lost his mind," Alex shouted. "Get Jerome and Stefan! *Now!*"

A wind blew through the room, bringing Gryphon. "What do you think you're doing, *kingling?*"

Aaron's eyes darted to the sorcerer for half a second. Alex took advantage and turned to run, but Aaron expected it and charged her. He rammed his sword forward, and she felt searing pain as tendons ripped in her shoulder. The moment he drew blood, everything changed.

"Alex!" Michael screamed, dashing to her.

She cried out and tried to run. Aaron lunged for her again, so she threw her hands up and sent him flying across the room with a wind.

"Alex?" Stefan arrived with Jerome and raced to her side. Aaron was back on his feet, but Michael stood between him and Alex with his sword drawn, hesitating.

Aaron smirked and held up his own sword, stained with Alex's blood, and Michael attacked. Alex knew all his moves and saw at once he was trying to disarm Aaron, but Aaron was vicious. After only a few strikes, Aaron knocked Michael's sword out of his hand and punched him in the face. He hit the ground hard, and Aaron's attention returned to Alex. Just then, a hulking form flew forward and tackled Aaron. As Jerome and Aaron tussled on the ground, Stefan pushed Alex behind him.

Aaron fought like a crazed animal and quickly threw off Jerome with abnormal strength. He leaped to his feet and turned to go after Alex again, but Gryphon appeared between them and raised his hand, imprisoning Aaron behind a ring of chest-high flames.

He spun, realized his predicament, and pointed his sword at Gryphon. "Can't fight like a man? You'll never be enough for her," he snarled.

"Maybe not, but she'll never have to fear me," Gryphon said.

Regret flashed across Aaron's face for an instant before the anger returned. He turned to her with a menacing smirk on his face, and Alex recoiled against Stefan. Her arm was warm and sticky, her sleeve and bodice soaked with blood. When she'd tripped, she'd bit her lip, and now a bitter, metallic taste coated her tongue.

"Birch," Gryphon called.

"Megesti," Alex said, so softly only Stefan would have heard it.

With a thundercrack, both appeared.

"Aaron!" Megesti rushed to him, but Jerome grabbed him and shook his head. Birch looked around and quickly focused on Alex and Stefan, the latter seeming ready to kill anyone who came near.

"What is going on?" Birch demanded.

Harold shook his head. "Aaron attacked Alex."

"That's impossible," Megesti said. "Aaron would die before he hurt her."

"I wouldn't believe it if I hadn't seen it myself," Michael said.

"I would," Stefan said.

"Lynx. Kharon." Gryphon summoned them.

"Are you all right?" Stefan asked. Alex nodded, tears welling in her eyes. Stefan stoically wrapped his arms around her as she pressed her face to his chest and cried.

Lynx appeared beside them. "What is this?"

"Aaron's gone mad," Stefan said. "He stabbed Alex."

The sorceress gasped. She sniffed and immediately moved Stefan's arm to inspect Alex's shoulder.

"What do you think it is?" Gryphon asked Birch.

Alex watched the older sorceress slowly walk around Aaron, going to stand by Gryphon once Lynx had tied a piece of Stefan's shirt to stop the bleeding. Aaron growled at her as she came closer.

Birch glanced between the Aaron before them and the Aaron in the wedding portrait on the wall behind the thrones.

Aaron opened his mouth, but Gryphon slammed his hand shut, and Aaron's voice vanished. "I've heard enough from you."

Michael asked, "How did you—"

In her mind, Alex heard Gryphon say, *Simple-minded mortal.*

Gryphon, don't—

If he ever lays another finger on you, princess, it won't be Stefan who ends him.

"General Wafner, please block the door. Gentlemen, are you ready to contain Aaron if he tries anything?" Birch asked, finally reaching the front of the circle.

"We are," Stefan said. Michael, Megesti, and Kharon approached Aaron and stood in a circle around the flames.

"Gryphon, stay with Alex. At the first sign of trouble, get her out of here," Stefan commanded.

"Gladly." Gryphon tried to get in front of Alex, but she stepped beside him.

"Remove the flames," Birch said.

The instant the flames dropped, Aaron charged through Michael and Megesti and raced toward Alex. She was prepared and thrust her hand up, sending a gale force wind across the room that threw Aaron back against the wall and held him there.

"Give him back his voice, Gryphon," Birch said.

"He doesn't smell right," Lynx said.

"Smell right?" Stefan asked.

"You're right," said Gryphon. "Something is off." He opened his palm, and Aaron's voice returned.

"Let me down, you useless little witch, or so help me, when I break free, I'll remind you who is in charge in this kingdom."

"Why do people keep calling me a witch?" Alex asked, crossing her arms.

"You've been called that?" Lynx asked, wide-eyed.

"It's the worst insult anyone can call a sorceress," Birch said. "All mortal witches are frauds, so when they call you that, they are accusing you of having no power."

"What's wrong with him?" Megesti asked.

"Gryphon, I don't like it when you use your gifts without consent, but we need answers." Birch turned to Alex. "I'll take over, dear."

Birch raised her hands, and vines shot out of the stone and wrapped around Aaron's arms, holding him against the wall.

Gryphon approached. When Alex scurried after him, he held up his hand to stop her. "I don't think you want to see this."

"I need to. I need to help him."

"Help him?" Lynx asked. She scrunched up her nose. "He stabbed you."

"That isn't my husband. If someone did something to him, I need to know."

"And if it's just him?" Stefan asked.

Alex swallowed. "Then I need to know that too, so I can decide if I'm willing to stay."

"I suspect a curse or a possession," Birch said. "It would explain the violent behavior, the eyes, and the fixation on a specific issue."

"What issue?" Michael asked.

"His jealousy of me," Gryphon said.

Aaron struggled against the vines, but he still wore a smirk. "Cocky little Head, aren't you? Not everything is about you, *fire pumpkin*."

Gryphon glared at him and took a few steps forward before Aaron spit in his face.

"Keep your hands off my wife, boar."

Gryphon grabbed Aaron's face, and his eyes flashed blue. Only a few seconds later, the sorcerer screamed and jumped back.

Aaron laughed. "Got a little shock, baby Ares?"

"He's cursed," Gryphon said, rubbing his hands. "It's an Ares curse, an ancient spell."

"This whole thing reeks of your mother . . . or your hexa," Lynx said.

"So now what?" Jerome asked.

"We try to heal him," Birch said.

"Try?" Alex felt her stomach knot. "You mean you might not . . ."

"The only sure way to remove a curse is to have the sorcerer who crafted it remove it. We're going to try to break someone else's curse."

Aaron smirked at Alex. "The price of your strength is harder to bear than you expected, isn't it, witch?"

Tears streaked Alex's face as she turned back to Birch and Gryphon. "Please, we have to remove it. I need to know which version of him I married before I decide if I'm staying in this marriage because I will not spend my life cowering from a king like my father did."

Birch ordered Stefan, saying, "Get your things and take her away from here."

"I'm a Cassandra—"

"I'm sorry, Alexandria, but it isn't safe. You and Gryphon are the targets of his rage. You cannot be here. Gryphon is an Ares and more experienced with Ares curses."

"What am I supposed to do?"

"Go to Warren. Be with your father," Birch said.

"My father is here. He's been helping Guinevere plan the funeral."

"You still must leave. Go with Stefan and Lynx. They'll protect you. When you get there, find your father's general and tell him what is happening. Jerome and Edward will handle Aaron's duties while you handle your father's," Birch said.

Alex's heart was beating so hard she couldn't breathe.

"I'll get Jessica to join you here," Stefan said.

"No," Birch said. "We'll need people who have known Aaron for a long time—the Wafners, Megesti—they'll know if what we're doing is working."

"What about the queen?" Megesti asked.

"Aaron is all she has left," Jerome said. "I don't believe she can handle this."

Birch nodded.

"Michael," Alex said, breathing deeply. "Stay with Jessica. She'll need your support, and she'll need to help the queen with the funeral so she doesn't get suspicious."

"But Alex—"

"No. You're Aaron's guard now too. Stefan, Lynx, and Randal will protect me."

Stefan nodded to Michael. Lynx came up beside Alex and put her arm around her shoulder, hugging her.

"Jerome, take care of Aaron for me." She walked up to her husband and looked at the vines that held him. "I know you're in there . . . somewhere. Remember that I love you."

Aaron leered. "Goodbye, witch."

Alex spun around and walked out of the hallway with Stefan and Lynx on her heels. A short time later, she was in her suite, packing a few things.

When Edward arrived, he held her. "Alex, tell me it isn't true."

"That's not our Aaron. And that's why I need you to stay. You and Jerome have to keep the kingdom running while Birch, Gryphon, and Megesti try to fix him. No one can know that he's cursed or that the King of Datten is incapacitated."

"Where does everyone think you're going?" Edward asked.

"Jessica will let news of my miscarriage slip to some noble-women. They'll assume I've gone home to heal in private. You can use that story to postpone the funeral too."

Edward kissed her forehead. "Randal won't be back on duty until tomorrow, and I don't want you there without both generals. If everyone thinks you're in Warren, go to your moth-er's castle. I'll make sure no one realizes Aaron is unwell."

She paused. "What if they can't fix him?"

"Don't think like that. I have complete faith in them and in Aaron too. He'll come back to you. He just needs time."

"Thank you," Alex whispered.

After Edward left, she met Stefan and Lynx in the stable and cracked them all to Verlassen Castle.

CHAPTER 40
GRYPHON

ryphon listened to the mortals chatter away.

Michael asked, "How many times can we delay a funeral before people get suspicious?"

"With the southern lords wanting to attend and the kingdom learning of Alex's miscarriage, we have some time," Jessica said, "but the issue is how we'll keep his mother from finding out about this. She'll notice if Aaron isn't around."

"We'll handle Guinevere and the lords, right, Jerome?" Edward said. The general nodded.

"What a mess this is," Jessica said.

Birch said, "All right, mortals, off to bed. We still need to figure some things out, but there isn't anything else you all can do here."

Michael hung back as the others shuffled out. "You'll get us if there's any change, right?"

"Of course," Kharon said.

With the mortals safely out of the room, Gryphon rolled up his sleeves. He strode the length of the hall and stood in front of Aaron.

"I thought you'd have run off with my wife," he snarled.

"No, she was pretty clear that I'm to stay here and fix you." He turned to Birch. "Where do we start? I cause chaos. I don't fix it."

"That's exactly what this is," Megesti said. "He's given into his chaos—his jealousy from you being here and around Alex. It seems to have caused his fears to magnify and bleed into his less pleasant parts, like his temper. Does that help you figure out who caused this?"

"I know who it was," Gryphon said. "It was either my mother or my hexa. An Ares cursed him, and although we are a large and powerful line, only two sorcerers would have a reason to go after a mortal king."

Kharon groaned. "How do we undo a curse from an Ares without the line of Cassandra?"

"We have one," Birch said, pointing at Megesti.

"He's too close to Aaron," Kharon argued.

"Between Alex and me, I'm more removed," Megesti said.

"I know she's closer, but she's the healer," Kharon said. "There's one gifted heal—"

"Of course it's her, but she can't help. It's not fair to ask her to watch her husband suffer like this," Birch said.

"That's ridiculous. Bring her back and let her heal him," Kharon said.

Gryphon shook his head. "We don't even know if she can, and I'm not risking her."

"Maybe that isn't your call to make, Gryphon," Kharon snapped.

"Enough. Birch is right. We sent Alex away for her safety and to keep her from seeing this. Are you really ready to announce defeat after an hour and bring her back to face this?" Megesti pointed at Aaron, still pinned to the wall.

"Can we at least knock him out? That smirk makes me want to set him on fire," Gryphon growled.

"I'll make a sleeping potion," Birch said. "But you and Megesti might have to force it down his throat."

Gryphon chuckled. "With pleasure."

"None of that," Birch scolded. "Right now, you see him as an inconvenience. He has the love of the sorceress you have feelings for. He's the reason you'll be waiting almost a century for your chance with Alex. How do you think that will go if he tragically dies now, decades before his time?"

"The guilt would destroy her," Megesti said. "He's my friend, and I couldn't live with myself. And she loves him a thousand times more than I do."

Gryphon grunted. "Then let's get to work before I knock that smirk off his face myself."

TORIAN TIMELINE

Sorcerers arrive	No one knows
Founding of Datten	year 0
Founding of Warren	50
Founding of six Southern kingdoms	50-100
Merlock arrives in Datten	1469
Megesti is born	1483
King Arthur of Warren is born	1484
King Emmerich of Datten is born	1503
Prince Edward of Warren is born	1510
King Emmerich is crowned king of Datten	1516
Prince Daniel of Datten is born	1522
Prince Aaron of Datten is born	1530
Princess Elizabeth of Warren (Alex) is born	1533
Princess Elizabeth vanishes and Prince Daniel dies	1538
Princess Alex returns home to Warren	1550
Princess Alex is taken by Moorloc	1550
Datten brings Princess Alex home	1550
Present day story	1551

KINGDOMS

DATTEN

Motto: Honor above All

Royal Family
King Emmerich (1503–)
Queen Guinevere (1504–)
Dead Prince Daniel (1521–1538)
Prince Aaron (1530–)

House of Wafner
Jerome (General of Datten) and dead Lady Gwendalin
Seven children: Patrick (Stefan), Jessica, dead Ryan, Arthur, Samuel, Olivia, and David

House of Merlock
Merlock: royal sorcerer and king's advisor
Megesti: sorcerer apprentice and Merlock's son

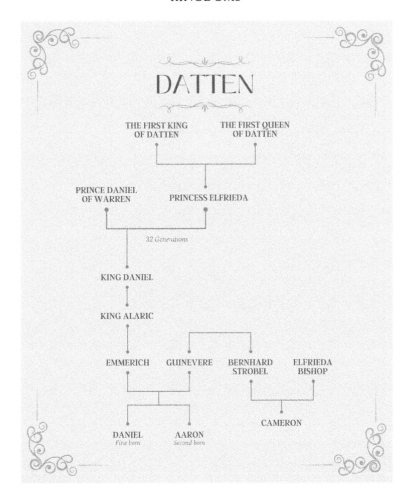

KINGDOMS
WARREN

Motto: Prosperity through Courage

Royal Family
King Edward (1509–)
Dead Princess Victoria (1451–1538)
Princess Elizabeth aka Alex (1533–)

House of Nial
Randal (General of Warren) and Lady Judith
Three daughters: Abigail, Diana, and Edith

House of Bishop
Matthew (retired general) and Lady Lillian
Three sons: Marco, Aiden, and Julius

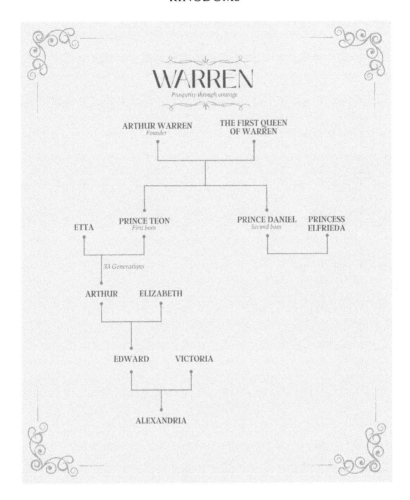

WARREN

Prosperity through courage

ARTHUR WARREN
Founder

THE FIRST QUEEN
OF WARREN

ETTA

PRINCE TEON
First born

PRINCE DANIEL
Second born

PRINCESS
ELFRIEDA

33 Generations

ARTHUR

ELIZABETH

EDWARD

VICTORIA

ALEXANDRIA

KINGDOMS

BETRUGER

LEGACY NEVER DIES

Motto: Legacy Never Dies

Royal Family
King Harold (1525–)

House of Macht
Bruno (Head Guard of Betruger)

SORCERERS OF TORIAN

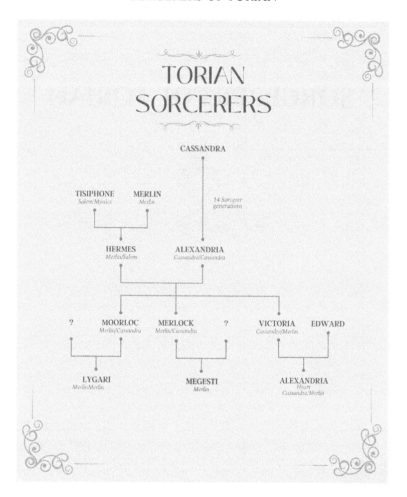

TORIAN SORCERERS

CASSANDRA

14 Sorcerer generations

TISIPHONE
Salem/Mystics

MERLIN
Merlin

HERMES
Merlin/Salem

ALEXANDRIA
Cassandra/Cassandra

?

MOORLOC
Merlin/Cassandra

MERLOCK
Merlin/Cassandra

?

VICTORIA
Cassandra/Merlin

EDWARD

LYGARI
Merlin/Merlin

MEGESTI
Merlin

ALEXANDRIA
Heart
Cassandra/Merlin

ARES

- orange
- chaos and violence

CASSANDRA

- gold
- healing and premonitions

CELTICS

- light green
- plants and peace

HADES

- grey
- death related

MERLIN

- violet
- varies

MIRE

- brown
- earth powers

MYSTICS

- royal blue
- mind control

POSEIDON

- dark blue
- water and weather

SALEM

- maroon
- fire and explosions

TIERE

- dark green
- animal powers

HEAD

- one of two strongest born in a generation
- logic ruled

HEART

- other strongest born in a generation
- emotional ruled

PRONUNCIATION GUIDE

Ares: Air-ease

Bernhard: Burn-hart

Betruger: Beh-True-Grrrr

Cassandra: Cas-an-draw

Celtic: Kel-tick

Datten: Day-ten

Ferflucs: Fair-f-looks

Hades: Hay-dees

Lygari: Le-garh-ee

Kirsh: K-ear-sh

Kruft: K-ruff-t

Merlin: Mer-lin

Merlock: Mer-lock

Mire: Mirr-ah

Moorloc: More-lock

Mystics: Myst-ics

Nial: N-aisle

Ogre: O-grah

Oreean: Or-ian

Poseidon: Poe-sigh-done

Rassgat: Ras-gat

Salem: Say-lem

Tiere: Teer-rah

Torian: Tore-Ian

Warren: War-en

GLOSSARY

Betrayer: term used for a sorcerer who tries to kill or severely wound their own family. Appears as three x's stacked on top of each other on the left inner forearm.

Bond marks: a mark that a mated pair of sorcerers share. Each is unique, made up of their line marks, and can appear on the back of either shoulder or neck.

Hexa: sorcerer grandmother.

Hexen: sorcerer grandfather.

Line marks: images used to show the ten sorcerer lines.

Magician: insult that implies a person has no power as all human "magicians" were frauds.

Pearls: magical spheres that show the past (clear), present (white), and future (black).

Returned one: a sorcerer who dies but is brought back.

Sorcerer line: also known as a line, this is the legacy of sorcerers born from a founding sorcerer. For example, the line of Merlin includes all Merlin sorcerers born from him with Merlin powers.

Sorcerer awakening: a time in a sorcerer's life when they go through puberty and subsequently receive their powers and learn which line they are.

Sorcerer: sorcerer who identifies as male.

Sorceress: sorcerer who identifies as female.

Sorcerous: sorcerer who identifies as neither male nor female, nonbinary.

Titan: strongest sorcerer of a particular line.

Usurper: a special sorcerer born every two or three generations who can borrow or siphon the power of sorcerers around them. Only one can ever be alive at a time.

Witch: insult that implies a person has no power as all human "witches" were frauds.

ACKNOWLEDGMENTS

ALWAYS first. Thank you to my husband, Steve, and my children, Lillian, Katrina, and Zack. They believe in me, love my characters, and give up time with me to write my books.

To my mom, Elke, and stepdad, Al, thank you for supporting all my crazy dreams.

My amazing friend Andrea who is always there for me and gives me the best ideas and lets me ramble at her until I figure things out. I love you more than you know! And her cat is a lovely purrball.

To my amazeball friend Brittany you are AMAZING and I can't thank you enough for taking on my crazy.

To my amazing online BookTok and Bookstagram friends, thank you for bringing a smile to my face and giving me a safe place to vent and talk books and cry when I needed. To my fantastic author friends I found online—you are shining lights in my dark days. Killian, Nikki, Tiffany, Amanda, Sonja, Penelope, Ruby, Rosalyn, Laura, Bekah, Jillian, Lynn, and countless more—you all make writing so much more enjoyable!

To my ferflucsing photographer, and FRIEND Brittany Nosal—I hate the way I look in photos, but you made the entire process painless and, more importantly, made me feel beautiful and gave me photos I love and can use knowing they captured the real me in all my happy, loving craziness! You are the best.

Thank you to the team of Intrepid Literacy. Lauren, you are

the CEO but so easy to talk to. Brooke, you were amazing and kept me on track.

Sam, my amazing developmental editor! You love my characters a much as I do and I know they are always safe in your hands!

To my cover designers, Alan and Ian—I cannot thank you enough for making magic again! I love my covers.

S. E., I can't thank you enough for keeping me on track and keeping things rolling. You are so easy to talk to you and I value you so much.

Supriya my amazing copy editor! Thank you for helping me keep things consistent and making sure people can read my words.

Thank you to the amazing Kickstarter fans who helped me make some special editions of my books!

Allie Burton

Alpha reader Andi 😊

Anna

Anthea Sharp

Ashley Cook

Billye Herndon

Brenda (lepnut)

Brittany

Dead Fishie

Danielle Jewinski

Eden Cooper

Elise

Emma Adams

Eriko

Gary Phillips

Halee Brewer

Holly Colvin

Jen W

Jennifer L. Pierce

J.L. Henker

Jo Holloway

Julianne

Kat Swank

Katherine Shipman

Kathy Storms

Kelly Kilpatrick

Killian

Lissette & Crow Robert

Lynsey

Marissa

Megyn "Crimson" MacDougall

Mercedes Cooper

Meredith Carstens

Mirabelle Huynh

Nicola Mckenna

Nicolette Andrews

Nikole C.

Olivia Atwater

Pat McDaniel

Rebecca

Rosie Wylor-Owen

Samantha D.

Seamus Sands

Sergey Kochergan

Shabana

Shanon M. Brown

Simon Mark de Wolfe

Springbrookorbillabong

Yuyu

Yvette

MARISSA! Marissa Atchison! The amazing super fan who helped bring both of my kickstarters to life. Not only is she an amazing and all around fantastic indie author supporter, but she is a wonderful friend and a mother of five! She is a true inspiration to me and I aim thankful to call her my friend!

ABOUT THE AUTHOR

Photo by Brittany Jean Photography

Alice Hanov was born in Germany and then raised on Pelee Island in the middle of one of the Great Lakes, spending her days imagining grand adventures in the woods around the island. She has never stopped writing and has a degree in rhetoric and professional writing from the University of Waterloo. Alice lives in Ontario with her hubby and three kids, various pets, and many, many books. You can visit her online at alicehanov.com.

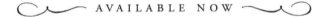

CONTINUE THE ADVENTURE

WITH

The Last True Heirs

SNEAK PEEK
AVAILABLE ON
ALICEHANOV.COM

VISIT

alicehanov.com

FOR MORE INFORMATION